GONE
FOR
SOLDIERS

By Jeff Shaara
Published by The Ballantine Publishing Group:

GODS AND GENERALS
THE LAST FULL MEASURE
GONE FOR SOLDIERS

GONE
FOR
SOLDIERS

JEFF SHAARA

BALLANTINE BOOKS
NEW YORK

A Ballantine Book
Published by The Ballantine Publishing Group
Copyright © 2000 by Jeffrey M. Shaara

All rights reserved under International
and Pan-American Copyright Conventions. Published
in the United States of America by The Ballantine Publishing Group,
a division of Random House, Inc., New York,
and simultaneously in Canada by Random
House of Canada Limited, Toronto.

www.randomhouse.com/BB/

Library of Congress Cataloging-in-Publication Data
Shaara, Jeff, 1952–
Gone for soldiers / Jeff Shaara.— 1st ed.
p.   cm.
ISBN 0-345-42750-5 (hardcover : alk. paper)
1. Lee, Robert E. (Robert Edward), 1807–1870—Fiction.   2. Scott, Winfield,
1786–1866—Fiction.   3. Mexican War, 1846–1848—Fiction.   I. Title.
PS3569.H18   G66   2000b
813'.54—dc21   00-022745

Maps by Mapping Specialists Ltd.

Manufactured in the United States of America

First Edition: May 2000

10 9 8 7 6 5 4 3 2 1

To my friend Ralph Johnson,
who for thirty years has been my Winfield Scott

Where have all the young men gone?
Gone for soldiers, every one . . .

—Pete Seeger
"Where Have All the Flowers Gone?"

TO THE READER

ONE OF THE MOST OVERLOOKED STORIES IN AMERICAN HISTORY is our involvement in a war with Mexico, from 1846 through 1848. The most obvious reason why the Mexican War is overlooked is that it predates the Civil War by only thirteen years. Such proximity to the most horrific event in our nation's history easily explains why history books often pass over this more *minor* of wars, and skip quickly to the events of the 1860s.

While not all wars are as momentous as World War II or our Civil War, to that generation which lived through the experience no war is ever unimportant. The most significant result of the Mexican War was the amount of land the United States acquired, extending our boundaries to most of the limits we are familiar with today. Compared to other wars, the cost in human life was minimal, if that term is ever appropriate. The war was short, lasting only two years, and the actual fighting involved only a dozen significant battles. But what the history lessons often overlook is the extraordinary cast of characters who first experienced the horror of combat during the Mexican War. And it is that cast of characters that brings this book to life.

This story primarily follows the exploits of two men, Robert E. Lee and Winfield Scott, from March 1847 to the final days of the war in 1848. It is the story of the relationship between old and young, the commander and the subordinate, the veteran soldier and the untested engineer. Throughout this story we are introduced to many other characters, an extraordinary cast whose names are familiar not only to historians but to those with even a casual interest in the American Civil War.

We are a nation hungry for heroes. That observation has become nearly cliché in recent times, but the passion inspiring that hunger is still profound. Our interest in the Civil War is testament to that passion. Some have strong loyalties to these characters because of which color uniform they wore. Thirteen years before the outbreak of the Civil War, there was no difference in their uniform. The issues that would tear apart our nation in 1861 were uncomfortable disagreements in 1847. The soldiers fought under one flag, and their loyalty was to one commander. In Mexico, so many of the familiar names would fight side by side.

To many of us, these characters are appealing because they represent something fundamentally decent; they stand as examples of dignity and honor holding firm despite the shattering collapse of their world. There are many who hope that we would be capable of such decency today.

It is impossible to study the Mexican War without seeing the parallels to our own time, to the amazing similarities to Vietnam, and the conflicts that war brought home. If anyone believes that the noisy shame of political behavior is a recent phenomenon, the Mexican War will seem modern indeed.

The events in this story are true, and the participation of each character is as close to exact as I could make it. But this is not a history book. The story is told through the thoughts and the voices of the characters themselves, from their own points of view. However accurately I have tried to portray each character, in the end each must be my own interpretation, a product of research into much personal material, original sources, letters, diaries, and journals written by the men themselves. Much of that research is marvelous discovery, a surprising journey through their own personal histories that can alter a preconceived notion, or eliminate a much repeated myth. The final result is a story that often surprises. It is, after all, a story about . . . all of us.

JEFF SHAARA
APRIL 1999

INTRODUCTION

I N 1844 THE UNITED STATES IS VERY MUCH A NATION FEELING ITS youth. Since the country was doubled in size by the Louisiana Purchase, there has been a passion for expansion, for pushing the boundaries farther west, a mission to bring the new enlightenment of the "American Ideal" to the entire continent. To politicians in Washington, this expansion is justified not just by an enthusiasm for our system of government, but by official policy. The document is the Monroe Doctrine, and the rallying cry becomes *Manifest Destiny*, as though it is not only in the nation's best interests to expand our influence, but the best interest of anyone whose culture we might absorb. This practice has already resulted in bloody conflict with several Indian Nations, notably the Seminoles in Florida. It also leads to a showdown with the British over the Oregon Territory, a threat the British defuse by backing away.

In summer 1844 the independent nation of Texas is annexed by the United States. The territory of Texas had been part of Mexico itself, only became independent in 1836 when Mexican leader Antonio Lopez de Santa Anna was defeated by Sam Houston at the Battle of San Jacinto. This defeat followed Santa Anna's highly publicized massacre of the defenders of the Alamo, in San Antonio.

To the Mexican government, led by the moderate General José Joaquin de Herrera, the loss of Texas is a severe blow to Mexican pride. While Herrera favors negotiation to resolve differences, specifically the growing border disputes, loud voices of ultrapatriotism within his country consider the loss an outrage, an assault on the sovereignty of Mexico, which must be avenged.

In December 1844, Texas is officially granted statehood. The decision is controversial. Because it was admitted as a slave state, many in the north opposed Texas's inclusion. However, as a necessary ingredient of Manifest Destiny, even opponents concede that the land, and the passion for expansion, make Texas a valuable treasure.

The Texans consider their border to extend to the Rio Grande River. To the Mexicans, Texas stops at the Nueces River, some one hundred miles farther north. The land in between the two rivers is mostly barren and uninhabited, but both sides begin making moves to secure the land for their own cause.

To protect the new wave of citizens that move into the disputed area, President James K. Polk sends a military force of nearly three thousand men, under the command of General Zachary Taylor. This so inflames the spirits of many Mexicans that Herrera cannot hold power, and he is replaced by General Mariano Padredes, an ultrapatriot who immediately declares that Mexico is in a state of "defensive war" with the United States.

As the wheels of war grind forward, neither side seems to understand the forces driving the other. The Mexicans are far from accepting Manifest Destiny as legitimate, and the Polk Administration has no grasp of the nationalism and fiercely proud protectionism that so motivates the Mexicans.

As Taylor's forces move into the disputed territory between the two rivers, Mexican General Ampudia marches troops northward, intending to turn Taylor away. While politicians in both capitals seem helpless to find some middle ground, some way of avoiding the inevitable war, Taylor confronts a sizable Mexican force at Palo Alto, a small crossroads village. The resulting fight is the first engagement of the war, and is a decided victory for Taylor and the Americans. The Mexicans retreat to a strong defensive position at an old riverbed called Resaca de la Palma. Taylor pursues, and defeats the Mexicans again. The Mexican forces have no choice but to retreat below the Rio Grande.

With the spilling of blood, the disputes move beyond the angry protests of politicians. The diplomatic wrangling gives way to the harsh reality that the dispute over boundaries and the inability of each culture to understand the customs and needs of the other, has but one possible outcome. Even the voices of reason in both capitals are powerless to stop the momentum. On May 13, 1846, President Polk convinces Congress to declare war on Mexico.

As the momentum for war rolls forward, President Polk is approached by Colonel Alexander Atocha, a representative for the exiled

Santa Anna, who lives now in Cuba. Atocha proposes that if Santa Anna receives Polk's support in his return to power in Mexico, the charismatic Santa Anna will calm the angry voices, and with his considerable influence over the weaker political figures in Mexico, he will stop the war. In August 1846, Santa Anna is allowed to quietly pass through the American blockade of Mexican ports. Upon reaching Mexico City, he has little difficulty assuming command of the Mexican military. Despite what Santa Anna had promised Washington, his first act is to organize an army of more than twenty thousand troops and march them north to confront and destroy the forces of Zachary Taylor.

In February 1847, at the Battle of Buena Vista, Taylor's greatly outnumbered forces defeat Santa Anna in a battle that comes to symbolize much of the war itself. Santa Anna relies on old customs, his cavalry, and employs the European methods of fighting war, unchanged for centuries. Taylor cannot rely on strength, so he relies on technology: the American artillery is significantly superior, and ultimately controls the field.

Taylor then bogs down in the great expanse of wilderness in northern Mexico, and Washington understands that if the Mexicans are to be defeated, victory will have to come from another front. It is General-in-Chief Winfield Scott who proposes an assault by sea, to invade Mexico through the port of Vera Cruz, to take the fight straight into the heart of Mexico.

In the field, the American soldiers are a mix rarely seen in military history. The regular officers are a strange combination of old and new, veterans of the War of 1812 and the bright young graduates of the United States Military Academy at West Point. It is not a smooth blend. Zachary Taylor's methods are loose, and discipline and drill are foreign to him. The younger officers take to their duty with enthusiasm, but feel frustration with the poor planning and execution of the commander's decisions.

At Palo Alto and Resaca de la Palma the younger officers and their men experience war for the first time, and they learn quickly that it is not necessarily conducted in the manner they had been taught in the classroom or as instructed in the camps.

As the army is reinforced, Taylor's numbers swell with volunteers, men who seek some marvelous adventure, a chance for glory or, better yet, wealth. If the volunteers have enthusiasm for a fight at all, they know nothing of discipline, of the ways of the army, of drill and rank. Many of their officers are volunteers as well, and they are often as undisciplined as their men. While Washington frets over Taylor's lack of initiative in pursuing the war, Taylor's mission stagnates and his army suffers from a lack of discipline and the lack of focus that only comes from marching into the guns of the enemy. And though Taylor is seen by many back home as a great hero, if there is duty to be performed, or glory to be found, it will have to come from the spirit of a new commander.

MAJOR GENERAL WINFIELD SCOTT

Born July 13, 1786, near Petersburg, Virginia, he is raised by an extremely strict mother, who does not hesitate to apply the whip. She dies when he is seventeen, and her lessons stay hard within him. He grows into a huge man, takes pride in his strength and ability to win physical disputes, remarking often on his *"great power of arm."* Aware always of the social class structure of eastern Virginia, he never seems to make the grade, is usually awkward and socially clumsy. He attends school in Williamsburg, cannot find acceptance from the elite, aristocratic youth who dominate the social scene, is considered too plainspoken. Though he is never a farmer, many assume he is a product of that simpler class, and he is often accused of reaching beyond his own breeding. He attends William and Mary for one year, but has no patience again for the social elitism, and drops out. He finds employment in a law office, and is allowed to observe the trial of Aaron Burr, where he meets Thomas Jefferson and Andrew Jackson. The experience shapes him in ways he does not yet understand, and gives him a solid appreciation for the intellectual power behind the founding principles of the nation. It is an admiration and a loyalty that will be tested throughout his military career.

In 1807 he volunteers for military service with local defense forces and personally captures a British shoreboat which is discreetly searching the coast for supplies. He arrests the British officers, though there is no official hostility with Britain, and so creates an international incident, which very nearly starts the War of 1812 five years early. Chastised by President Jefferson, he returns to the law offices, but cannot escape the lure of the adventure he finds as a soldier. He seeks out the army again, finds the rumbling threats from the British creating new positions in a growing army, and in May 1808 he receives a commission as Captain of Artillery. He reports for duty though he has never fired a cannon. He is ordered to New Orleans, immediately shows no understanding of life under the command of temperamental superiors, and is charged with misconduct for a variety of poor decisions, but can only be found officially to be "unofficer-like."

Anxious for life in combat, he is thrilled to be ordered to Baltimore in 1812, as the tensions with Britain continue to grow. In June, when war is declared, Scott is promoted to Lieutenant Colonel, is assigned to duty in northern New York, on the Niagara frontier. He begins to believe that President James Madison has no instinct for military operations, watches in amazement as the army commanders above him are appointed only as a reward for their good service during the Revolution, thirty years earlier. It is yet another example of his impatience, and his indiscreet judgment of superiors, that will surround him in controversy most of his career.

In service against the British threat along the Niagara River, he endures what he sees as the complete ineptness of his commanders, creates controversy and nearly ends his own career by performing operations without orders. But as the war goes favorably for the British, the country cannot afford to rely on aging obsolete commanders, and Scott's successes on the field are finally celebrated in Washington. As the frail commanders blunder their way into retirement, Scott's rise to prominence is assured, and he receives promotion to Brigadier General. In his most significant action, he defeats a much larger British force in the Battle of Lundy's Lane, near Niagara Falls, where he receives a severe shoulder wound. In 1815, while he waits anxiously for return to combat, the war ends.

He visits France, wearing the mantle of a military hero, feasts upon the attention he receives. He observes the foreign curiosity about this strange American nation, so unlike the monarchies of Europe. He is inspired to speak out for the American system, begins to consider himself a custodian of the nation's honor.

He marries Maria Mayo in 1817, and fathers seven children, but only three daughters survive childhood. His career takes him far from home, and even in peacetime he is not an attentive husband and father. Maria tailors her life accordingly and never seems to resent his absence.

He grows older learning none of the lessons of diplomacy, feuds with Andrew Jackson, another man of great ego, and another hero of the war. When Jackson is elected President in 1828, attempts are made to repair the rift, and the two men recognize the importance of their professional relationship; however, a friendship never develops between them.

In the peacetime years, Scott settles into the comfortable life as a senior commander of the army, gains considerable weight, and continues to build a reputation for fairness and efficiency. He oversees the actions of various Indian conflicts, travels to Charleston to put down the secessionist rebellion of 1832, and defuses the Aristook War in New England. In 1841 he receives promotion to Major General, and the following year he is named General-in-Chief.

He uses the peacetime years to great advantage, continues to shape the army into the most modern of its day. He carries well the lessons learned in 1812, insists on developing the artillery first, proposes that the soldiers should be full-time and professional. As events begin to heat up on the border with Mexico, he actively plans strategy from his office in Washington, but learns quickly that the new President, James K. Polk, is a man driven first by political loyalties, and Scott does not play the game.

As Zachary Taylor languishes in northern Mexico, Polk's cabinet can no longer ignore the strategy that Scott proposes. Supported by the navy's senior commander, Commodore David Conner, and finally by Secretary of War Marcy, Scott succeeds in convincing Polk that the invasion plan is the best way to win the war, and that Scott himself is the best man to lead the charge. With great reluctance, Polk orders Scott to Mexico.

Arriving first in south Texas, Scott immediately pulls the best units from Taylor's army, with the explanation that bringing fresh and untrained troops into the war would consume too much time. Taylor fumes, and when Scott arrives to meet with him, Taylor simply stays away. The two men never speak during the war.

Surprisingly, Scott ignores Taylor's insubordination, proceeds with his plan, and brings much of Taylor's army to the Gulf coast. As he organizes his staff, he sorts through the records of many fine officers, chooses men he believes have special talent, including one man who has built a distinguished reputation in the Corps of Engineers.

CAPTAIN ROBERT EDWARD LEE

Born January 19, 1807, at Stratford Estate, eastern Virginia, he is the son of Henry "Light-Horse Harry" Lee, an illustrious hero of the American Revolution and a product of one of the more aristocratic families of Virginia. Lee's ancestry includes two signers of the Declaration of Independence. His relationship with his father is fractured at best. His father's later life is marred by debt and a scandalous reputation for business. Eventually Lee's father is forced to leave his family and Virginia behind, and dies in Cumberland Island, Georgia.

Lee attends West Point, and graduates in 1829 second in his class, achieving notoriety for the extraordinary accomplishment of never having received a single demerit in his four years as a cadet. What should be a year of celebration for Lee is changed dramatically when his mother, Ann Carter Lee, dies in his arms. His devotion to her has always been magnified by the disgrace she has endured from her husband's failures, and throughout the remainder of his life Lee is never far from the awful moment of her death. He embodies his mother's quiet piety, and Lee's religious faith hardens into a strong foundation that he will rely on to guide him through his entire life. He is devoutly fatalistic, believes completely that every event of his life is a result of God's Will.

He marries Mary Anne Randolph Custis, an only child and a descendent of Martha Washington. Her father's estate of Arlington is perched on a prominent hillside across the Potomac River from the capital.

Though often away with his various duties, Lee makes the extreme effort to be home with his family at Christmas, and for several years each visit seems to produce a child, seven in all, who all survive to adulthood.

Lee's high standing at West Point provides him a position in the much sought after Corps of Engineers, and Lee excels at every post he is assigned. He assists in designing many of the forts along the Atlantic coast, from Florida to New York. In 1837 he travels to Missouri, where he takes on his most outstanding task as an engineer—rescuing the port of St. Louis by rerouting the flow of the Mississippi River, thus washing away shallow bars of sand that had blockaded the port. His success earns him accolades from the civilian officials of the city and a promotion to Captain.

In 1840 he returns to Washington, where he resumes duty repairing and constructing the various eastern forts, spending much of his time at Fort Hamilton, New York.

In June 1844 he is assigned duty as one of the designated commissioners to observe the final examinations of the West Point cadets. Here, he becomes reacquainted with General William Worth, who had been Lee's own commandant, and establishes a friendly relationship with the army's commanding general, Winfield Scott. Lee leaves the Point having no idea of the impression he has made on his superior officer.

Lee begins to feel frustrated by the duty he regards as increasingly routine, and he finds little challenge in the constant repair of the existing forts. In early 1846 he is distracted by excited talk of the activity along the Rio Grande, and follows the diplomatic wrangling of the day with great interest. But his duty keeps him at Fort Monroe, often observing the departure of ships filled with men he knows, who are bound for the activity in south Texas. Without warning, in August 1846, Lee receives orders to report to San Antonio, Texas, to the command of General John Wool. A month later he reaches his new post.

Texas is a different world for Lee, and Wool's men are not yet active, thus Lee uses the time to explore the old-world charm of the city. He visits the Alamo, which still shows signs of the slaughter at the hand of Santa Anna. In San Antonio he first begins to understand that this new duty might become very different from anything he has yet experienced.

Wool's command begins to march, separates from the bulk of Taylor's army, moves farther west in an attempt to locate and possibly confront Mexican forces rumored to lurk just below the Rio Grande. Still an engineer, Lee assists in the building of a bridge for Wool's troops to cross the river. But there is no enemy to be found, and while Wool receives continuing reports of Taylor's bloody duels against the Mexicans, Wool's troops spend long days marching in pursuit of rumor, rushing forward to confront an enemy that simply isn't there. As Taylor's star rises as a result of his first victories of the war, Lee begins to understand Wool's frustration, and while under Wool's command, Lee never sees a Mexican soldier.

Busy with his new duty of smoothing the primitive roads and providing bridges for the troops to cross the various rivers, Lee is painfully aware that Christmas, 1846, is the first he has not spent at home with his young family. In mid-January 1847, Lee is surprised to receive an order to leave Wool's command and join the staff of Winfield Scott, on the Texas coast. Weary of rumor, Lee goes to great lengths to verify what has been circulating around the campfires for weeks. Scott himself is commanding a new force, and much of Taylor's army is leaving the wilderness for the ships in the Gulf.

Lee spends his fortieth birthday on horseback, makes the dusty journey imagining what the duty might be like under the eyes of the commanding general himself. The rumors follow him still, reports of great hordes of Mexican soldiers, the threat of battles yet to come. He reaches the coast, anxious to learn for himself what so many of the experienced officers seem to understand. As the army comes together on the Gulf coast, the troops ignore the politics, know nothing of the diplomatic chaos, the argument over borders. The mission is now simple and straightforward.

For the first time in his life Lee becomes part of a different kind of army, commanded by a professional soldier, a man who knows how to fight a war.

Captain Robert E. Lee

1. LEE

March fifth, 1847

THEY HAD SAILED EARLY, CUTTING SOUTHWARD THROUGH THE quiet water, the rugged coastline barely visible to the west. Lee had moved to the bow of the tall ship, staring out quietly, tasting the salt air, the cool wind that pushed into the great sails above him. At first he was alone, but then more of the officers were moving forward, and like Lee, they stared to the front, watching for any sign, the first glimpse of the rest of the great fleet.

Lee glanced to one side, saw a small figure, thought, My dear friend Joe . . . you look awful. He would never say that to the man's face, knew Johnston was embarrassed, sensitive about his seasickness. The agony had been on Johnston's face even before the ship had left Tampico, and it made no difference if the weather rolled them about or, like this morning, was ghostly calm. Joe Johnston would never be a sailor.

Lee moved toward him, eased along the heavy wood rail. "You all right, Captain?"

Johnston, weary, his eyes heavy, looked at Lee, nodded, said nothing. Lee glanced at the dome of exposed scalp on Johnston's head, looked away, would not let his friend catch him staring. He knew Johnston was a vain man, frustrated with the baldness that had shown itself when he was still young. He had a small frame, thin, and some at the Point had even used the word fragile to describe him. It had made Johnston furious, and Lee knew his vanity had been a form of self-defense. Johnston had begun to comb his hair straight forward, covering his high forehead. But today there was none of the self-consciousness, and Lee could not be pleased about that, knew it meant that Johnston was feeling sick indeed.

Lee, still looking away, pointed out beyond the bow. "We'll be there soon I think. The masts should come into view first."

Johnston nodded, looked now toward the horizon, his expression a mix of hope and a silent plea for the trip to end.

Lee put a hand on Johnston's shoulder, felt the rough wool of Johnston's coat, felt Johnston sag beneath his grip. He pulled his hand away, thought, Maybe best to just let him be. He leaned out again on the rail, and now the sun had come up, full above the flat ocean to the east. He looked toward the warmth, felt the energy, felt a light salty breeze drifting across the deck. There was a new sound now, birds, the high call of the gulls, gathering, dancing in the air, near the stern of the ship. He looked up, smiled slightly, stared into the deep blue of a cloudless perfect morning. Suddenly there was a voice, behind him, high up on the lookout.

"Ship ho!"

The men around Lee pressed forward, and Lee stared again to the front, saw now a fleck of orange, a brief flicker of sunlight reflecting on . . . something. The others saw it as well, the soldiers betraying their excitement, while all around them the sailors seemed only to do their work, and if they paid any attention at all to what lay in front of them, they would not reveal it to these men who fought on land.

Lee saw more reflections now, and someone had a pair of field glasses, passed them along the rail, and as each man took his turn, there was a smile, a small sound, recognition. Now the glasses came to Lee, and he raised them up, and the flecks of light were suddenly clear. He felt his heart thump hard in his chest, could not help but smile, thought, Yes, a ship! He lowered the glasses, offered them to Johnston, who took them and without looking, passed them along. Lee wanted to say something, encourage his friend, to help him put the sickness aside somehow. Still Lee's attention was drawn to the front, where there were a great many more reflections, and it did not take the glasses to see that before them, spread across the wide gulf, was an enormous fleet.

The first big ship was plainly visible now, and Lee could feel the *Massachusetts* turning, the helmsman steering General Winfield Scott's flagship to a path closer to the warships. Lee was still feeling the excitement, examined the big ship as though he were a small child. He was stunned by the size, the great rows of small black eyes, the enormous firepower of the big man-of-war. He had seen ships like this before, near the forts in the East, but this was very different, moving past so close, the view from the deck of another great ship, so near the mouths of all those guns. Lee stared into the open gun ports, felt a sudden chill. My God, he thought, the pure power. So much artillery in one place. He had never seen a naval bombardment, certainly had never seen two great ships at war, swirling around each other in a violent fury of sound and smoke. He blinked, thought, No, you have never seen much of anything to compare to this.

The warships had been here for a while now, had blockaded the Mexican seaports, keeping the arms and supplies away from Santa Anna's army. The *Massachusetts* moved past the man-of-war, and now Lee could see out across the open water. In the distance, spaced apart in strategic formation, were more of the men-of-war, but they were the farthest ships from shore. Closer in Lee could see more detail of the smaller ships, some masted, some with steam, black smoke belching from fat smokestacks. Beyond were smaller boats, all sizes and shapes, and now he saw clusters of . . . he strained to see, now turned, looked for a sailor, someone who knew. One man was carrying a coil of rope, moving by with quiet efficiency, and Lee said, "Excuse me, seaman. Do you know what those might be?" The sailor looked out where Lee pointed, and other officers had turned to hear, waited for the man's answer. The sailor took his time, enjoying the momentary celebrity.

"Yes, sir. Those would be surfboats, sir. Oar-powered, like on whaling ships. I expect that would be how you all will be going ashore."

Lee turned back to the boats, could make out the shapes now, bobbing slowly beside the larger ships like rows of wooden shoes. He felt the chill again, thought, For all the firepower in the big ships, the invasion would after all rely on these surfboats, the very small and very vulnerable craft that would carry Scott's great army to the shore. He still stared out, said in a low voice, "Then we should pray for good weather."

The sailor said nothing, moved away to his duty, while Lee scanned the shoreline. At first, all along the coast the horizon was nearly unbroken except for the gentle roll of sand hills. But now Lee saw something new, distant shapes, square, a church steeple, all enclosed by a long low wall. It was Vera Cruz.

He stared that way for a long moment, thought, How will it happen? Will we sail in close, bombard the wall? How do we land those tiny boats? Perhaps . . . we could move inland from below, come at them from behind. He understood forts, had built enough of them himself, knew that the big guns would face the sea. The glasses came back to him again, and he raised them, scanned the old city, then farther to the north, beyond, on an island, another wall, this one larger, taller, an enormous fat rock sitting alone, as though a piece of the city had broken free, drifted away, anchoring a mile off shore.

He tried to remember the name. He had studied this place at West Point, San Juan de Uloa. Surely . . . no, we will not move straight into that place. Far too dangerous, a hundred guns, maybe more. Uloa had stood against invasion for centuries, and Lee thought, We are not that strong. He was suddenly the engineer, thinking of the great fort as he had the projects on the East coast. They knew something of engineering, he thought, they had some skill that maybe even now we do not completely understand. How are we to know, after all? We do not have the experience, most of our forts have never seen an enemy, may never see one. Will they stand up like Uloa, become a symbol of our strength? Or, will our enemies just find a way to avoid the strength, the power of the guns, as surely we must do here. There is a lesson in this, Engineer. For all your training, all your skill, someone will find a better way, a way to defeat your fine work. Pay attention, learn from this, perhaps use it in the future. He turned, pulled his gaze away from Uloa, looked again at the sky. He felt helpless, grateful it was not his responsibility, thought, That's why General Scott is here, why the commanding general of the army will lead this invasion himself. He became excited again. My God, what we will do here . . . this is *important*. This will make history. Whether we succeed or not . . . no, we will succeed. That too is why General Scott is here.

There were sounds now, coming from the other ships, and Lee saw for the first time sailors lining up along the rails of the closer ships. Lee glanced up the tall mast, saw Scott's red and blue flag, waving a crisp salute to the fleet. He could hear the sounds clearly now. All through the great mass of strength, across the decks of two hundred ships, were the soldiers who had waited in patient misery, and the sailors who worked around them. Now, the misery and the work was put aside. A dozen bands began to play, spreading a cacophony of sounds across the water, but above it all was the sound of men cheering. Lee felt the men around him stiffen. He turned, saw General Scott emerging from below.

Scott climbed the short ladder, his huge hands pulling on straining ropes, the steps slow and ponderous. He wore a grand uniform, the gold braid draped over the shoulders, the long hat punctuated by the thick feather. Lee looked carefully at the old man's heavy round face, saw fatigue, more than the effort at climbing the steep stairway. Lee was suddenly embarrassed, glanced at Johnston, who stood stiffly now, as he did. The general appears to be in some discomfort, he thought. He looked down, scolding himself, No, it is more likely the strain, the enormous responsibility. He looked up again as Scott reached the deck, saw Scott take a deep breath, one hand on the broad expanse of his stomach. Scott glanced briefly at the men who stood at attention, but stared past them, moved forward. The staff stood aside, watched quietly as the big man moved to the rail, and now the only sound came from across the still water, from the other ships. Lee heard the cheers grow louder as the troops saw him, and Scott seemed to respond, stood taller, his discomfort gone. Lee saw a smile spread across the older man's face, Scott enjoying the moment, the great figure in blue and gold standing large on the deck of his flagship. The commanding general had arrived.

"CAPTAIN LEE, YOU WILL ACCOMPANY US."

Lee saluted, did not hesitate, followed Scott down the narrow passageway. Scott had rarely spoken to him, and Lee had not expected to go with the others, was not even sure where they were going.

He waited at the rail while Scott climbed slowly down onto the deck of the smaller boat, a steamer named *Petrita*. He looked at the faces below, now looking up at him, was surprised to see Joe Johnston, standing unsteadily among a cluster of young staff, and a few old and very senior commanders.

"Any time now, Captain."

The words came from below, from General Twiggs, a tall, grim man whom Lee had barely met. Lee started to salute, thought, Not the time, get over the side, *now*. A sailor stood by helpfully as Lee moved to the ladder, and Lee nodded to the unsmiling seaman, climbed down to the boat.

Scott did not look at Lee, turned, said, "We may proceed."

From a platform in the bow of the small steamer, Lee saw a different uniform, very navy, very dignified. Johnston sidled closer to Lee and said quietly, "Commodore Conner, himself."

Lee nodded dumbly, thought, This much brass in one place . . . amazing. He saw Conner nod to Scott, and Conner gave his own order to a sailor at the helm. Suddenly the steamer coughed a great black cloud and began to move. Lee steadied himself, saw the others move to the security of the railing, and he looked at the old faces, ran the names through his mind, David Twiggs, General Worth, General Patterson.

Nearly hidden by Scott's frame was a younger man, frail. It was Scott's son-in-law, Major Henry Scott, the man who struggled to endure the confusion about his name, the odd coincidence that the commanding general's daughter would marry a man with the same last name. The younger Scott served as his father-in-law's chief of staff.

The steamer was clear of the big ship now, churning its way toward the distant shoreline, pointing just south of the city walls. Lee moved beside Johnston, whose discomfort was still evident. Johnston gripped the handrail, looked painfully at Lee. "There was nothing at West Point about boats."

Lee smiled. He had no idea what to say, but saw another face, much younger, both hands anchored to the rail on the far side of the boat, wearing the same look of agony that possessed Johnston. Lee had met the man in Texas, another engineer. Lee caught his attention, nodded pleasantly, but the young man glared at him, seemed to glare at everything. Lee noticed the man's white-knuckle grip on the handrail.

Johnston said, "Lieutenant Meade shares my . . . affliction."

Lee said nothing, was still distracted by the power of the other men around him, thought, Why are we here? I still don't understand what this boat ride is about.

He could see Scott up on the platform, talking to Conner. Conner was a tall, thin man, elegant in any uniform, but he did not compare in physical stature to Scott. Lee thought of West Point, of meeting General Scott for the first time, both men serving on the Visitors' Board. It was not that many years ago, but Scott was not as . . . large then. There was always the unmistakable feeling from anyone near him, that sense of . . . Lee tried to think of the right word, perhaps aura. General Scott's position, his authority was certainly intimidating. But even the old guard, the veterans who knew him from 1812, had to admit that no one else could ever dominate a conversation, no one else could ever be the center of attention, when Scott was there.

Lee watched the other generals now, gathered below the platform, maneuvering for position, each trying to be a part of the conversation taking place above them. Now the younger Scott came toward the junior officers, looked with disdain at the suffering of Johnston and Meade, and said quietly, "You may move forward, gentlemen. The commanding general will advise us all of his plan."

The young man turned quickly away, officious and curt, and Lee followed him forward, thought, What must this be like for him? Your wife's father, that kind of presence.

Scott turned to speak to the officers now gathered close to him.

"Commodore Conner has suggested this stretch of beach south of us to be the landing site. I am pleased to agree. I am asking the commodore to command the landing forces until such time as they are ashore. The navy has done a commendable duty here. Once we are on land, it will be the army's turn."

Lee could not take his eyes from Scott, was riveted by the deep voice, the sheer mass of the man commanding everyone's attention. Abruptly, Scott turned away, and now the only sound was the steady cough of the steam engine. From the bow of the boat a sailor called out, "Sir! Commodore, we have an audience!"

The men looked toward the walls of the city, now close enough that they could see it clearly without field glasses. Lee moved to the rail, could see motion along the wall, saw hands waving, hats in the air. They cannot know, he thought. They cannot know who is on this boat. But still . . .

They were too far away from the sound of cheering, but clearly, the people of Vera Cruz were not at war with these *yanquis*, the Mexican people's greeting more like a celebration. Lee glanced up at Scott, was surprised to see the general waving back to them, a wide smile on the old man's face. Lee shook his head, thought, But this is a *war*.

Scott said, "As I suspected. They're glad to see us." He turned, looked to the junior officers. "A lesson, gentlemen. Despite what we may have been told, this fight is about liberation, after all. They can see our strength, they know we're coming ashore. You'd think it was a grand parade. Well, we'll give them a show."

"Sir! Off to starboard!"

The sailor's tone of voice struck Lee, something deadly serious about it. Lee looked out to the right, beyond the city, to the great fort, could see the trail of white smoke rising above the wall. He looked at the sailor, saw the man staring hard at Uloa, thought, What?

He heard the sound, the air above them ripped by the scream of the ball, and just beyond the boat the sea was punched by a heavy fist, water rising up suddenly in a tall plume. Lee looked at Scott, saw his face twist into disappointment, the party interrupted. Now Conner made a quick motion to the helmsman, and the boat lurched to one side, turned away from the fort.

"We're a bit close, don't you think, sir?"

There was a tremble in the voice, and Lee turned, saw the ashen face of George Meade, still gripping the handrail. Scott did not look at Meade, waved a final greeting to the people lining the walls of Vera Cruz.

Conner said, "Best not give them another shot. Might improve their aim. A direct hit might be cause for concern. With your permission, sir."

Scott nodded toward Conner, turned to the men again and, smiling broadly, said something Lee did not hear. Lee stared out at Uloa, waited for the next puff of smoke, the next gun to fire. He held the handrail in a firm grip, so hard he began to shake. He caught himself, loosened his hands, looked down at his white palms, felt the cold stab in his chest. Yes, he thought, it *is* a war. And no matter what has already happened, no matter the fights that have already passed, that was *yours*, your first taste of combat, the first time anyone has ever fired at *you*.

The boat was moving back out to sea now, and as Lee stared back at the great old fort, Scott and Conner and the others were watching the beach, eyeing the key places, making the final plans for the great invasion.

2. SCOTT

MARCH EIGHTH

CONNER HAD HOPED TO LAUNCH THE TROOPS OUT OF THE great ships the next morning, but that night the stars were suddenly swept away by swirling clouds, the strong winds churning the calm water into a froth. It was a norther, and the sailors had been through it before, knew that along the Gulf coast these storms would blow up without warning, strategy and planning be damned. If the soldiers feared the worst, curled up into the quiet agony of the tossing ships, the sailors knew it would not last, because as suddenly as the black skies roared over them, the storm would be gone.

The cabin was small, but it was the largest space on the ship, what would normally be the captain's quarters. Now, the dark office in the ship's stern was for the commanding general. The young Scott stood off to one side, his boot idly prodding the corner of the glorious Persian rug, the one piece of grandeur Scott had brought with him. Scott ignored him, did not consider the young man a part of the conversation now filling the small space.

In front of Scott, Conner sat straight, hands by his side, calm and unsmiling. Off to one side, General Worth sat nervously, pulling at his uniform, glancing around the room, his legs bouncing. Behind the small fat desk, Scott stared at a piece of paper, read slowly by lamplight, the oil in the lamp rocking back and forth with the motion of the ship. He had received these dispatches before, in Texas, and the anger still came, but he was inured to it. He had been too angry at Washington for too long. Now came the frustration, the numbing sense that there was nothing he could do. He stared at the dispatch, the words now a blur, felt the great weight of weariness, thought, You are getting old. He shook his head, said, "What the hell is the matter with these people?"

No one spoke, knew Scott did not require an answer. He put the paper down, looked at the calm face of Conner, said, "The quartermaster at Brazos says there are no supply ships. Should have been a dozen more from New Orleans by now, more after that. But . . . nothing. No wagons, no horses, no reinforcements."

Scott leaned back in the chair, took a long deep breath, felt the familiar heat in his chest, the back of his neck, said, "This is Washington's fault. They have placed every roadblock . . . caused every delay."

Conner studied Scott carefully, and Scott thought, He's discreet, waiting for an opening. All right, go ahead, Commodore. Conner said, "General, I am well acquainted with General Jesup. Surely, he is doing the best he can—"

"It's not Jesup, not the damned quartermaster's office. It's higher than that, much higher."

Scott looked at Worth, saw the man's discomfort, felt a stab of uneasiness, thought, This will make the papers . . . anything said around him always makes the papers.

"General Worth, do you object to my tone of voice?"

Worth seemed to flinch, his hands clasped now, twisting together. He leaned back in his chair, shook his head. Scott saw Worth's attempt to appear calm. Worth offered a weak smile and pulled his hands apart before saying, "Uh, no, not at all, sir. The commanding general is entitled to his views."

Scott grunted. "Spoken like a politician." He looked at Conner now, said, "That's the problem, you know. They all talk like politicians. Every damned one of these generals is running for President. Or at least, that's what Polk thinks."

Worth sat upright, said, "Sir! That is simply . . . inaccurate. I have no ambitions in that regard!"

Scott looked at him for a long time, tried to read the man's face, saw indignation. "No, certainly not, General Worth. Would you say the same for General Taylor, General Quitman, General Pillow . . . ?" Scott laughed now, moved his huge frame forward, leaned heavily on the desk.

"Commodore, it is clear to me that President Polk has determined that I am to sink or swim with these men and these ships we currently have on hand. I am certain he expects me to sink, and take this army with me."

Worth was wide-eyed, the hands twisted together again. "Sir!

That is scandalous! To suggest that the President does not care for these men—"

"He cares very much, General. Sorry for offending your delicate sensibilities, but I have no doubt that Mr. Polk wishes to see the name of every one of these men at the ballot box. And if my plans do not succeed, Mr. Polk is confident that those soldiers who survive will gladly place their vote for *him*." He paused, looked for a reaction. "And not for *me*."

Scott winked at Conner, smiled. "Mr. Polk is assuming, of course, that I have my own ambitions."

Worth seemed put in his place, sat slumped in the chair. Scott thought, that will give him something to chew on. Let that one get around, President Winfield Scott. They think I'm hard to serve under *now*.

For a long moment there was no sound but the groans of the moving ship. Scott glanced up toward the thick curtains drawn shut over the wide glass across the rear of the office. The air was thick and warm now. The place needs more windows, some breeze, he thought. He glanced at Conner, saw no change in the man's expression. Do all naval commanders act like him? Total dedication to duty, no distractions. Makes sense, if you spend all your time in a dismal place like this. I never would have made it in the navy, would have wanted to stay up on deck, put a bed right outside, fall asleep feeling the wind like an infantryman ought to. The silence was growing thick, and Scott pulled himself back to the matter at hand, moved papers on his desk, saw one, headlined, *Current Roster*. He moved his finger down the list of ships, smaller boats, said to Conner, "Are we ready?"

Conner seemed relieved that the conversation had resumed, said, "If this is all the strength we are going to receive, then, yes, we are ready."

"The storm? Any estimate how long it should last?"

"The winds have already calmed a bit. A few hours more, perhaps. It likely will be a clear dawn."

Scott nodded, glanced down at the paper, felt the weariness again, breathed the stale air. Enough of this. He stood slowly, felt the stiffness in his knees and the ship's slight roll. He reached out and caught the corner of the desk with his hand, steadied himself. "I'm tired of ships. No offense, Commodore. But I'm as ready as those men out there to put my feet on dry land. If it's a clear dawn, then we go." He smiled at Conner, said, "I hope your cannoneers can shoot straight. If the Mexicans try to stop the landing, you'll be shooting over our heads."

Conner did not smile, said, "We will give you our best, sir."

Conner stood, bowed slightly. Worth was up as well, moved quickly to the door, where the young major held it open. Scott looked at his son-in-law, raised his chin slightly past perpendicular, signaling *out*, and the door closed. Scott turned to the wide curtains, pulled them open, stared out at small flecks of light, the only evidence that the water around him was a mass of ships. He felt the ship list to one side. With his hands on polished mahogany, he waited for the ship to rock back again.

Yes, slower now. Conner was right, the storm is passing. Conner, so prim and utterly efficient. Marvelous, General. You probably offended him too. Your greatest gift. The rest of them deserve to be offended. Why aren't they like him? Is there a difference because he's navy? All these old soldiers, they're leftovers, relics. They all want to see me fall on my face, and every one of them wants to pick up the pieces, turn some failure of mine into his own personal success, go back home to his own private parade.

He thought of the younger men, the lieutenants and captains fresh from West Point. He had traveled there often, especially in the last few years, had made a point of meeting them, speaking to the graduating classes.

Training professionals for this job is invaluable. We have lost too much, suffered too many casualties to officers who came by their title because they happened to be from aristocratic families, happened to be *gentlemen*. He thought of his generals, the men Polk had appointed to command his troops. We're all just old fools, veterans of a war that ended thirty years ago. If any of us falls on our face, it's those cadets who will pick us up, the young officers who will save our skin. The damned parades had better be for *them*.

He stared out at the flickering lights, above them even more lights.

Yes, *stars*. Conner was right: a clear dawn. Finally, we can go to work.

MARCH NINTH

The stars did not lie. The dawn's low clouds quickly thinned and then drifted off. By late morning the smaller gun ships had lined up along the beach, their crews staring anxiously past the flat beach to the rolling sand dunes beyond. Conner's men had supervised the loading of the surfboats, each now filled with a mass of blue, slipping through the slick calm of the water toward the shallows along the beach.

Scott stared through field glasses, watching the motion of a hundred oarsmen, the song of the oarlocks the only sound in the stark silence, replacing the bands and the sailors who had cheered him when he first appeared. The men were as focused as he was. He raised the glasses slightly, looked past the small boats, scanning the white dunes, where he saw small black shapes. He felt his heart jump. *Soldiers . . . the Mexicans . . .* But no, there was no movement, the dull shapes were simply clusters of brush, scattered along the dunes.

He lowered the glasses. *Easy, old man. They'll be there soon enough. Leave it to the navy, to those guns. We have many guns. The Mexicans will not show themselves, not yet. They'll hit us when we're the most vulnerable, when the first boats reach the beach.* He thought of the Mexican commander there, General Morales. He knew nothing about how he would respond to this glorious opportunity to turn the Americans away. He was not sure of Morales's strength, knew Uloa could hold a garrison of three thousand men, and in the town, that big damned wall . . . there could be thousands more. He felt a sudden deep uneasiness. He had never doubted the plan until now.

Sixty surfboats, half what I need. Damn Washington! It will take three trips for each boat, we will land one division at a time, twenty-five hundred men, and if the Mexicans are patient, and pick the right moment, even their cavalry can ride down that beach and cut us up piecemeal.

He pounded his fist on the rail, thought of Conner. *Those gunners had better be very very good.*

The sun was moving on toward the west, and he tilted his head back, let the clean and cool air chill the sweat on his face. He put the glasses down and watched as the line of surfboats jumbled together, a cluster of brown and blue working its way to the beach. The queasiness returned, and he shivered. Around him the staff was staring out intently, waiting, as he had been, for the first sounds, the response from Morales's troops to this invasion of their soil. He looked down the rail, saw a row of field glasses, all pointing out, felt the helplessness again, thought, *This is not how it should be. I should be* out there, *with them,* leading *them.*

It was so long ago, that marvelous awful war, crossing the Niagara River, straight into the guns of the British. Then, he had been in the boats with his men, jumping ashore past the dead of both sides, leading his men up to take the British guns. It had been quick and glorious, and he had stayed close to his men, sharing the pure joy of watching the redcoats pulling away, leaving Scott and his men their precious cannon.

The Americans could not hold the fort, they were simply too few, and once the British regrouped, their strength pushed the Americans back into the river. He had been captured, the price he paid for a brief truce that allowed his men to retreat. He thought of the newspapers, the response from the feeble old men, the generals who ran *that* war. In their eyes it was humiliation, a defeat, but he knew better, he had seen the respect in the faces of the British. And his troops, they understood what he had sacrificed, what they had *all* done. They had stood up to the greatest fighting force in the world, and, for a time, had pushed them back.

He looked at the field glasses in his hands, raised them again, found the line of small boats. The ninth of March was a date he would never forget. He had received his first star, the promotion to Brigadier General on this same date. He did not believe much in signs, thought, If it is a coincidence, it is a grand coincidence. He lowered the glasses, saw in his mind the piece of paper he had read a thousand times. *March 9, 1814.* My God. Thirty-three years ago. It cannot be so long. . . .

"Sir!"

He tried to clear his head, heard the rumble of a cannon. He looked toward the shore and a puff of white smoke rising from a small gunboat.

Around him, men were pointing. He raised the glasses, thought, It has begun. Behind him a naval officer hurried close, said, "Sir! The lookout reports enemy cavalry, back in the dunes. We fired a shell from the *Tampico*."

Scott nodded. He said nothing, simply stared hard at the dunes, waiting, expecting to see a mass of dark shapes, thick lines of horsemen. But the dunes were still motionless. He lowered the glasses. The Mexicans are very patient indeed.

The officer cleared his throat, said, "Sir, the boats are holding their position, close to the beach, as per plan. The commodore is awaiting your final order, sir."

Scott looked at the man, saw grim efficiency, nodded slowly, said, "You may signal the commodore to proceed."

The officer saluted Scott, moved quickly away. Scott turned again toward the shore, and suddenly there was a sharp blast, one gun firing from below, the deck jumping beneath his feet. It was the signal, *his* signal, to land the troops.

He saw the motion again, the oars reflected in the sun. His weariness was gone now, the anxious twist at his belt had subsided. He strained to see through the glasses, felt his heart pounding. Go on, go on. He still waited for the sounds of a fight, scanned the dunes again, still saw nothing.

Damn, old man, you should be *out there*.

IT HAD BEEN DARK NEARLY FOUR HOURS. HE HAD STOPPED LOOKING at his pocket watch, would not let down, turn away, still expecting the assault at any time. There were lights all along the shore, fires up in the dunes, and closer, the lights from the smaller ships, and everywhere the eerie silence. The Mexicans had still not come.

Leaning against the rail, he looked down into black water, listened to the slow slap of waves against the ship. Suddenly, there was a streak of light, and he looked up, followed a long arc of fire coming out from the shore. He gripped the rail, waited for more, watched the streak of white fading. He realized it was a rocket, the signal from the commanders.

"Sir, we are ashore."

Scott turned, saw his son-in-law in the dim light, a rare smile splitting the young man's unlined face. Scott looked at his watch. *Eleven o'clock.*

"Losses?"

The young man seemed surprised at the question. "Sir, there were no losses. The landing was unopposed."

"I am aware the enemy did not oppose us. But, surely, there were casualties, a boat sinking, somebody falling overboard." He saw the puzzled expression on his son-in-law's face. It can't have been *this* easy.

The young Scott saluted. "Sir, I will investigate the matter."

Scott nodded, and the young man moved away. Behind him, another man cleared his throat. Scott grunted, turned, thought, Why can't they just *speak* to me?

The man snapped a crisp salute, said, "General, your boat is prepared. With your permission, sir, we can take you ashore. The commodore respectfully advises that your objective and his mission have been satisfied. The army is once again on land."

Scott smiled, thought, A man who speaks with frankness. Refreshing. "You may advise the commodore that the last of the army is leaving his command."

The man still smiled, said, "Um, sir. I apologize for overhearing your inquiry. You were asking about casualties, I believe?"

Scott stopped smiling. "How many?"

"None, sir."

Scott said nothing. Eight thousand men, sixty surfboats, thousands of enemy troops close by . . . and no casualties?

The officer held out his arm, pointed along the rail. "The boat is this way, sir. At your convenience."

The man saluted again and Scott returned it, still absorbing the news of their resounding success. He took a deep breath, felt himself straighten, was suddenly full of the old energy. By God, this was a victory! A one-shot victory! Let Washington swallow that!

He turned toward the bow of the ship, could see along the railing, several of the staff still watching the shore. He looked at the faces, some now looking at him. He tried to remember names, scanned past the younger faces, saw the taller man, not so young, watching him with clear sharp eyes, the face of experience, thought, Yes, the engineer. Good.

"Captain Lee. It seems we have accomplished our objective. Are you ready for duty?"

Lee stood straight, said quietly, "Certainly, sir."

Scott scanned Lee's face, glimpsed a spark, a short quick nod, expectant, briefly piercing Lee's composure. Lee seemed to be waiting for more, leaning forward slightly. The rest of the staff also moved closer, waiting for Scott's command.

"Gentlemen, let's go ashore." Scott moved away, back toward the waiting boat. He turned and said to Lee, "You the least bit curious just what duty I'm talking about, Captain?"

Lee's expression did not change, and he said, "Curious? Certainly, sir. I am at the general's disposal."

"I recall that you built forts. Along the East coast, I believe."

"I assisted in the preliminary construction of several works, yes, sir."

"Good. Just the man for the job."

Scott moved to the opening in the rail, saw the naval officer who had informed him that the landing craft was ready and other sailors waiting. Lee said, "May I ask . . . what job, sir?"

Scott pointed out through the darkness, toward the mass of lights, the glow of the city off to the right.

"The enemy has chosen to let this army come ashore unopposed. That was a mistake. He apparently believes he can stay behind those walls, and defend himself. It's up to you, Captain, to convince him he has made another mistake."

Now Lee's expression changed, and Scott saw a puzzled look. They reached the gangway, and Scott saluted the naval officer before moving down toward the waiting boat. Lee followed, said, "I'm not sure I understand, sir."

Scott did not answer. He prepared to step down into the smaller boat, saw the boat's commander, a cheerful man with a thick beard, who said, "Welcome aboard, General. We will be under way at your discretion, sir."

Scott landed hard on the deck, felt the boat move slightly with him, said, "You may proceed, Commander."

Scott moved heavily to the bow, the boat listing slightly. Lee stayed close behind him. Scott glanced back, saw the rest of the staff file into the boat. The commander gave a brief order to a helmsman, and two sailors pushed away from the big ship with long poles. As the boat began to move, Scott felt the chill, the breeze picking up, the heavy darkness of the early morning closing around them as they moved away from the big ship. He did not look at Lee, but he could feel him close by, staring out at the lights of Vera Cruz, protected by the great fat wall.

Scott said, "You certainly understand how forts are built, Captain. Then I assume you understand how they can be destroyed."

3. LEE

March eighteenth

THE GUNS AND SUPPLIES WERE UNLOADED ON THE BEACH AS quickly as the soldiers could move out of the way. The headquarters had become a simple cluster of tents, dug in tight to the rolling dunes, out of range from the big guns of the city. The command's first priority had been to move the troops, spreading them out into an arc to enclose Vera Cruz, preventing any supplies or Mexican troops from reinforcing the garrison in the city. The Americans had spread out in the rough country with slow progress, and they came to appreciate how glorious the weather had been for the landing itself. As the army moved, cutting its way inland through the soft dunes, it was as though the deep sand sucked the energy from their legs as they staggered toward the thick brush. More storms blew in, making the sand firmer, the footing more solid in exchange for the misery of chilling rain. The winds increased, whipping up the sand that coated the men's exposed skin, their beards, in a gritty film that worked its way into their eyes, noses, and mouths. Soon every crease in their clothes was covered as well, and these men marched, heads down, slogging uphill. The patter of the rainfall was punctuated by the sound of the men spitting, hoping to rid themselves of the particles they ground between their teeth.

But soon the arc was complete, Vera Cruz was cut off, and the army now stood squarely in the face of the enemy who waited quietly behind the big walls.

The Mexicans had shown no sign of an advance, no attempt to push out against the American lines, to break out of the city. Even Uloa was quiet, the massive firepower in the old fort silent, waiting for Scott's next move.

It was not all quiet. To the west, along the main road that led inland, Mexican horsemen picked and prodded at the Americans from behind, some seeking a way into the city, to join the forces there, or to bring in valuable supplies. The skirmishes were usually brief, and often it was one sharp volley from the Americans that drove the enemy away. As the strength and resolve of Scott's forces became apparent, the Mexicans learned to attack in small numbers, lightning quick, using the guerrilla tactics that torment an immobile army. If the calm from the city gave the soldiers some rest, the bands of Mexicans inland meant that no sentry could let down his guard, and that no one was really immune to attack.

Lee was becoming used to the soft sand now, led a gun crew through the winding trail, between the dunes, out of sight of enemy sentries in the city. Behind him the men heaved against the cannon, a big twenty-four pounder, and rolled it very slowly forward, fighting the sand's resistance. Lee stopped, waited patiently, watching the wheels again cutting deep furrows. The men gathered themselves once again, lifting with one loud grunt. The gun inched forward again.

The men were grateful that they moved the guns at night, under the cover of darkness to avoid detection and to avoid the heat. They knew that as the guns were brought forward, close enough to put their shells over the wall, the Mexican guns could reach them as well.

The sand began to harden as the terrain flattened and the trail straightened beyond the dunes. Lee heard the sound of shovels, pointed the way, and now the men could see a glow of light. A lantern, hung from a pole, shielded on the back side by a wide black tent so the Mexicans could not know where the guns were being placed.

Lee moved to the gun pit, the men with shovels climbing out, making way as the crew rolled the gun forward. The men held the gun from behind with ropes, guiding it slowly down into the pit, the barrel resting just above ground level.

Lee nodded, said quietly, "Very well, gentlemen. Good work, all around."

The night's stillness was broken by small sounds, whispered conversations, the click of shovels. The gun crew was busy looking for a place to make camp.

Lee watched the work, thought, What remarkable energy. They have been in the ships for so long, I suppose this is a relief, even if the work is hard. I hope it is enough. He looked out toward the city, the pattern of lights familiar now, thought, They must know what we're doing, they cannot just . . . wait. We're not going to simply march away.

He heard a man move up beside him, turned, saw a sergeant, a young face, reflected in the light of the lantern. "Sir, you think we ought to keep going? Probably three or four hours left till daylight. There's two more guns in this battery, still on the beach."

Lee read the exhaustion in the man's face, knew the crews would be in worse shape still. "Not now, Sergeant. Let it go. They need some rest."

"Be a sight easier if we had some horses, sir."

Lee had heard that before, nodded quietly. The man moved away, and Lee stared again at the city, thought, Yes, it would be much easier if we had horses. But for whatever reason, they didn't give us any.

Earlier in the evening he had been called by Scott to attend another senior meeting. Lee had thought it would be about strategy, but it had not been a meeting at all. The staff and several senior commanders had sat quietly while Scott blew out his anger about the horses. The landing had put eight thousand men ashore, and less than a hundred horses, but worse, there were barely a dozen wagons. The navy had done their job with astounding efficiency, had landed a great mountain of supplies on the beach, but anything moving inland had to be carried by hand. Each box, each roll of canvas, had to be carried through sand and swamp and prickly pear cactus by cursing, sweating soldiers. And, as Lee had directed for several days now, the big guns would be pushed, lifted, and dragged as well.

For a long moment he tugged at his collar, tried to let the cool air, any breeze reach his skin. He had not stopped moving all night. He was not used to sleeping in daylight, and so, as the days wore on, and the army prepared itself for whatever was next, he rarely slept at all. He tried to read his watch, squinted in the dim light, guessed, maybe three o'clock? He felt a sting on his arm, brushed at it, then his face, tiny pinpricks on his forehead, his cheeks. He wiped his face with his hand, felt the assault spreading now to every part of his body, even inside his clothes.

He resumed moving, brushing, scratching at himself, waving the air in front of him. He thought, No, not again, *move*. He hurried past the gun crew, some men lying flat on the sand, already looking for the blessed sleep, and now he heard the curses from them, men slapping themselves, fighting back at the sudden torment. Behind him the men with the shovels stopped their work, watched the new arrivals fighting against this unseen enemy. There was laughter, and one man called out,

"It ain't no use, boys. You can't see 'em. Can't even feel 'em. Might as well just let 'em in, 'cause they're gonna take over anyhow."

Lee knew the man was right, it happened each time he stopped moving. You could barely see them in the daylight, some kind of flea that seemed to rise up out of the sand. He watched the men on the ground still rubbing their arms, legs, faces, and the sergeant was up now. "Captain, the men want to keep at it, sir. We heard about the fleas. Best we keep moving. If you don't mind, we'd like to go get those guns."

The men were all standing now, and Lee saw them already moving away, back toward the trail. He took a deep breath, felt something fly into his mouth. He spit sharply, felt his throat twist into a knot, spit again. Hard to get used to that, he thought. Glad Mary wasn't here to see this. He spit again, thought, A fine show from a Virginia gentleman. His face was contorted by the awful bitterness from his mouth. The sergeant was watching him, suppressing a laugh, and Lee said, "By all means, Sergeant. The faster we get the job done, the less time we have to stay *here*."

MARCH NINETEENTH

Lee had been out on the far end of the line, performing a last minute inspection of the most distant gun positions, and was moving through the narrow path his men had cut through the thorny brush. Behind him was Lieutenant Beauregard, the brilliant young man from Louisiana. Beauregard was a small, wiry man, handsome, who wore a short clipped point of beard. He was always neat, the uniform perfect, nothing out of place, and Lee had begun to see that Beauregard brought that same attention to detail to his engineering skills. Lee had not known him long, but he knew the man's reputation as an engineer was already well-established. He'd come to the army's attention first by his West Point standing. Beauregard had been second in the class of 1845, the same ranking Lee had achieved sixteen years earlier. Some of Beauregard's detractors had said the Louisianan's high rank was due to his age, graduating at twenty-nine, much older than his classmates. Lee had never considered the young man's age to be any reflection on his abilities, took for granted that all the junior engineers were younger than he.

They moved quietly. The daylight was fading, and he could hear Beauregard behind him, slapping at the bugs that swarmed over them from the deep brush. The trail turned a blind curve, and Lee stepped past a palmetto, his coat slapping the stiff green fronds. In front of him he saw a soldier facing him, pointing a pistol at his head.

"Who goes there?"

Lee ducked, heard Beauregard shout, "Friends! Officers!"

Lee could see the man's face, his wide, panicked eyes. The barrel of the pistol aimed past Lee, then jerked back toward him again. Suddenly there was a bright flash, a deafening sound, only a few feet from Lee's face, and the soldier was hidden by the cloud of white smoke. Lee stood up straight, felt his heart pounding. The smoke slid away into the brush, while the boy stood staring at them, his face a map of raw horror. Lee put his hand up, said, "It's all right. We're not hit."

Behind him, Beauregard was looking down, feeling his chest, then rubbing his hand along the blue coat. "You missed. Thank God."

The soldier dropped the pistol, stared at the two officers for a moment, then suddenly began to cry. Behind the man, along the trail, more men appeared, sentries, the men who guarded the army against the guerrillas. Now a sergeant appeared, pushed the boy aside, saw the pistol on the ground, looked at Lee, said, "What? Anyone hurt? Damn! I knew it. He's too green for this!"

Lee held up his hand. "No, we're all right. He was just . . . a bit jumpy. We were too quiet, surprised him."

The sergeant removed his hat, said, "Sir, this will be reported to my commander. It is inexcusable. Might I ask, sir, your names? For the report."

Lee looked at the boy, who was sobbing now, thought, This will ruin him, he'll never be a soldier after this.

"I am Captain Lee, this is Lieutenant Beauregard, of the general staff."

The sergeant turned, looked at the boy, the anger spilling over. "You hear that? You damned near killed . . . by Jesus, you damned near killed General Scott's staff! What's the matter with you?"

Lee moved closer to the man. "It's all right, Sergeant. No harm done. File your report as required. But, it was an accident. Could have happened anywhere."

The sergeant looked at Lee, pulled a paper from his pocket, a small stub of pencil. He looked at Lee's coat, then leaned his head to the side, stared under Lee's shoulder. "Uh, appears, sir, he didn't exactly miss."

Lee looked down, raised his arm, saw a black rip in his coat. He felt his breath suddenly punched away, then pulled open the coat, saw the bullet had not penetrated. He let out a deep breath, blessed relief, thought, I didn't feel it . . . but that was very close. Thank God.

Beauregard stood beside him, leaned close, looked at the ripped cloth, said, "Well, now, Captain Lee, another inch or so and your service might have ended right here."

Most of the artillery was in place, gun crews waiting impatiently for the order to begin the great assault. The waiting meant that the other war would continue awhile longer, the fight against the small creatures that kept up their relentless assault on their new visitors. Most of the men had never seen some of these strange and exotic pests: scorpions, snakes, a tiny black ant with an amazing bite, outdone only by the torture from the yellow flies, or worse, huge black horseflies. And of course, there were the fleas.

Lee took his place beside Totten, while his commander, the old engineer, inspected Lee's work, examining the placement of the guns. Lee had been nervous about this at first, wondered if the gun pits were deep enough, if the angle of fire was correct. Under other circumstances, Totten was his friend, and the two of them often enjoyed the quiet social scene. But the duty of the engineers was very different now. In Mexico, Totten was all business, brought the keen eye of a senior commander to the work of his engineers. Lee could not help feeling nervous, intimidated, as he watched Totten's quiet inspection. He thought of West Point, recalled his nervousness, the intolerance he and his superiors had for any mistake. He tried to push those recollections away, but felt as though he was again very young, very much under the eye of someone who would find any fault. Totten was no longer the friendly face, but the no-nonsense engineer and the man Scott would hold responsible for the success of his plan. Lee had already begun to accept that their relationship might never be as it was before, that this duty would change all of them, the relationships, the social informality. Now, it was only about doing the job, and doing it right.

Some of the guns were aiming nearly perpendicular to the big wall, others were pointed higher, so they would launch their shells in a high arc. Totten had still said nothing, but stopped now, stepped down into a gun pit. The crew stood respectfully aside. Lee tried to follow Totten's gaze, tried to visualize the trajectory of the shell. Totten leaned down, looked along the barrel of the twelve-pound gun, said, "Too high."

He looked up at Lee then, the message clear in the expression, and Lee said, "Yes, sir. It will be corrected, sir."

Beyond Totten, Lee saw an officer approaching quickly, then another, reacting to the sudden presence of the chief engineer. The first man was clearly in command, a familiar face Lee had met while placing his battery. The man was older, gray hair peeking out from beneath his hat. He glanced unsmiling at Lee, spoke to Totten.

"Excuse me, Colonel. Captain Francis Taylor, Company K. These are my guns. Is there a problem, sir?"

Totten appraised Taylor, said, "Are you certain of your aim, Captain?"

Taylor glanced at Lee again. The other officer moved up beside Taylor, and Lee noticed another young man. His angular face flushed, he glared fiercely at Totten. Lee thought, Careful, young man, don't be too defensive.

The younger officer said, "Pardon me, Colonel, but I intend that these guns do more than bounce their shells off a stone wall. They're not big enough to do much good anyway. We figured . . ." He paused, looked up at Lee. "We figured it would do the most good to drop these shells behind the wall. Should cause much more damage to the enemy. Sir."

The man had spoken with a slow, deliberate drawl. Lee had heard the accent before, thought, Virginia, the mountains.

Totten was eyeing the young man. "All right, young lieutenant. If Captain Lee agrees with your strategy, then I concur."

Totten climbed out of the pit, straightened his uniform, said to Taylor, "I admire confidence, Captain. Let's put it to work."

Totten turned close to Lee, said quietly, "As you were, Captain. Give me a moment."

Totten moved on, and Lee saw his hand go up as Totten engaged in a brief reunion with an older officer, a man Lee did not know. Lee backed away from the guns.

Taylor motioned to the young lieutenant, said to Lee, "Captain, forgive the lack of subtlety of my young lieutenant. Have you made the acquaintance? He's another Virginian."

Lee looked at the young man, who seemed suddenly self-conscious. He held Lee's gaze briefly before his sharp blue eyes darted away. Lee held out a hand, said, "He handled himself well, Captain. Lieutenant, I'm Captain Lee."

The young man hesitated a moment, then took Lee's hand briefly, withdrew his hand quickly. "Jackson, sir. Thomas Jackson."

The blue eyes again glanced past Lee. The man backed slowly

away, and Lee saw a small grimace of discomfort on his face, thought, He is not accustomed to being sociable. It's apparent he would rather be with his guns than making small talk with a senior officer.

Lee could see Totten approaching again, said, "A pleasure, Mr. Jackson. When the time comes, I'm sure you will make good use of these guns."

Abruptly, Jackson straightened, stood stiffly, said, "We're waiting for the order, sir. We just want a chance to fight. One good fight."

Lee noticed Totten moving farther along the gun pits and beckoned to him. "Excuse me, gentlemen." He quickly moved toward Totten, who was already down in another gun pit, the inspection continuing. Lee glanced back at the two officers, thought, Strange comment. He shall get his fight. I hope it's to his liking.

MARCH TWENTY-FIRST

"Our guns aren't big enough! If we're going to knock those walls down, we need something else besides these field guns." Scott paused now, looked around the group of men, each looking to the man beside him, hoping someone had an answer Scott would approve of.

Lee sat beside Totten, the chairs arranged in a semicircle in the hard sand. Scott sat at a small field desk, at the mouth of his tent, his round face reflected by the light from a great fire. Lee glanced in the direction of the bright light. He thought it was a bad idea, providing so large a target for Mexican cannon, and he wondered how obvious their position would be with the night broken by such a large ball of light. Scott had not seemed concerned, had insisted two aides stay close to the fire and keep it high, the heat rolling toward the tent, in hopes of keeping the tormenting insects at bay. Lee realized now that across the camps of the men there were more fires, some nearly as large as this one. If they were all targets for anxious gunners in Vera Cruz, at least no one could tell that close to this one was most of the command of the entire American army.

He looked around the circle of men, saw Worth and Patterson, and straight across from him, the craggy frown of General Twiggs.

Twiggs stared at the ground near Lee's feet before saying, "We don't need guns. We just need men. Take it to 'em. The Mexicans can't stand up to this army. Full out assault."

Lee looked at Scott, saw the deepening red in his face. Scott looked around the circle. He focused on General Pillow. "Anyone else agree with General Twiggs? Anyone else feel we should just march right up to those walls? Anyone have some information about the enemy's eagerness to surrender that I am not aware of?"

Lee watched Pillow, who seemed to wilt under Scott's glare. Pillow glanced to the side, looked at Worth, who said, "They can't win. Surely General Morales understands that. If we show them we're willing to launch an all-out assault, he'll give up the city."

Scott leaned back, rubbed a heavy hand across tired red eyes, and slumped in the chair. He took a long deep breath, before saying quietly, "It'll look good in the papers too. Lots of good old man-to-man fighting, blood in the streets, our boys giving it their all, for the Cause. And then, we can explain to the American people just why we gave them a such a butcher bill. Or rather, the President would make sure *I* explained it."

Scott looked around the circle again, said, "Gentlemen, you ever hear of *saving face*? Everything I have learned about the Mexicans tells me that coming out of a fight with their honor intact is more important than who won the damned fight. They'll surrender the city, and that big damned fort, when it's the right time, and it will have very little to do with how much blood we shed. Morales isn't about to surrender because he's scared of our strength. He can't show he's scared at all. He'd disgrace himself." Scott shook his head. "This is a foreign country, gentlemen, a foreign culture. We're not fighting the British here, people like us, people who see things the way we do. War is about knowing your enemy. It is not necessary to spill blood, our blood, if we can defeat Morales by letting him keep his honor."

Lee looked at Worth, watched a patronizing sneer spreading across his face. Worth cleared his throat and said, "Excuse me, sir, but if we defeat Morales, how does he keep his honor? Isn't losing a disgrace? Hard to imagine anyone saving face when he's just had his city occupied. Or are we not planning to occupy Vera Cruz?"

Scott closed his eyes briefly. Lee felt a sudden frustration, thought, Surely he has a plan. Why do they show such disrespect?

Twiggs leaned forward now, still staring at the ground, and said, "So, General Scott, do you have an alternative plan? How do we convince the enemy to surrender without *fighting* him?"

Scott glanced at Lee, said, "We are already in position for a siege. I believe it's the best plan."

Twiggs grunted. "A siege!"

There were muttered comments from the commanders, a small laugh from Worth, who said, "Forgive me, General, but a siege might take a while. My understanding is . . . we don't have that luxury."

Scott nodded. "Yes, General, point well taken. We have three, maybe four weeks before the fever season hits. It is crucial we move inland, gain altitude before then."

As was his custom, Pillow stood to speak. Lee looked at the fresh uniform, always neat, as though the small thick-waisted man was always dressed for a formal review. Lee could see him preparing, a brief strut, a quick turn, all designed to capture everyone's attention.

"General Scott, am I to understand that your plan is to effect a siege on Vera Cruz, defeat the enemy therein, gather this army for a bold move inland, all before the *el vomito* destroys this army?" He paused for dramatic effect. "Ambitious, to say the least."

Scott noted Pillow's arrogance with grim silence, and Lee could see it plainly now, what they all knew from the beginning. Gideon Pillow was President Polk's law partner, was commanding troops despite having no great experience other than an oily skill at political maneuvering. Lee watched Scott, thought, Of course, he thinks Pillow is here to spy on him, a conduit straight to the President. And he's probably right.

Lee felt his own frustration growing, had begun to understand Scott's anger. He shifted slightly, began to raise his hand, hesitated, and Totten leaned close, whispered, "Speak up, Captain."

Lee stood, glanced at the faces of the others, saw Scott now watching him, and Scott said, "Yes, Captain? Ideas or complaints?"

There was complete silence until Lee said, "Sir, I believe the siege can be accomplished in short order. It is understood now that the army's guns are not large enough to inflict damage on the walls of the city, and I believe Uloa is stronger still. However . . . we have another resource."

Scott was watching him intently, nodded, a silent command, *Continue.*

"If we could call on the navy . . . make use of their guns. On shipboard I saw cannon as large as sixty-four pounders. Those would be more than adequate to inflict extreme damage on Vera Cruz."

Worth leaned forward, said, "Captain Lee, we have already considered at length a naval assault against the city. Perhaps you were not present. The guns of Uloa would inflict serious loss on our ships if they came close enough for a bombardment."

"No, sir, not a naval bombardment. I propose . . . I respectfully suggest that we relocate . . . bring some of the larger cannon ashore, at least the thirty-two pounders. My men can dig them into gun pits alongside the army's guns. The men are already accustomed to hauling equipment by hand. With the navy's help, we could create a formidable artillery force. Sir."

Lee sat down slowly, felt himself sweating, waited for someone to speak, but there was silence. Scott still watched him, stared at him for a long moment, and Lee felt the gaze, was suddenly self-conscious, looked down, flexed his fingers, thought, Well, *I* thought it was a good idea.

Scott slapped his hand down on the small table, said, "Let's give it a try, Captain. I will make arrangements with Commodore Conner. You will have all the armament and manpower you require."

Scott looked at Totten. "Colonel, you stand by your engineer?"

Totten nodded slowly, looked up at Lee, said, "Absolutely, sir."

"Good. Captain, I like men who have enough of a brain to come up with helpful suggestions. I already have enough complaints. You will command the placement of the naval guns yourself. Once they're in place, you will notify me."

Lee felt his heart thump, tried to speak, felt his throat tighten, fought it, said in a rough croak, "Yes, sir."

Scott stood, and the meeting was over. The commanders were quickly up, moving away without a word. Around Lee, the other staff began to gather, murmuring, and Lee felt a hand on his shoulder, a brief pat, and then another. He saw smiling faces, Johnston, even the young Scott, and finally Totten smiled, said, "Well done, Captain. You may have a talent for making powerful friends. But be careful. Not everyone appreciates a junior officer who catches the general's eye."

MARCH TWENTY-SECOND

The navy had responded with surprising enthusiasm, sailors dragging their guns through the brush as the army crews had before them. Even the ranking naval officers understood that Lee was in command, and older men accustomed to their absolute authority on the great ships followed his instructions. The sailors strained and groaned as the army crews had, placing their guns throughout Lee's batteries, and the awful assaults of the fleas did not slow the work. To the sailors, the work was something new, shovels and sand, and to the soldiers, it afforded them a new kind of camaraderie and competition—the navy men not merely transportation workers, but fighters as well.

Lee watched as the huge gun barrel was lowered by block and tackle, setting the massive iron down on a makeshift gun carriage. The barrel settled heavily, the timbers below groaning, and now the crew swarmed over the gun, lashing the barrel to the thick wood, while

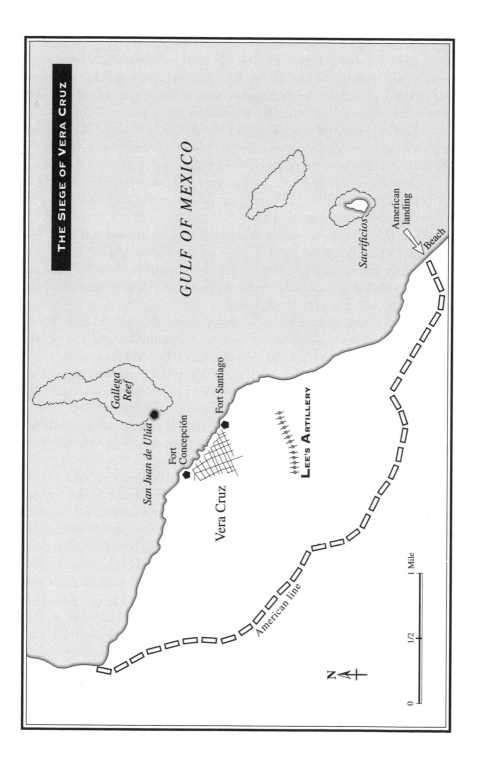

THE SIEGE OF VERA CRUZ

GULF OF MEXICO

Sacrificios

American landing

Beach

Gallega Reef

San Juan de Ulúa

Fort Concepción

Fort Santiago

Vera Cruz

LEE'S ARTILLERY

American line

N

0   1/2   1 Mile

more men with shovels began to move the sand again, close around the gun pit, erecting a small round wall. Lee had given the instructions once, did not have to repeat himself, the sailors tackling the dirty work with a glee that made him smile. The gun firmly in place, he looked out toward the dunes, knew another was coming, the last of this battery. Very soon, he thought. We are almost ready.

A small group of sailors moved out of the brush, the men straining under the weight of wooden boxes. Good, he thought, powder and shell. If this is to be a siege, we will need a great deal of both.

Out of the corner of his eye he saw an officer carrying a box. The officer smiled, said, "You taking good care of my guns, Captain? Not sure I can trust an old army man."

Lee knew the voice, returned the smile. It was his brother. "Smith! I knew you were here . . . still on the *Mississippi*, I believe?"

Smith Lee set the box down, walked toward his brother. He put his hands on Lee's shoulders, said, "Appears . . . we're a team. At least for a while. What would Mother say?"

Lee nodded, said nothing. Smith's comment surprised him. He always believed his older brother had been his mother's favorite, the handsome one, sure to capture the fair hearts. Lee had seen some of the letters between them, soft and tender, his mother always anguishing that Smith had chosen the navy, and so would rarely be home. Lee had felt his mother's death as deeply as any event in his life, but he had been *there* and Smith had not. Lee had always wondered if Smith felt any guilt about that, or if he resented his younger brother holding on to that special, awful moment, his mother dying in his arms. Lee felt uncomfortable now, and Smith, still holding him by the shoulders, said quietly, "She *would* be proud of you. Look at this. Look at the responsibility. Every officer I meet says, 'So, you're the brother of General Scott's engineer. That's really something.' "

Smith backed away now, and Lee saw that his brother was embarrassed as well. They were not often together, and these moments were rare. Around them the men had stopped working, watched the two with curiosity. Smith turned, saw the sailors moving up, said, "Hold it. Let's find out where we need to be." He turned to Lee now, bowed slightly. "Captain Lee, will you direct us to our proper position?"

Lee thought he heard something in his brother's voice, a tease, an edge of sarcasm, but Smith looked at him with no trace of humor on his face.

Lee said, "Yes, very well. That dugout there, beyond the twelve-pound howitzer. It should accommodate the next gun. The range is seven hundred yards. Adjust your aim to strike the wall immediately to your front. You may place your men behind, with their supplies in the dugout farther back. They will construct a trench parallel to the defensive works, there, for cover from enemy artillery. They can make camp back beyond that brush line. A trail has been cut."

He stopped, saw the grin again, and Smith saluted him, something Lee had never seen, said, "Aye, sir," then turned, said to his men, "The captain's instructions were plain. Proceed!"

The sailors moved quickly toward the open gun pit, and Smith began to move away as well, glanced back at Lee, nodded, said quietly, "Yes, proud indeed."

March twenty-fourth

He paced impatiently, watched a group of sailors groaning under the weight, hard men covered by the sand and sweat of an unfamiliar duty, strong hands holding thick ropes and levers and long poles, positioning the last of the huge cannon. In front of the long line of batteries, the ground was clear, all obstruction removed. There was no longer any reason to hide the guns from the Mexican lookouts. The order had come straight from Scott: coordinate the batteries, and fire when ready. He watched the sailors, thought, Give them time, let's do this right. His brother was commanding the closest naval battery now, and Lee saw him climb up from a deep pit, sweating, his uniform covered in sand.

Around Smith the sailors were only partially dressed, having shed the blue outer shirts without embarrassment. But the officers had to keep decorum, and despite the heat and the work, their coats stayed on. Smith rubbed sweat from his face, cursed. Lee felt the tension give way, smiled, was about to tease his brother when he heard a crackle, then a long low sound above him, growing louder. He looked up, saw a streak of blue cutting the air, and behind him, near the trenches the men had dug for their own protection, the ball dropped with a deep *thud* and plowed into the sand. There was a quiet moment, the closest men backing away from the impact of the heavy shell, and then no one moved, the men staring at the strange crater in the sand. Suddenly, the sand rose up in one great blast, a sharp explosion of black smoke and dirt. The men yelled, a great release of tension, cheering the close call with raw excitement. Lee wanted to shout something, felt the same burst of excitement, the cold in his chest, but held it back. He looked toward the city. He could still see the wisp of smoke, thought, There are no surprises now. They know we are here.

He looked again at the final crew, and they were watching him, their work complete. He looked at his brother, who was smiling, waiting, as they all waited, and he felt his throat tighten, thought, *Remember this.* This is how a soldier feels. God help us. He stepped up on a small mound of dirt, the commander's vantage point, said, "You may begin, gentlemen. Fire!"

MARCH TWENTY-SEVENTH

It had been three days, and he could see it clearly, stared out through field glasses at gaping holes, great piles of rubble that had been the walls of Vera Cruz. Around him the guns still shattered the air, the crews black with smoke and powder, ducking into the trenches when a response would come from the guns in the city.

Close by there was a blast, a great flash of light and sound, and he heard screaming, stared through the smoke, moved toward the explosion, trying to see the result. Men were scrambling toward the wounded, and he thought, *Smith.* He fought his way forward, saw one man's body torn nearly in two, a great black stain in the sand, and another man, a sailor, his leg twisted horribly to one side. There were men beside the sailor now, the man screaming still, and Lee stood back, watched as the others carried him away to the rear, back where the hospital had been set up. It had been a surprise to Lee, something he had never thought of. A *hospital.* Men were wounded, dying, and if the Mexican batteries were losing the fight, or if their guns were old, less accurate, they could still do damage. They could still kill his men.

He saw his brother then, pointing, shouting to his crews, the big gun roaring out a volley, answering the Mexican shell. Thank God, he thought. I had not thought of this either. My brother, right next to me. I could watch him die. He fought those images. Focus. Do your job.

He moved back to his vantage point, raised the glasses again toward the enemy positions. Still he was torn, the man after all was his brother. There is no time for that. I have no right. He looked toward his brother again, hidden again in a great fog of white smoke. But I cannot ignore it. *God protect him.*

He glassed again toward the city, could see a fresh opening in the wall, and through it, the city itself, bright color, a wall, a painting of . . . something. He stared at that one spot, caught a glimpse of motion, a small cart, a horse, maybe a donkey. There was a flash, a smaller shell, striking the painted wall, then he could see nothing, the image hidden by the smoke and debris.

He lowered the glasses, shook his head grimly, thought, It is a city, after all. The people, civilians. The plan had been sound, the smaller field guns would not waste ammunition firing at the wall. He thought of the strange young lieutenant, Jackson, had seen him working his guns with a terrifying energy, knew that Jackson's guns, many of the smaller field pieces, were dropping shells right into the city itself. He had seen the smoke, could see it now, great billowing black columns rising from the wooden houses.

The destruction, the casualties, must be horrific. Don't do this, he thought, you cannot dwell on that, on what these guns might do to those people. They have an army in there, and they have commanders, and it is up to them to stop this. It is not up to me.

He moved the glasses along the wall, gazed past the ragged openings, saw motion out in front of the wall, a carriage, small flickers of color, flags. He strained to see the carriage moving out toward the American lines, far to his left, disappearing now from his view. Strange, he thought, someone trying to escape.

He felt something turn in his chest. Or, perhaps the cart was carrying a flag of truce. He looked down past the batteries, the crews still working methodically, the guns firing in rhythm with each other, as they had for three days. They had not seen what he saw, and he watched for a moment, had become used to the scattered blasts of smoke and sand, the Mexican artillery trying in vain to silence the batteries. But for a long moment the only sound was the steady firing of his own guns. He thought, There are no shells, no incoming rounds. The Mexicans have stopped shooting.

He felt a small panic, thought, If it's a truce, you should order a cease-fire! Stop them! But that was not up to him either. You could be wrong, you don't know what is happening. He felt a wave of frustration, each blast from his own guns punching him now, and he looked down the line, shouted, "Cease fire. Conserve powder!"

The men looked at him, and soon the guns nearest him fell silent. He shouted again, "Pass the word, conserve powder!"

He saw officers motioning to him, men in blackened uniforms, faces stained with the thick smoke and powder. They began to acknowledge him, and then men were moving away, spreading the command, and all down the line of batteries the guns stopped firing. His ears were ringing, the silence a strange sensation, and he saw some of the officers moving toward him. He stepped down from his vantage point, felt the need to explain, said, "On my authority . . . resume firing only on my command." The officers nodded, no one questioned him, and they moved away, back to their guns. He felt suddenly very alone, thought, Just for a few minutes . . . only a few minutes.

Behind him there was commotion, and Lee turned, was surprised to see Totten, moving toward him quickly. Totten was breathing heavily, said, "You have heard?"

Lee thought, Be careful. "Heard, sir?"

"You may stand down for the present, Captain. It seems your siege was successful. General Morales . . . the Mexicans have surrendered."

4. SCOTT

MARCH TWENTY-SEVENTH

THE CARRIAGES PULLED AWAY, DRAWN BY THE BEST HORSES their Mexican hosts would provide. Above the brass ornaments and rich leather trim flew the flags of France, Spain, and England, the fragile symbols that had allowed the men in fine suits, the well-spoken dignitaries, to pass unmolested through the American lines. Scott looked at the document they had left him, held it carefully in his hand, admired the gold seal of the Governor of Vera Cruz. He smiled, then looked at the staff, at Worth, who had met the first carriage inside the lines of his men. Worth took it upon himself to serve as escort, bringing the dignitaries straight to the commanding general. Scott knew it was only Worth's curiosity that prompted him to do so, wanting to know what these men brought with them, whether Scott had been right after all. Now Worth stared out, watching the last carriage passing beyond the last line of his muskets, lurching on the rough road back toward the city.

"I didn't know . . . there were Europeans in the city. We were fortunate."

Scott shook his head, said, "I doubt Washington knew there was so much European influence anywhere in these parts. We should pay attention to that. This time, they used their influence to convince the Mexicans of what the Mexicans already knew. They had no defense, the city was lost. Now, the Mexicans can claim the surrender was coerced by the Europeans. And, so, they save face." He paused, smiled again. "Nothing fortunate about it."

Worth did not look at him, thought a moment, said, "They said General Morales resigned."

"Of course he did. He turned over command to some junior officer, some brigadier, so Morales could say he never actually surrendered himself. It's all very simple once you understand the way they think, General."

"Still, we are very fortunate."

Scott felt a tug of annoyance. "Fortune had very little to do with this, General. We had the right strategy, and we carried it out."

"Forgive me, sir, but I meant . . . we are fortunate that we do not have to engage Uloa."

Scott let the anger slip away, was surprised that Worth understood that, thought, For once I agree with him. I did not want a siege of that place.

"Quite right, General," he said. "I had hoped they would concede the fort as well. According to this agreement, they will open up Uloa by tomorrow, march their men out and send them home on parole."

"Do you believe they know what that means? Do their soldiers understand parole?"

Scott shrugged. "Probably not. They will do what their commanders tell them to do. Mexican soldiers are not allowed to think for themselves. In their culture they are the bottom rung of society. Some *generalissimo* will probably round them up, and send them back out to fight us. But I'd rather fight them somewhere else, and not in that big damned fort."

Scott could feel Worth's willingness to talk, thought, Victory does that, makes everybody *cozy*. Suddenly we're all good friends. Scott did not look at him, thought, I'm not in the mood to talk to generals. He moved away from the tents, leaving Worth alone, walked along one of the trails, while behind him the young major emerged from a tent, scurried to catch up with him.

He moved behind the lines of his troops, men rising up from the sandy ground, stopping to watch him. He saw the uniforms, mostly filthy, but the faces were alive, smiling, men calling out to him as he moved past. They know, he thought. The word has already spread. One voice boomed loudly, "God bless you, General Scott!"

He stopped, looked for the face, saw a huge man, a thick dark-bearded sergeant saluting him. Others were moving closer, in all manner of ragged dress, their uniforms barely evident from the coating of sand and dirt. Some men were shirtless, self-conscious now, covering bare chests. He waved to them, made a point of returning the big man's salute, said aloud, "None finer, anywhere. Be proud, gentlemen!"

There were calls now, hats waving, and he moved forward again, still smiling. No, we did not want to march up against the walls of the city, not the generals, not the soldiers who would lead the way. The cheers are as much for that as they are for me. This is good for them, for their morale, their confidence.

If we had started this fight with blood, if we had taken this city with great loss, it would be very different, it would change the way they would see this, the way they would see everything that follows. It might have taken something from this army we could not get back. Still, they cannot believe it will be this easy. We won here without firing a musket, without a single one of them facing the muskets of his enemy. If there is confidence, there may also be arrogance, cockiness. They may believe it will always be this simple. The troops can afford that, we can let them draw strength from that. But I have to make damned sure the commanders know better. *Their* arrogance can cause disasters, and I still do not know them well enough. Which ones can I trust? Worth, Twiggs, they're regular soldiers. Pillow? There's a disaster waiting to happen. And once we leave here, move inland, confront an enemy who may be more real than any in this army believe, how much control do I have over them after all?

He did not hear the troops now, began to think of strategy, maps, the road that led away to the west.

Out beyond the safety of the American lines, the guerrilla bands were still harassing the troops, and Scott turned his thoughts in that direction. We must first clear them out, open that road. We have succeeded in our job here, now it's time to move inland, climb those hills, get out of this damned swamp. And the reports from the doctors, a few men already feeling the effects of the *el vomito*. I've seen some of the afflicted, the awful toll it took on them. Men lying in coiled masses of sweat and filth, nearly paralyzed by the gut-twisting sickness. Even the Indians in the area could offer us no remedy, nothing that worked on these *yanquis*. If it should spread . . . No. We will not allow it to spread. We will move. We will get out of this place.

He moved through some scrub trees, climbed a sand hill, saw his men now spread all through the thick brush. One man sat on a horse just ahead of him. Scott felt the annoyance return, spoiling his mood. Twiggs, of course. Horses are in short supply, but he will damned well sit on one.

The young Scott, his son-in-law and chief of staff, was beside him now, and Scott glanced at him, said, "The sooner that man is out of my sight, the better. When we move inland, he will lead the way. Let him ride that damned horse at the head of his troops."

The young man said nothing, followed again as Scott turned and moved back toward the headquarters tents. There was more cheering now, more men moving closer as he walked, and the bad mood slipped away again, the calls from the men lifting him. I truly miss this, more than anything else, he thought. It has always been like this, even in the old days, the old war. The men understand what is most important. They appreciate a good solid victory, and none of them have an eye on a newspaper headline. None of *them* are running for President.

He thought of Zachary Taylor. Scott had received word of the great victory at Buena Vista, a fight Taylor had won against Santa Anna himself, in some remote godforsaken place up north. The victory had been costly to Taylor's army, meant that Taylor would be unlikely to send Scott any more help, and that Taylor himself would not do much more campaigning on his own. He simply had too few men holding fort in the middle of a huge part of Mexico that simply was not worth fighting for. Even Santa Anna knew that. The Mexican general had withdrawn from Buena Vista claiming a great victory, even though Taylor had beaten back his army with barely a third of the Mexican's strength. Now, Santa Anna would be in Mexico City, gathering strength, making those speeches that dictators always know how to make, rallying the people against their enemies from outside, blinding them to Santa Anna's own abuses, his brutality to his political enemies, his thievery of Mexican resources.

Scott felt the bad mood return, could not think of Santa Anna without his stomach balling up into a hard cold knot. It was President Polk and those fat politicians in Washington, who had allowed Santa Anna to come back to Mexico. He thought of Sam Houston. He would be a good one to have here, instead of some fossil like Twiggs. Houston had beaten Santa Anna, driven his army out of Texas, and so the Mexican people drove Santa Anna all the way to Cuba. But Houston is a politician now, he thought, enjoying the rewards of the good victory, retiring into the quiet life of the dignified hero. Too bad.

Scott had not been in Washington when Santa Anna's representative came to call. The man had offered assurances that if Santa Anna was allowed back into Mexico, he would take control again, and prevent the war from happening in the first place, negotiate a just peace for both sides.

Polk had believed him, sent the order to the Gulf, telling the navy to allow Santa Anna to pass through the blockade. Scott had blown sky-high when he heard about the order, had not understood how the Mexican people would allow Santa Anna to simply walk in to

Mexico City and take command again. But beyond that, he wondered how the United States government could support putting a dictator back into power.

He could see the headquarters tents, felt his stomach turn, thought, You do this every time. When will you let it go? Enjoy your *own* damned victory? He could hear the calls from the men again, their noisy salutes. He exhaled deeply.

No, you can never let it go. Listen to them. They want something to fight for, they believe in what we're doing here. They believe in this command. It is for them, for the men, that I can never let the stupidity just pass by. I cannot allow politics and intrigue to stand in the way of our duty here. Destiny has had a hand in this. Santa Anna knew his people better than we did, knew how weak the Mexican government was, knew that one strong man can always push aside a weak, floundering government. And if he never had any intention of negotiating with us, if all he wanted to do was secure his own power by making a war against the *yanquis*, then, well, here we are. He has a war. We are on their soil, and we have nowhere to go but to their capital. That's the only place we will *win* this war. It's time to move.

"GENERAL SCOTT, ALLOW ME TO INTRODUCE MY REPLACE-ment."

Conner's voice was slow, steady. Scott watched him, thought, He has more control, more dignity, than I would have now. Behind Conner, the younger man stepped forward. Scott noticed that he was heavier than Conner, round-faced, serious. He looked at Scott, nervous, uncertain, and Conner said, "General, this is Commodore Matthew Perry. Effective immediately, I am turning over command of the naval forces here to him. Be assured, General, he is quite capable."

Perry held out a hand, and Scott reached over the small table, felt a hard, firm grip, thought, Well, at least he has that right. Scott looked at Conner again, saw a strange nervousness, the calm dignity failing him, Conner's eyes reddening, revealing the sadness of the moment, the man's final duty. Scott said, "When will you leave?"

Conner seemed resigned now, weaker, the control gone.

"Tomorrow, sir." Conner paused, seemed to search for words. "Sir, I want you to know . . . the orders were not unexpected. My term of command has been expired for some time. Washington has been gracious in allowing me to continue here while our operations were under way."

Scott saw Conner studying him, thought, He expects me to blow up again, more stupidity from Washington, changing commanders in the middle of a military operation. But he had seen the change in Conner as well, the man's health slipping away. He could also tell that he was watching a man whose job is done, who has accepted his own passing. No, it's not anger, not now, he thought. It's just sadness. Damn.

He looked down, said, "Commodore, you have done your country proud. All my reports will reflect that. Without the navy's assistance—"

Conner held up his hand, "Please, sir."

Scott stopped, thought, No, he knows all of this. Save it for a speech. He looked at Perry now, saw the nervousness was gone, and Perry said, "General, my command will continue to cooperate with your every requirement. I am pleased to make my first report, sir. You may expect horses and wagons in the next few days, weather permitting. Your requests for additional troops have finally been answered favorably. Several regiments of volunteers are sailing this way as well. By the end of the week, your situation here should be somewhat improved."

Scott looked at Conner, who was smiling now, and Scott understood what Conner had done, allowing Perry to make the good impression. Scott stood noisily, the table suddenly rocking as he leaned forward again. He held out his hand, grinned at Perry, said, "Commodore Perry, you may bring me surprises like this any time." He paused, squinted a bit. "You're not, say, running for *President*, are you?"

APRIL TWELFTH

He had ordered Davy Twiggs to move out first, with a screen of dragoons, William Harney's good cavalry leading the way. The first objective would be the town of Jalapa, nearly eighty miles from the coast, and well above the fever zone. But Twiggs had not yet reached Jalapa when word came back to headquarters: They had found Santa Anna, and a considerable number of Mexican troops. If they had not known Santa Anna's plans, they understood now that the Mexican commander intended to keep the *yanquis* close to the coast.

Scott had left Worth in Vera Cruz, to handle affairs there, acting as a temporary military governor, commanding a division of regular soldiers. Worth would not only keep the peace with the Mexicans, but his men were more disciplined than the volunteers, and so would keep peace among themselves. Twiggs commanded regulars as well, and Scott was clear that the spearhead of the inland drive would have to consist of the best troops. Patterson's division of volunteers had marched behind Twiggs. Neither Twiggs nor Worth had any enthusiasm for depending on the volunteers as an effective fighting force.

Scott was still far behind the advance of Twiggs's men, riding with a large escort, more of Harney's dragoons. The march was uneven, slowed by cavalrymen still growing used to the new horses, many bought from local farmers, ranchers. Scott had heard the clamor, the men trying to maintain control, keep a calm firm hand over the fresh mounts. But then he would hide a smile, wait patiently as the quiet discipline of the escort was shattered by the sudden wild galloping of an unbroken mount, the helpless cavalryman shouting curses at the horse that carried him into the rugged brush.

They had come past small patrols of foot soldiers, the rear guard from Patterson, protecting the road from the guerrillas, and always, Scott had heard the blessed cheers.

As they moved farther inland, the ground began to roll, the sand giving way to hard, dry dirt. The flat scrub brush of the beach changed as well, great knifelike plants, their strange, long dark leaves, with sharp serrated edges, standing tall in vast thickets of wiry gray vines. As the march took them higher, the dirt grew harder still, and the angry vegetation began to thin out, opening into wide patches of bare earth. Here, the enemy was the wind, blowing great clouds of dust across the road, choking the men, slowing the horses, nearly stopping the march.

He rode up a long rise, after climbing several big hills today, and the change in altitude was obvious, the cooler, dryer air filling them all with fresh energy for the march. He began to see stretches of small trees, healthy, more green than the dull gray and brown of the coast. He stopped, moved the horse off the road, stared out to the front, admired the stunning view of Orizaba, the great mountain that never lost its crown of snow. You could see the peak from the coast, from the first day the ships had sailed close, but now it was much closer, much larger. He stared for a long moment, thought of the mountains up north, New York, Pennsylvania. *We thought they were huge, imposing and impossible to climb.* He laughed quietly. The staff instinctively moved closer, waiting for him to say something. He held up a hand, *No, nothing,* stared still at the great peak, buried under a thick cap of snow. *My God, we could never have imagined this. Those dark hills with the thick green, the dense blanket of pines ... hills indeed. This is a mountain.*

He had never been intensely religious, had left that to his wife, and the immense spectacle of the mountain suddenly brought her into his mind. Dear Maria, you would appreciate this. God's handiwork, the spectacular reminder when some of us forget.

He turned the horse, gazed down the line of blue horsemen stretching out behind. They had stopped with him, waited patiently, and he thought, We should keep moving, but he was enjoying this small pleasant moment, Maria's image still with him. He did not think of her often, had never felt painfully alone, or gone through the torment of homesickness. No, *this* has always been my home, and she understands that. She has her social circles and my daughters to fuss over her, and if I am not there, my reputation, my notoriety, certainly is. He laughed again. She no doubt prefers it that way.

He had not thought of her on their anniversary, had only remembered it weeks later, when the big guns were punching the walls of Vera Cruz. It had been thirty years, and he had suddenly marveled at that, thought of it again now. That is special I suppose. *She* certainly didn't forget. There was probably some celebration, some gathering of local ladies to support her sorrow that I am so far removed. She will enjoy that. But she won't say anything about it to me.

Her image began to drift away, and he watched the cloud of dust, hanging low behind them, kicked up by the horses of his men. He looked toward the front now, the air still clear, a stunning blue sky, thought, Keep moving. Scott could picture Twiggs in his mind. The man's broad shoulders still hard, Twiggs sitting high on the horse, glowering at his men through his rough gray beard. Twiggs knows only one way to be a soldier, he thought. Sometimes, that's a good thing, act first, think about it later. But not this time. Patterson's message had been straightforward. There are a lot more of them than there are of us, and Santa Anna has the high ground. Patterson hinted that Twiggs was ready to charge straight ahead, and Scott knew he would have to be there to take charge personally. If those two start arguing, for all I know it could lead to a duel. I'm like a damned father, breaking up squabbles between unruly children. He felt a sudden impatience, looked toward the dragoons, waiting for him to continue the march. All right, he thought, let's go.

He focused again to the rear, scanned the flat horizon, the dust slowly clearing, the road empty except for a distant squad, the rear guard, sentries who would keep the guerrillas away. He thought of Worth, waiting in Vera Cruz, enduring the painfully slow arrival of the supplies. There were still not enough wagons, and fewer horses, but the navy was still insisting the ships were en route. Worth would stay on the coast, prepare the transportation as quickly as the ships appeared.

Commodore Perry would do the job. Scott had no doubts about Perry, not anymore, but still he thought of Conner, the old man sailing north now, going home. Damn, there should be some better way, some recognition. He'd earned it. So many commanders in this army, great peacocks in puffed shirts, men who will earn very little recognition, but *they* will be remembered because they know how to get their names in the newspaper. And one very good man is sailing back home to be forgotten.

He moved the horse back into the road, spurred his mount into a trot toward the front, heard the staff moving into line behind him. He crested the long hill, looked again at Orizaba, then beyond, toward the foothills that stretched far to the west. Patterson's column is up there, close, he thought. He didn't know Robert Patterson well, just that he was another gray-haired veteran of 1812, and that the rough old Irishman was the only man who seemed capable of commanding the volunteers. Scott knew Patterson's son was in his father's command, the young man a rugged copy of the commander. They're probably together now, he thought, the young man's a Texas Ranger, Ben McCulloch's bunch. The Rangers had already built their own reputation as a ruthlessly straightforward fighting force, though some were saying they were out of control. Scott worried still about that.

We have our hands full of problems with the volunteers. But the Texans bring something else, a different spirit, a violence born of revenge. Certainly, no one else in the army has such a hatred of Santa Anna. That's a challenge for Patterson, to keep them in line. If they stay focused on the enemy, maybe that will spread to the other volunteers, point them all in the right direction.

The horsemen were moving now, more dust was rising, another hill stretching around a long curve. The road was good, hard, a few big holes the men would have to march around. But it was a road an army could appreciate, a road that would lead them straight to the enemy. He thought of Cortez, centuries before, moving another army on this same road. The Spaniards killed nearly everyone that met them. Cortez had no way of knowing that his men carried something far deadlier than guns. In the end, the strength, the power, of the Spanish did not matter. If there had been no fight at all, Cortez had brought disease, the awful plague of smallpox that decimated the Indians. The conquest had been absolute. Scott had heard comparisons, the political enemies of Polk condemning the army, another conquest of a helpless people, thought, But there is no comparison. Cortez came for gold, to expand the Spanish empire. This is a fight for . . . His mind seemed to lock up on one thought. He knew the term *Manifest Destiny*, that somehow it was part of being an American. God has decreed our rights to the entire continent, a chosen people. It was always the justification, the response to the critics, to those who opposed Polk, and so opposed the war.

I don't know much about being *chosen*. A soldier fights for . . . duty. We always fight for duty. Here, our duty is clear. This is a war about boundaries, borders, a dispute that could not be settled any other way.

He felt a headache coming, a hard knot in the base of his skull. He blinked hard, fought it, twisted his head to the side. The young Scott was beside him now, said, "Sir, can I get you anything?"

Scott looked up, squinted into the bright glare of the sun, said, "No. Dammit, I'll tell you when I need something." He turned, looked behind him, saw the other staff officers watching him, waiting calmly for some command. He focused on one man, saw the man's eyes searching the horizon, intense, curious. Scott continued watching him for a moment, thought, I have no idea if he'll ever be a soldier, but it seems he's a damned good engineer. Maybe more, something in the eyes. More than just another *college boy*.

"Captain Lee, move up here. Ride with me."

Lee seemed startled, focused on him now. The horses parted, and Lee pushed through, moved alongside Scott, said, "Sir?"

Scott said nothing, stared again at the magnificence of Orizaba.

Lee followed his look, said quietly, "Beautiful, sir."

Scott nodded, twisted his head again, pulled at the still-growing headache. "Yes. Beautiful. You fight a war before, Captain?"

Lee seemed surprised at the question, said, "Uh, no sir."

"No, I suppose not. You don't have the gray hair. Been a long time since this army had to fight."

Lee said, "Some of the others here fought the Indians, the Seminoles."

"Yes, yes, but a real war. Mobilize the army, march off under big damned flags, brass bands, the whole country rallying around the Cause."

Lee said nothing, waited.

Scott continued, "Can't say the whole country's rallying around *this* cause. You have any idea why we're fighting here, Captain?"

Lee hesitated, then said, "Yes, sir, we have our duty. The army must perform as ordered. Those decisions . . ."

"Those decisions are made by someone else. The army is told what to do, and performs accordingly. That the way you see it, Captain?"

Lee seemed uncomfortable now. "It's how we were taught, sir."

"Hmmm, yes, taught. I didn't spend much time being taught, Mr. Lee. Forty years ago nobody gave much thought to West Point. We went out and did the job the way we thought it ought to be done. No demerits given in the field. No one to scold you on failing your lesson. You make a mistake, your men die. Too many men die, they pull you out, stick you somewhere else. You think all these West Pointers can handle that, Mr. Lee? The army's a bit different out here where it counts. You don't find any of this in a textbook."

He stopped, thought, Easy. No need to preach, not to this one. He's no youngster. "We will find out, though, won't we, Mr. Lee? As much respect as I have for the institution, for the *place*, now, we'll find out if I can depend on the men it has sent me. We'll find out if college boys are up to fighting a war."

Lee said nothing, and Scott thought, I hope he has a thick skin. I need people around me who don't get so damned touchy every time I say something to ruffle a few feathers. He waited, saw Lee staring ahead.

"I have absolute confidence in the men of this command, sir. Forgive me sir," Lee said, "But if you have respect for West Point, then you should have respect for the men who made the grade. We are not just . . . college boys, sir."

Lee still stared ahead, and Scott smiled now, had heard the slight edge in Lee's voice. "I admire your pride, Mr. Lee, and I accept your advice. This time."

Lee seemed uneasy, said, "My apologies, sir. If I was out of line—"

"Never back off, Mr. Lee. I pushed you, and you pushed back. That's not always a good idea, you understand. But I had to know how you felt. We have a long road in front of us, Captain. I'm still learning who I can depend on." The smile was gone and Scott sat quietly for a long moment, then said, "The damnedest thing is, Captain, this time it's my show, I'm in charge. I can't even depend on Washington, not even the President." He turned, looked back at the young major.

"Bring me the order, find that order from Polk."

The young man reached back, shuffled through a saddlebag of papers. Scott said to Lee, "I keep it close by as a reminder, in case any of those puffed-up gray-heads start arguing with me."

The young man moved up, handed Scott the paper. Scott opened it, read out loud, " 'It is not proposed to control your operations by definite and positive instructions, but you are left to prosecute them as your judgment . . . shall dictate. The work is before you and the means provided . . . in the full confidence that you will use them to the best advantage.' "

Scott looked at Lee. "You hear that, Captain? *My* judgment, the President has *full confidence*. I just wish . . ." He paused again. "There's a flaw in this plan, Captain. Any military commander would understand this. There has to be accountability, there's always accountability. But the President is saying here, I'm on my own. Polk has detached himself from the strategy, from the consequences, from the *responsibility*. I'm supposed to be happy about that. And damn it, I'm not. Why?"

Lee thought a moment, said, "Sir, you asked me if I knew what we were fighting for. A better answer might be . . . that we're fighting for the good of the country. We're carrying out the instructions of the President."

Scott nodded, held the paper out toward Lee. "Well, Captain, you heard the instructions. I'm to *handle it*. No moralizing, no flag-waving, no hurrahs for our grand old Constitution. Mr. Polk has made a war, and now he's handed it to me. And, I'm not supposed to be concerned about why."

Lee stared at the big mountain, thought a moment, said, "It's still duty, sir. We're here because God has put us here. If the President has given you discretion, then that is the hand of God as well. We can't . . . I'm sorry, sir, but the duty is clear. You have a responsibility to carry out your instructions. If the instructions are . . . vague, then you must use the judgment that the President has granted you." Lee seemed suddenly embarrassed, awkward, said, "Forgive me, sir. This is not my place."

Scott sniffed, rubbed his neck, trying to massage the headache away. "I *asked* for your opinion, Captain. You might find it interesting that my wife would agree with you. She'd see the hand of God in all of this. We're put here just like that big damned mountain, just another piece of God's plan. I wish I could just . . . accept that, Mr. Lee. If my duty is just to fight this war, then *how* I fight it is how I will be judged. I'm not supposed to care *why* I'm fighting, or just what the hell we're really doing here. If you and my wife are correct, then in the end I'll just have to answer to God and nothing else will matter. Problem is, in the meantime I'm answering to the government, and the American people. I suspect God is more forgiving."

They rode in silence now, and Lee let his horse slowly back away, resumed his place in line. Scott still looked at the big mountain, thought of the delicious misery of the old war. At Niagara, leading the men through the heavy snow, the raw beauty pushed aside by the duty, the job at hand, move the men, find the enemy. When this is over, he thought, then I can worry about what this was all about, whether this was a *good* war. He glanced to the side, expected to see Lee still, but no one rode beside him, and he thought, Does Captain Lee ever have fear? Is he so comfortable in God's hands that he is not concerned with mistakes, or pain . . . or death? I should ask him, he thought, I would like to know.

He could see a horseman, moving toward him down the long hill. The dragoons stopped, moved aside as the man came close. The man rode up quickly, saluted, said, "General Scott, a message for you, from General Twiggs. Sir, General Twiggs is preparing to assault the enemy."

Scott leaned forward, close to the man's face. "*What* enemy?"

The courier leaned back, wide-eyed, said, "Uh . . . the Mexicans, sir. There's a whole bunch of 'em."

Scott felt the headache erupt into a wave of fire in his neck, felt as if his face was exploding, the anger boiling through him completely. He shut his eyes, clenched them hard, thought, We should kill Twiggs now, save countless lives. And it would feel so damned *good*.

"Son, did General Twiggs give you any further message for me, any specifics on just what he is facing? Does the general know how many of the enemy he has found? What about General Patterson?"

The courier seemed genuinely scared now, shook his head slowly. "No, sir. General Twiggs had some words with General Patterson. There is disagreement, sir. General Patterson was angry too, sir. That's all I can tell you."

Scott nodded, the heat now controlled, a hard, manageable simmer. Thank God Patterson's closer. He outranks Twiggs. He can pull rank, stop him from making some damned stupid mistake. Surely he knows that.

He looked toward the dragoons, said, "Let's move. We have a new urgency. It seems General Twiggs would rather fight this war by himself."

THE DRAGOONS LINED QUICKLY OUT ON THE ROAD, SITTING stiffly on their mounts, saluting him as he passed. He ignored them, focused on the flag, a small flutter over the heads of the men in charge. He saw Twiggs now, and Patterson, the two men waiting for him with a wide gap between them, a symbol of their obvious disagreement. Scott clenched his fists on the straps of leather, glanced at Twiggs, thought, There he sits, proud of this, as though whatever happens here is all his responsibility, the man with the *good idea*.

Scott rode close to Twiggs, who did not move, stayed tall in the saddle, hard and gray, silent, the only expression coming through the man's eyes, a grim stare, defiant. Patterson dismounted now, and Scott nodded toward him, polite, held up a hand, said quietly, "Excuse us, General Patterson. I would like a word with General Twiggs alone, if you don't object."

It was not a request, and Patterson nodded quietly, backed away. Scott climbed down from the horse, did not look at Twiggs, knew Twiggs would carry through the performance, would not dismount just yet, would maintain the annoying posture, the man's stubbornness filling the air, choking away any disagreement.

Scott's head still pounded, the pain hammering behind his eyes. His body stiff from the long day's ride, he eased out of the saddle, moved away from the horses, noticed for the first time the amazing ground out to the west. He put a hand on his forehead, still did not look up at Twiggs, said, "General Twiggs, walk with me. Alone. *Now.*"

Twiggs climbed down from the horse, and Scott was already moving away, thought, If he has so damned much energy, he can catch up to me.

He walked out through low brush, short green plants, climbed a slight bare rise, thick dirt giving way to his boots. He reached the crest, stopped, remained focused out to the west. The anger was boiling beneath the headache, and he tried to sort through the thoughts, what he would say now, felt weary from fighting the headache. He knew that was probably a good thing.

I have no patience, no energy for this. So watch what you say. You know how this goes, what happens next. You lose control, shout at him, and his pride makes him resign, and we start a feud that lasts for years. Washington gets involved, reputations are damaged, careers end. Good God, we cannot afford this, not here. I need all of them, but I need them to understand that we will do this *my* way.

He stared at the prominent peak to the west, realized now it was farther away than he had thought, was much larger, tall, ragged rocks, deep ravines of thick green stretching out toward him, toward the place where Twiggs had halted his troops. Scott began to scan the land carefully, saw a straight wide river to the left, winding gently past the large hill, guessed now at the height of the hill, four, five hundred feet above the river. The main road stretched forward right into the base of the hill, began to turn, disappearing into the smaller rises. He began to see detail, bits of color on the hill itself, high up, and down, near the base, smaller rolling hills, the deep cuts, ravines, thick brush broken by small clearings and rocky outcroppings. Twiggs was beside him now, breathing heavily, and Scott ignored him, stared at the sight in front of him, more details now, small clusters of motion. My God, he thought, that's one big rock. And it's covered with an army. And cannon. A great many cannon. He felt a sudden odd respect, a surprise, thought, It's *them*. It's the Mexicans. They're right in front of us, and they have very good ground.

He looked at Twiggs, saw the grim old man watching him, still angry, defiant, ready with the hot argument. Scott felt the headache suddenly drifting away, his mind clearing, and he looked again at the Mexican position, the great fat hill, said, "Pretty amazing, isn't it?"

Twiggs's face contorted in confusion. A low mumble of sounds, hardly words, came from his lips. Scott felt the tension and the anger easing away, replaced by the sheer spectacle in front of him. He pointed to the hill, said, "Up there, that high knoll in front of the larger hill. Must be ten, maybe fifteen big guns dug in there. Over there, two more strong batteries, nearly hidden by that brush. They control the road, that's for sure. Anybody tries to push through there gets an artillery barrage from three sides. Amazing."

He felt for his field glasses, but they were in the saddlebag, and he turned to Twiggs for the first time, said, "Give me your glasses, let me have a look at those troops up there."

Twiggs handed him the glasses numbly, and Scott held them up, focused. "Just as I thought. How many men in a Mexican division, General? Three thousand, maybe more? There's pockets of men all over that hill, all along the base. Could be three or four divisions, and God knows how many are *behind* this big damned hill. Let's see, a division the size of ours, say, one like yours. Maybe the same size. And they're up high, on the hill. Wonder who's in charge? This large a force, good chance it's Santa Anna himself."

Scott began to feel a strange humor, thought, No, there will be no shouting. He just doesn't see it like I see it. I will explain it to him.

"General Twiggs, I received a report of what you intended to do here. I certainly misunderstood, or the courier had it all wrong."

Twiggs began to speak, and Scott held up a hand, said firmly, "I'm not through, General. Let's see, you're down here, all this low ground, not much good cover. If you use the road to move up close . . . well, no, that's no good. Can't forget about all that artillery up there. So, it seems pretty clear that if we launch some kind of straight-ahead point-blank assault, it would be more than a disaster, might lose every damned man we have. No one would suggest that as a good idea, I'm certain of that. Not under my command. Of course, that's just *my* opinion."

He handed the glasses to Twiggs, stared out quietly for a long moment, could feel Twiggs slowly deflate beside him, the stiff defiance flowing away. After a long moment Scott said, "Now, General, you were going to tell me something about a plan?"

He could hear Twiggs let out a long breath, and Twiggs said quietly, "I have reconsidered, sir. Perhaps the commanding general would offer a plan of his own."

Scott turned, looked at him, hard, straight in the eyes. Twiggs looked down, and Scott felt the humor gone now, thought, Enough of this. His jaw tightened, his voice a low growl, he said slowly, "I will not mock you, General. I will not embarrass you in front of anyone else. But I will not tolerate bullheadedness."

Twiggs said nothing, nodded slightly.

"The President has given me absolute command of this operation," Scott went on. "I expect my generals to accept that. You're a veteran, General, you've earned your rank, your command. You may not agree with my strategy. But you will respect it."

Twiggs looked at him now, the defiance gone, replaced by his old tired eyes. "Yes, sir. I understand, sir."

Scott turned, stepped back off the rise, waited for Twiggs, the thin man feeling his way down through the soft dirt. Scott said, "General, the rest of the army is right behind us. I believe it's time we come up with a way to get those people off that big damned hill."

5. LEE

THE CHAIRS WERE SET OUT IN THE USUAL HALF CIRCLE IN FRONT of the tent, the commanders making their way in from their camps, the general's staff already seated in their usual places. The chair beside Lee was empty, and no one had yet been assigned to fill it. Colonel Totten had returned to Washington, had gone north on the *Princeton*, the same ship that had carried Commodore Conner. Lee glanced at the chair, thought, He will be missed. He is missed now. It was a comfort having him there to back up his engineers. Lee was now the second ranking engineer with the army, and his only senior, Major John L. Smith, had been ill for weeks, had stayed behind in Vera Cruz.

The commanders finally settled into the chairs, some still carrying a piece of their supper. Lee could still smell the marvelous smoke from cooking beef, had already filled himself, a great pile of meat and some strange vegetable he had never seen before. He felt the pressure, the hard pull from his belt, thought, No, this will not do. I cannot return to Mary and claim that going to war has made me obese.

He saw Johnston now, eyeing Totten's chair, and Lee smiled, motioned with a tilt of his head, but there was motion from behind, and quickly someone else moved into the chair. Lee saw that it was Beauregard, and the young man seemed to inflate, his chest puffed up. He leaned in and whispered to Lee, "Good evening, Captain. It seems I will be part of the meeting tonight."

Lee nodded. He had never seen Beauregard at a staff meeting before, thought, He has been out here for a while, probably done some scouting. Good, maybe we'll find out what General Twiggs's plan was, what he was going to attack.

Scott emerged from the tent, faced the seated officers, and Lee saw he was chewing something, Scott's face a mask of determination. Scott moved to his chair, sat behind the small table, did not speak, still worked his jaw against something stubborn. He stood up, glanced at the others, stepped back around the tent and made a harsh hacking sound as he expelled the unforgiving mass of food. There were stifled laughs from the men, and Lee could not help a smile. Scott returned, his mouth empty, and sat, saying to no one in particular, "Damnedest strange food in this place."

Scott looked at the faces as though he noticed them for the first time, said, "Anybody try those little green things? Thought they were like some kind of fruit, a berry or something. Won't make that mistake again. Never chewed on something that chewed back. Felt like I was cooking from the inside out."

There was more laughter, unbridled this time, and Pillow stood up, said, "Quite, General. It's the indigenous produce. I believe you are referring to the rather aggressive pepper they have here. It's called the jalapeño, I believe. Nasty little creature." Pillow laughed, and no one joined him. He sat, and Lee saw how smug Pillow was, nodding slowly to himself, so proud at having cleared up any mystery for the commanding general.

Scott stared at Pillow, said, "We are grateful for your keen insight into the local agriculture, General. If this command requires a food taster, I shall call on you."

There were more laughs, and Pillow nodded, serious, said, "Certainly, at your service, sir."

Scott ignored him now, put his hands on the table, paused for a moment, then scanned the circle of men, said, "Gentlemen, up there, on that high ground to our west, General Santa Anna has maybe thirty-five cannon dug in, and a best estimate of twelve, maybe fifteen thousand troops. They are firmly entrenched, and completely control the main road. Any advance into that position would be . . . costly." Scott glanced at Twiggs, but Twiggs ignored him, staring hard at the ground. Beside Lee, Beauregard began moving, twitching, and Lee glanced at him, saw Beauregard's fingers nervously tapping his leg, moving faster now. Lee thought, It's like . . . we're in school. Yes, Mr. Beauregard, you may speak. Lee raised the back of his hand to shield his mouth hiding his smile.

Scott noticing Beauregard's fidgeting, said, "Lieutenant Beauregard, please give us your report."

Beauregard jumped to his feet, the chair beneath him knocked backward, a clatter that produced small laughs around the circle. Beauregard tried not to notice, said, "Thank you, General Scott. Per the orders I received, dated the thirteenth of April, signed by the commanding general himself, and sanctioned by Major General Patterson—"

"Lieutenant, save all the lawyer talk for your court-martial. Just give us the damned report."

The men laughed again, and Scott sat back, ignored the response to his attempt at humor. Beauregard seemed to stagger, and Lee heard a small, high groan. Then Beauregard tried to speak again, coughed, cleared his throat.

"Sorry, General. My apologies. Sir, the enemy is in position as you indicated. It is a very strong position, and cannot be carried by a frontal assault. The enemy's right is firmly anchored by the river, the Rio del Plan, and his center controls an area of deep ravines and steep rocky hills that our troops could not assault in any kind of organized strength. To the enemy's left and rear are two hills, El Telégrafo, the larger, upon which he has constructed batteries and fortified heavily, and the smaller hill, Atalaya, which is occupied by an unknown number of troops as well. These hills completely control the main road. I have scouted the only possible avenue which we may use to attack effectively. If we can locate a route through the deep ravines to the enemy's left, our right flank, it is possible we can fight our way through and thus turn the enemy's flank."

Beauregard stopped, sat down, and there was a silence, the commanders all absorbing the report. Scott leaned forward, said quietly, "*That's* a report, Lieutenant. Fine work." Scott looked at Twiggs, who still stared at the ground in front of him. Scott said, "Do you have any questions, General Twiggs? Is our situation . . . clear?"

Twiggs looked up, nodded slowly, did not look at Beauregard, said, "Quite clear, sir."

"Good. Now, Lieutenant, have you found a way through that rough ground? How can we reach the enemy's rear by that route?"

Beauregard stood, the swagger now gone. "Uh, well, I'm not sure sir. But I can make another survey of the area, penetrate farther this time."

Scott held up a hand, said, "No, that will be all. Fine work. You are dismissed, Lieutenant."

Beauregard glanced at Lee, looked at the faces watching him, said quietly, "Dismissed, sir?"

"Yes, Lieutenant, fine work. That will be all."

Lee watched Beauregard slink away, with his shoulders hunched down, the small man's pride damaged. Lee thought, He looks almost like a child. He suddenly felt sorry for the young man. Give it time, Lieutenant. You are after all a good engineer. There will be a place for you here.

Beauregard disappeared into the darkness, and Lee felt the silence. When he turned his attention back to the meeting, Scott was staring at him. He felt a sudden knot in his throat. Scott said, "Well, Captain?"

Lee thought, What did I miss? The faces were watching him now, even Twiggs, and Lee said, "It was a thorough report, sir."

"Yes, yes, Captain. But we need someone with a bit more experience. There is too much at stake. If the lieutenant's plan is sound, then I would prefer *you* to verify that. It is up to you to find the route."

Lee felt a cold lump growing in his chest. "Me, sir?"

Scott leaned toward him, and Lee saw the sharp glare in his eyes, the general's impatience rising. "Captain, we are faced with a considerable force of the enemy. As our most experienced engineer, we *should* be able to rely on you to read the ground, and find a way to move our people into the enemy's rear. Is this not why you're here, Captain?"

Lee felt the cold spreading, saw only the face, the eyes boring hard into him. "Certainly, sir. I will begin immediately, sir."

Scott's face seemed to calm, his eyes softer now. He sat back in his chair, nodded toward Lee. "This is an opportunity, Mr. Lee. A chance for the engineers to prove their value. Show some of these, um, *veterans* what West Point training can bring to this war."

Lee thought he saw a flicker of a smile. He glanced at the others, their faces still focused on him. Lee felt more relaxed now, thought, An opportunity, yes. And a challenge. "Thank you, sir. I will do my best."

"Tomorrow morning, Captain. We're counting on you."

LEE FOUND A SMALL TABLE OF HIS OWN, PROBABLY BORROWED from a local farmer, but no one had protested, and now he needed the space to work.

He spread out the paper, adjusted the lantern, could see the pencil lines Beauregard had made, the rough sketch of the terrain. He moved his finger along one line, running out to the right of the main road, the line curving around the shape of a long ravine and then suddenly ending. That's as far as he went, he thought. That's where I have to begin. He scanned the sketch of the two hills, focused on the smaller one, thought, If it's not too steep, we can move cannon there, drag them up by hand if we have to. It could be a very important position, a spot from which we can shell the enemy from behind. Lieutenant Beauregard said there were troops up there. I must find out how many.

He thought of the enemy, the Mexican troops dug in hard to the rough high ground in front of Scott's army. Out away from the camp, you could see their fires, small flecks of light that spread up and out, the main road snaking away, disappearing right into those hills. And General Twiggs would have sent his troops straight ahead.

There was a sound behind him, boots on dry grass, and Lee heard a low voice. "Captain, you mind a bit of company?"

Lee turned, saw Joe Johnston move into the light, stop, hesitant. Lee pointed to a small chair, said, "Not at all, Joe. Sit. Please. Just going over the map. For tomorrow."

Johnston sat down, leaned forward, looked over the map, said, "You taking any troops with you?"

Lee shook his head. "No. Can't, too obvious. We need to stay out of sight. I'll take that young man, Fitzwalter. He was out there with Lieutenant Beauregard, knows how far they got, where they stopped."

Johnston nodded, still studied the map. "You know, Robert, you'll be pretty close to those Mexicans out there. Won't be easy for us to come get you. You could be captured."

Lee nodded, smiled. "Well, yes, Joe, I had thought of that."

Johnston leaned back. "Oh, no, Robert, I didn't mean to throw any bad—"

"It's all right, Joe. It takes some getting used to, certainly. Engineers don't usually have much business up close to the enemy. Even Vera Cruz, the shelling. The enemy was still out *there* somewhere, behind a wall. Never thought of them as soldiers. Tomorrow, I have to get somewhat . . . closer."

The two men fell silent, seemed to both be enjoying the faint sound of a harmonica, muffled sounds of men moving about, fragments of conversation, all the sounds of an army at rest. Johnston gazed out over the camp, small fires reflecting in his eyes. Lee followed his stare, saw small circles of men, could hear the murmurs of their conversation, an occasional comment from a card game. Some men sat alone, staring across the open ground as he was. The sudden, nervous whinny of a horse drifted over from out near the makeshift corral. Shadows were moving, a shout broke the calm. Johnston said, "Rattlesnake, probably. The horses don't care for them any more than we do. Smart horses."

Lee stared toward the corral, the horses quiet now, said, "Never dreamed of such a place, so different. It's as though God gave this land . . . anger. I've seen bugs, snakes before. But not like this. You don't dare walk barefoot, don't dare take a quick swim in a water hole."

Johnston laughed, said, "Wolves. Heard talk of wolves. Expected to hear them by now. That howl. Nothing like it, makes your hair stand on end. It's like they're calling for you." Johnston seemed to shiver, said, "And, if that's not enough, we have an enemy out there on high ground with a whole lot more muskets than we have."

Lee looked again at the map, at Beauregard's pencil lines, said, "This is the real thing, Joe. All the training, all those years we spent laying brick and slapping mortar, working on the rivers. I thought that would never change, we'd grow old doing the same job. Now we're out here in some place God may not want us to be. It's hard to believe He is happy watching us fight a war."

Johnston leaned forward, pulled the thick wool of the coat tighter on his small frame, shook his head. "Maybe. But we're going to fight it anyway. And General Scott expects us to win. That means we have to go all the way to Mexico City. We'll be in for some serious action. I never thought . . ." He stopped, looked at Lee, pointed toward the wide field of small fires.

"Look out there, all over the camp. Even the card playing is quiet. This is no party. They're preparing for it, every man looking deep inside himself, asking the same questions, making his own peace." Johnston took his hat off, held it in his hands, stared at it. "No one plans this, Robert. No one says, 'I'm going to join the army so I can fight a war.' You and I have been doing this for what? Eighteen years? After a while you never expect to see something like this. Some of these boys are straight out of the Point, the class of 1846, they're going straight from the classroom to combat. What will that do to them? They'll see the army very differently than you or I do, Robert. War might even become . . . normal to them. You and I, we have lives to go home to, families. This war will end, and we will go back to doing what we always did before. But those boys, their lives will never be the same. All they'll know about life is fighting a war. Peacetime could be very dull."

Lee looked at Johnston, the small man outlined in the firelight. He felt a light breeze, pulled his own coat tight, said, "I rather like . . . dull. Can't imagine I'll ever miss this, miss the kind of duty I have to do tomorrow."

Johnston said, "I can't agree with you, Robert. I've been giving it a lot of thought. I plan to request a new assignment."

Lee was surprised, sat back, tried to see Johnston's face hidden by the darkness. "You want to leave the Engineers? Why? To do what?"

"It's been *eighteen* years, Robert. Eighteen years of drawing maps and measuring riverbeds." Johnston stood now, turned toward the fires, stood quietly for a moment, then said, "This may be the only chance I ever have to be a part of something like this. This is combat. I'm afraid, if I don't do this now, I may never get another chance."

Johnston turned toward him, and Lee saw his face in the lamplight, saw a flash of something in his eyes, thought, He's . . . serious. Johnston said, "Robert, I'm putting in for transfer to the infantry. I've heard some of the senior commanders talk about the young officers. There is a concern about their inexperience, their youth. They need people who have some seasoning." He laughed and shook his head. "I'm forty years old, Robert. That's enough seasoning for me. I'm not ready to grow old drawing maps."

"But, Joe . . . infantry? You want to lead men into fire?"

"Sure. What could be more interesting than that?"

Lee shook his head. "I never thought about it like that. I spent my whole career trying to become as efficient as I could be at what I do. I never thought one day I might just stop, go do something else." He looked down at the map again. "It's enough of a challenge to understand what General Scott expects me to do. His understanding of what an engineer does is not what I had expected. He assumes I know how to be a scout."

"You afraid?"

Lee shook his head, looked at Johnston again. "It's just a bit riskier than anything I've done before. I have to focus on the task at hand. I would hope that would keep the fear away. Focus on the job. Would you be afraid? No, I don't suppose you would. You want to charge off into combat."

Johnston laughed, and Lee smiled, said, "I thought I was beginning to understand General Scott. He just expects people to do their job, to carry out his orders. He has high standards."

"Word is . . ." Johnston paused, chose his words carefully. "The word is, General Scott has adopted you, has taken a special interest. What you did at Vera Cruz caught his eye."

Lee shook his head. "No, I haven't done anything conspicuous." He felt his stomach turn, the evening meal reminding him suddenly he was not in Virginia. He put a hand on his stomach, flexed, prodded, said, "Is there—resentment? I haven't tried to put myself in a favorable position."

Johnston laughed again, shook his head, said, "Don't worry about it, Captain. We all have our duty. You just seem to take to yours with a bit more . . . efficiency. Perhaps you need more time like this, right now. Sit out alone in the quiet and let all that energy go for a while. It's nice to see you relaxed a bit. There's plenty of time later for efficiency. Can't say I envy you, that close under the eye of Old Fuss and Feathers. The junior officers are pretty happy to let you have that kind of attention."

Lee felt his stomach calm, rubbed his hands together. An image of the hard face of General Twiggs rose in his imagination. "Happy to hear that. May not be the case with some of the . . . senior officers."

Johnston stretched his arms high, yawned. "Just do your duty, Captain Lee. Maybe some day *you'll* be a senior officer. That's why they're jealous, you know."

Lee began to feel dread, had not seen things the way Johnston did, thought, *Jealousy* has no place here. The army is no place for politicking. We all have our duty, the focus should be there. He thought of General Pillow now, the posturing, said, "I suppose . . . I am naive."

Johnston put a hand on his shoulder, stepped past him. "Perhaps you are, Robert. That may change tomorrow. Good night, Captain."

"Good night, Joe."

Johnston tapped Lee's arm and strode away.

Lee looked at the map again, the lines now a blur, the weariness complete. Lee felt a yawn rolling up inside him, couldn't hold it down, stretched out his arms, the yawn pouring out. He rolled up the map, thought, Tomorrow . . . just, do the job. This is, after all, what all the years, what all the training and preparation, was for, and all the duties in so many places. It's all that General Scott expects. But, yes, this is the real thing.

APRIL FIFTEENTH

The two men slipped through high brush, between thick willows, clusters of scrub oaks, moved down into a deep gorge. Fitzwalter led the way, stopped, glanced back toward Lee, waited as Lee moved deliberately, quietly, stepping carefully past smaller brush, deep green and brown, vines and clusters of thorns covered with small white flowers. Lee looked at the younger man, saw that his face was a dark red crust of sunburn. Fitzwalter was breathing heavily, and Lee thought, He's nervous. So am I. He nodded silently, pointed, *Go on.*

They climbed out of the gorge, hands briefly holding on to loose rocks, small cascades of dirt behind them, moved then into a narrow field of rocks. Lee stopped again, looked up to the left. El Telégrafo

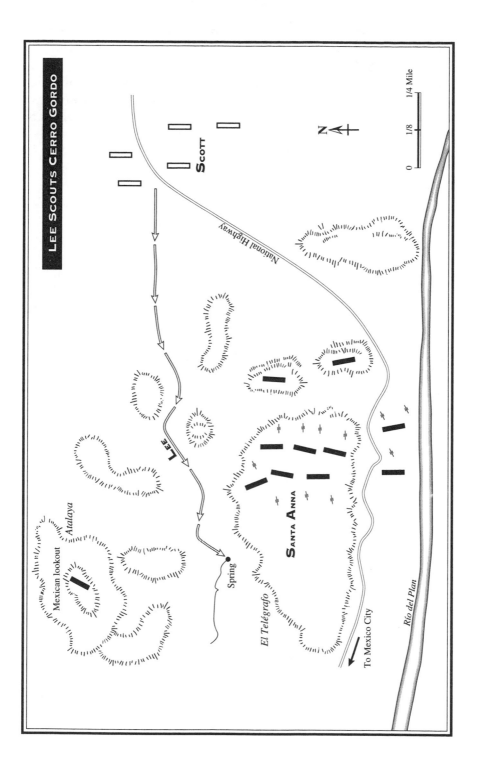

LEE SCOUTS CERRO GORDO

Scott

National Highway

Lee

Mexican lookout
Atalaya

Spring

El Telégrafo

Santa Anna

To Mexico City

Río del Plan

N

0   1/8   1/4 Mile

was nearly five hundred feet high, and for the first time Lee studied more than jagged rocks. He could see color, flags, small flashes of motion. It was Santa Anna's army. He felt the ice in his chest, moved quickly, ducked behind a tall thorny bush, peered around the edge, thought, Surely they will see us. He waited, watched for a long moment, no commotion, no one seeming to notice this small intrusion on their flank. He saw Fitzwalter standing out in the open, gazing in all directions, felt a sudden anger.

"Take cover!" he whispered harshly, and pointed angrily toward the big hill, thought, Doesn't he see them?

Fitzwalter looked at him, smiled, moved up close to Lee, said quietly, "Captain, we best keep moving. We got a long way to go yet."

Lee took a deep breath, felt a little foolish, thought, Keep moving, Captain. They're still a long way away.

The rock field was long and narrow, a dry creek bed that lay between rolling mounds of grassy dirt. The rocks were small and round, moving underfoot, and they walked with care. Lee thought, No twisted ankle, not here. That could make for a very uncomfortable day. Fitzwalter reached the end of the rocks first, moved into the brush, stopped, waited for Lee. Lee looked up, his foot kicked a small rock and he stumbled, the rock rattling noisily. He steadied himself, felt his stomach knot up. *Noise*, Captain. We can do without noise. He moved closer to Fitzwalter, who whispered, "This is it, Captain. As far as Lieutenant Beauregard got. You're in the lead now, sir."

Lee looked again at the mountain to the left, stood on his toes, tried to look ahead, out over the brush in front of them. The ground fell away, a small depression, more grass and dirt. Beyond, the ground rose again, seemed to dip and roll in all directions, small deep cuts, shallow ravines. He made a quick appraisal, thought, Yes, this is an excellent place to hide troops.

He could see the small hill now, Atalaya, and he raised his field glasses, saw something square and dark on the peak, thought, Not guns. It's a *tower*. He lowered the glasses, said in a low voice, "A signal tower. They're using the smaller hill as a lookout. That would mean . . . only a few troops." He pulled a paper from his pocket, a small pencil, began to make a sketch, thought, We have to get closer, move between the two hills. When the main road runs out behind the big hill, we have to know *where*.

He folded the paper and tucked it away, nodded to Fitzwalter, moved into the brush. There was no trail, and he thought of the sappers, the men who worked with the axes and machetes. Yes, they can cut through this, open it up. They moved down into a small ravine, dirt walls rising on both sides, and he glanced again toward the big hill, could not see it now, thought, Yes, very good. He reached out to one side, grabbed a rough limb of a willow, broke it, let it hang, marking the trail. Now the brush cleared away again, more rocks, and Lee stopped, felt his chest tighten, his breath coming in shallow gasps. He stared straight ahead into a tall wall of rock. Fitzwalter, beside him now, said, "Not this way, Captain."

Lee did not respond, looked to the right toward a low place in the rocks, moved that way. He tried to see what lay beyond and began to climb slowly. The rocks were large, as big as a man, and he climbed with both hands, stopped, looked out to the side, saw another old creek bed. He lowered himself down, pointed that way, and began to move into more brush.

He felt the sweat now, the sun moving overhead, and stopped, wiped his face with a handkerchief. Fitzwalter moved up beside him again, said, "Water, sir?"

Lee saw the canteen in the young man's hand. He shook his head and pointed toward the front. "Just a short way. Let's find the creek bed again."

Fitzwalter put the canteen away. He would not drink alone. Lee smiled and thought, That's all right, young man. You have nothing to prove to me. He reached up, parted a cluster of brittle thorns, and heard Fitzwalter's sudden yelp.

When Lee turned around, he saw the young man pulling a long thorn from his gloved hand. He looked at Lee and whispered, "Sorry sir, this is some rough stuff."

Lee closed his eyes for a moment, felt the sting of the sweat again, nodded, said, "Use care, Mr. Fitzwalter. This is not the time to be careless. We are surely very close to the enemy."

Lee turned, moved through the brush, felt the thorns stabbing his side, scraping his coat. He pushed forward, leaned hard against a mass of thick branches, took one step forward, and suddenly the ground fell sharply away. Lee slid down a rocky bank, dug his heels in, but the ground was hard and still he slid down, until finally his feet stopped him at the bottom. He felt himself breathing again, a shower of dirt and rocks sliding down around him. He waited for the sounds to stop, looked up behind him, saw Fitzwalter standing above him, looking out ahead self-consciously, observing something other than his captain's clumsiness. Lee stood, brushed at his clothes, wiped at the thick cake of dust glued to the sweat on his face.

Yes, young man, the point is well taken. We will both be careful.

Fitzwalter eased himself down toward Lee, and Lee pulled out the glasses again, could see Atalaya much closer now, one flag extending from a small wooden structure. He turned, glassed up at the larger hill, saw cannon, the movement of gun crews. He could see the guns pointed away, out to the left, toward the Americans' camp. He lowered the glasses, felt the excitement return, thought, We're behind the guns. We are beyond their flank. He pulled out the paper again, noted the trail he had pushed through, sketched the battery on the big hill. They *expect* us to come straight at them. General Twiggs would have done exactly what Santa Anna wanted him to do. Of course, that's the way wars are fought. He continued to sketch on the paper, thought, Santa Anna was probably educated by the Spanish, the old European methods. It's the same way wars have been fought for centuries. You stand up straight and look your enemy in the eye, and the stronger man wins.

He thought of West Point, the old lessons, the textbooks. Of course, it was all Napoleon, massed strength against massed strength. And it should be no different here. Santa Anna expects us to fight by the *rules*. He suddenly felt very odd, as though some dark place had opened up in his mind. He looked around, thought, Here you are, so focus on the job at hand, figure out how to cut a trail through this . . . mess. You're not paying attention. There is something much more important here than hacking a trail through brush, the duty of one engineer. This is strategy, this is what a good commander must do. This is how General Scott will win this war. We don't have the strength or the ground. So, we use guile. He wrote again, made notes on the map, felt his heart beating. You will remember this, Captain. They did not teach us this in class. What would Napoleon say?

He folded the map away, looked for Fitzwalter, saw the young man in the distance, hands on his knees, staring down at the ground. Now Fitzwalter looked at him, motioned, *Come here.*

Lee moved that way, saw the young man point down. Lee leaned over, could see small arcs, half circles cut into the hard gray dirt. *Horses.* It's a trail. He followed the line of tracks, saw them disappearing into more brush, but the brush was thin, and he moved that way, the young man close behind. The trail was on flat hard ground now, wound down through more shallow ravines, past a small cluster of taller trees. Lee looked up to the left, watching the big hill, thought, We're still in cover. This will do just fine. He moved quickly now, easing his way forward, kept one eye on Atalaya. If they're lookouts, they may be watching for us. Don't get careless.

The trail began to wind to the left, and he kept moving, past more of the taller trees with their canopy of thick green tops. He glanced up, thought, Oaks, but no, they're different, small leaves, unfamiliar. You're not in Virginia, Captain.

The trail straightened out again, leading out past the trees, beyond the shorter brush, into another rock field. He stopped, thought, Easy, no cover out there. He looked at both hills, realized Atalaya was on the right, thought, This is it. We're between the hills. This has to go right out to the main road. He looked toward Atalaya, could see small clumps of brush, some larger trees, looked again toward El Telégrafo, rising to the left. He clenched his fists, wanted to laugh. This is ... amazing. We're in the enemy's *rear*. And so far, they have no idea. He glanced up at the sun, nearly straight overhead, looked for Fitzwalter, the canteen, thought, We're nearly finished here, a little water would be fine. The young man was not on the trail, and Lee felt a sudden dread. No, don't go off exploring. Not now.

Then Fitzwalter emerged from a line of tall, thick bushes, motioned to Lee, excited, whispered, "Sir, this way. There's a spring."

He was gone again, and Lee followed, could hear it now, the marvelous sound of bubbling running water. He reached a clearing, saw Fitzwalter on the far side of a great fat log, a long dead tree. The young man's head disappeared, then bobbed up from behind the log, dripping with the delicious coolness. Lee smiled, climbed a small rise, reached the log, leaned his hands on the rough old wood. The spring was small, a few feet across, feeding a stream than ran noisily through a channel of rock, a small ditch that carried the clear water to the pass between the two hills.

Fitzwalter pulled his canteen out, knelt down, reaching toward the water. Lee watched him, thought, God has provided. Make note of *this* on the map. He waited for the young man to fill the canteen, but saw Fitzwalter suddenly freeze, the canteen just above the water, and now there were noises, the sounds Fitzwalter had already heard. Lee looked beyond the spring, saw a trail leading up through the rocks of the big hill. The sounds were louder now, and Lee felt his chest turn cold. *Voices.*

The young man scrambled back over the log, and Lee helped, pulled his arm sharply, then pushed him away down the short hill. Lee dropped down behind the log. He could hear the voices plainly now, Spanish. The men suddenly appeared on the trail, moving toward the spring. Lee looked down, saw a flat open space beside the log, lay flat out, slid himself hard under the side of the log. He could see underneath the log through a small dip in the ground, could see the motion of the water. He began to push down the log with his left foot, digging with his heel, shoveling dirt along past his feet. The dirt was soft, and blessedly quiet, and he cleared out a small space against the log, thought, How close are they? Maybe once more. He dug his heel into the dirt again, pushed his leg straight. He could hear the voices clearly, thought, All right, enough. He pulled himself tightly into the dampness of the dirt, under the old wood, pulled his legs together, his chest pressing hard into the log above him. He lay his head back slowly, felt his hat give way. He turned his head, stared into the narrow space under the log.

He could see the boots of the soldiers now, dull black leather. He counted . . . four men. His eyes were filled with sweat now, and he felt the awful burn. He blinked it away to clear his vision. His heart was throbbing, the dusty smell of the old wood filling him, and he held on to his breath, tried to calm himself, keep the sounds away. His right arm was free, and he felt his pistol in his belt, thought, No, only if you have no choice. They will leave soon. Patience. Just . . . pray. *God help me. God protect me.*

The talking continued, men filling canteens and bottles, and now there was laughter, words Lee did not understand. He stared at the boots, all gathered beside the spring, saw two of the men moving away. The talk was cheerful, friendly good-byes, and the two men moved up the trail, out of Lee's sight. Thank God, he thought. He felt his breathing calm, his chest not pressed as hard into the log. Patience, he thought. Just two more. Now one man called out, and Lee felt his heart freeze. He gripped the pistol, but the words were a greeting, not a call of alarm. Then there were more voices, moving closer, and Lee closed his eyes, heard the footsteps in the rocks. Eyes open now, he saw more boots, different this time, one man in gray, one in shiny black. He tried to count. Four more men, maybe five.

There was laughter again, more canteens filled, one man kneeling, suddenly leaning down, and Lee's heart jumped. He could see the man's face, dark red skin, a black mustache, his coal-black eyes looking straight at Lee, then away. The man plunged his face into the water. Lee watched him splashing the water, saw a brief glimpse of the face again, then the man was up, moving toward the log. Lee felt the log move slightly, a sudden hard pressure against his chest, the man leaning against the log, the heels of his boots inches from Lee's face. Lee felt the pistol again, thought, If one of them should come around . . . take a walk back here. He suddenly thought of the map in his pocket. You cannot be captured. He felt his breathing again, his lungs filled with the damp smell of his own sweat, his chest pushing painfully against the gray wood above him. No. Patience, he thought. They're just socializing, getting water. But if they have nothing better to do . . . you could be here for a long time.

The man above him was telling a story now, the others listening, small comments. There was laughter, the man pausing, continuing now, and Lee thought, It would be nice to understand this. Who would ever have thought we'd have a war with someone who spoke Spanish? We all learned French. Not much good now. If I knew Spanish, I might learn something, pick up some piece of information. He listened to the words, heard more laughter, the storyteller growing more enthusiastic. One word was repeated now, emphasized, *esposa*. Lee knew that one. Wife. No military secrets there. There was a great burst of laughter, the story concluded. The man stood, moved away from the log, and for a moment the voices grew quiet. Lee heard footsteps on rocks, thought, They're moving away, but no, not all of them. The spring was blocked from his view again, another man bending low, another conversation.

His left leg had grown numb. He closed his eyes again, blinked through more sweat. Turning his head slightly, he looked up, straight at the gray wood above his face. If I am to be here a long time, I had better be comfortable. He tried to flex his left hand, pressed hard into wet dirt between his leg and the ancient wood, the fingers barely able to move. No, nothing I can do about that. He could feel the sweat now, blending with the dampness beneath him, soaking his uniform. He began to feel a coolness. At least you're in the shade. He shivered, a sharp chill, felt his nose twitch. No, God, no, there will be no sneeze. He flexed the free hand, thought, Bring it up slowly, you can reach your nose. But he could not see his right arm, was not sure how much of his right side was exposed. If the right arm moved . . . no, keep it still. He clenched his face into a tight frown. There will be *no* sneeze.

He concentrated on trying to relax, conscious of his breathing. He could hear the steady, low voices of a simple conversation between friends. He was suddenly aware of a pain in his back, between his shoulders. He had not noticed it before, tried to shift his weight slightly, and the pain suddenly knifed into him. No, he thought, don't move *that* way. He flexed his shoulders. What is it? A rock? Some small pointed thing in just the wrong place. He shifted his weight again, felt the rock settle slowly into his back, the pain now just a dull stab. I could have swept that rock away, he thought, just one more second. Another message from God. You will stay awake.

H
E HAD LOST TRACK OF TIME, COULD FEEL SUNLIGHT WARMING his right arm, thought of the watch in his pocket, unreachable now. The numbness in his leg was now complete, his left hand ached with crushing agony. He faced straight up, his eyes closed, opened them when there was a change in the voices, when the boots moved away on the rocks, or worse, when more of them came down the trail to the spring.

His mind had taken him away, drifting off into darkness, the pains and the agonizing stiffness held aside whenever his mind would allow. He had stopped listening to the blur of meaningless words, just the dull sound of the voices kept rolling through his mind, holding him there, tight against the ancient log. He thought of the log itself, began to wonder, how old? He thought of the taller trees he had seen, but this was much larger, fatter, two and a half, maybe three feet across. And very old.

He had seen nothing else this size in the area, and he thought, Maybe . . . they were all cut, when the Indians were here, maybe even before Cortez. This land might have been thick woods, changed now, by time, by man's hand, or, by the hand of God. If this was Virginia, it would be a mass of rot, soft and crumbling, full of bugs, might not even be here at all, long gone, eaten away by weather. He stared up into the dark, tried to see detail in the wood, but it was too close, too dark. It's almost petrified, rock hard, he thought. Probably hollow. How old, I wonder?

His eyes began to close, and he felt himself slip into a light sleep, then the pain from the small rock dug into him, jarring him into awareness. No, he thought, you cannot slip away. Stay here, stay alert. All it would take is one man, one observant soldier, catching a glimpse of blue behind the log. He gripped the pistol again, thought, Would I have time? I'd take one of them for sure. They would be surprised, off guard. They might not even have weapons, maybe a knife. He felt his stomach curl into a knot. Not a knife, God help me, not a knife. He could not help it, his mind holding the awful image, imagined the blade pushing, slicing inside his gut. He shuddered, blinked hard, No, I do not want to die like that, to feel it like that, the slow, painful horror. No knife, no bayonet. His mind was filled with the awful images, something he had never actually seen, the stuff of nightmares, and he fought it, tried to push it away.

If there is an officer, he would have a pistol, and he felt better now, thought, Yes, there must be an officer, coming to the spring with his men, sending them back up to their posts. Maybe . . . these are all officers, the privilege of rank, and this spring is their social gathering place. He took a deep breath, quietly exhaled, licked his lips, felt their dryness. At least Fitzwalter got a good drink of water. He felt his heart jump: *Fitzwalter,* did he get away? There was nothing from the voices to hint that a prisoner had been captured, surely there would have been excitement. He felt relief, thought, He probably made his way back. It might be the only chance I have, the only way anyone will find me. There would be no search party, not out here, not in this place. Silence, discretion, was still important. It would be too risky, could reveal the army's plans. One engineer was not worth that.

He could feel the warmth again on his right arm, thought, Surely the sun is going down. If I don't return to camp by dark, they will have to assume I'm captured, or worse. And so, tomorrow, another engineer will follow the same trail, maybe Fitzwalter will lead Lieutenant Beauregard again. Maybe they will get as far as the main road. It doesn't appear I'm going any farther than this.

He opened his eyes again, focused again on the voices, the sounds of the water. He heard small splashes, a cruel tease, and he opened his mouth slightly, felt the crusty dryness. He moved his tongue, a stump of dried leather, the inside of his mouth like rough wool. Stop this, you cannot think on that. Focus on something . . . anything else. He tried to turn his head, to see the boots, but his neck was stiff, a twist of pain moved down the wetness of his back. No, just stay still. Patience. His eyes closed, and he suddenly thought of Mary, the sound of the water taking him back to the fountain, the gardens of their lovely mansion. It was high above the Rappahannock River, and across, you could see Fredericksburg.

He was there now, the broad grassy hill, great oak trees, walking with Mary down along the river, tall, thin Mary, walking with that regal stiffness, always on parade. We were so very young, too young for her father. He did not approve of this soldier coming to call on his only daughter. I suppose he expected someone more fitting to his heritage. George Washington Parke Custis, the grandson of Martha Washington, and painfully aware of the responsibility of that. His house was more of a museum than a home, a storehouse for the artifacts of Washington's presidency. No, Lee thought, Mr. Custis wanted a caretaker for the legacy, someone worthy of the honor. Thank God for Mrs. Custis. Women have a different view of marriage. It has to begin with romance, soft words and tenderness. That is what mattered to Mary, and to her mother.

Lee smiled now, could not help it, remembered the nervousness, his hands and voice shaking, catching her alone, a brief moment without supervision in the kitchen, and the awkward proposal. Her face, the shy smile ... the moment began to fade and he thought, What would she say to me now? Robert, you are filthy and you will not come through that door until you have seen the washtub. . . .

He worried about her, even now, thought, She was sick again this winter. How much of that is my fault? I missed being home for Christmas. The first time, since the beginning, since the wedding. No matter the duty, no matter how far away, there was always a way to get home. There was never anything so important that I would not spend Christmas with my family. Until now. And it seemed ... He smiled again, could hear the teasing, his friends at the different posts, Fort Monroe, Fort Hamilton. Every visit home seemed to produce another child, another Lee, seven now, and he remembered the joke, "Captain, you're producing your own army." He focused again. The first Christmas apart. God cannot be pleased.

He tried to clear his head, opened his eyes, felt all the pains come back, the awful thirst, growing worse now, his breathing painful, labored, the awful stiffness in his chest. He tried to open his mouth again, but the numbness had come up his back into his neck, his jaw. He tried to think about that. It's better than pain, I suppose. God's gift. The body grows quiet, still, numb, like ... dying. Perhaps this is the way, the blessing God gives us when death comes, the relief from the awful pain. He blinked, scolded himself. Stop this, Captain. You are not dying. You're supposed to be a soldier. You must endure this. He blinked again, felt something flicker into his eye, dust, some piece of the wood finding the vulnerable place.

He held his eyes closed, but there were no tears, nothing to help. All right, use this. It is another distraction. Perhaps ... He felt suddenly like laughing. It is another test. God is playing with you. What have I done, why this torment? He fluttered his eyes, tried to brush away the piece of debris, felt angry now. Please. He fought it again, tried to calm himself, scolded again.

Patience, Captain. That is the test. Patience. Nothing has changed. The voices were still there, and he flexed the fingers of his right hand, felt the pistol again, thought, If they find me now . . . how much good will this do? Can I even grip the handle, pull the trigger? I'm as petri-fied as this log. He suddenly felt a great sadness, thought, This is how it will end, under a log at the feet of the enemy. Even Fitzwalter doesn't know where I am by now.

He began to drift again, could hear a strange voice, far away, a dream from some deep place. He tried to see the face, but there was no one there, the old man's voice a strange echo. He tried to remember to picture the face with the voice, thought, Yes, I know it's you, it has to be. The old man's words were a jumble, nonsense, and Lee fought through it, tried to see his father's face. He never dreamed about his fa-ther, did not recall much of the early days, the old man rarely around, always in some kind of trouble, some shameful scandal. I wish I had known him back then, the old days, the Revolution. He was a hero to his country, Light-Horse Harry. I could use a hero right now.

The old man's voice was gone, and now Lee saw the face of his mother, it came to him in a sudden shock of recognition, and he felt light-headed now, dizzy. He tried to hear the voice of his father again, did not want to see her, but he could not push her image away. She was staring at him, calm, clear-eyed, and he was suddenly very small, and very ashamed. I do not have the right, he thought. I cannot feel sorry for myself. I must be . . . He held the word away, did not want to hear it, his mind fighting her image. She seemed to smile at him now, and he could not fight it, felt the great awful sadness, could see her in the bed, so fragile. He leaned over her, held her, her eyes still looking at him, the only piece of her still alive, and he knew what she was saying. I must be . . . *strong*. Because she cannot, because there is no one else now. It is my duty. It will always be my duty.

He felt something on his right leg, his eyes suddenly wide, his mind snapping into focus, a sudden burst of clarity. He tried to lift his head, to see, raw instinct, his face bumping the log. He lay flat again, helpless, felt the movement, the small pressure, delicate, deliberate steps across his knee, then up, closer to where his hand gripped the pistol. Now it was gone, and he felt his breathing again, his heart beating, thought of the dreaminess, the images, thought, A strange land with an amazing selection of creatures. Another reminder. Do not sleep.

He tried to see out to the right again, but the stiffness held him tight. His arm was still warm, the blue wool soaked through with sweat. There was still sun, and he thought, How long? Three, four hours? There can't be that much daylight left. He thought of Scott now, the old man's angry eyes. Will he worry? He's an old soldier, and he understands the cost of war. Maybe I'm part of that cost. He thought of his father again, his similarities to Scott. It had never occurred to him, and he thought, Both of them warriors and neither of them politicians. Strange, I feel like I know General Scott better than I knew my own father. General Scott doesn't understand the rules, who you can offend and who you can't. So he ends up offending everyone. At least out here he outranks all his political enemies, all the other generals with their own ambitions. He remembered Scott reading him the order now, Polk's vague instructions, command without interference. So, Washington has given him all the responsibility, and the war is his to win. And his strategy is correct. I know that, I have seen it, seen how it can be done. And I'm stuck under a log.

He was suddenly aware of a difference, something unusual. He forced his head slowly to the side, looked under the log, to the spring. The boots were still there, the voices still low and calm, but now the light was fading. It was getting dark.

He stared at the boots, spoke to them in his mind, *Go on!* Get back to your camps! One man moved away now, a louder voice, *adios,* a laugh, the sound of rocks colliding. The light was fading quickly, and he saw motion, more boots, moving away. He heard the voices moving now as well, one man yawning, stretching, then the sound of rocks again. He strained to hear, the voices now nearly gone, and then he could hear nothing at all. He waited, stared out toward the spring, could feel the air, cooler still. He closed his eyes, endured the piece of debris in his eye, the annoying intruder, thought, Push it all away, clear everything, every sound. You must be certain.

It was another ten minutes, maybe more, and he turned his head, stared up again at the darkness of the log. He moved his right arm now, slid his hand along the hard dirt, his shoulder loosening, giving way to the motion. He pressed his hand down, tried to lift himself, tried to slide his back across the wet dirt. He tried to turn his head to the right, worked the stiffness out of his neck. He could see out beyond the log, pulled again with his right hand, slid farther out in the open. He raised the hand now, brought it to his face, blinked as his finger found the eye, rubbing, hard rough probing. He blinked hard, the debris now replaced by the intrusion of dust and grime from his finger. The spring, he thought, the water. God help me.

He tried to move his right leg, realized now both legs were completely numb. He pulled himself clear of the log, his legs dead weight, saw movement, under the log, and now a large hairy spider moved into the open, stopped, and Lee stared at it through watery eyes, thought,

Yes, sorry old fellow. No doubt I was the intruder. He slid his legs farther out, rolled to the side, unclenched his left hand, slowly, painfully, moved his arm down his leg, began to massage it. The feeling crept into his legs, the slow spread of the tingling, the awful prick of a thousand needles. He rubbed harder, worked the stiffness out of his hand, tried to lift his head, and suddenly his hat fell off, rolled on its brim down the short hill. He felt a laugh trembling inside him, but he knew he could not make a sound. He looked down at the hat, thought, Well, thank you for doing that *now*. He was completely clear of the log, looked back underneath, saw the stain of wetness, saw now the small pebble that had been under his back, a tiny cone of rock. He leaned over, picked it up, slipped it into his pocket, thought, I will remember *you*. He tried to stand, leaned against the log, slowly pulled himself up, and now there was a sound, behind him, from down the hill. He reached for the pistol, felt the ice in his chest, saw motion, the brush moving, then a figure, a man. It was Fitzwalter.

The young man moved quickly up the rise, and Lee saw the smile, a toothy grin, and Fitzwalter whispered, "Quite a day, eh, sir? Thought they'd never leave."

Lee tried to speak, fought through the dryness in his mouth. "Where did you go?" The words tore at his throat.

"Right down there, sir. Just in those bushes there. I could see 'em just fine. Could see you too, sir. If they'd a found you, I was ready." He tapped the pistol in his belt. "We'd have made some noise, that's for sure."

Lee nodded, could see the young man's excitement, thought, Yes, remember this day. You will never have another one like it.

"Uh, sir, I reckon the Mexicans won't mind if we have a taste before we leave?"

Lee looked at the spring, nodded, said, "Quickly. We have a long walk."

Fitzwalter climbed up on the log, swung a leg over, landed with a thump on the other side. The noise startled Lee, and he looked up the trail, thought, Easy, we still may not be alone. Fitzwalter moved to the spring, bent down, took a long drink. Lee looked down into the water, pressed his hands on top of the log, thought, Swing your leg over . . . well, no, not just now. He tried walking, moved stiffly down to the end of the log, saw a great dark hole, the log hollow. He eased around, moved up closer to the spring. Fitzwalter backed away now, his face soaking wet, still smiling broadly.

Lee looked down into the spring, the water reflecting the last daylight like a fountain of diamonds. He knelt in the boot tracks of the Mexican soldiers, reached into the water, felt the cold shock in his hands, brought them up to his face, opened his mouth, then again, wiped at the crust of dirt. Not today, he thought. It was not my time. *Thank You.*

He stared at the water again, leaned down closer, now drank, paused, caught his breath, then drank again. He felt the dryness wash away, smiled, stared at the water. He thought of a swimming hole, some wonderful place very long ago, then plunged his face into the icy coolness with a child's pure joy.

THE FIRES WERE LOW, MOST OF THE STAFF HAD SETTLED INTO their tents. Lee moved quietly, the stiffness in his legs complete, the weariness pressing down on his shoulders. He heard Fitzwalter moving close behind him, thought, Young legs. He'd have made it back an hour faster.

There were still a few men near the fires, and they began to move toward him, recognition, small greetings, and now hands came out, enthusiastic relief, the men gathering around the dusty engineer. Lee said nothing, could hear the curiosity, felt grateful for the concern, saw Joe Johnston now, and Johnston said, "Welcome home, Captain. Long day?"

Lee smiled, nodded, said, "Long day."

The men around him gave way, and Lee focused on the larger tent, began to move that way, Fitzwalter still behind him. He saw the young Scott emerging from the tent, drawn by the commotion, and the young man seemed surprised to see him, said, "Captain, you survived. The general was concerned."

Lee saluted. "Thank you, Major. Captain Lee reporting. May I see the commanding general?"

The young Scott studied Lee's face now, a look of concern, leaned closer to Lee, said, "You all right, Captain?"

"Could use something to eat, actually." Lee felt a dryness in his throat, thought, The canteen, looked behind him, saw Fitzwalter looking around, eyeing the staff. Fitzwalter suddenly threw up a salute, stood frozen, wide-eyed, and Lee saw now the tall grim man moving around a low fire. It was Twiggs.

The old man ignored Fitzwalter, looked at Lee, said, "You find that road, Captain?"

Lee felt suddenly sick inside, the weariness magnified by the glare from Twiggs.

"Sir, we discovered that we can move between the two hills. Atalaya is occupied only by a signal detachment."

Twiggs grunted, and now Lee felt a large heavy hand on his shoulder, heard the voice of Scott. "General Twiggs, shall we take this conference inside? The night has ears."

The two commanders moved into the tent, and Lee started to follow, then stopped, glanced back at Fitzwalter. He saw the canteen, thought, I suppose it will have to wait. Fitzwalter would not follow now, could not be a part of the high level meeting. Lee saw his face, the disappointment, thought, Be patient, young man. You'll have your chance. He looked at the young Scott, said, "Major, can you secure some rations for Mr. Fitzwalter?"

The young Scott moved quickly, said, "Certainly. This way . . ."

Lee held up his hand, and Fitzwalter waited, and Lee said, "Mr. Fitzwalter, this was a fine day's work. You should get some rest. I suspect that tomorrow we'll have a job to do cutting through that brush."

The young man nodded, stood straight now, snapped a salute toward Lee. "Sir. Good night, sir."

Lee returned the salute, then moved into the tent. Scott was sitting behind the table, and Twiggs sat as well. Lee saw there were no more chairs. Scott reached for the lamp, turned up the light, the yellow glow now surrounding Lee. He suddenly felt unsteady, the light and the shadows swirling together, and he blinked hard, reached for the table, leaned heavily, holding himself up. Scott leaned forward, said, "You eaten anything, Captain?"

Lee straightened, slid his hands off the table, said, "No sir. I was hoping . . . there would be something here. I know it's late."

Twiggs said, "You find the road?"

Twiggs had not changed his expression, and Scott said, "We will hear the captain's report in a moment, General."

Lee felt the twist in his gut again, thought, *The road.* If that was the mission then this was not a good day after all. Scott looked at Lee again, said, "Difficult day, Captain?"

Lee thought of Johnston's question, thought, I must look awful. "Yes, sir. Somewhat difficult, sir. We had to make some effort to avoid capture. But we located a good route between the hills. The smaller hill, Atalaya, is lightly defended."

He stopped, pulled the map from his pocket, unfolded it, laid it on the table. Scott leaned forward, slid the map slightly toward the light, studying Lee's drawings. Twiggs sat back, did not look at the map, and Lee glanced at him, felt his patience slipping away, thought,

This is important. At least look at it, try to understand. Twiggs looked up at him now, and Lee felt himself flinch, instinctive, thought, No, let it go. It's only the fatigue. This is General Scott's concern, not yours.

Scott said, "Good, very good. Captain, tomorrow have your men begin work early, clear the trail. As soon as it is suitable for artillery, notify me. This time, take some muskets, a good escort. The Mexicans will certainly detect something, might try to interfere."

Twiggs said, "They won't believe it. Won't pay any attention. They expect the fight to be right in front of them."

Scott leaned back, said, "That's the idea, General. As long as they stay up on those hills, the surprise will be ours. I have ordered General Worth to march his men from Vera Cruz. We need the strength, need those men here more than we need anyone on the coast. We'll discuss the plan of attack when he arrives. Good night, General."

Twiggs knew the signal, stood, nodded to Scott, passed behind Lee, said nothing, moved out of the tent. Lee glanced at the chair, and Scott pointed, nodded, said, "Have a seat, Captain. So my engineer got a little close to the enemy? Quite a feeling, eh? Well, tell me about it. I want to hear a good story."

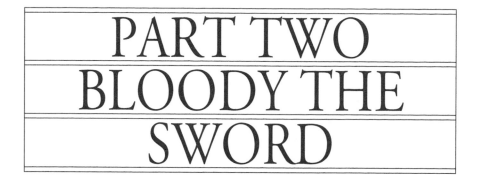

PART TWO
BLOODY THE
SWORD

Major General Winfield Scott

6. LEE

April eighteenth, dawn

THE WORK WAS COMPLETE. THEY'D CLEARED A CRUDE ROADWAY that could even support the movement of the field cannon. The plan of attack was plain now to all the commanders. Twiggs would lead the hard thrust around the Mexican flank, following the trail Lee had discovered. Behind Twiggs, Worth would move in support. Directly in front of the Mexican position, Patterson's volunteers would demonstrate, all noise and bluster, men lined up in battle formation with all the show of some grand parade. The show was for Santa Anna, to convince him the attack was indeed coming straight at him, to occupy his attention while Twiggs moved into position from behind.

Lee had been up early, working with his sappers until dark. He had overseen every detail, every turn of the trail, and even when the work ended, the details stayed with him. He had spent a long sleepless night, staring into darkness, thinking of brush and rocks and the men with machetes. And always there was the specter of the main road, the great wide highway behind the Mexican position that led to Mexico City, the road that Lee had not found.

Now with the dawn he had risen with the rest of the army, making ready for the day to come. He stayed close to Scott's quarters, drank a cup of the sweet coffee that had been a gift from a local farmer, a man who did not see the Americans as invaders. Lee had not thought much about the locals, had naturally assumed they would be hostile to this violation of their territory. But the people showed the army a different face, and the gifts from the ranchers and farmers were common and much appreciated.

I do not really understand that, he thought. They don't seem to know much about government, or care who is in command. If they are left alone, then the outside world doesn't seem to matter. He swirled the coffee in the cup slowly, looked into the thick blackness, thought, They have enough to be concerned with surviving. This land is not like Virginia, there is no great bounty of fertile soil. God has given these people a challenge. I don't understand why.

The army had passed by many of the small churches, simple buildings of stone and clay, but inside, all the grand artifacts of old Catholicism, rich stained glass, brightly colored paintings and sculptures, mostly of the Virgin Mary. The symbols of veneration for the Virgin were everywhere, some form of statue or painting adorned nearly every home, visible to anyone who passed by. He knew there had been some trouble in Vera Cruz, some of the American soldiers, volunteers mostly, taking exception to the different practices of the country's dominant religion. Some had destroyed the statues, or simply stolen them, and even the churches themselves had suffered vandalism, the citizens sometimes abused by taunts and insults they could not understand. The outbursts of hate and intolerance were an embarrassment to the army, a challenge to Scott's authority, and a horrifying mystery to Lee. Lee had been relieved when Scott finally responded directly, issuing the orders restricting access to the citizens. The civilians and all aspects of their culture were simply off limits. But Lee had begun to feel that even Scott could not change the ignorance that powered the intolerance of the volunteers.

Lee finished the coffee, thought, Maybe one more cup. He stood, moved toward the mess wagon, began to feel that turn of the machine in his chest, his body fully alive, the effect of that wonderful little bean. No, he thought, that may be enough. This is much stronger coffee than what the army provides.

It had been light for nearly an hour, and as Lee moved toward Scott's tent through the early morning light and haze, he could see activity ahead, a lone man on a horse, finally more of the staff. It was General Twiggs. Twiggs dismounted, saw Lee, stared at him for a moment but said nothing. Lee felt the dread again, always felt the dread when Twiggs looked at him. He moved quickly now, saluted, said, "General Twiggs, good morning. A fine day for a fight."

Twiggs looked at him curiously, remained silent. The general turned away, and Lee thought, Why do you even attempt it? He obviously has no use for you. Probably has no use for anyone, not even General Scott.

There was commotion in Scott's tent, then the big man emerged in one great flow of motion. Lee stared wide-eyed, had rarely seen Scott in full dress uniform, the bright gold sash, medals polished, gold epaulets on his shoulders, all the great pomp and display of command. Scott stood for a moment, looking slowly over the camp. He seemed to be waiting for the men to notice him. Now the cheers came, slow at first, then some of the men moved closer and more picked up the call, the sound echoing well out across the rugged ground. Scott stood motionless. Lee smiled, thought, He loves it, the affection of the men. Lee glanced at Twiggs, saw his grim impatience, and he thought, Of course, this is why he and some of the others don't like Scott. The cheers are never for them.

Scott held up his hand, the signal to the staff to disperse the soldiers, to get them to move back to their posts. Lee could hear the orders, officers gathering their men into formation. The sounds of the army were muted, tense, and even the foot soldiers had to know that today something would happen. They could all see the Mexican position, knew from where the cannon watched them, where the soldiers were dug in, waiting for them with bayonets.

Leaving his staff behind, Twiggs moved toward Scott. Scott looked at Lee, said, "Captain, you feeling fit this morning?"

"Yes, sir. Quite fit, sir."

"Good. General Twiggs, are your men ready to follow my engineer?"

Twiggs nodded, "We understand the plan, sir. I have ordered two brigades to move beyond the big hill and make straight for the vicinity of the main road. One brigade will follow Captain Lee and seize the smaller hill." Twiggs paused, looked at Lee with no expression. "We are prepared as ordered, sir. We will provide your captain with three twenty-four-pound guns from Captain Steptoe's battery. If he can get them up that hill, he may place them as he sees fit."

Lee nodded, said, "Thank you, sir. They will be put to good use."

Ignoring Lee, Twiggs said, "General, we are ready to move out on your command."

Scott moved to a fat white horse, pulled himself up with a soft grunt and sat heavily. He looked out across the camp.

"General Twiggs, take advantage of your guide. Captain Lee knows the ground. You may proceed. I will see General Patterson and make sure they put on a good show."

Twiggs snapped a salute, climbed his horse, watched as Scott moved away. He looked down at Lee now. "Captain, you have a horse?"

Lee felt the man's imperious glare again. "Yes, sir. Right over there, sir."

"Well, get to it, Captain."

Lee moved quickly, climbed his horse, pulled the animal close to Twiggs, who said, "Stay close to me, Captain. I'll cut you loose when the time comes."

Twiggs spurred his horse, his staff moving in behind him. Lee hurried to catch up, thinking, Cut me loose? I'm supposed to be his guide. He doesn't know the land. Lee felt a burn spreading in his chest, could suddenly taste coffee again, thought, Stop complaining. This is a war. And you're about to ride right into the middle of it.

T WIGGS HAD MOVED HIS MEN FAR ALONG LEE'S TRAIL BEFORE the Mexicans began to respond, and even then it was little more than a nuisance—brief, scattered musket fire, a few skirmishers. As the troops moved farther beyond the flank of El Telégrafo, they came into sight of the lookout on Atalaya, and Lee could see the flags waving frantically, signaling the troops on the big hill.

Behind Lee the troops moved quickly, following the trail quietly. He led the way, Twiggs close beside him, silent and grim. Lee watched the man's face, noticed a change coming over him, as though some aspect of the fight was reflected in his eyes. The old general's eyes were sharper now, more alert. Lee understood then. Twiggs's anger was not directed at Scott or him, but out *there*, at the enemy.

Lee moved the horse carefully down a slope, the same place he had fallen on the scouting mission. But the slope was smoother now, the rocks hauled aside, the grade made less steep by good work from men with shovels. Lee waited for Twiggs to move his horse down beside him, could hear a light chatter of musket fire, from in front, the few Mexican soldiers on the smaller hill firing at the growing mass of blue snaking toward them. Far in front of Lee the Americans had a skirmish line of their own, clearing the way of any Mexicans who might be waiting to ambush the column. The skirmishers were close to Atalaya now, and Lee thought, Some of that firing may be from our own men. But we are still too far away. Twiggs was ignoring the sound of muskets. He looked back to his men, waiting for the first foot soldiers to reach the slope.

"Come on, dammit! Let's move!"

Twiggs's voice startled Lee, who thought, Please, quiet. We have too far to go yet. Not everyone knows we're here.

Twiggs spurred the horse, scowled at Lee. "You coming, Captain? Let's *move!*"

Lee drove the horse quickly beside Twiggs, keeping his eyes on Atalaya. He could see small wisps of smoke curling skyward from the musket fire, then he heard a sharp zip, slicing through the brush beside him. He looked to the side, saw nothing but stillness. He looked again at Atalaya, felt a thump in his chest. Well, *that* was something new. The enemy, indeed.

They moved along the path through high brush, and since Lee could not see the big hill any longer, he thought they were still hidden. Twiggs had stopped to give orders to a courier. The man rode quickly away, and Lee thought, What message? We have to keep moving. No, Captain, that is not your concern.

Twiggs did not look at him, moved his horse to the front, past Lee, and Lee spurred his horse, again moved beside the old man. The brush gave way, parted into the wide rock field, a flat path cutting down the center, cleared of rocks by Lee's workmen. They were much closer to the smaller hill now, and Twiggs stopped, said, "All right, Captain. There's your damned hill. Give my men a few minutes, and you can have it." Twiggs turned, shouted, "Colonel Harney, up here on the double!"

Lee cringed again at the volume from Twiggs, looked at Atalaya, thought, Well, surely our presence is no surprise by now. He heard horses behind him, saw an officer riding hard, moving close, an older man, grim-faced, handling the horse with the skill of a cavalryman.

The man saluted, and Twiggs said, "Colonel, that's your hill. Take two regiments, clear them away! Charge them to hell!"

Harney saluted, and the other officers began to give the call. Twiggs moved off the trail, said to Lee, "Move out of the way, Captain."

Lee pulled his horse aside, watched the column of blue troops moving past quickly, the sweating faces of men whose eyes stared to the front. Lee felt his chest pounding, could hear the chatter growing from Atalaya. He raised his field glasses, could see the Mexican soldiers firing down the hill, the brush below the skirmish line draped in a light cloud of smoke from the musket fire. Now the sounds grew louder, the rattle of muskets straight out in front, and then voices, shouts, as Harney's soldiers swept past the skirmish line and began climbing the hill. Lee strained to see them, looked out just above the brush and rocks in front of him. A mass of blue spread up from the base of the hill, moving higher, and he could see the Mexicans suddenly running, disappearing over the crest of the hill. The men in blue reached the lookout post, and Lee saw the flag cut down, Harney's soldiers continuing to spread out over the crest of the hill in pursuit of the enemy. Lee lowered the glasses, his hands shaking. He looked at Twiggs, who was still watching Harney's men.

Twiggs glanced over at Lee. "There's your hill, Captain. Get your damned cannon up there, if you still think you can."

Abruptly, Twiggs spurred his horse, moved away toward the front, his staff hurrying to keep up. Lee felt a small wave of panic, thought, What's he doing?

Lee could hear a new wave of musket fire, Harney's men now moving beyond Atalaya, still pursuing the Mexican retreat, a steady flow of sound and smoke, moving toward the big hill. On the lower slope of El Telégrafo he could see the Mexican soldiers, retreating in panic, men climbing frantically to the safety of their strong defenses. Harney's men were still chasing them, and the voices carried back to Lee. No, he thought, there should not be a general engagement, not yet. He turned, rose up in the saddle, listened, thought, The demonstration, General Patterson's attack hasn't started yet. The enemy will put all their energy back here. We will be cut off.

He yanked the horse around, spurred hard, moved back along the trail. Seeing the next regiment of infantry, waiting, officers talking calmly, Lee stopped the horse, shouted, "Where is Captain Steptoe? I need his guns!"

The officers looked at Lee. One man shook his head; another, a young major, said, "Well now, Captain, I'm sure Captain Steptoe is back here somewhere. What you planning on doing with his guns?"

Lee felt an explosion boiling up in his chest, took a deep breath, fought it, thought, Get control, clenched his jaw and said, "I need a courier, *now*, to locate Captain Steptoe. By orders of General Scott, Captain Steptoe is to move three twenty-four-pound guns to the front, under my direction. I do not have time to explain."

Lee saw another officer, followed by a man holding a small flag. He knew the face, fought for the officer's name, an older man who sat tall in the saddle, broad-shouldered, who did not have to shout to be heard. The man moved close, said, "You would be Captain Lee, the engineer."

"Yes, sir." The name flowed into Lee's mind now, and he said, "Yes, Colonel Riley. Sir, I need to locate Captain Steptoe."

"He's coming. You still think you can get up that hill?"

Lee felt relief, thought, He knows my orders, thank God. "Yes, sir."

"Well, good luck, Captain. My men are moving out to the right. You get those guns up there, you can make our job a good deal easier."

Riley nodded to Lee, moved his horse off the trail, said to his officers, who still looked at Lee, "Let's move out. By the right flank, march!"

There was a surge of motion behind Riley, and the blue wave began to flow out through the brush. Quickly, the trail behind him was clear, and Lee saw a young man riding hard, waving at him. The man stopped the horse beside him, a cloud of white dust blowing over them both as the young man said, "Sir! Captain Steptoe, at your service. Where do we place the guns?"

Lee could see them now, rolling forward, each pulled by a pair of horses. He turned and pointed. "Up there."

Steptoe nodded, then shook his head, said, "That's what they told me. It's a hell of a haul."

Lee said, "Then we had better get started."

Steptoe said, "The horses won't do. We'll need some men. There's not enough manpower in my crews."

Lee saw the major again, Riley's man, leading another column of infantry forward. The man moved up to Lee, the annoying indifference gone now, said, "Captain, Colonel Riley has ordered me to provide you with any help you need."

Lee felt a wave of relief, thought, Thank you. Whoever is responsible . . . thank you. He pointed to the hill again, said, "Right there, gentlemen. Right now."

7. SANTA ANNA

APRIL EIGHTEENTH, MID-MORNING

HE HAD SLEPT LATER THAN USUAL, WAS STILL IN HIS TENT, THE rich white silk billowing softly, rustled by the light breeze. He sat at the dark wood table, held the silver knife in his hand, reached out to stab at the dark slice of meat. He nodded to the chef, a small quivering man in a white apron, "Yes, this will do. If there is nothing better to be found, I will sacrifice."

The chef withdrew, and Santa Anna ignored the relief in the man's face, studied the rest of the grand breakfast, the rich red of the strawberries, the sharp smell from the ripe cheese. He picked up a piece of the dark brown bread, stale and dry in his hand, turned it over with a look of disgust, tossed it out the opening in the tent. How hard can this be, he thought, how difficult is it to provide the basic comforts? They can bring the meat, the fruit, but no one here can bake a simple loaf of bread? Are we so far from the comforts of the city that I must be tolerant of those who cannot do their job? He stabbed at the berries, stuffed one in his mouth, the sweetness soothing him.

I will be lenient, this time. That incompetent chef is fortunate that God has granted me such patience. And, today, I would rather have only the pleasant tasks. I will repay God for His kindness. Today, I will destroy the American infidels who soil our land.

He drank from the silver goblet, the wine warming him, sat back in the deep velvet of the chair, put a hand down on the thigh of the left leg, prodding and probing the dull ache. It bothered him every day, but especially in the morning, when the artificial limb was first attached. He still tried to do it by himself, but his patience would slip away, and he would shout for the doctor, the man whose only job was to comfort any pain that might torment him. The leg was fastened tight now, would serve Santa Anna as well as anyone could expect. But the pains brought the reminder of the bungling doctors, the incompetent men who had done the operation that had taken his shattered leg away.

The wound had come at the hands of the French, occurred during their retreat from their brief conquest of Vera Cruz, nearly ten years before. Santa Anna had risen again to command the army, a command no one thought he would ever see, not after the disgrace of the loss of Texas. But when Vera Cruz fell to the aggression of the French, an embarrassing surrender to a small force, Santa Anna could not stay away, could not ignore the inner call to duty, the passion that consumes anyone who calls himself a patriot. He had assumed command of the Mexican forces still scattered around the city, demanded that the French withdraw, and his presence and the threat it represented was enough to intimidate them into leaving. But Santa Anna had paid a heavy price for such an easy victory—a round fired from a retreating French cannon that shattered his leg. He had nearly given up then, his spirit flowing out through the awful wound. Despite the clumsiness of the doctors who took the leg, his life was spared, and though there had been a time when he had wished for it, eventually he came to understand that God was not yet ready for him to die. Every day since, the pain reminded him that being a patriot required more than waving a flag or blustering like a politician.

He pulled at a narrow leather strap, tightened the leather collar to the skin of his stump, his face twisting at the pain, thought, It is why I am out *here*, after all, where the cannon point east, toward the heart of the invaders. The politicians who hide in the soft comforts so far away, they are not the patriots, they are not Mexico. It is the soldiers, the people, and *they* know the difference, *they* have learned that there is no one in Mexico City who will defend the honor, no one who can repel the invaders, no one who has the power of God behind him as I do.

He drank from the goblet again, thought, More wine perhaps, it should be a day for celebration. He motioned to the servant standing outside the tent, a small thin man who ducked inside, said quietly, "Yes, Excellency?"

Santa Anna studied the empty plates on the silver tray, thought, Perhaps something sweet as well. The chef always has something saved for me, something to make me smile.

There was noise outside the tent, and he looked past the servant, saw an officer, the man's uniform already showing the dust of the rocky ground. The man was speaking to a guard, who replied, "No, not yet. It is not yet time. He is not yet through with his breakfast. Come back later."

Santa Anna put the goblet down, ignored the servant now, said aloud, "He may enter. This is a glorious day. I will be patient."

The officer moved slowly into the tent, his hat in his hand, glanced at the silver, and Santa Anna saw the excitement in the man's rugged face, the sharp black eyes darting around the tent.

Santa Anna said, "You are Colonel Reyes, yes? Tell me what has you so agitated, Colonel."

Reyes bowed deeply, saying, "Excellency, you must see it. The *yanquis* are moving into formation for their attack. We have been scouting the camps, and we can see them moving into position."

Santa Anna set the goblet down on the table, nodded slowly. "It is a marvelous sight, is it not, Colonel?" He smiled, deep satisfaction transforming his expression. "An army preparing for its own destruction. I have seen armies before, all the dress and the banners and the music. The *yanquis* play music as well. It is one thing I respect. It is the one part of them that is *civilized*."

He leaned forward, placed his hands on the table to support his weight while he pulled his right leg under him, the stiff wood left leg still out to one side. He strained to pull himself up to his feet. Reyes stared wide-eyed, uncertain of the proper protocol, finally held up his hands. "Excellency, may I assist?"

Santa Anna was on his feet now, the pain that gripped his thigh holding his face in a tight frown. The servant had moved close, and Santa Anna ignored him, said to Reyes, "Colonel, you will not speak of this. I do not require anyone's assistance. There is no weakness here. None! Do you understand?"

"No, certainly not, Excellency. My apologies."

Santa Anna moved out from behind the heavy table as his left leg swung forward slightly, like a pendulum beneath him. He stepped to the opening in the tent, straightened himself, pulled at the short coat of the uniform, ran his hand up to his throat, the stiff tall collar wrapped tightly around his neck. He turned to one side to gaze into the small mirror that hung against the side of the tent, stared a moment at the wave of his hair, the brown giving way to a slow spread of gray. He smiled at that, thought, Fifty-three years old and only now does God remind you that you are no longer a young man.

But He has not taken away what the people see, He will never take that away. The Americans were foolish enough to believe I would return to my home to betray my people, that a patriot would walk on his own land and tell his people not to fight. The *people* knew why I came back, and even the politicians—those weak traitorous fools who had prayed for my death—even they knew that when I marched again into Mexico City, they could not stop fate, could not stand in the way of Destiny.

He still looked into the mirror, ran his hand across his chest, straightening the row of small medals, thought, Yes, there is no one else, there has never been anyone else for these people, and the people know that. Now, it is time to show them what a patriot must do. We must destroy our enemies.

He examined the rest of the uniform, the rich gold braid draped from his shoulders, ran his finger over the top of the epaulet, touched the small brass figure of the eagle. Now they will see, the *world* will see what the Mexican people already know in their hearts. Even God will sit back and admire the glory of it, even He will be impressed watching me destroy my enemies.

He stepped into bright sunlight, saw the troops close by rising at his appearance, the men standing stiffly in line. He ignored them, moved past the thick fat rocks that surrounded his camp, past the grand carriage that had brought him to this wonderful place, this perfect ground to fight a battle. He glanced briefly at the horizon, the distant mountains rising up as a gathering of great sentinels, silent and respectful, waiting for the day to unfold. He stopped, looked all around, thinking, Yes, it is more than just the people, it is the land, all of it, every part of Mexico smiling on this glorious day. He stepped close to the horse, saw the groom standing back behind, looking down, respectful, fearful, tucking the thick brush behind his back.

Santa Anna ran his hand over the horse's rich black coat, touched the black mane, the strong animal nodding to greet him. He put his hand on the harness, saw the gold trim, the buckles and hooks all bathed in gold leaf. He looked back at the carriage, the driver standing quietly to one side, head down, prepared to hear some command. He scanned the carriage itself, more gold leaf, admired the ornate designs of pure grandeur, wiped spotlessly clean by the servants. Pride welled up inside him, and he stood back from the horse, thought, Not even Napoleon was so loved, so respected. If he was here now, he would fight for *me*. Even *he* would know that his name could not rise over this land with so much glory as mine. And today, that devil himself, that fool General Scott, he will know what it means to face the anger and the fury of *this* Napoleon.

He moved past the carriage now, while his honor guard, the handpicked men who stayed close to him wherever he was, the men whose loyalty would never be doubted, moved into formation at a discreet distance behind him. He examined their uniforms, quietly inspecting the gray and white accented by the gold on their shoulders, the stiffly creased clean white pants. He nodded his quiet approval, then turned away and moved up into the rocks. He climbed stiffly, stepping across small round boulders, moved past the taller uneven rocks, some larger than the carriage. In between were thick masses of dull green brush, a patchwork spread all along the rise of the great tall hill, El Telégrafo. A trail had been cleared for him, and the guards stayed back, knowing not to help him, not here, where the troops could see.

He moved over a small crest, past a wide shallow pit dug into dirt and rock, where the cannon were mounted. The cannoneers stood quietly as he passed, but he did not see them. Instead he was focused on the dull brass of the guns, the great power, the hard instruments of death. He moved through a gap in tall rocks, a dark passageway, nearly a tunnel, with a small shaft of light from a split in the rock over his head pointing the way. He was still climbing, felt the pain in his left leg easing, working itself out with the movement. He tried to pick up speed, felt his heart pounding, the exertion of the climb holding him back. Finally, he stepped into a clearing, and could see all across the face of the big hill. He moved toward a thick mass of troops with muskets, and they began to cheer.

He stopped. He always waited for this moment, when the troops would let their emotions flow out toward him, their love and their loyalty too strong to hold back. He knew the officers would try to keep the men quiet, but it never worked, and he would sometimes scold the officers, pick out some nameless lieutenant, would even threaten him with arrest, but he knew it was all a playful tease, even if the officers did not. Now, he just let them have their voice; no words, they would not dare to speak his name, just a song, a loud, joyous cry.

He fought to keep the stern look on his face, always aware of the solemn nature of the ritual. He met the gaze of the officers who watched him carefully, saw one young captain staring at him in silent fear. Santa Anna stepped toward the man, moved very close, leaned into the man's face, said, "Do your men have some problem with discipline, Captain? They sound like nothing more than a mob."

The young man tried to speak but the words were choked away, and Santa Anna backed up a step, said, "Well, we shall see if they obey you in combat. I will be lenient this time. But I will remember you, Captain. Do not give me cause to doubt your efficiency."

The young man shook his head, saluted him, still had no words, and Santa Anna moved again to the trail. Hiding his smile, he thought, It is good for them to see the discipline, the danger. It is part of being a soldier, after all. A bit of fear will make them better in the fight, keep the fire moving forward. They should all carry the knowledge of what waits for them if they fail.

In front of him, a line of riflemen stood, men who had emerged from a fissure in the big hill, the gray of their uniforms blending into the rock, the line stretching in a great curve beyond his view. The sounds came from them as well, as though a single voice. He saw more officers, more of the fear, but he was growing tired of the game. One man pointed out beyond the face of the hill. He stopped, looked past the thick brush and jumbled rocks close to him, the hill dropping away into a rolling tumble of brush and dirt and small hills. He saw more cannon below, more lines of troops standing with their muskets in salute, a vast show of the strength of his numbers, the infantry uniforms a variety of colors and designs, reflecting their different commands.

He saw more men pointing out now, to the east, but he would not turn his eyes in that direction: He knew what he would see. Slowly raising his gaze, he could see where the ground flattened out, and beyond the base of the great hill, the low ridges gently rolled, revealing patches of dull green, and beyond, the neat blocks of dark blue. His heart jumped, and he smiled, could not help it, the moment adding to the glory of the day. Yes, there they come. They will march straight down the road, and in their arrogance they will tell themselves we are weak, that we can be brushed aside. He studied the neat squares of blue, saw motion now, the flicker of flags, saw men on horses moving behind the dark mass. Yes, bring them forward. March to your deaths.

H E HAD CLIMBED HIGHER, SAT NOW ON A WIDE FLAT ROCK, HIS stiff leg to one side at a painful angle. He still waited for the assault to begin, but the neat blue lines kept their distance, stayed too far away to have their strength counted. He stared out through field glasses, thought, They cannot be so strong after all. There are not that many. He had not known the enemy numbers, had never received an accurate report from the men who escaped Scott's invasion of Vera Cruz. He knew his own numbers, down to the last gun, and felt a strange impatience. *You dare to approach us with such small strength? It does not even look like an army, merely one division. I had thought the devil Scott would know what I would bring to this fight.*

He felt suddenly insulted. *How dare the yanquis believe I am so weak! Did they not believe I would confront them? Did they believe they could simply march across the heart of Mexico unobstructed?* He was angry now, clenched his fists, shouted, "You will all die!"

He ignored the men below him, the faces watching him, the cannon primed, prepared for the first wave of assault from the blue enemy who had only then begun to creep forward. He looked out through the glasses again, his anger billowing out of his impatience for the assault to begin.

Why do they wait? Has the devil Scott realized the foolishness of his plan? Perhaps it is the soldiers themselves. They know what waits for them, perhaps it is they who will not obey, they who will not march into certain disaster. Why should the yanquis be different from any other army, after all? The generals may be fools, criminals, but it is the soldiers themselves who understand what war truly is. They must know the evil that commands them. And perhaps by now they know who *is up here waiting for them. They know, as the people of Mexico know the power behind* this *command.*

He suddenly slid down off the rock, the guards moving up quickly to assist him, and he waved them away, said aloud, "They are too slow. I have no patience for this." He stepped back behind the rocks, moved through the stiff brush, feeling hungry again. He thought of wine. *Yes, I should summon the chef.* He glanced out to the north, out beyond the big hill, saw smoke drifting up from the thick rolling ground near the far hill, the smaller rise they had told him was Atalaya. He saw men moving on the rocks below him now, his soldiers, scrambling up toward the cannon pits where the gunners still waited for the enemy to come close.

"What is that? Who are those troops?"

He stepped out on a narrow ledge of rock, looked down into the thick underbrush and rugged ground at the base of the hill. Nothing. No movement. He heard sounds, a short chatter of musket fire. He looked again into the dense thickets between the two hills.

The voices of his men rose up the hill to him, the soldiers scrambling toward him, some calling out, pointing back toward the ground below. He saw an officer, the man's gray uniform torn, the white shirt a smear of dirt. As the man pulled himself into a gun pit, he called up to him, "Excellency, the enemy!" The man stopped, doubled over, his chest heaving from the climb.

Santa Anna felt the raw power of anger as he stared down at the soldiers coming up toward him, more men now emerging from the thorny brush farther below. He looked again at the wisps of white smoke drifting up out of the deep rolling ground between the hills, shook his head, feeling the full fury of what he was seeing building in his chest. He shouted, "Cowards! It is only cavalry! You run from a few horses!"

He looked at the young officer, the man now backing away, shaking his head, and Santa Anna shouted, "You! These are your men! You have run away from a scouting party! I will see you hang!" He backed away from the edge of the rocks, his fury full red on his face. He moved past his guard, ignored the other officers who had gathered behind him, men who heard the sounds, who had seen the smoke. Climbing back toward his own perch, he saw the face of the young officer in his mind. He imagined his sword cutting the man down, killing him in front of his own traitorous troops. His anger complete, the man's image swept away. How do I endure these cowards? he asked himself. I will have to order cavalry to push the *yanquis* away. We should already have had horsemen between the hills. It is carelessness. There will be punishment.

He climbed up to his flat rock again, flexed his hands, tried to relax, to revive the morning's bright promise. He looked out again to the masses of blue still gathered to the east. Laughing, he shouted at them, "You still delay, *yanqui*. Has no one taught you how to fight a war? Bring your men here. Their fate awaits them."

He heard more sounds then, again from the north, from the direction of the smaller hill—the chattering of muskets, voices of men, faint cries, shouts. He looked that way, saw more smoke rising. Around him, men began to see it with him, officers close by moving toward him, one man calling, "Excellency! We have reports! The enemy is advancing beyond our flank!"

Santa Anna looked at the man, saw a group of officers gathering, some still pointing in the direction of the sounds. He shook his head, said quietly, "You are all cowards. If you knew how to be soldiers you would stop this foolish panic. The enemy is right where I want him to be."

At great peril to themselves, the officers murmured protests, but he would not hear it now. His patience exhausted, he turned away from them, looked again at the blue mass to the east, raised the glasses. He studied the distant flags, the blue-coated officers on horseback, saw more motion, the blue masses beginning to march forward, and he smiled, nodded, said quietly to himself, "They have played their games. Now, they will come."

8. LEE

H E LED THEM UP THE SLOPE OF ATALAYA, THE MEN STRAINING against the ropes, pulling the field guns over the ragged ground. Where the hillside was steep, they would gather close to the gun, shoulders under the thick barrel, hands gripping the wheels, lifting and pushing until the next level spot gave them relief. He looked above him, toward the top of the hill where the cavalry waited. The men Harney had left back were keeping tight control of the precious high ground. Lee felt anxious; he could hear the musket fire all out through the thickets toward the big hill, but he forced himself to focus again on the curses and groans of the men who pulled Steptoe's guns up the hill.

He saw Steptoe himself pulling on a long rope, as more of his men moved to help, inching the wheels of a twenty-four-pounder up and over a narrow ledge of rock. The gun moved more easily, and Steptoe pointed the way. He stopped and smiled at Lee, said, "We've made it, Captain. By damned, we're doing it!"

Lee pointed to the crest of the hill, the ruins of the Mexican lookout tower. "There! Put it back behind the crest. Protect yourself with the contour of the ground."

Steptoe smiled again, said, "Yes, sir. That's what we're here for."

The gun moved past Lee. More men were moving up, backing over the ledge, another rope, wheels appearing, shirtless men with broad sweating backs giving the final groaning push, lifting another gun up to the flat ground. Steptoe, already there, issued quick and precise orders. Lee felt his anxiety easing as he looked toward the big hill where Harney's troops still pushed the enemy back. He saw the thin white smoke rising, could hear the musket fire echoing out of the ridges and thickets between the two hills.

Then Steptoe was beside him, and Lee turned, saw the third gun moving into position, the crews swarming over them. Steptoe said, "You have a target in mind, sir?"

THE GUNS HAD BEEN FIRING FOR SEVERAL MINUTES. LEE HAD stayed close at first, but could see clearly that Steptoe knew his job. The young man directed the aim with precision. From his vantage point, Lee could now see the enemy's response to the flanking move by Twiggs, the Mexican commanders finally moving men and guns around the defenses on the big hill, confronting the flanking assault. But Steptoe had the range, and as the Mexican gunners began to answer the sudden assault from Atalaya, many of their guns were shattered into silence.

Just below the Mexican entrenchments, Lee could see scattered patches of blue. Harney's men were pinned down, helpless against the Mexican muskets just above them. Harney had gone too far, could not call off the pursuit of the retreat from Atalaya, the Americans infected by the success of their attack. There were waves of smoke from the volleys of the Mexican muskets, drifting over the face of the big hill. Then Lee heard a new sound, far to the left, from the far side of El Telégrafo. Patterson's demonstration had begun, finally, and Lee thought, Yes, hold them. If more of the enemy moves this way, we could be in serious trouble.

Lee wondered about Twiggs's whereabouts. He thought, What am I supposed to do now? I should be . . . somewhere. He thought of the road, the main highway leading west out of the Mexican position. I can still find it. I *should* have found it before. Maybe that's where Twiggs is. He looked at Steptoe, but the young man was scrambling back and forth between the guns, and Lee thought, No time to be polite. He won't mind my leaving. He moved back down the hill, encountering more soldiers coming up toward him, carrying heavy wooden crates filled with powder and shell. The men, grunting and cursing, climbed past him. Lee reached the bottom of the hill, saw a private holding his horse, the man clearly disgusted with the duty, and Lee said, "Thank you, soldier. You may resume . . . uh, you may return to your unit."

The private was gone without a salute, and Lee moved the horse toward the trail; it shied slightly from the sounds of the fight above

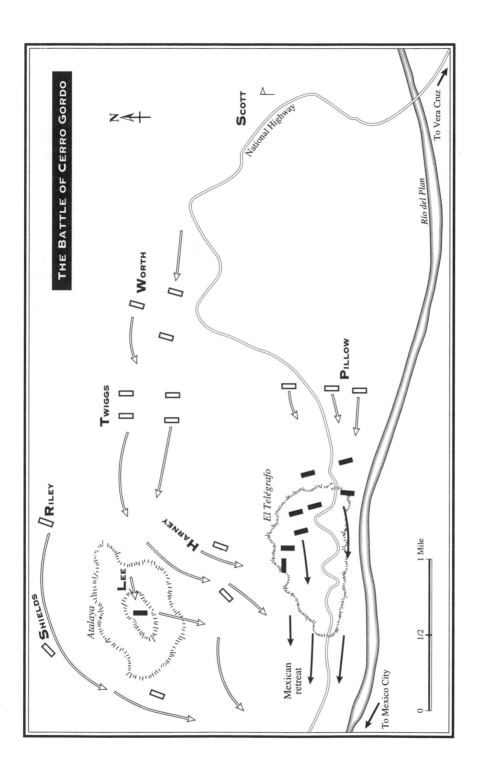

THE BATTLE OF CERRO GORDO

N

SCOTT

WORTH

National Highway

TWIGGS

RILEY

SHIELDS

Atalaya

LEE

HARNEY

El Telégrafo

PILLOW

Río del Plan

To Vera Cruz

Mexican retreat

To Mexico City

0   1/2   1 Mile

him, the thudding impact of the shells against El Telégrafo and the
response from the Mexican guns. He patted the horse's neck to calm it.
A new wave of musket fire broke out to the right, beyond Atalaya. Lee
thought, Colonel Riley, General Shields . . . it's the rest of the division.
They're in the rear!

He rode along the desolate trail, felt strangely alone, swallowed
by the sounds of the fight above him. He spurred the horse harder, the
trail still empty in front of him. Reaching a patch of open ground, he
stopped the horse, realizing that he had ridden right out in the clear.
He could see both hills now, on either side of him, the bright streaks
from the big guns ripping the air high overhead. He looked up, absorbed the stunning sight, bright orange coming from Steptoe, and from
the big hill, the blue of the copper Mexican shells. He stared up, felt
childlike again, watching one shell explode too soon, a bright burst of
blue fire, thought, My God, I'm in the middle of it. I'm . . . *underneath*
it. He could hear shouts, orders, and looked around frantically, thinking, I'm in the wrong place . . . move to cover. He saw blue, a line of
men emerging from the brush, and he could hear the words. *English,*
thank God. The soldiers moved toward him, and Lee saw an officer, a
young lieutenant, a thin blond man carrying a small sword.

"Sir! Do you know where Captain Holcomb is? We are supposed
to be . . . up there. Lieutenant Jeff Garrett, sir, Company E. We're supposed to link up with Company B."

The man was out of breath, and his men began to gather around
Lee. Lee pointed up the trail, said, "Follow me. There's cover up
ahead." He suddenly remembered the spring, the rocky trail that the
Mexicans had used. "Yes, come on!" He spurred the horse, moved out
of the open into thicker brush, stopped, waited for the men to catch
up, thought, This is ridiculous. They can't follow me like this. Get
down! He dismounted the horse, and the men were with him now, and
he said, "This way, up here!"

They followed him up a short rise, and he pushed past the thorns,
saw the great dead tree. He felt a breath of relief, Yes, you found
it. He could still see his imprint in the dirt, the small dug-out place
beneath the log. He moved quickly around the log, pointed at the
small opening in the rocks, said to the lieutenant, "There. That goes
straight into the enemy's camp. Be careful . . . I'm not sure what you'll
run into."

Garrett looked around, appraising. Then he looked at the spring,
saw the footprints in the mud, the trail. He turned to Lee and said, "I

don't know you, Captain, but appears you're a mighty good scout. We'll find Captain Holcomb soon enough." He turned to his men, said, "Quiet! Let's do some sneaking!"

Garrett scrambled quickly up into the rocks, the men filing behind him, and Lee backed away, moved around the log, climbed his horse and rode back to the trail.

He saw more troops moving into the trail, some marching in formation, others lying on the ground. Lee moved among the wounded men, his eyes fixed on their bloody clothes, saw other soldiers tending to the wounds. He halted his horse, dismounted. A man stood holding his side, his shirt ripped open. A loose flap of skin hung from his chest, a great dark stain on the man's pants. Lee thought, Help him, do something. He moved close, knelt down beside him, but the man did not look at Lee, merely stared at the ground with wide eyes, his face ghostly, pale. He rocked slowly, his breathing coming in sharp, short bursts. Seeing the man holding his own body together, blood flowing through his fingers, Lee felt the sickness rising in his gut, wanted to back away, move far away from the horror. He fought it, forced himself to say, "Can I help you, soldier? What can I do?"

The man still did not look at him, continued to rock, and Lee stood straight, thought, He cannot survive this. He is . . . *dying*.

"It's all right, Captain. We'll take him, now."

Lee turned, saw two men holding a litter, a dirty white cloth tied to two fat sticks. Lee backed away, watched them roll the man over, and the man did not protest, stared ahead calmly, still held his side with both hands as they laid him out on the cloth.

"Ready . . . up."

The two soldiers moved away, carrying the man back down the trail. Lee watched them disappear into the brush, thought, He was alive, but . . . he was waiting to die. He knew it. Lee felt a cold chill. That's the hand of God, the gift of peace. He turned, looking for his horse among the confusion of more men, more litter-bearers and, scattered out through the brush, more wounded. One man screamed, a sharp high wail, and then another. The sounds multiplied, some men praying, loud calls to God, some not uttering words at all, just a haunting inhuman wail.

Lee climbed onto his horse, intending to go, but the sounds held him for one awful moment, the voices blending with the sharp thunder from the hills. The horrible chorus of war filled his mind, consuming him, and he closed his eyes, said, No, do not do this. Take control. He spurred the horse, moved past the men until the trail abruptly stopped. Lee thought, This is the end, it's as far as we could go without running into the enemy. But it should be far enough. The highway—the main road—has to be near here. He stepped the horse carefully through the thorns, over another rocky creek bed, where he could see movement again, more blue troops, shouts, the sharp crack of muskets.

Musket fire came from very close now, straight in front of him, and he dismounted, thought, Get down, you are too close. He moved slowly, pushed his way through a dense undergrowth, and was suddenly looking at a wide clearing, El Telégrafo up to the left.

Far out in the clearing there was a great flow of men, some wagons, broken guns, horses, all moving away from the big hill. Lee led the horse up a small rise, walked out onto a hard, flat road. He looked out, both directions, saw that the road ran straight into the big hill, then curved to the right, toward the main Mexican position. He clenched his fists, said aloud, "The road! It's here!" He suddenly felt ridiculous, but there was no one watching him, and he thought, You were close after all. I wonder if General Twiggs knows?

He saw a wagon now, moving quickly toward him, and he backed away as it clattered past, its wild-eyed driver staring ahead. The man wore a strange uniform, short gray coat, and Lee felt his heart jump. Mexican! The road began to fill, more Mexican soldiers coming out of the brush, some moving straight from the big hill. Lee pulled the horse off the road, stood at the edge of the brush, thought, You're in the wrong place again, Captain.

They did not pause to look at him, their flow was unstoppable, the raw panicked retreat of a beaten army. He pulled his pistol, thought, Prisoners, perhaps . . . but there are too many. He felt suddenly helpless, a spectator watching as Santa Anna's troops scrambled away from their enemy in a confusion of strange and colorful uniforms, men in solid gray, some with red coats, gold and white, tall round hats dropping away as they ran from the soldiers in blue.

He moved slowly up to the road again, looked across the flat open space. In the distance he could see the river, and all across the ground the great flow of men was spreading. From the big hill cannon began to fire, the sounds streaking out above him. The shells landed far out in the field, great flashes of fire blowing gaps in the retreat, shattering pieces of the running men. More men streamed past close to him, and he read the panic in their eyes, their wild animal stare, men running from something inside them, some beast that took control, that took their fight away. They carried no muskets, no weapons at all. One man suddenly fell forward, facedown into the hard road, and Lee expected him to get up quickly, to run again. The man struggled to stand, and Lee saw the blood, the man's back a dark stain. The man took a step, then fell facedown again, hitting the ground with a sharp smack. Lee stared at the man, who lay motionless. He began to feel sick again, some part of him wanting to pull away from the horror, but he could not look away, saw more of the Mexican soldiers run into the road, saw a wagon rumble past them, one man reaching up, trying to grab the horse, secure blessed escape, but the man could not hold on, was knocked away, fell into a heap. He fought to stand up, but the ground came alive with a blast of fire and dirt, just missing the wagon. Lee backed away, stared at the scene, saw what was left of the man. The shock was wearing off now, the horror becoming one great mindless blur as he watched the death of the enemy, the collapse and destruction of an army.

From the west came a new rush of sound, voices, shouts, and he saw a mass of blue push into the road, thought, Riley, the flank. There was even more musket fire now, and the tide of the retreat moved away from the road, Mexican soldiers running hard for some safe place where the guns could not reach them.

He looked toward the hill, high above the road, saw the flashes from the guns, but there was too much smoke, the hillside bathed in a thick white fog. He felt his heart pounding, thought, I have to see what is happening.

Pulling out his field glasses, he scanned the big hill, found a gap in the smoke. He could see troops again, American troops, the Mexican guns turned, firing into the retreat of their own soldiers. Then he saw a flag, held tight by the sharp breeze. It was the Stars and Stripes. He lowered the glasses, thought of General Scott, Yes, you did it! This was your plan, and it worked. The sickness was gone now, replaced by something new, unexpected, and he was smiling, felt pride in the old man, pride in the army. My God . . . we have won!

Men in blue began to flow past him, Twiggs's men, officers with swords raised, hoarse voices urging their men forward to pursue the enemy. General Scott should be here, Lee thought, this was his fight. He should be right here, to see this. I will tell him, explain what this was like. He felt something open up inside him. He climbed on his horse, stood high in the stirrups and watched as more of the men in blue swept down from the big hill. He raised his hat, waving it high over his head, began to yell, something he had never done, to cheer the men, to cheer their commander, his voice blending with all the other sounds, sweeping away the horror of war. He could feel it inside of him, opening up some new place, the sounds deafening, glorious, the magnificent joy of victory.

9. SCOTT

APRIL NINETEENTH

H E WALKED ACROSS THE RUGGED GROUND, STEPPING OVER THE rocks and the littered remnants of Santa Anna's army—clothes, boots, guns, flags. The Mexicans' retreat had been so rapid, there was no organized withdrawal, no gathering of valuable equipment, no salvaging the tools of war.

The victory had been complete and overwhelming. Scott understood now that Santa Anna had ignored the flanking movement. Even when the mass of blue began to appear between the two hills, the bulk of the Mexican forces had stayed tight in their defenses, still looked to the front, still expected the main assault to come straight at their strength. When Twiggs's men opened the flank attack with full fury, when the guns on Atalaya began to throw deadly fire into exposed Mexican positions, the surprise and panic had been complete, and the Mexicans had suddenly fled.

All around him stood prisoners, men with eyes downcast, their sadness and dull anger revealing their shame. Tattered strips of uniforms lay scattered, men with dirty bandages on arms and legs, one man's head wrapped in a bloody white turban. They moved in a single file line slowly down through the brush. He watched as still more emerged from the rocks, and he thought of counting them, could see dozens, maybe a hundred, prodded along by men with bayonets. He had heard the first estimates, over three thousand prisoners in all. He knew he could not feed them, and had already decided to parole them, to turn them loose and hope they went home. If they chose to join Santa Anna again, they would have to fight them again.

The soldiers were watching him, and he could hear their cheers, exhausted men who felt that rare sense of pride, unique to the soldier.

Two armies faced each other with deadly intent, and one prevailed. There was no doubt, no disputing the result, no arguing that either side could have claimed victory. He listened to the sounds of his men, thought, Santa Anna cannot go back to Mexico City and convince his people that he won this one. If there is any kind of government there, someone who can make decisions about peace, this will tell them that we are here to win. And we are coming straight at them.

He eased down through the rocks, saw his staff, an aide holding his horse. He took the reins, climbed the horse, sat solidly in the saddle, gazing up over the high ground as a swarm of blue pulling wagons came down from the hill. Very good, he thought, we can use those. Mexican wagons are something we will not set free. He saw more of his men climbing down from the hidden cracks in the hill, saw men carrying bundles of muskets, one man toting a thick bunch of swords like a sheaf of wheat. The men put their captured prizes into piles, guided by officers, and there was backslapping, joyous talk. Men began to point in his direction, and he heard the cheers again. He waved to them, could not help but smile.

Enjoy this, he thought, this is no Vera Cruz. *This* is better than a siege. I don't like sieges. I'd rather face the enemy, and drive him away. *This* is a victory.

He saw more men waving at him, heard shouts, and the men were not just cheering, but were moving toward him, calling to him. An officer with a short thick beard came forward, his coat open. The man was breathing hard, but was all smiles, and he said to Scott, "General . . . we have quite a prize here, sir."

Scott looked toward the wagons, smiled, had been through this before. "Spoils of war, Lieutenant? What is it?"

"Sir, I had heard General Santa Anna has a wooden leg. It seems, sir—" The man stopped, took a breath, still grinning widely. "It seems, sir, that now *we* have it."

Scott's eyes opened wide and he said, "Are you certain, Lieutenant? I cannot imagine Santa Anna making a retreat on one leg."

"Sir, we have his carriage, his personal belongings. There is silver, uniforms, and . . . a considerable amount of money, sir."

Scott looked behind him, said to an aide, "Notify the provost. Have guards posted at that carriage."

He looked at the lieutenant again, said, "We'll keep the carriage intact, Lieutenant, protect Santa Anna's property for a while. That could come in handy. My guess is that he has more than one wooden leg. I see no reason to protect that."

The lieutenant snapped to attention, said, "Sir, it would bring a great deal of pride to the Fourth Illinois if we could keep the leg. My men put up a hell of a fight, sir."

"I thought you might have something to say about that." He smiled again, said, "It's yours, Lieutenant. Take good care of it."

The soldiers whooped loudly, pounding their lieutenant on the back, congratulating him and themselves on their great trophy. Scott laughed, before turning his horse toward the road. That's a trophy to take back home, he thought. Every man in that regiment will have a story to tell, give birth to his own legend.

With his staff following him, Scott moved along the road, down into the rugged landscape, rode past the big hill. The signs of a fight were scattered everywhere. Besides the debris left behind by the retreat, broken muskets, pieces of wagons, shattered and broken cannon dotted the landscape. But most of the Mexican defenses were untouched, had been abandoned before the Americans could even try to reach them.

He looked out to the right, could see the smaller hill, tried to remember the name, thought, Captain Lee's hill. He could see the Stars and Stripes up there as well, saw the cannon still in place. He stared out that way, thought of his engineer, the scouting mission, the good plan. There is no good strategy without good men to carry it out. This time, one engineer might have made all the difference. It was the only way to make a fight here, and it worked. We cannot afford brute force, we don't have the strength. Maybe my commanders will understand that now, maybe Twiggs will see how this worked, maybe he learned something. Maybe we should pay a bit more attention to what these college boys have to say. This army could have been held up here for days, charge after bloody charge, thrown all our strength away against these rocks. Instead, a three hour battle and the enemy is swept away. Good work, Mr. Lee.

He moved the horse along the main highway, moved out past the big hill, where the scattered remains of the Mexican retreat spread all over the flat ground, all down along the river. Men in blue were moving through the debris, some were pulling bodies together, lining up the Mexican dead for burial. Now he saw more bodies, and a small group of men already at work with shovels. These dead bodies wore blue, and he stopped the horse, thought, For God's sake, don't count them, but he couldn't help it, ran his eyes along the awful sight . . . fourteen. He saw two men emerging from the brush, dragging another corpse, laying the body heavily at the end of the row. The men saw him now, saluted with bloody hands, and Scott said, "You have many more out there, gentlemen?"

The men did not seem impressed with Scott's presence, looked at him with no expression. This response surprised him, but he thought, No, take no offense. Look at the job they are doing. *That* is the priority here.

One man shook his head, pulled the hat off a balding head. A rough beard muffled his voice. "Quite a few, sir. It's a rough place. The boys gave it their best, sir." The man looked down at the bodies again. "I been hearing . . . lots of fellas been saying the Mexicans can't fight. They ain't no match for us. I expect . . ." The man paused, rubbed a shirtsleeve over his eyes. "I expect these boys here found out otherwise." The man pointed to the gravesite, where the shovels lay still now, the men all watching Scott. "We best be gettin' back to work, sir."

The man moved toward the fresh dirt, picked up his own shovel, and Scott spurred the horse again, thought, It's always the same. Every fight, every victory, someone has to do . . . this. What I have to do is send the letters, notify the War Department, give this place a name, so the people back home will know where their sons, their husbands, died. He thought of the map, a small village beyond the hills, Cerro Gordo. That's the name, he thought, that's what this day will be called. The Battle of Cerro Gordo. He rode past the graves, stared out down the wide road, recalled the man's words, thought, You're right, young man, I've been hearing the same thing, some of our people think we will walk into Mexico City without firing a shot, that the Mexican army has no fight. But there will be more of this. The veterans know it. The younger ones are just finding out. And they'll just have to get used to it. They're soldiers.

"WE WILL MOVE OUT TOMORROW, MARCH GENERAL Worth's division to Jalapa. I don't expect any resistance." The commanders watched Scott, some nodding in agreement. He paused, sat back in the chair, said, "The official reports will go out to Washington very soon. The Secretary . . ." He glanced at Pillow " . . . and the President want to know what happened here. They expect to hear the worst. It will be a delight to give them good news. However, I want to caution anyone here who feels they should present their own version of events. There is only one official report."

There was silence, and Scott looked at the faces one by one. Twiggs was looking down, shrugged his shoulders slightly. Scott thought, No, not him, he could care less what Washington thinks. He saw Patterson looking at him, nodding slowly in quiet agreement. Next to Patterson, Pillow was nervous, moving in his chair, and Scott thought, Of course.

"Yes, General Pillow, you have something to add?"

Pillow stood, turned, briefly nodded to all the others, as though greeting them for the first time. "Sir, I just want to be sure that the official report gives credit where credit is due."

"And what do you want credit for, General?"

Scott saw Patterson squirming slightly, and he thought, You should be nervous, General. You're his commanding officer.

Pillow said, "Sir, given that there was considerable activity on our right flank, I just want to be sure that the actions in the enemy's front are not forgotten. My brigade succeeded in forcing the enemy before us to surrender. It should be so noted."

Scott watched as Pillow sat down, saw the prim satisfaction of a man who has shed light on his own importance. Scott looked at the others, said, "Very well. I will make the appropriate investigation, and if your claims are accurate, if you, General Pillow, did in fact cause the enemy to surrender, it will be so noted."

The others murmured their reactions, and Scott felt suddenly very tired, thought, No more meetings. Not today, not for a while. If I had the power . . . not ever.

"That's all for now, gentlemen. I will have your orders for the march to Jalapa soon. You are dismissed."

The men stood, and no one spoke, there was none of the social banter typical of the men in command. He watched them move away, thought, They are not friends, not even cordial. I suppose that's good. Hard for them to conspire some plot against me if they can't stand each other.

He saw Patterson standing alone, seeming to wait for the others to move away. Scott stood and asked him, "Can I do something for you, General?"

Patterson looked at the ground, then slowly looked up at Scott. "A moment, sir?"

Scott pointed toward the tent, stepped toward the opening, said, "Would you be adding something to General Pillow's report?"

It was sarcastic, and Scott expected some indignant response, the same response he always seemed to get from the rest of them. But Patterson shook his head, seemed to struggle for words, finally said, "Sir, for the sake of accuracy . . ." He paused, frowned. "My feeling is that General Pillow's version of events is not entirely accurate."

"I'm not surprised."

"Sir, please understand. I am aware that General Pillow is my subordinate, but it has been made clear that he has the President's ear. If he does not perform quite as efficiently as he should, it might not serve the interests of your command to make mention of that."

"General, give me your version of what occurred this morning under your command."

Patterson moved inside the tent, sat in the small chair, said, "General Scott, at the appointed hour, the order was given to General Pillow to advance his brigade in demonstration against the enemy. The order communicated specifically that if General Pillow discovered an opening in the enemy's defenses, he would pursue that opening to our advantage. In fact, sir, General Pillow was considerably delayed in moving his troops into position. The demonstration did not begin as ordered, and when his troops were finally in position, the enemy had already begun to withdraw. For him to claim credit for the surrender is . . . amazing, sir. I don't know what else I can say."

Scott moved behind the table, sat down, reached behind him to a small wood cabinet propped up and fastened to a tent pole. His hand wrapped around a bottle of brandy, and he clamped two small glasses between his fingers, turned, set the glasses on the table.

"General Patterson, will you join me?"

Patterson looked at the bottle, said, "Gracious of you, sir. Thank you."

Scott poured the brandy, corked the bottle, slid one glass toward Patterson, said, "I am not a great proponent of spirits in camp. I try to make an example, practice temperance around the men. It is not always . . . easy." He paused, said, "General, my report to the Secretary will be accurate. Despite my caution to the commanders, no doubt there will be private versions of the Battle of Cerro Gordo. Hell, every battle and skirmish we have here will be written up by somebody. We're fortunate not to have very many reporters following after us down here. We're too damned far away from their comfortable offices. But if the reporters aren't here, doesn't mean they aren't expecting a story. Some of our commanders are only too eager to oblige."

Patterson sipped the brandy, stared at the small glass, said, "Never seen so much . . . intrigue."

Scott laughed, said, "There's always intrigue when you get so many peacocks together. We're in close quarters here, no room for anybody to strut. Some of you may not like each other, and God knows, none of you likes me, but ultimately none of that matters. Not here, not while we have an enemy out there. And despite what some of our people believe, Santa Anna is a very dangerous enemy who still means to drive us to hell. What Washington thinks about all this is not my concern. My concern is what this army will do in the field. If General Pillow did not perform, then it is up to you to bring him up to speed, make sure it doesn't happen again. We were damned lucky this time, the timing was on our side, the element of surprise is what won us that fight. The collapse of their army was a humiliation, an outright embarrassment. That's worse than any military defeat. I doubt Santa Anna will let it happen again."

"I'll try to control him, sir. Keep a tighter watch."

"All you can do, General. Gideon Pillow may yet learn to command an army. It's your job to make sure he doesn't kill too many of our people doing it."

Patterson stood slowly, the man's age showing itself in the stiffness with which he moved, how his face was cut deep by the long years of being the good soldier. He said, "Thank you for the brandy, sir. It was a privilege."

Patterson began to move out of the tent, and Scott said, "General, have you given thought to the volunteers? Their enlistments are coming due."

Patterson turned, a frown darkening his expression, and said, "Actually, sir, I had hoped the problem would work itself out. A sizable number of my men have another couple of months left. I have made considerable effort to convince them to reenlist. I am distressed to say that thus far . . . it has not been successful."

Patterson moved back into the tent, sat again, said, "I had thought most of them would stay, understand that this was something worth doing. But all I hear is that they're a long way from home, and not very happy about it."

Scott rubbed his face with his hand, said, "Replacements are supposed to be on their way. I can't give you any numbers. Hell, a while back Secretary Marcy promised me another twenty thousand men. If I believed every promise I got from Washington . . ." He shook his head, stared down at the desk. "If they want to go home, it's their right. How many you expect to lose?"

"Nearly all of them, sir. Perhaps four thousand."

Scott let out a deep breath. "I would have thought half that."

"Sir, I thought we might resume the march to Mexico City, that it might be a powerful incentive to make them stay with the army by taking them farther inland. There could be something of the patriotic fever, some call to duty once we got closer to another good fight."

"General Patterson, I appreciate wishful thinking when it's in my favor. Consider that the volunteers have already been difficult to manage. They are not accustomed to life in the army. If you force them to stay beyond their term of enlistment, I would imagine they might become even more of a discipline problem. They might begin to feel like prisoners. We can't afford that. This army has already suffered the embarrassment of the deserters."

Patterson winced, and Scott thought, Of course, he takes that personally. It has to be a sensitive subject. Scott said, "It's an unfortunate fact of life, General, that patriotism does not always work. Sometimes, it backfires altogether."

Patterson seemed to sag, said, "Sir, someone must take the blame or at least share the responsibility for the desertions. It is one thing to have a man simply run away, refuse to fight. It is quite another to have him go over to the other side, and take up arms against his comrades. I have never known of this before. I am horrified, sir."

"It is no one's responsibility in this army, General. First of all, most of the desertions happened under General Taylor's command. But, no, I'm not about to make a fuss over that. Too many people already making such a commotion over whose feelings have been trampled on. Fact is, we cannot overestimate the power of the Church, not down here. If I'm correct, most of the . . . uh . . . St. Patrick—"

"I believe they are now referred to as the San Patricios, sir."

Scott shook his head. "Yes, I was right the first time. These St. Patrick fellows decided, I suppose, that they wouldn't fight against their fellow Catholics. Religion runs a lot deeper than army training. No commander, not even Zachary Taylor, can be blamed for that. Unfortunately, it doesn't help the prejudice in this army against Catholics, not one damned bit."

Patterson stared at the ground, still seemed weighed down, said, "I will carry the stain, sir. The volunteers have not made anyone's job a simple one. Now some of them may end up shooting back at us. I do not understand. . . ."

Scott took another sip of brandy. "It will never happen. Can't believe any American would ever shoot at his own countrymen. Put it out of your mind, General. We need to deal with the problem at hand, which is your volunteers who intend on leaving this place altogether."

Patterson nodded slowly. "Thank you, sir. Yes, we must focus on these men now."

Scott sat back. "Consider, General, that the longer we wait and the farther inland we take them, it will be much more difficult eventually to move them to the coast. Waiting until the summer months would be barbaric. We'd be sending many of them straight to their deaths. The *el vomito* would consume the lot of them."

"What would you like me to do, sir?"

"Muster them out now. Send them on to the coast before the hot weather gets here. We'll hold the army at Jalapa, hope like hell some reinforcements arrive. Worst thing that can happen is Santa Anna has time to gather a new army. Not much we can do about that anyway. We can't go after his capital with seven thousand men."

"The volunteers will be grateful, sir. This will calm a lot of tempers."

"If the reinforcements don't get here soon, someone will have to calm mine. You're dismissed, General."

Patterson seemed to hesitate, and Scott asked, "Something else, General?"

"Sir, yes, I suppose this is as good a time as any. You are aware that my specific assignment here was to command the volunteer division. Since there is no certainty the division will be reinforced, I am requesting transfer, sir. I would like to apply to the Secretary for reassignment, with your endorsement, sir."

Scott leaned forward, smiled. "You want to leave this wonderful place?"

Patterson's expression remained serious, and he said, "Sir, I have not done the job I had hoped to do. I'm afraid I cannot just put aside my responsibility for the deserters, or the discipline problems with the volunteers. When my division marches back to Vera Cruz, I should like to accompany them. It seems appropriate, sir."

Scott said nothing, could see it now, the defeat in the man's face. I would never let him go, he thought, we need the veterans, the good commanders. But he is gone already. And if he stays here, he could make mistakes. We cannot afford mistakes. Scott said, "You are a fine commander, General. But I respect your wishes. Prepare your request, I will endorse it."

Patterson stood again, said, "Thank you, sir."

Patterson saluted, moved away quickly, and Scott reached behind him, pulled the bottle of brandy out again, thought, Now I need one more. He looked at the papers on the table, the official report he had already begun to write. He looked outside, saw aides gathering at a coffeepot, thought, I should get going on this damned paperwork. If Washington understands that I may actually be capable of winning a battle, they may even send some support.

He thought of the volunteers, men itching to go home, to leave the fight and their duty behind. They had signed twelve-month enlistments. A mistake, he thought. You can't assign duty by a calendar. They should have signed up for the duration of the war, committed to staying until the job was done. Not much of a Cause to them. I had thought Manifest Destiny might be important to more than just the politicians. Apparently not. It's a good thing we don't run the army like a democracy, let the troops vote on whether this war is worth fighting. Maybe we'd *all* be heading back home.

He set the bottle back in the cabinet, sipped from the glass, thought, All right, enough. You've given the volunteers more attention than they deserve. There is only one priority now, and it's a big damned city, and we will need more than seven thousand men to do the job. He picked up a paper, read it over, thought of the commanders, Pillow, the rest, all hoping to see their name in print. The junior officers, he thought, that's what these reports should be about, the men who *did* the job, who led the attack. He thought of Lee now, his quiet dignity. There should be more like him. Do the job, and instead of standing around waiting for a medal, do the next job. To hell with these gray-headed peacocks.

10. LEE

APRIL TWENTIETH

T HEY SANG AS THEY MARCHED, ENERGIZED BY THE COOL AIR, and no one complained that the road seemed to be uphill the entire way. Jalapa was not a long march, the town only a few miles beyond the village of Cerro Gordo, but the change of scenery was dramatic. As they climbed into cooler air, the dull greens of the dense brush opened up into brightly colored checkerboards of rich farmland. Where thorny thickets had spread over dusty hills, the land here was flatter, wide patches of deep green fields of corn and beans and rows of short thick fruit trees. If the men from New England and the Atlantic coast had thought Mexico was a hostile wasteland, they were startled to see this change, how the countryside opened up in soft and pleasant scenes that reminded many of them of home.

Lee rode with Worth's division, and soon the rest of the army would follow, making camp around the larger town. He wore his heavier wool jacket, had not needed it since the cool nights on the big ship. Around him the march moved quickly, and he could hear laughter, the troops' spirits high as they seemed to draw strength from the land. He had thought of home all along the march, so much of this fertile land so familiar, but there was still one stark difference. No matter how much the lush green brought back thoughts of the rich valleys and vast farms of Virginia, in the distance stood the vast amazing beauty of the tall mountains, the reminder that this was still a very different place after all.

He moved past a small farm where a single mule stood tied to a makeshift plow. The farmer looked at him with a wide smile, the strange mix of white teeth and burnished ruddy skin the color of the reins Lee held loosely in his hands. The farm was small, a flat stretch of freshly plowed dirt, and beyond, a small orchard around a crude house of low stone under a flat roof. He felt pulled in by the man's cheerfulness, smiled back at him, and the man waved.

Lee thought, How easy it is to judge. This place is so much like western Virginia, and how I've seen those people struggle to survive. We shake our heads and take our patronizing attitudes back to our grand estates and have no idea that those people can in fact be quite happy. This man is not struggling. He works his farm and maintains a home, and here he stands watching some great army pass by, and clearly he does not see this as some horrible invasion. We are a curiosity, and this is a day to remember, something interesting to tell his children. And his father probably told him the same stories, more armies, moving both ways, always some war down here, some revolution, and always the farmer waits until the armies pass by, then he picks up the plow and goes back to his field.

He rode closer to the orchard, saw white and pink flowers scattered through the trees, a soft sweetness on the breeze. Surely they believe God is protecting them, he thought, that God is here, in this bounty. He had become increasingly impatient with the hostility, the prejudice against the Catholic church, even among the officers. Some of it came from the desertion of the San Patricios, but Lee did not understand how the church could have had any part in that, how someone's faith could have pulled at a man's honor, betraying his sense of duty. It is in a man's heart what he fights for, he thought. If they had thought this fight was wrong, or our cause was unjust, they should never have come here at all, should never have accepted the duty. Whatever they do now will be judged by God, and surely it will not matter to God to what church they placed their loyalty. But the people here, the citizens . . . I must find out, see how they worship. They are a devout people. There is something to be respected in that, even if they are . . . different. Surely God has given them that. It is not for us to judge.

He could see more buildings up ahead, the outskirts of the town, more flat rooftops on stone houses, the tiny homes huddled tightly together. He could see a few taller buildings, two stories, some clearly providing cramped living space above a family business. Along the road people were gathering, lining up on both sides. The soldiers began to speak to them, receiving greetings, cheerful salutes in return, some delivered in Spanish, which the men did not understand. Lee saw more smiles as the people watched the army move past, and he was struck by their politeness, how the people did not seem to be anyone's enemy. He was unsettled by their behavior, how different the emotions of this day were than yesterday's. He wondered if these people had seen what he had, the destruction, the death, would they have received their visitors in the same way?

More sounds up in front of him captured his attention. From the tone of the outbursts, the soldiers must have been reacting to something new. Finally, Lee could see the women, a cluster of bright colors, soft dresses, flowers in black hair. The women were smiling as well, not just offering a pleasant greeting, but something more, a playful teasing, waving to the troops seductively. The troops were becoming noisier, some men slowing the march, trying to speak to the women, and officers began to shout, calling the men to order. Lee rode past the women now, smiled at the show of flirtation, saw one woman draw a long-stemmed rose from her blouse, toss it toward him. Lee caught the rose, could hear the men behind cheering him, the voice of one man, "How 'bout that, Captain. She 'pears to like you."

He was suddenly embarrassed, thought, Give it back, I should not be accepting gifts. He looked at the woman again, her rich olive skin, round dark eyes, could not help himself, thought, She is truly . . . beautiful. He caught himself, turned to the front, felt the burn in his cheeks. As you were, Captain. He looked at the rose, marveled at the deep luscious red, God's handiwork. I did not thank her . . . and he glanced back, saw all the women focused now on the men behind him, saw her handing another rose to another soldier, and he smiled, faced front again.

We should not be so easily flattered, he thought. There is simply a marvelous beauty in these people. He held the soft flower to his face, filled himself with the wonderful smell, and now a sudden flood of guilt began to rise in him, and he tossed the rose over his shoulder. This is for the men, some of them will seek this kind of comfort here. They do not have the discipline of the officer. We must avoid temptation.

There were different smells now, and Lee felt himself pulled toward a familiar delicious warmth. He saw a fat stone building with a small smokestack. Through an open window he saw a long row of dark brown bread, and then the baker, spreading fresh loaves in the window. Lee felt his mouth turn wet, watched the steam slowly drift above the feast, thought, Perhaps I should look into *that*. It could provide a treat for the headquarters staff. He smiled, thought, Temptation indeed.

APRIL TWENTY-SECOND

He did not stay long in Jalapa. After only one day of rest, he was on the march again, riding along with General Worth to occupy the next small town, Perote. General Scott sensed that there would be no organized threat from Santa Anna, not for a while, nor did he believe the army would find much resistance moving farther along the highway. Perote was not merely another small trophy of war, but the gateway that would lead them next to Puebla, the second largest city in Mexico, and a place that Scott believed would be the site of the next major confrontation.

They could still see the remnants of the retreat, mostly the wagons, broken down from the hard ride, their drivers and passengers leaving them where the axles had given way. Out in front, the skirmish line had picked through anything that might hold some value, or some threat, and Lee had become accustomed to the debris, did not feel as shocked as he had been at first by the waste and destruction of the battle.

Worth had asked Lee to come, and Scott expected quiet for a while, had no reason to keep his engineer, now his chief scout, close at hand. Lee had looked forward to the ride, had not yet spoken to Worth alone, out from underneath the enormous shadow of the commanding general. Most of the older generals were strangers to Lee, and before Mexico were faceless names that filtered down through the hierarchy of command. If a junior officer heard anything about men like Twiggs or even Zachary Taylor, it was by some rumor, a scandal perhaps, some suggestion of misbehavior. But William Worth had been commandant of cadets at West Point, had been a mentor to the entire class in those days when young men appreciated an officer who took the time to teach. One of those young cadets had been Lee.

He knew Worth was a Texan, and would fight the Mexicans if only for that reason, but he also knew that Worth was a good soldier, and a commander who would not shame his men. If he had one maddening trait, one that was sure to always create a controversy with Scott, it was Worth's strange habit to see the ghosts of the enemy as though a battle were always around the next bend. Zachary Taylor had experienced Worth's panic, sending his men out through the countryside chasing an enemy who simply wasn't there. It was a reputation that followed Worth south, and Scott had no use for panic.

They rode for a long while without speaking, and Lee had wondered why he was there, thought, You can't assume he remembers you. It's been a long time, and after all, he is a major general.

In the silence, he had stared out toward Orizaba, the grand mountain now out to the left. Scott had assumed Santa Anna to be near there, scrambling to gather men and equipment, salvaging what he could of the scattered pieces of his army. Lee looked again at the debris along the road, thought, I suppose Santa Anna doesn't have to explain this to anybody. He's a dictator, there is no one to sit in judgment, no one to blame him for the loss. He has all the ways of appealing to his army, can still tell them they're fighting for their country. There's a big difference between being an invader and being invaded.

That difference arouses a very strong sentiment in these people, at least to their army. The people, the private citizens, don't seem to be concerned. They have seen their share of governments, of dictators. As long as Santa Anna can rally the army, as long as he shows power, then he *is* the power, until someone else comes along with more power. He began to feel naive, thought, This isn't new. This is the way most countries are run. It's easy to understand why Americans have a sense of superiority, why the government sees this war as necessary. We're like missionaries, spreading the Word. Maybe one day that word will reach every corner of the earth, Manifest Destiny. God's will. He looked at Orizaba again, suddenly felt a chill, thought, You're thinking like a politician. Or a preacher. Better to think like a preacher.

He glanced at Worth, the older man riding stiffly in the saddle, thought, He hasn't changed so much, still the thick curly hair, something youthful in his face not really showing his age. Lee estimated, counted the years, thought, Mid-fifties, I suppose. Worth looked at him now, said, "You're mighty quiet, Captain. What's on your mind?"

Lee cleared his mind, looked at Orizaba again, said, "Mighty fine view here, sir. Spectacular."

Worth tilted his head, said, "More going on in your head than that. Don't mean to pry. I had hoped we could clear the air."

Lee was puzzled, said, "Clear the air? I don't understand, sir."

"Captain, let's be precise. You are now the property of General Scott. You're the fair-haired boy, the general's rising young star."

Lee felt a wave of embarrassment, began to protest, but Worth interrupted, "Let it go, Captain. I knew you'd take exception to that description. Doesn't matter. It's accurate. Every officer in the army knows it. It's interesting, actually. There was a time when talk like that described me. Did you know I was on his staff? I was there when he made his reputation, the victory at Lundy's Lane. God, it's been how long . . . it was summer, 1814. There were not very many of us then, and we stood up to the finest army in the world. Hell, we flat out whipped them. It was his finest hour as a soldier. And we all shared in that, the glory, the recognition. But not for long. He absorbs the light around him. No one else can claim much attention when he's the star. Since then, I've never known Winfield Scott to take a shine to anybody. He seems to need to protect that attention, make sure it doesn't drift off to find some other hero. But for some reason, he's noticing you. You should be flattered."

Lee did not respond, recalled Joe Johnston's words, the night before his mission at Cerro Gordo, wondered how many of the senior officers saw Scott's attention as some sort of favoritism. A protest formed in his head, *Surely they are mistaken.*

Worth continued, "Don't assume anything good will come from it, Captain. Scott must have some selfish use for you. He sure as hell has no use for me. And even I'm better off than Davy Twiggs, or that damned fool Pillow." Worth glanced at Lee before going on, "You think I'm talking out of turn? Make you uncomfortable? Good. We're even. General Scott makes me uncomfortable all the time. Make no mistake, Captain, I'm not his enemy, whether he believes that or not. There's no one in this army better to be leading troops down here. No one in Washington either. Now, there's a mess."

The words had come toward Lee in a flurry, and the engineer was uncomfortable now, but not for the reasons Worth might have thought. The youthfulness was gone from Worth's face, and Lee saw something bitter, angry, a hard cold stare replacing it.

I don't understand why he says these things, Lee thought. *I do not believe General Scott is so . . . petty. No, this is not your place to comment. He has waited a long time to say these things. It may not be accurate, or completely truthful, but he clearly believes it.*

After a long moment Lee said, "I'm honored the general would take me into his confidence."

Worth looked at Lee again, shook his head. "You always going to talk like a cadet?"

"Sorry, sir. It's . . . habit."

"Can't argue with that. All your habits still good ones? You still keep sober?"

"Why, yes, sir. I've never felt the need to be . . . intoxicated. I can't say I understand those who do."

"I'm wary of men who claim to be champions of sobriety. They're either liars or madmen. Or . . ." He smiled, looked away. "Maybe they're in line to be commander." Worth paused, then said, "How about a good swear word now and then? I recall, that wasn't in your repertoire either."

"Uh, no sir. Can't say I have mastered the use of profanity. There's enough flowing around without my contributing to it."

"It's an art, Captain, a convenient skill. You should learn how to use it, but it requires some discretion. It can be an effective weapon, if used properly. Most of these men don't understand that. They consider it an obligation to start cussing as soon as they get away from their mamas. But a well-placed curse can punctuate effectively, enforce a point. You should try it sometime. I'm certain General Scott would be a good instructor."

Lee shifted uncomfortably in his saddle, scanning the horizon. He said nothing.

A long silence passed between them before Worth said, "I wish I knew why he dislikes me so."

"Sir?"

"Even in the old days, even when he would visit the Point, I hoped he would allow me some of that glory, the recognition. But he would never speak of the war, barely acknowledged that we had served together. It was as though I was merely a staff officer, nothing more."

Lee was surprised, thought, But you *were* a staff officer. Surely, there is more to this. But he's serious, this really bothers him.

"Sir, I have learned that General Scott has a healthy dislike for most all the commanders. I can't say I understand that myself. He has to endure . . . forgive me, sir. I don't want to say anything inappropriate."

"Nonsense, Captain. I appreciate your views."

"I don't understand the conflict with Washington. He is under enormous pressure to win this war, and the army doesn't get support." Lee paused, feeling his discomfort welling up in his chest. "I've said too much, sir. Forgive me."

"I'm not in the best of health, Captain. After this war is over, I'll probably retire. Makes me a bit fearless when it comes to Washington. You hear about Senator Benton?"

Lee shook his head. "No, sir."

"Thomas Hart Benton, the esteemed senator from Missouri.

Good friend of Polk's, a good Democrat, makes all the right speeches, delivers the vote for his party. Few months ago, the President goes to Congress with a list of promotions, mine included. One of them is for the good senator to become a lieutenant general. Just like that, the highest ranking officer in the army. Complete command. Never mind that he's a civilian."

Lee noticed that Worth's expression had hardened, his lips set in a thin line.

"Apparently, Captain Lee, Senator Benton had ambitions to become a war hero, expected the President to reward him by sending him down here to run the show, win the war and grab the headlines. And his friend James K. Polk thought that was just a dandy idea. Word of all this came down to General Scott, while he was still in Texas." Worth laughed, shook his head. "You must not have been at headquarters yet. You'd have learned something about profanity for sure. Half of Texas heard the explosion. A few congressmen went to the President and gave him the best advice he'll ever get, said drop the Benton promotion. For the army's sake, he did."

Worth was laughing still, and Lee felt a wave of depression.

"I don't understand that, sir. This is serious business. This is a war."

Worth looked at Lee, serious again, said, "Captain Lee, you are not especially . . . political, are you?"

Lee looked down, said, "I try to keep up with events, sir."

"It's not a criticism, Captain. You are blessed. You don't carry the infection. Simply put, Winfield Scott is a Whig. The president is a Democrat. Their politics don't . . . blend well. What makes one look bad makes the other look good. And they both want to look good."

There was a silent moment, and Lee looked out toward the mountain, thought, Yes, you are naive, Captain.

"There is more to command than I would have thought, sir."

"That's right, Captain. It's a hell of a way to run a war."

H E WAS STILL BESIDE WORTH, BUT THE CONVERSATION HAD faded away, drowned out by the steady rhythm of the horse's hooves. The focus now was forward, the first glimpse of the low buildings and tall church steeples of Perote. The line of skirmishers stayed far out in front, and Worth had strengthened them. Nearly a full regiment marched in a wide line of battle, prepared for a sudden assault by an army Worth was convinced was lying in ambush. As they drew closer to the small town, the quiet was broken by a burst of sound. Lee sat up straight in the saddle, stared forward, and Worth said, "Muskets! He's there! I knew it! We could be in serious trouble, Captain. The whole Mexican army could be up there."

Worth turned, shouted to an aide, "Advance, double quick! Move!"

The officers gave the commands, and the troops did not hesitate, had known the order could come any time. Lee moved off the road, watched the soldiers surging past, and behind them the wagons bunching up, the guards fanning out, protecting the supplies from the inevitable assault.

Worth was staring out through field glasses, said, "I don't see anything yet . . . there must be . . . wait, horses . . . there, off to the left."

Lee raised field glasses, studied the small town quickly, saw the dark mass of a very old stone fort that guarded the town. The muskets were still firing, and Lee could see a dust cloud, moving out south of the town. He thought, I don't think that's an army. It's not much of a fight.

Worth was still glassing, said, "The major force must be beyond the town. That appears to be a small detachment, the scouting party for the main body. No major problem yet." He looked at Lee. "That's why we keep the march tight, the wagons well-guarded, Captain. It could come at any time. If we're not prepared, it could be a disaster. We're giving Santa Anna too much time to put another army together." He looked back toward his staff, said aloud, "Let's proceed, gentlemen."

They resumed the march, moved down the long hill, the town quiet now. Lee looked out over rocky hills, thought, How could Santa Anna have put together another army? From where? Could this have been just . . . guerrillas? He rode behind Worth, studied him, the man staring out across the rocks, still expecting the sudden roar of an attack. Lee followed Worth's gaze, thought, I have no business second-guessing him. I suppose it's better to be prepared for the worst. He studied the rocks again, thought of the guerrillas. If I was a bandit, that's where I would be. Not much we can do about it. Hard to chase anybody in country like this.

A squad of skirmishers was gathered near the road now, and the rest of the regiment began to file in closer. All threats from the small raid were gone. A younger officer stepped forward to address Worth. "General, we cleared them out. There were a few in the town, probably have families here. They didn't seem serious about making a fight. Took off after a few shots."

Worth removed his hat, stared out to the south, said, "Lieutenant

Longstreet, you keep a sharp eye out. They're clever. Post a strong guard. We'll make camp in the town."

Longstreet glanced at Lee, appraising, then looked at Worth again, said, "They won't stand up to us, sir. A few well-directed shots and they scatter like birds."

Worth grunted, said, "Overconfidence is dangerous, Lieutenant. If Santa Anna brings his whole army down on us, it will take more than a few well-placed shots to repel him."

Longstreet looked at Lee again, and Lee could see a small frown of frustration on the young man's face. He knows, thought Lee. It's only the guerrillas. Keep your tongue, young lieutenant. Lee nodded slightly, said nothing, and Longstreet saluted, said, "With your permission, sir."

Worth returned the salute, said, "Stay alert, Lieutenant."

A small group of horsemen came out of the town, more of the advance guard, the men who would check the houses, draw fire if they had to, to make sure there was no ambush still waiting. The men rode up, and Lee saw a man with a bandaged arm, thought, I've seen a great deal of that lately. He stared at the wound, the man moving as though the bandage was not there, and Lee recalled the horribly wounded man at Cerro Gordo, the man's quiet resignation. There must be something, some word from God, telling you whether or not you are going to die. Of course, God would give you that, offer you some kind of peace of mind. But there are many now, men like this one, the wounded who come back. They still have the fight in them, they do not focus on their injury. It is past, behind them, I suppose. That is . . . amazing. Could I do that, just ignore it, go back to work, hide the memory of that wound? Maybe that's what truly makes a soldier.

Some of the men were pointing back to the town, their voices rising in excitement, and a young lieutenant called out, "General, you have to see this!"

The man reined his horse, still excited, and Longstreet said, "Easy, Mr. Pickett. Make your report."

"Excuse me, sir, General Worth, the fort, we thought it was empty, like some of those others we seen. No, sir. It's full of guns, powder. And, sir, there's even prisoners."

Worth said, "Prisoners? What kind . . . locals? Criminals?"

"Beggin' your pardon, sir, no. They're Mexican army prisoners. Officers. Still wearin' fancy uniforms and all."

Worth looked at Lee with a cold grim stare, said, "Bait, Captain. Let our guard down, and they hit us. Keep a sharp eye, gentlemen. Let's go have a look."

They moved quickly into the town, and Lee could see the civilians now, moving out into the street, cautious, then slowly opening up, their smiles appearing again. Just like before, he thought, they're glad to see us. It's very strange.

They rode up to the old fort, the door flanked by four American soldiers. Lieutenant Pickett was down quickly, moved to the entranceway, said, "General Worth, welcome to Fort San Carlos de Perote. After you, sir."

Lee followed Worth inside. They moved through a dark hall, and Lee felt his nose curl up, a thick cloud of wet stench, the distinct smell of human waste, blending with something more, worse, the stale odor of death. He lowered his head, tried to breathe in short quick bursts, thought, I wouldn't want to be a prisoner *here*. They moved into a large low-ceilinged room, and Lee could see boxes, crates, cloth bags, all marked in Spanish.

Worth moved forward, leaned down, said, "Muskets . . . Spanish made. Pretty old." He stood up, looked at the young officer, said, "You said prisoners, Lieutenant."

"This way, sir. Through here." They moved again into a dank hall, and Lee could hear voices, low, absorbed by the damp stone walls. He saw a heavy wooden door, held shut with a fat iron bar. Worth pointed, and Pickett pulled the bar away, pushed the door open.

There was dim light, one small opening high on the wall, and Lee felt a damp rush of air, and more of the awful smell. Worth stepped into the room, and Lee could see past him, two men, struggling to stand. The lieutenant was right, Lee thought. They're officers . . . high-ranking officers. Their uniforms were filthy, and Lee could see one man still wore a medal, dull brass, hanging loosely from his coat. Worth stepped around, moved to see the light on the men's faces, and Lee saw now, the gaunt unshaven faces, hollow eyes.

Worth said, "Good God! I know these men!" He looked at Lee. "Captain, how's your Spanish?"

Lee stepped closer, shook his head.

"Almost nonexistent, sir."

"Mine too. Well, we'll do the best we can. Captain, may I present to you General Juan Morales and General José Landero."

Lee looked closely at the faces, and the men glanced at him, then focused their eyes straight ahead. They seemed to waver slightly, then stood at attention. Lee said, "Morales . . . the same . . . the commander of Vera Cruz, sir?"

Worth held out a hand, and Morales took one slow step toward him, raised a hand, spoke slowly, *"General Worth."*

Worth shook the man's hand, then suddenly released it, and Lee could see a twist of pain on Morales's face. Worth looked at the man's hand, said, "I'm sorry, General. You are injured."

The man rubbed his hands together, seemed embarrassed. He put his hands behind him, stood again at attention.

Worth said, "General Scott was right. The loss of Vera Cruz was a disgrace. This is their punishment."

Lee moved closer, the light now reflecting on the men's faces, and he saw their weakness, the slow starvation in their hollow eyes.

"Sir, what do we do with them?"

"We liberate them, Captain. These men are under parole. They were released from Vera Cruz with our assurances of safe passage. If we need any proof that they have observed their parole, consider that Mr. Santa Anna saw fit to put them in prison. Hell, they've been here now probably two weeks or so, don't even look like they've had a scrap to eat. He just left them here to die. That's proof enough for me."

Worth pointed toward the open door, said, "General Morales, General Landero, you may, uh, *vamos.*"

The two men looked at the door, and both bowed slowly and with great dignity.

Morales said quietly, *"Gracias señor, muchas gracias."*

The two men moved unsteadily toward the door, and Worth said, "Probably haven't been fed in a while. We scared off their guard. They might never have been fed." He looked at the young officer, said, "Lieutenant, make sure these men get rations. Get them cleaned up, and when they're fit, they can go on their way. I don't expect they'll be any trouble to us, that's for sure." He looked at Lee.

"Captain, since you represent General Scott here, you have any objections?"

Lee said, "Uh, sir, I would not presume to represent General Scott. However, under the circumstances, I agree with your actions."

"Good. So when General Scott breathes fire at me for making this decision without asking him, you can tell him just that. He'll listen to you before he listens to me."

Worth moved out into the dark hall again, said, "Dismal places, prisons. Let's get out of here."

They moved toward the front entrance, and Lee watched the two Mexicans step slowly into the daylight. They held their hands over their eyes for a few seconds, and Morales smiled, bowed politely again to the American soldiers who were gathering around them. Morales glanced at Landero, said aloud,

"*Viva General Scott.*"

11. SCOTT

May second

SCOTT EASED INTO THE SOFT LEATHER CHAIR. HE LEANED FOR-
ward and ran his hand across the rich oak of the desk's top, felt
the inlaid leather along the edge, thought, Nice, very nice. We
should always have a camp like this. Now he sat back, settled once
again into the wonderful softness of the chair. Taking his time, he
examined the short round man who stood before him, the man's fine
suit, the colorful trim of his shirt, the fine silver on the strange necktie.
He slid a piece of paper across the desk, turned the writing toward the
man and said, "You understand, it is the official policy of the United
States government that the army simply *take* whatever we want." The
man glanced down at the paper but did not read what was written there.
Scott thought, He speaks English, but that doesn't always mean he can
read it. He pulled the paper back, said, "Sir, allow me to read this."

He looked up at the man's face, saw quiet concern, a growing sadness. "President Polk sends me a great many letters. I even read some of
them. Like this one. 'If you continue to insist that only the resources
made available by the government can sustain your army, and those resources are not being provided in a manner you find satisfactory, then
the only reasonable alternative is for the army to lay claim to the territory it now occupies, and secure food and forage from the citizens of
the hostile nation by whatever means necessary.' "

He waited for a response. The man nodded slowly, and Scott
thought, He looks like he's going to cry. Scott set the paper aside, said,
"*Señor*, despite my government's willingness to ride roughshod over
your citizens, I have no intention of *taking* anything. We are neither
bandits nor pirates, despite what President Polk would suggest. Under
my command, the army will negotiate fair prices for the goods we re-

quire. Jalapa is prosperous, your authority covers an area that has a great many productive farms. I am sure we can arrive at a reasonable agreement. As mayor, uh, *alcalde,* you can appreciate the benefit this kind of relationship will have on your community. It is up to you to convince your people of the wisdom of cooperating with us."

The man's energy seemed to return, and he smiled now at Scott, said, "Yes, General. There is no need for you to see Jalapa as your enemy. Your enemy is not *here.*"

"Excellent, *Alcalde.* I will have the quartermaster accompany you to your merchants. His staff is authorized to negotiate in the name of the United States Army. A good day to you, sir." Scott rose, shook the man's hand, and the young Scott led the *alcalde* from the office. Alone now, the general moved around the desk, walked toward a large window and stared out into bright sunshine, said aloud, "A little diplomacy." He shook his head and thought, They don't think I know anything about negotiation. You don't just rip your way through a foreign country, grabbing and destroying anything you want. I'm not Attila the Hun, for God's sake.

His son-in-law returned to the office, said, "Sir, excuse me, but General Twiggs is here to see you. He is insistent, sir."

Scott looked at the young man, thought, How much energy will *this* require? "Fine, show him in."

Twiggs stood in the doorway, took a moment to compose himself, then moved stiffly into Scott's office. He held his hat in his hand and said, "General, a moment?"

Scott pointed to the chair, and Twiggs eyed it, ran his own hand across the desk's dark wood, pressed down hard as though testing its strength. He sat, appraised Scott for a moment before speaking, "Quite a nice place. The people are . . . surprisingly . . . uh . . ."

"They're surprisingly gracious, General. The governor wouldn't take no for an answer, insisted the army make use of his home. The mayor just left, is going to speak to the farmers, see about opening up a supply line for us here."

Twiggs seemed at a loss for words, shook his head. "Not what I expected."

"It's all in how you treat them, General. Just a little respect. Washington thinks we should stampede through here. They have no sense of how these people can help us. We cannot make war against an entire nation with an army as small as ours. Our fight has to be with their government, and their government is one man. The surprising thing to me is these civilians don't much seem to care about us being here. I had always thought Santa Anna was some great national hero, like their version of George Washington. He's more like their version of James K. Polk."

Twiggs said nothing, and Scott thought, He's never been political, probably doesn't get the joke. Good thing Pillow isn't here. A silent moment passed between them, and Twiggs shifted in the chair. Scott broke the silence, "What's on your mind, General?"

Twiggs sat up straight, stared down at the wide desk, said, "I would prefer, sir, that you not insult the President."

Scott smiled, thought, So, he *did* get it. Give him more credit next time.

"What can I do for you, General?"

"Sir, the threat from the guerrillas is increasing. We can't send wagons into the countryside without attracting a raid. If they think we're the least bit vulnerable, they appear out of nowhere. The cost in supplies, and even in men . . ." Twiggs paused, searching for the right word. " . . . is unacceptable. We had two men killed last night, ambushed. We sent out a cavalry detachment, but they didn't find anything. They're like cockroaches."

"I'm sorry about your men. I've been hearing a great many reports in the past few days. It may be that what we're facing is all the force Santa Anna can muster. He can't have much organized strength. His army collapsed at Cerro Gordo, and I suspect so did much of his ability to recruit new troops. Most of the troops he had are long gone, probably tending their farms." He paused.

"General Twiggs, I don't have much stomach for a drawn-out fight with a bunch of guerrillas, but it may be the only fight we'll have. Do *you* have a solution?"

Twiggs looked up quickly, and Scott saw the spark, a rare show of enthusiasm. Obviously this was the opening Twiggs had come for. "I think we should organize a special squad," Twiggs said, "Maybe the Texas Rangers, send them out on a specific mission to hunt down the guerrillas. Show no mercy. It's the only thing those people will understand. They're nothing more than thieves. Treat them like thieves."

Scott said nothing, looked at Twiggs, who stared past him, out toward the wide window behind Scott's desk. Scott thought, He never looks me in the eye.

"You can send out patrols if you like, General," Scott said, "but I don't think it will do much good. As you said, they'll be as hard to catch as cockroaches, and it's their countryside. If you think the Rangers will have some positive effect, then see to it. I may work on another remedy."

Twiggs stood, bowed curtly, said, "Thank you, sir. If I may be excused . . ."

"Dismissed, General."

Twiggs was quickly gone, and Scott looked again at the letter from the President, thought, It's the same kind of problem. Maybe it needs the same kind of solution. He looked toward the door, saw the young Scott coming in, said, "Major, is the *alcalde* still outside?"

The young man replied, "I believe so, sir. He is waiting for the quartermaster's staff."

"Good. Go get him. I have another proposition for him."

The young man moved outside, and Scott sat back in the chair, studied a painting on a far wall, a beautiful woman in a floor length dress, long black hair flowing beneath a bonnet of bright flowers. Something wonderfully . . . primitive, he thought, unspoiled. How many conquerors have torn through this land, how many revolutions brought by the ambitious against the corrupt. And then the ambitious *become* the corrupt, and so another revolution. This time, *we* bring the ambition, and *we* fight the corrupt. And all the while the people adapt, and survive, and live with whatever rule of law hovers over them. Well, General Twiggs may be right. We'll try another rule of law.

He heard the outside door open, and the *alcalde* hurried in, holding his hat in both hands.

"*Sí*, General Scott, what can I do?" The mayor smiled and nodded his head.

"Sir, we have a problem. Unfortunately, it is also your problem. General Santa Anna has been forced to resort to fighting us with bandits, guerrillas, causing us a great deal of trouble. It makes it difficult for the men to keep their . . . kind attitude toward your people. I'm sure you understand. However, it has occurred to me that you might know someone who, quite by accident of course, has some direct contact with the guerrillas. Perhaps you can find some way to communicate with them, encourage them to . . . curb their activities."

The *alcalde* seemed concerned, shook his head, and Scott thought, Give him a moment. Let him have his protest of innocence. The man thought, then said, "General, I do not know . . . these men, they are *banditos*. We do not support what they do."

"No certainly, *señor*. However, if we go after them, we will kill them. It would be a sad affair. Some of these men probably have families, *señoritas* here in town. A sad affair indeed."

The *alcalde* stopped smiling now, and Scott thought, Yes, he is beginning to understand.

The *alcalde* said, "It would be a very sad affair, General. Still, I do not know what I can do."

"I have an idea, *señor*. Since I cannot communicate directly with the guerrillas, I will do it through you. I believe it is a prudent policy to levy a fine for each raid against our men and supplies. You find a way to convince them to stop their raids, and no one will be forced to pay. If the raids continue, then the army will levy a fine. Let's see, a fair amount would be . . . three hundred dollars. For *each* raid. And since I cannot hope to collect that from the guerrillas, and since I cannot, in good conscience, take money from the courteous people of your community, the most reasonable policy is that I will collect it from . . . *you.*"

He watched the man's expression grow grimly serious, thought, Good, he understands politics *and* war.

The *alcalde* straightened his coat, trying to achieve an air of formality. "General Scott, I cannot say to you that I have any means of contacting the *banditos* . . . the guerrillas. But I can assure you that I am outraged by their actions, and I will not tolerate this kind of activity under my authority as *alcalde*. I am not afraid of General Santa Anna. It would be a reflection on my, um, weakness if the raids were to continue."

"Yes, *señor*, I believe you're right. I do not believe you to be a weak man."

The man bowed quickly as he backed slowly away, before turning and slipping past the young Scott.

General Scott sat back, a smile of satisfaction on his face. "Major, it's a talent. That's all, just a talent."

He stared out the window, felt the sun on his face and said, "I don't think there will be much more of a problem with the guerrillas."

MAY SIXTH

The ship had eased into the wharf at Vera Cruz, pulled to the landing by the longshoremen. No one noticed the tall, thin man who made his way carefully down the ramp, his pale corpselike face standing out in stark contrast to his black suit. The man had obviously suffered for most of the trip, as many suffered, especially those who did not spend much time at sea. He stopped at the bottom of the ramp, tried to take in a deep breath and clear his lungs of the stale air of his quarters on the tall ship. His stomach still ached, still sore from the misery that had rolled over him as the ship rocked and pitched southward. He put a hand on his gut and closed his eyes as though in prayer. When he opened them, he watched as a sailor, a thick dark man who did not look at him, carried his bags down the ramp. The sailor set the bags down heavily on the wharf before turning and walking silently back to the ship.

The man moved to the larger cloth bag, picked it up, straining under the weight. He prodded it and a smile of satisfaction came across his face. He ran his hand over the smaller bag, fat with papers, picked it up, hoisted the larger one over his shoulder and began to move unsteadily. He was startled to see sailors suddenly blocking his way, an officer and two men behind him wearing pistols. He dropped the bags, looked at the pistols, and felt a sudden wave of the familiar sickness churning inside.

The officer said, "Good day, sir. May I ask your destination?"

The man still looked at the pistols. He moved one hand, pointed a bony finger toward the bags and said, "My orders. I am here on official business. I am here to see General Scott."

The sailor smiled, glanced at one of the guards behind him, said, "Well, sir, General Scott's whereabouts is privileged information. I can tell you, though, the general is not presently in Vera Cruz. What kind of business did you have with the general?" The officer looked at the bags then said, "You a salesman? You come a long way just to sell . . . what? Might you be selling guns? Perhaps you are also here to see General Santa Anna. He might be a better customer."

The sailors all laughed, and the man felt a deathly helplessness, his brain a jumble of words. "No, sir. I am a clerk. The chief clerk, actually. That is, I have been sent . . ." He looked at the smaller bag again, said, "May I be allowed to retrieve my papers? They will provide an explanation."

The officer nodded. "The *chief* clerk, no less. Well, Mr. Chief Clerk, you be careful going into that bag."

The man reached down, his eyes again drawn to the pistols. He opened the leather clasp on the bag, felt inside, his heart racing. Finally he pulled an envelope out of the bag. He stood, felt light-headed, and nearly slumped to the floor before the officer grabbed him by the arm.

"Whoa there, steady."

The man tried to straighten, felt the officer's hard grip under his arm. He took a deep breath, his head starting to clear, and said, "Thank you. It's all right. I've been on that ship for too long."

The sailors laughed again, and the officer said, "You'll get your land legs in a bit. You might feel the ground rocking for a while. Let's have a look."

The officer took the envelope, opened it and read the letter. His eyes wide-open, the officer looked at the man, shook his head as though in disbelief, read again. "I'll be damned. Official business indeed."

An army officer moved across the wharf and said to the naval officer, "A problem there, Lieutenant?"

The sailor held the papers out. "No problem at all Colonel. We got us an official visitor here. All the way from Washington."

The colonel took the papers and examined them. "Well now, this is a surprise."

The man felt a wave of relief, thought, *Finally,* and said, "Nicholas Trist, sir. As you can see, I'm here under instructions from the President and the Secretary of State. I wonder if either of you gentlemen can arrange for me to reach General Scott?"

12. LEE

May eleventh

ITT WAS NEARLY DARK, AND A GLORIOUS SUNSET FOLLOWED HIM INTO the town. He had returned from Perote, after days of making a detailed inventory of the guns and stores they had found in the old fort. It had not been a pleasant task, a mundane detailing on paper of matériel the army would probably never use. He did not understand why Worth would assign the job to him, since it did not quite fit his duties as an engineer. But worse, the work took place in that awful dark place, where the smell reminded Lee of old dungeons and torture chambers he had read about.

Worth had finally agreed to let him go, could find no more reason to retain the services of Scott's engineer. Lee had begun to wonder if Worth's keeping him at Perote was some aspect of the strange hostility between Worth and Scott. It was almost as if he were a hostage or a prisoner of war of that odd and unstated battle. Even Worth's brief good-bye had been curt and angry, and Lee had left feeling depressed, as though his relationship with Worth would never be the same. As he rode along the ragged highway, he tried to recall the Point, when Worth was his mentor, his friend, giving Lee the benefit of experience.

That was a long time ago, he thought. What experience has made Worth so angry, suspicious, even . . . afraid? He believes Santa Anna is always there, always a danger, speaks of him as larger than life, some kind of all-powerful demon. General Scott will not listen to it, but General Worth's staff has to. Does that mean eventually his fear will become theirs as well? How will that affect his men? Lee remembered Worth's concern about his own health. It doesn't show on his face, he still carries the energy of a younger man, but he doesn't expect to stay long in the army. Maybe he's afraid of that. He's come as far as he can. There's nothing left to look forward to.

Lee moved through the streets of the town, his mood somber, as he ignored the calls of the merchants, the craftspeople who held out their wares, blankets, and baskets. He could not help but stop beside a wagon filled with strange and beautiful birdhouses, the man selling them smiling a wide toothless grin. Lee knew he had made a mistake, that if you stopped, they would pour out the salesmanship, hold you tightly until you bought something. He tried to smile, nodded through the man's flow of words, finally said, "No, *señor, gracias.* Not now. Maybe . . . later."

The man was still speaking to him, held up one of the birdhouses. It was made of some type of delicate wood, trimmed with colorful feathers. Lee's mood darkened even more as he thought of his children, how far away he was from them. The birdhouse would have made a wonderful gift. But, not now, this was not the place to indulge in sentiment. He moved away, tried to ignore the rest of the merchants, but one woman approached him holding a thick bunch of roses, the wonderful scent finding him, adding to his sadness. He nodded toward her, smiled faintly, as though to say, Sorry, I must go.

The army was used to this now, the town taking advantage of the wealth of new customers, these *yanquis* who moved among them with the swagger of heroes. The relationship between the citizens and the soldiers was still a pleasant one, and the army handled even the occasional problem, a fight perhaps, or some abusive treatment of a civilian, with swift discipline and the townspeople's tolerance.

He began to hear new sounds, quiet conversation, the laughter of children, the evening meals prepared in dozens of small homes. He also caught the smells, the roasting of meat, the strange stew with the rich brown gravy, and then of course, his weakness, the bread, fresh and hot and wonderful. The effect of his unsatisfactory departure from Worth was gone now, and he could not help a smile, thought, Nothing smells as good as freshly made bread. The lamplights were taking effect now, spilling from the homes into the quiet streets. Even the aggression of the shopkeepers had given way to the peace of the cool evening.

He began to see soldiers, heard sounds more familiar, voices in English, a different laughter, jokes and tall tales. He moved toward a group of men in blue, and he was saluted, saw a familiar face, heard his name. He was suddenly very tired, thought of the bread, felt his stomach grumble, heard his name again.

"Captain Lee! Sir!"

He looked for the voice, saw a young lieutenant moving toward him, waving. Lee stopped his horse. He saw the resemblance immediately, the man a younger copy of Joe Johnston, small and thin, but with a quiet air of assurance.

The young man said, "Captain, I'm glad to see you. We were hoping . . . Captain Johnston has been asking for you."

Lee felt a twist in his gut, said, "How is he? Is he all right?"

"Oh, yes, sir. But he's been hoping to see you. We didn't know when you might return. If you have a moment . . . this way, sir."

Lee climbed down from the horse, said, "I recognize you. You are his nephew."

The young man was already moving away, stopped, looked at Lee, said, "Yes, sir. John Preston Johnston, sir. I am honored you would remember me."

"Not at all, Lieutenant. Your uncle has told me a great deal. Class of 1843, I believe?"

"Indeed, sir. Thank you."

There was a pause, and Lee felt awkward, didn't know what else to say. The young lieutenant saw the look on Lee's face and said, "Perhaps we should go now, sir."

He followed the young man past more soldiers, some men carrying plates of food. Lee's senses were overwhelmed by smells now, roasted meat, chicken. He wanted to stop, thought, Surely . . . one minute, just a plate, but the young man was moving into a glow of lamplight. He stood in an open doorway, said, "This way, Captain."

Lee followed, moved through the door, and the smells suddenly changed. Lee felt his throat draw tight, fought for a breath. He could see across the room now, a row of low beds, wounded men, soldiers, doctors standing, moving slowly among them. Lee scanned the faces, saw the young man again, waiting for him, standing at the foot of a bed. Lee blinked hard, fought past the odor, but suddenly remembered his mother, her sickbed, the awful, terrible time, the smells . . . like this. Medicine and sickness . . . and death. He still fought it, pushed hard at the image, could not face those memories. He looked again at the men in the beds, thought, Now they will have the images, their own horror. I don't understand why it has to smell like this. He began to take small, tight breaths. He stepped into the room, moved toward the young man, saw Johnston now, his friend looking up at him with black eyes.

"Joe, how are you?"

Johnston nodded, raised one arm, pulled the sheet back, and Lee saw a heavy bandage on his other arm. Johnston said weakly, "Cerro Gordo will be memorable for both of us. While you were off finding a way to get promoted, I wandered out with a reconnaissance patrol a little too far in front of General Pillow, nearly walked right into a Mexican picket line. This one went clean through. But . . . the other one's worse." Johnston moved his hand lower, pointed to his hip. "Allow me the dignity of not showing you this one, Robert."

Lee tried to smile, put his hand on Johnston's shoulder while he fought for the right words. "You healing . . . getting better? Surely, you'll be out of this place soon. Any word yet what they're going to do with you?" He felt a sudden cold chill, said, "They sending you home?"

Johnston pulled the sheet over him again, said, "Wouldn't hear of it. The doctors say I'll be back in action in a few weeks. Say I'm healing nicely. Not sure what's so nice about it. Best reason I can think of to get healed up . . . is to get out of *this* place. Besides . . ." He looked at his nephew. " . . . somebody's got to take care of this young firecracker here. He's artillery, you know. Couldn't interest him in being an engineer, he had to play with the big guns."

Lee looked at the young man, saw his red-faced embarrassment. "What unit, Lieutenant?" Lee asked.

"Magruder's battery, sir. Captain John Magruder."

Johnston shook his head, said, "You believe that, Robert? Not only does he want to shoot cannons, but he wants to do it for the most disagreeable man in the army."

The young man seemed wounded, said, "Sir, I have been told in no uncertain terms, if you want to see a good fight, follow Captain Magruder. I only hope to be of capable service."

Lee smiled. "Joe, I'm certain the lieutenant will perform to Captain Magruder's expectations. There is a great deal to be learned under the command of a man like John Magruder. He is nothing if not . . ." Lee paused. " . . . if not a perfectionist."

Johnston laughed, but the sound was cut short and his face twisted with pain.

Lee leaned close, thought, No, my fault. He felt suddenly helpless, said, "I'm sorry, you shouldn't be laughing, not good for the stitches. Can I get you something, Joe? Anything?"

Johnston closed his eyes for a moment, the pain easing, and he said, "No, you're right. Laughter hurts the worst. That's why I wanted *you* here." Johnston looked toward his nephew, said, "If anyone asks you, Preston, Captain Lee is the worst joke teller in the army."

Lee smiled, thought, It's probably true. He felt his stomach protesting again. "Something to eat? It's supper time."

"Thank you, Robert. No. Not too much of an appetite, since the operation. That was very strange. They put me right to sleep. I never even knew they were digging on me. The doctor said it was called *ether*, some new drug. I never heard of it. Only one problem. Made me sick. Worse than the ship, if that's possible."

Lee glanced to one side, could see a doctor leaning over another man, thought, This doesn't seem like the place for advances in medicine. He felt his head beginning to swim from the warmth of the oil lamps. His stomach growled again.

"I'll visit you again, Joe. I have to . . . report to General Scott."

Johnston held up a hand, and Lee took it, felt a weak grip, set his friend's hand down by his side. He nodded to the young lieutenant before he backed slowly away, turned, looked for the blessed door. He moved outside, felt the cool air now, took a long slow breath. Even from the beginning he had expected it, prepared himself for the horror. He thought of the wounded men at Cerro Gordo; it was a shock, but you accept it, the sounds, the screaming, the things a man says when he's dying. But even those memories fade, the blood is cleaned away, the pain is treated. But . . . I never expected this, I never expected the awful smell. What is it, I wonder? Is it the wounds themselves, the blood, infection? He pushed hard again to keep the image of his mother away. No, it is no one thing, no thing that can be described. It follows the wounded men everywhere, and it stays with them until they are healed or they die. There is no other relief. God help them.

He moved out into the dark, past the men with the plates of food, took another breath, thought, You have a lot to learn about being a soldier, Captain.

H E EASED DOWN FROM THE HORSE, CLIMBED THE WIDE STEPS TO the porch of the grand old stone house. There were more horses standing to one side, and beyond, a small cluster of aides talking quietly. The porch was not lit, and he strained to see in the dark, stepped up carefully to a wide veranda, the roof supported by heavy columns of stone. There was a glow of light now from the front entrance, and he moved that way, stepped through the doorway, saw that the glow came from a lamp on the desk of Scott's receptionist, a frail, anemic sergeant. The man smiled, seemed relieved to see Lee, and he stood and saluted.

"Captain Lee, welcome back, sir."

Lee saw tension in the man's face, how he glanced toward the rear of the house. "Good evening, Sergeant Dunnigan. It's good to be back. The general has found suitable quarters, I see."

Dunnigan nodded. Still casting glances toward the back of the house, he said, "Yes, sir. Did you . . . expect to see the general tonight, sir?"

Lee watched the man's twitching face. He had seen Dunnigan weather more than one of Scott's outbursts, thought, He's been the focus of the general's anger perhaps once too often. Lee followed Dunnigan's glance, could see the outline of light around a wooden door.

"The general's office?"

"Yes, sir."

Lee studied the man's face again before speaking. "Have I come at a bad time, perhaps?"

"Well, sir, I expect there hasn't been a good time today. The general has been, uh, agitated. I don't make it a point to listen to the goings on back there, you understand, sir, but he's been meeting with some of the other big shots . . . uh, begging your pardon, sir. He's meeting with some of the commanders. Not sure how long it's gonna last."

There was a sudden burst of sound from behind the door, the loud angry voice of Scott: "If that rodent dares to show himself here, I want that sergeant out there to shoot him. I want many holes in that wormy little clerk!"

Lee looked at Dunnigan, who seemed even paler in the lamplight, and Dunnigan sat down, looked suddenly sick to his stomach. Lee thought, He doesn't seem like the type to shoot anybody. The sounds came again, other voices Lee could not hear clearly, then Scott again said, "I don't care, dammit! Major, send that letter tonight! The rest of you, get out of here!"

The door suddenly burst open, startling Lee, and he saw silhouettes coming down the hall, heard heavy boots on the wooden floor. Lee snapped to attention, saw faces now, Pillow, Twiggs, another officer Lee did not know, and a civilian, finely dressed. He saluted, watched them pass quickly by, ignoring him, and quickly they were out the door. He dropped his salute, glanced at Dunnigan, who asked, "You still want to see him, sir?"

Lee peered toward the light, said, "I must report. Excuse me, Sergeant."

He eased down the hall, softened the sounds of his boots on the hard floor, reached the open doorway, then the young Scott hurried out of the office, bumping Lee's arm. The young man said, "Oh! Sorry, Captain!" He was gone quickly, and Lee waited. Hearing nothing from Scott's office, he slowly stepped into the light.

Scott stood staring into the darkness through a closed window, and Lee glanced around the large room, thought, We're alone. Not sure this is a good idea . . .

Scott reached down, grabbed the handles along the bottom of the window, grunting heavily as he lifted, but the window would not budge.

"Damn!" He lifted again, still no movement from the window, and abruptly turned, red-faced, stared at Lee with furious eyes, said, "Somebody teach these Mexicans how to build a house!"

Lee waited for more, and Scott's expression seemed to go blank, the anger suddenly wiped away.

"Hello, Captain. Come in. Haven't seen you . . . Have you been away?"

Lee nodded, said, "Yes, sir. I was asked to accompany General Worth to Perote. Your orders, sir."

Scott shook his head, moved to the wide chair, sat down heavily. "Yes, yes, Worth. Of course. Glad you're back. I hope General Worth is comfortable in Perote. Not too many demons there for his liking?"

Lee had seen this kind of anger before in Scott, thought, Be careful. He has a strange way of remembering details. Just be grateful he's not angry at *you*.

"Sir, General Worth has secured Perote. I will make a full report, sir."

Scott stared down at the desk, clasped his hands together under his chin. Lee waited, and Scott said quietly, "Sit down, Captain. I'll hear about Worth later. You have any idea what's happening around here today?"

"No, sir. I just rode into town."

"Seems we have a visitor. The President has sent an emissary, a representative of our government, to begin discussing peace with Santa Anna. Would you assume, Mr. Lee, that someone charged with such an important role should bring some legitimacy, some experience, some diplomatic seasoning to this enormous task?"

Lee nodded, thought, He doesn't expect an answer. Scott put his hands on the desk, spread his fingers on the polished wood, slowly brought his fingers together into two great fists.

"*I* certainly would think so, Mr. Lee. Instead, they send a lackey, a clerk, excuse me, *chief clerk* of the State Department. Someone they can control and manipulate, someone who, if he succeeds, can be quickly pushed aside so the President can claim credit, and someone who, should he fail, is easily expendable. And on top of all of this . . ." Scott paused, and Lee could see the redness returning, the eyes glowing as though a hot fire were burning inside him. "On top of all this, they give this clerk the authority to overrule my command. He comes here with a piece of paper that authorizes him to stop all military activity if he happens to think it's a good idea!"

Lee waited, and there was a silent moment, so he said, "Sir, forgive me, but has General Santa Anna indicated he wants peace?"

Scott stared at Lee with a hot glare that made Lee sink into the chair.

"Of course not! Santa Anna is probably in Mexico City by now, trying to convince his people they should still try to stand up to us, telling them he's going to drive the godless *yanquis* into the sea! No, Mr. Lee, this idea, this concept that is so astounding in its stupidity, comes from Washington! And you know why? Because we have generals here who have so little respect for this command that they are sending frantic letters to Polk and Marcy telling them that we are in fact doomed to failure! We can't win! General Pillow . . ." Scott paused, clenched both fists, held them off the desk. Lee could see the whiteness of the knuckles, the slight quiver of his fists, as though the man's anger was boiling out into his two hands. Scott loosened his fingers from their grip, his hands settling onto the desk again, and growled, "*General Pillow* has even offered the most highly regarded opinion that it is *I* who cannot win!"

He looked at Lee again, his calm returning. "And so, Mr. Polk looks at Mr. Marcy and they wring their hands and say, 'We need peace! Quick, before it's too late!' "

Lee felt a wave of helplessness. "I don't understand why they feel . . . I mean, sir, we have won every major fight. How can they not believe the war is going in our favor?"

Scott leaned back in the chair, seemed to relax, his massive frame deflating slightly, and he said, "We have prevailed in every fight we have had. Hell, even Zachary Taylor won when he had to. Our greatest challenge has been bringing the Mexicans out to fight in the first place, and now there might not be enough of a Mexican army left to stop us at all. We came here with an untested army, with a crew of junior officers who have done everything to make their nation truly proud. But none of this matters in Washington, because, Mr. Lee, we are too damned far away. We are out here all alone without their valuable assistance. So, this clerk, this Mr. Trist, has come to rescue us, to prevent our certain destruction."

Scott closed his eyes, and Lee felt a growing frustration, his heart pounding, the heat rising in his face. What is the matter with those people, with Washington? Why don't they let this man do his job?

Scott opened his eyes, seemed suddenly very sad, said, "Mr. Lee, I have considered requesting my own recall, sending a letter to Secretary Marcy saying, 'Fine, you want Trist, or Pillow, or Thomas Hart Benton to run this war, fine, it's all yours.' "

"You can't do that, sir."

Scott let out a long breath. "No, Mr. Lee. I can't. I've been in this army for too long to just step aside, hand the reins to some incompetent fool. It took me years to work my way into this position, years of serving under old men who wore their uniforms because it made them look good at parties. When they gave me that first star, when President Madison signed the paper that made it official—*General* Winfield Scott—it was the proudest day of my life, Mr. Lee."

Scott paused, and Lee said, "Sir, this army is behind you. No one here believes you will fail. There must be some way to make them understand that we need a good commander, that this is a serious affair down here, men are dying for their country. This is not just some political game."

"All wars are political games, Mr. Lee. Winners and losers. Armies fight and men die, but it is the government who wins or loses. Mr. Polk wanted this war, and Mr. Santa Anna has obliged. And the army will fight it, and yes, Mr. Lee, men will die. It's the system. We play our roles. You have your duty, I have mine. I just wish they would allow me to perform mine."

Scott stood slowly, moved to the window again, grabbed the handles, gave a halfhearted pull.

"Been wrestling with this damned thing all day. This place could use some air. Gets stale in here."

Lee moved over to the window, said, "Allow me, sir?" He thumped the window along the bottom with the flat of a fist, then again across the top. "Try it now, sir."

Scott pulled, and the window suddenly opened, a rush of cool breeze flowing into the room. Lee backed away, thought, Maybe making it look so easy wasn't such a good idea, but Scott began to laugh. He moved back to his chair, sat down, still laughing, his face flushing again, but not in anger, something else, something Lee had rarely seen.

Lee sat as well and waited. He felt uncomfortable, watching Scott as the general put a hand on his broad stomach, shaking, his eyes filling with tears. Then Scott pounded the table, and the laughter began to ease. He shook his head, pulled out a handkerchief and wiped his eyes.

"Wonderful, Mr. Lee. Truly wonderful. All that is right with the world in one simple demonstration."

Lee looked at the window, thought, Right . . . with whose world?

Scott said, "You see? Cut right through it, didn't you? I fought that damned window all day, probably took a year off my life in simple aggravation. Just like everything else around here. All these commanders, all the gray-heads, and those fools in Washington. Instead of so many angry words, and so much posturing, leave it up to you, to the young men who have no other agenda, leave it up to you to cut through it all and simply get the job done. Reminds me of 1812, same thing I went through. Had to practically ignore orders, make my own plans, carry them out before some old fool had time to stop me. Dangerous practice for a military man, but I was right, I knew I was right."

He put the handkerchief away, shook his head, leaned back in the chair.

"And I'm right now, Mr. Lee. Any day now, reinforcements will arrive. Took me a while to learn about that, because the guerrillas killed one of our couriers. We don't have an effective communication line between here and Vera Cruz. With Patterson and the volunteers gone, even with the reinforcements, our strength here will barely reach ten thousand men. The plan is simple, has to be made simple in order to work. We don't have the luxury of maintaining a strong garrison at Vera Cruz and Jalapa. I'm bringing them all in. As soon as our new troops arrive, we're moving on, advancing the entire army to Puebla."

Lee considered for a moment what Scott was telling him. "Sir, we will have to fight for Puebla. It's a major city."

"Maybe. Not sure about that. It will give us a pretty clear message how much of an army Santa Anna has left. That's why we need every man."

Lee thought again for a moment, and Scott shouted, "Sergeant! You still awake?"

Dunnigan appeared quickly, seemed to shake slightly. "Right here, sir."

"Sergeant, go find my son-in-law. I need to send another letter."

Dunnigan was gone, and Lee said, "Sir, excuse me, but are you intending to pull away from the coast? That will cut off our communications—"

"By God you're right, Mr. Lee! That's just what I'm going to tell Washington. They ignore most of the letters I send them, but they won't ignore this one. Effective with the arrival of our additional strength, all units will report to headquarters, to resume our operations toward Mexico City. We will operate as one unit, with one base of supply, which will be wherever we happen to find ourselves. I believe we can sustain this army by keeping a good working relationship with the citizens."

Lee felt a growing sense of alarm, thought, This could be a mistake. A huge mistake.

"Sir, how will we receive orders? We must still answer to Washington."

Scott looked at him for a long moment, and Lee felt the pressure of the gaze. He sank back in his chair.

"You remember the orders I read to you, Captain," Scott said quietly. "The President's instructions? This operation will be run at my discretion. *Your* orders will come from right *here*. I need to know the right men are behind me, men I can count on to do their jobs. War is a good teacher, Mr. Lee, and I am a good student. I have already learned where to look when I want something done *right*. I don't expect that to change. Do you?"

Lee didn't know what to say, suddenly realized Scott was talking about *him*.

"No, sir. Certainly not, sir."

"Good. As soon as we are prepared, we are marching to Puebla, capturing and securing the city, and then we will make a final march to Mexico City. Santa Anna may be able to convince somebody to fight for him, but he knows by now what this army can do. He knows by now that we intend to whip him. By the time we reach Mexico City, the door could be wide open."

Lee remembered the old lessons in the textbooks. He recalled how Napoleon, marching on Moscow, created such an awful disaster.

Scott was still watching him. The older man leaned back in the chair, stared up, and Lee saw his lips moving, thought, He's putting it into words, what he intends to tell Washington. This could be . . . very bad. The name suddenly came to him, and he said, "Sir, what of Mr. Trist? The, uh . . . clerk?"

Scott looked at him again, said, "Mr. Trist has the authority to deal directly with Santa Anna. He should be pleased. I will deliver him there."

13. SCOTT

MAY TWENTY-EIGHTH

H E RODE UP A LONG HILL PAST SHOPS AND HOUSES, COULD
hear the line of people shouting his name, heard other shouts,
all in Spanish, but the message and the mood was clear. The
citizens of Puebla were as enthusiastic to welcome these invaders as the
farmers of the smaller villages.

He reached the crest of the hill and looked out over the city, its
rows of squat buildings and tall church steeples spread out as far as he
could see. He stopped the horse, the staff staying behind him, and he
focused on the spires of the main cathedral. He thought, This is a big
damned city. This would be like marching an army through New
York, or Philadelphia. How can anyone see us as much of a threat?
There's eighty thousand people here. We're a curiosity, something to
break up their routine, but after we leave, after this war is over, little
will change here. This is a city of merchants and trade, and of course,
that big damned cathedral.

Beyond the edge of the city, he could see his army's campsite,
which was beginning to grow again. The first of the reinforcements he
had fought and pleaded for had finally begun to arrive, a brigade of volunteers, commanded by General John Quitman, another older man, a
regal, dignified lawyer from Mississippi.

The advance from Perote to the city had encountered guerrillas,
but the fighting was brief and sporadic, and nothing the *banditos* did
could slow the Americans down. He had passed by some signs of a
fight in the smaller villages, some little more than a single house guarding a nameless crossroad. The guerrillas would make a stand, maybe
one good volley at the advancing column of blue, but the volley was
answered with horsemen, Harney's cavalry, and the guerrillas were

145

swept away, disappearing into the hills and deep brush beyond the highway.

The city itself had been undefended, and Scott had heard the calls from Worth, the urgent need for reinforcements, the need to attack the city with full force. But even Worth had to finally admit that Santa Anna simply had no strength, no great army to stop the American advance. And, in a city this size, there was nothing to focus on, no single target, nothing really for Worth's men to actually attack. When they realized Puebla was completely undefended, Worth had moved his troops into the city without firing a shot.

Scott rode again through a large open square, framed by an old cathedral and the office buildings of the local government. It was becoming his routine now, a bit of luxury, a relaxing ride through streets where there were no signs of the war, no hostile presence of any kind. Even the staffs of the local politicians made no show of protest, and he smiled at men in black suits as he passed the government buildings.

He had another fine home as his headquarters, having learned that to refuse would be an insult. There had even been grand estates offered to the others, the commanders who had always found a reason to criticize Scott's acceptance of the luxury. Now they had luxurious accommodations of their own, and suddenly there were no complaints.

H E HAD LED HIS STAFF THROUGH THE IMPRESSIVE ENTRANCE OF the grand cathedral, and finally saw the interior of the magnificent Gothic building that so dominated the city. He had been met with an escort, a small unsmiling man in a white robe, who led him in a slow procession, to the soft murmuring and ponderous rhythm of an organ. Scott followed closely behind the man, who motioned silently and guided him and his men to their seats, a long padded bench covered in a rich brocade that lined the tall stone wall. The soldiers stood there, remained standing, as the man backed away slowly. Scott saw relief on his face, thought, All right, see, we can do this without disrupting anything. We're not savages.

Scott glanced out over the gathering of worshipers, looked again at the man in the robe, who waited patiently, his face showing mild frustration. The man motioned discreetly toward the bench, and Scott thought, Yes, I suppose I should sit. He glanced out at the faces, all watching him, saw a mix of people, men and women, even children, some of the faces dark, the black hair and burnt skin of the Indians, others fairer-skinned with lighter hair. Beyond them he saw a mass of

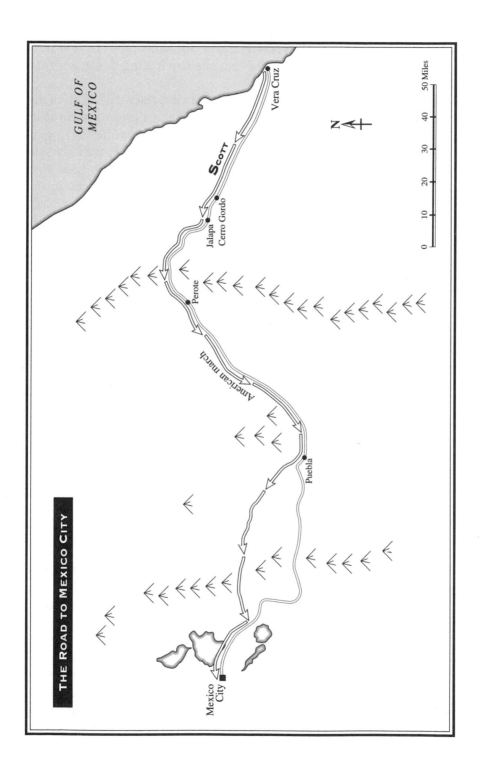

THE ROAD TO MEXICO CITY

GULF OF
MEXICO

Vera Cruz

Scott

Jalapa
Cerro Gordo

Perote

American march

Puebla

Mexico
City

N

0   10   20   30   40   50 Miles

blue. He was surprised to see the American soldiers, and the men were looking at him with wide eyes, seemed as uncomfortable as he was, as though they had all been suddenly caught participating in some forbidden activity.

He nodded at them, acknowledging their presence, and thought, They are not here because I am here. Not all of us are from the same background, not everyone in this army carries the annoying prejudice against the Catholics. I wonder, do they hide it, do they have to be discreet to attend the services here? Certainly they are here with permission. They must have sympathetic officers, or at least company commanders who have more enlightened views about religion. Still, it must be difficult for them, the few Catholics in a predominantly Protestant army.

A gracious and dignified committee of church elders had extended an invitation to the commanding general to attend a mass as a kind of welcome. It was certainly the same invitation that would be made to any military occupation. He had accepted gratefully. In fact, he had hoped for this from the first days in Vera Cruz, had hoped to satisfy his curiosity about the ceremony, the services, the devotion of these people. He would not simply arrive at his own convenience, march in, disruptive, and arrogantly assume that of course this commander of the *yanquis* would be welcome. The invitation had to come from the Mexicans, and now his original curiosity was replaced by something else—wonder. He sat and sensed the people's marvelous devotion, was impressed by the colorful formality and pageantry.

He glanced behind him and saw his son-in-law and the men who had come with him—some from the staff, a few higher-ranking officers. He looked for a brief moment at Lee, saw the engineer gazing upward, his attention captivated by the extraordinarily ornate decor, the stained glass and gold leaf, the vaulted ceiling and its flying buttresses. Scott looked up as well, and admired the richly colored mural on the ceiling, clouds and angels, a baby Jesus with his mother. The man in the robe was still waiting, and Scott saw an impatient frown, thought, Yes, all right, sorry, and finally he sat, and the other officers followed his lead, lined up along the soft bench.

The rich sounds of the organ filled the church, and he tried to look around, knew they were all watching him, thought, An extraordinary sound, marvelous. He saw a row of pipes, back behind the pulpit, could just see another man in white robes nearly hidden from view, seated, the man's head moving with the rhythm from the chords he played. Scott felt the wall behind him vibrating with the deeper tones, looked up again at the mural, thought, My God, the time, the effort, the craftsmanship. There is no doubting their devotion, the energy they give to their worship.

He saw motion behind the pulpit, and an old man emerged from a small doorway. He wore another of the flowing robes, this one white satin, lined with purple and gold. The old man moved slowly forward, climbed the short steps to the pulpit, looked across the crowded church, then turned and focused briefly on him. Scott nodded, smiled politely, thought, obviously he's the head man, but the priest seemed not to have noticed, looked again at his congregation. Scott was still smiling as he waited for the priest to acknowledge him, but the old man stared quietly out across the faces of the people. Scott's eyes followed the other man's gaze, and he observed that the faces were now all watching the priest. Yes, he thought, if you had any doubts before, now it is very clear. This man is the power in this place, not you, not the glorious blue uniform. That old priest carries more authority in this city than the politicians.

He looked at the grim stare of the priest, his unchanging expression. The man seemed to be waiting for the music to finish, and Scott thought, I have seen that look before, the confidence, the strength. He knows his place here, he understands better than we do where the people place their faith, their loyalty. The end of this war might come from them, after all, not the generals, not the armies. He glanced across to the far wall, the windows filled with the bright colors of the stained glass. This is what holds these people together, and no one, not Santa Anna, not us, can pull these people away from the power of this place. We had better take a lesson from this.

The small man in the white robe was moving toward him, held a tall thin candle in one hand, stopped, bowed slightly, handed Scott the candle. The general looked at the small flame, thought, I suppose . . . pass it down. He held the candle to the side, and the young Scott hesitated, made a small sound of protest, but Scott still held the candle out, thought, Take it, dammit. Surely there are more. Now the young man reached out, accepted the candle, and Scott saw the man in the robe frown, shake his head, and Scott thought, I did something wrong. Well, dammit, nobody told me.

The man backed away, quickly returned with another large candle, held it out to him, and Scott took it, thought, All right, hold on to this one. The man watched him for a moment, seemed to scold him silently, and Scott nodded, Yes, yes, I'll keep this one. Now there were more candles, and soon each of the officers held one, and Scott saw the others were all smaller, shorter. He looked at the tall candle in his hand. Yes, now I understand. I get the *big* one. All they had to do was tell me.

H E HAD TAKEN DINNER IN HIS OFFICE. HE HAD COME AWAY from the church service in a strange mood, did not want company, had no patience for the chatter from his staff. He had understood almost nothing of the priest's words, the Latin rolling over him with the rhythm of a song, a very long song. He had picked out a word or two, the ones similar to English, but it was frustrating, and so he focused on the sea of faces, all captured by the old man's words.

He knew there had been some mention of the war, since the priest pointed at him once, but still the old man had not looked at him, would not acknowledge the presence of this special visitor. That was . . . unusual, he thought. But it's my own damned fault. I expected . . . what? A ceremony, some grand show of thanks for gracing their service with my presence? I thought it would be a good thing, show the people we are sympathetic to their ways. They were certainly polite in making an effort to welcome us, but certainly they would have done just fine whether we were invited or not. Maybe that's the point, they have been doing just fine without all of us, without this war, without Santa Anna. We are, after all, temporary. This war will end, and it really doesn't matter to them who wins, or who sets up shop in Mexico City. Those people will still go to that church and listen to that old priest, and there will be change if *he* tells them to change. They're kind to us because we're here, and maybe they even see us as a threat, so they are gracious and polite and avoid trouble until we go away.

If Santa Anna marches through here, they'll probably be just as kind to him, and so, of course, he believes his people are behind him. He looked at the grilled slab of meat on his plate, felt the hunger rolling inside him, thought, I don't care for being reminded of this. In the end, what this army does, what I do, really doesn't matter much. I don't care for that at all.

His office was on the second floor of a marvelous old *hacienda*, another politician's show of grand wealth. He had become used to that now, had always been used to it back home, the old Virginia estates, always some requirement for political power. He stabbed at the meat, stuffed a juicy bite into his mouth, the glorious flavor of the smoke and fire. He nodded, thought, This is wonderful. Or perhaps a bit decadent, a feast reserved for conquerors. Yes, they are kind indeed.

The meat had come from a local rancher, and Scott accepted graciously. He had come to believe that these people did not offer their gifts out of fear, or the need to placate their invaders. They seemed proud and brought all manner of food and other gifts to the soldiers, as though perhaps they hoped the Americans might never leave. We have been seduced, he thought. We want to believe we have been carried here on some kind of wave of righteousness, spreading our superior morality, our God-given politics to the ignorant. We may be very wrong about that.

He set the fork down, stared at the plate, thought of the rancher, the small man in the formal suit who brought a huge, beautiful roast. The man seemed grateful that he had accepted, and Scott laughed now, thinking of the priest. Did this come from you, old man? Have you told your people to feed us well, flatter us with offerings? Surely they understand destiny as well as Washington does. These people have suffered the indignation of conquest and brutality, and somehow, despite whatever Santa Anna tells them, they must see us for what we represent. Even people who have never had true freedom must have some idea, some powerful instinct, for what it means.

The class system here is just as it has always been in Europe, and the leaders all believe that the mass of people at the bottom simply don't know anything, have no idea how to take care of themselves, must be disciplined and led by a strong hand. But they're wrong, have always been wrong, and if the *people* begin to understand that the power is *theirs*, that their numbers alone are a power that puts fear into the dictators and kings, then . . . change happens, and dictators become just as vulnerable as the people they hold down. Even that priest must understand this. And maybe he understands it all too well. Maybe we're a threat to his power as well.

He picked up a piece of hard black bread, held it in his hand, stared out a wide window, could see a church steeple nearby, thought, How can these people be inspired by a man like Santa Anna? He tried to picture the Mexican commander, was not sure just what he looked like, how he might stand at the head of his few remaining troops, what his speeches, his calls to the fight, might sound like. He thought, Whatever he does . . . it worked for a while. He mobilized an army. He might still make a war against us, still convince some of these people to fight us. But in the end we will win. We *have* to.

He laughed at himself. Yes, old man, you are well trained. This is one argument you do not have with Washington. You believe you are doing the right thing, that this is a just war, a necessary war, all the things a good soldier must accept with absolute certainty. And all of that is reinforced by these Mexicans, by their graciousness and their smiles, and their wonderful food. But Santa Anna has had some good soldiers too, and they believe something very different. We cannot be too confident. There may still be a fight to be had.

He thought of Trist, who had been with the army for weeks but had not yet met with him. Instead, Trist sent a series of letters, each one angering him even more. He's still just a damned clerk, Scott thought. He doesn't think there's a fight anymore, but no matter how much power he believes they gave him, this is my army, and my war.

He knew Trist had begun to correspond with foreigners in Mexico City, mainly the British representatives. He was angry that Trist had tried to reach the Mexican government as though this was just some argument to be solved by flowery words. Scott looked past his plate, saw a letter on his desk, the latest report of Trist's efforts, and he saw a round blot of brown juice on the paper, a careless spill from his dinner. He wiped at the juice, the ink beneath it smearing, thought, Yes, you damned fool, that's how significant your letters are, how effective your strategy. Wipe it away with my thumb.

He backed the chair away from the desk, stood, lay his napkin across the plate, saw Sergeant Dunnigan moving slowly into the room.

Scott said, "You been watching me, Sergeant? Not necessary to hover over me like some damned vulture."

Dunnigan shook his head. "Oh, no sir. I just thought you'd want me to remove your plate quickly. Sorry, sir."

Dunnigan seemed frozen to one spot, and Scott thought, How did he get this job? Scott said, "Take the plate, Sergeant. I won't bite you."

Dunnigan moved quickly, swept the plate and silver away in one motion. Backing toward the door, he said, "I hope you enjoyed the veal, sir. The rancher was particularly proud—"

"*Veal?*" Scott glared at the sergeant, felt his stomach turn. "That meat was *veal?*"

Dunnigan seemed stunned, nodded slowly, backed away as though expecting Scott to shoot him. "Yes, sir. I thought you knew that, sir."

Scott put a hand on his stomach, turned away, moved to the wide window, said, "Damn. Wish I didn't know. Try never to eat the stuff. Can't stand the idea. Horrible, barbaric. Baby cows."

Dunnigan paused at the door, said, "I am terribly sorry, sir. I will be certain no more veal is served at headquarters, sir. I will tell the cooks. . . ."

Scott turned, thought, Good God, he's going to cry. He pointed out the door, said, "Never mind the cooks, Sergeant. It's all right. You are dismissed."

Dunnigan was quickly gone, and Scott looked again at the window, said aloud, "Actually, if he just wouldn't tell me, we should have it again. I rather enjoyed it."

JULY FIFTEENTH

The rides through the city were becoming monotonous now, the routine an annoyance to endure, just as the fleas had once been. The weeks dragged on and the army was still not prepared to move. Scott knew that he was still at the mercy of Washington, the paperwork and the slow arrival of the ships that brought reinforcements to his army. When the calendars told them it was July Fourth, Independence Day, there had been a subdued celebration, nothing with the pageantry and energy the men would have enjoyed back home. The army was after all on foreign soil, held in place by forces they could not control, and few felt independent at all.

TRIST MOVED SLOWLY, SEEMED TO BEND EVERY JOINT IN HIS BODY as he walked into the office. Scott sat, watched him carefully, thought, A stiff wind could do damage to that man. He pointed to the chair, said, "There, Mr. Trist."

Trist seemed grateful, moved to the chair, paused, said, "Excuse me, General, but since this is our first meeting . . ." He held out his pale right hand, which quivered like a fragile old man's. "Sir, I am delighted to meet you. It is an honor."

Scott tilted his head, looked up at the man's sickly complexion, expected to see a patronizing smirk, the same kind of oily smile he always received from Gideon Pillow. But Trist was watching him patiently, his thin face almost sorrowful.

Scott said, "By God, you're serious." He pulled himself slowly up out of the chair, reached out, engulfed Trist's hand with his own, and Trist nodded his head repeatedly while saying, "Thank you, sir. I had thought . . . you might not have appreciated my meaning."

Scott motioned to the chair again, and both men sat, and Scott said, "You are right about that, sir. I haven't appreciated much of anything you've tried to do since you've been here. In fact, as long as Washington refuses to offer much support to this army, my attitude is entirely justified. Or, would you disagree?"

Trist looked down, stared at his hands, flexed his fingers, said, "My authorization, the orders you were sent regarding my authority . . ." Trist paused, and Scott thought, Of course, here it comes, pulling rank, reminding me just how much power he has. Trist said, "General Scott, I feel I have been misunderstood. I have no intention of telling you how to run this war. I feel the Secretary's letter is confusing, and quite possibly overstates my responsibility. I do not believe that Washington expects me to come down here and single-handedly end the war."

Scott leaned forward, said, "Well, Mr. Trist, so far we are in agreement. Continue."

"Sir, I have begun to make some overtures to the Mexican government."

"Yes, I know. The British, I believe."

"Yes, of course. The British are motivated to see this war concluded. I believe they are concerned that if we tend to pursue a policy of aggression anytime we have a border dispute, this may eventually mean a war with *them*. Despite our rather, um, shaky history, it is clear that the British would rather be our ally than our enemy. To that end, they have gone to some lengths to get assurances that the Mexican Congress can be persuaded to accept our terms. We have been told that with the careful . . . with the discreet application of the money I am authorized to spend, key individuals in the Mexican government will agree to a cessation of fighting."

Scott stared deeply into Trist's eyes, and Trist seemed to flinch. Scott felt a flood of heat spreading up the back of his neck, the weeks of simmering anger boiling into an explosion. He clenched his jaw to hold the fire inside. He spoke with a barely tempered ferocity, "Mr. Trist, are you telling me that you intend to end this war by bribing the Mexican government to stop fighting?"

Trist's face suddenly changed, and Scott saw a smile. Trist nodded. "I know. It sounds rather . . . outrageous. Please let me explain, sir. The Secretary has authorized me to distribute as much as three million dollars—"

Scott suddenly coughed, grunted, and a low sound rolled up again from deep inside. *"Three million dollars?"*

Trist nodded again, said, "Please, sir, let me explain. The British have received encouraging reports from some of the Mexican officials. The request has been made with some enthusiasm that we proceed with the transfer of funds. Even though my orders seem to give me the authority to proceed on my own, I admit I am uncomfortable. I cannot make such an arrangement without your permission, or your support."

Scott sat back, looked at the ceiling, his eyes following the lines of a delicate painting that swirled around the small copper chandelier. He suddenly felt like laughing, thought, This is truly amazing. All of them, Washington, perhaps the whole world, they're all going mad.

"Mr. Trist, do you know how much three million dollars will buy? For starters, that's exactly how much President Jefferson paid for the whole damned Louisiana Territory."

Trist nodded slowly. "Oh, yes, I know, sir."

"Even if Washington believes ending this war is worth that kind of money, do the British believe that these cooperative individuals include General Santa Anna?"

"Oh, quite so, sir. The word is that the general is eager to accept our proposal. I have communicated with his representative myself."

Scott closed his eyes, took a deep breath, looked at the still smiling Trist. "Santa Anna is willing to take your money. And in return he assures you he will surrender."

"That's what we are being told, sir."

"And Washington thinks this is a good idea?"

"Don't you, sir?" Trist paused, the smile gone, and he looked down, said, "General Scott, may I speak frankly?"

"At any time, Mr. Trist."

"Sir, if we can end this war by making a payment to the Mexican authorities, is that not a better way than the loss of lives? Is not three million dollars a good deal less than what this war is costing us to fight?" He paused, looked up again at Scott. "Sir, I am not a politician. I have no political agenda. If the war can be brought to an end, I am not concerned with what my reputation might be, or what the President will say. I am more concerned what it will mean to your men, and to our country. And . . . I am *authorized* to secure funds from the Treasury, and even, sir, from you."

Scott was surprised, said, "Noble of you, Mr. Trist. I'm not terribly accustomed to selfless motives around here. However, I'm also very doubtful that anyone in Mexico City will take your money and then tell their people they have lost a war without at least defending their capital, and oh by the way, now they are very rich. I doubt seriously that any of Santa Anna's share will end up benefiting the public good."

Trist nodded slowly. "Sir, my contacts with the British, and with the Mexican authorities, have been most encouraging. I understand there are risks, but this plan has the blessing of the President."

"I have no doubt of that, Mr. Trist. The President has no faith at all that I can actually win this war by fighting it. That is, after all, why he sent you down here in the first place."

"Please, General, do not judge me harshly. I am beginning to suspect that Washington, that perhaps even the President, is not in the best position to know what is happening down here. Frankly, sir, since I have been here, I have been impressed with the spirit of this army. They are certainly willing to make a fight. But, would it not be better to avoid one?"

Scott leaned back, folded his arms across his chest. "Tell you what, Mr. Trist. I'll agree to this plan, I'll even provide funds for part of this payment. But first I want to see a signed peace treaty. I want to see General Santa Anna's signature on a piece of paper. If he does that, it will be hard for him to change his mind. Your friends the British would have a serious problem if he did."

Trist smiled again, said, "Thank you, sir. That is the most I can ask for."

"And, after all, Mr. Trist, this will please the President. General Pillow can write him now that I have seen the light, that I have come around to Washington's way of thinking. I should caution you, however . . ." He paused, leaned forward, stared hard at Trist. "The war is not yet over. This army has been promised another column of reinforcements very soon. Once they arrive, we will begin the march to Mexico City. You may continue your talks however you wish, with one very important condition. You are traveling with this army now, and despite whatever your damned papers say, you are under my command. This is still a war, and this army will continue to operate accordingly. That means you will not discuss our operations, our troop movements, or our strategy with either the British or the Mexicans. Do you understand the definition of *treason*?"

"I understand it very well, sir."

"Good. Now, assuming we occupy Mexico City, we will likely need you to negotiate a treaty, whether we have to pay for it or not. My feeling is that there will only be peace when Santa Anna is utterly defeated and we have occupied their capital. *That's* how wars are concluded, Mr. Trist. You don't buy peace at a marketplace."

14. LEE

AUGUST EIGHTH

THE REINFORCEMENTS CAME IN SLOWLY, SOMETIMES ONLY A single company, or part of a regiment. But then the larger columns began to arrive, complete with the blessed wagons and fresh horses, and by the first week of August the army could count over ten thousand men fit for service. To the regulars, already veterans of this fight, the frustration of the wait was finally over.

With Patterson and the volunteers already on the boats carrying them home, the army was now organized into four regular divisions, two commanded as before by Worth and Twiggs, but in Patterson's absence, seniority fell to Gideon Pillow, and the other senior commander, John Quitman. The advance was to be staggered, Twiggs in the lead, the others following with only a few miles between each division. The guerrillas could still be a problem, but now, with a contingent of marines, and the uniting of the cavalry patrols that had been scattered along the road to Vera Cruz, all the army's strength could be put forward.

LEE WAS ON FOOT AS HE MOVED QUICKLY DOWN THE NARROW shadowy street, the faint first rays of daylight blocked by the tall homes. The army camps were spread throughout the city, and as long as there was no threat from Santa Anna, there had been no need for urgency, for keeping the men billeted together. The urgency had been more in keeping the men busy, avoiding the boredom and monotony that might cause discipline problems. For weeks now the troops had spent most of the daylight hours enduring the routine of drill, units gathered in every open square to practice the precision for fighting a battle that some were beginning to believe might never come.

As the weeks passed and the fresh troops arrived, the drills took on more meaning, and even the bored veterans felt a new energy when the word came down that finally the army might begin to move.

Lee could hear the voices beyond the dark street, the sound of a bugle. He quickened his pace, taking long strides over thick cobblestones. He passed a group of small children, boys with black hair, emerging from the narrow space between two stone houses. He could not hold back the smile, laughed as they marched in line with long sticks on their shoulders, one boy saluting him. Lee stopped, returned the salute, saw the young dark eyes examining his uniform, saw all the eyes focused on the pistol in his belt. He had a sudden uneasy feeling, thought, What do *you* know of Santa Anna? He heard the blast from a bugle again, thought, No time for this, said, "As you were, soldiers."

Ahead of him was brighter daylight, more voices, commands from drill instructors, more short blasts from bugles. He passed a wagon spilling over with colorful blankets and an old man who smiled at him and reached up to unroll a dark red blanket. The man nodded cheerfully, trying silently to convince Lee that the thick wool was truly a blessed bargain.

Lee smiled, shook his head, said, "No, *gracias.*"

There is no time for shopping, not today. He kept moving, could see the street opening up now into a wide square. The soldiers were lined up in thick rows, muskets on their shoulders. Lee saw the flag, the Fourth, one of Worth's regiments. Across the square another line of troops stood, others were marching in a tight formation, drilling. The troops close by were turning in line now, and Lee saw the officers in charge, one tall in the saddle, thin, unmistakably a veteran's face, the other a small man with a thick dark beard. The shorter man was shouting something, pointing to a mistake, a small collision near the end of the line. Lee smiled, thought of West Point, the drilling and marching and formations that became a part of every cadet. He looked again at the smaller officer, thought, Definitely young, probably a recent graduate.

He saw more officers on horseback, across the square, thought, The brass, I should check with them, ask someone there. He began to move again, tried to slip unnoticed by the frustrated officers, the jumble of troops now straightening out by the forceful pulls and tugs from the hands of profane sergeants. The younger officer turned, glared at Lee, and quickly the man's face seemed to soften.

Lee nodded and said, "Sorry. Don't mean to interrupt."

The man tipped his hat, and now one of the senior officers was riding quickly toward them, the horse's hooves clicking across the uneven stones of the street. Lee saw a colonel, the face familiar, and the man yelled, "Lieutenant Grant! Spend more time on your instruction and less on chatting with visitors! This is the infantry, mister, not your comfortable quartermaster post!"

The officer saluted, said, "Yes, sir. Sorry, Colonel Clarke."

Lee was embarrassed, thought, Wrong place for me to be. He waited for the colonel to ride closer, prepared his own apology, but the man turned abruptly, rode back toward the other horsemen. Lee began to walk again, glanced toward the back of the young lieutenant, both of the officers purposely ignoring him.

He said quietly, "My apologies, gentlemen, Lieutenant, uh . . . Grant. Please continue. Pay me no mind."

He moved past the end of the line of troops, heard more orders, another call to formation, more profanity from the sergeants. There is an edge now, he thought, an urgency. This is not like the past few weeks. They are not just filling the time. They know the wait is over.

He moved closer to the group of officers, saw Worth now, watching him, tense, frowning. Worth said, "Didn't expect to see you, Captain. Thought you'd be on the march."

Lee saluted, said, "We're pulling out shortly, sir. Sorry to intrude on your drill. Not their fault, sir." Lee looked at the grim faces all watching him now, and then, one smile, the small man easing forward on the tall horse.

Lee nodded quickly, then said, "General Worth, with your permission, I was hoping for a brief moment with Captain Johnston."

Worth was watching the drill again, made a motion with his hand, said, "Yes, yes, of course. Make it quick, Mr. Lee."

Lee moved toward the side of the horses, saw Johnston dismount, and Johnston said quietly, "What are you doing here? Where's your horse?"

Lee glanced at Johnston's arm, said, "Couldn't leave without at least making sure you didn't hurt yourself again. The horse threw a shoe this morning. He's being attended to."

"Thought General Twiggs was supposed to be gone already. They waiting on you just so you could make a social call? Sounds like you're holding up the war, Captain. General Twiggs will have your head."

Lee smiled, said, "All right, Joe. Social call over. You're right, I had better get back." He paused, looked again at the arm, said, "You all right?"

"You writing home to my mother, Captain?" Johnston laughed.

Lee looked down, felt embarrassed again, said, "Sorry, Joe. I just wanted to be sure. . . ."

Johnston reached out, put a hand on his shoulder, and Lee felt awkward. He wanted to pull away, thought, This is ridiculous. You shouldn't have come here.

Now Worth said, "This isn't some gathering for the general staff. Captain Johnston, if you intend to lead infantry in this army, you will pay more attention to drill and less to socializing! Captain Lee, don't you have somewhere to be?"

Johnston was looking at Lee, said aloud, "Right away, sir!" He nodded, said quietly, "Thank you, Robert. Get going, before we're both in trouble. Keep your head down. No more heroics."

Lee wanted to say something, watched Johnston move to the horse, climb up, saw a small grimace cross Johnston's face.

He saluted Worth, said, "With your permission, sir."

Worth returned the salute without looking at him, said nothing, and Lee moved quickly away. He walked back near the drilling troops, heard Lieutenant Grant shout an order, saw the troops suddenly wheel about in perfect precision, the muskets moving in rhythm, the men now standing at rigid attention. Grant did not look at him, and Lee slipped back down the narrow street, thought again of West Point, the impatient grumbling from exhausted young men who endured the marching and formation because they had to. They understand now, he thought, the drills, the discipline. Now, we're an army.

AUGUST TENTH

The road wound up through the mountains, an endless snaking trail of rocks and potholes, and no one still called it a highway. Lee rode back behind the staff and the flag bearers. He had learned quickly what they all knew, that Twiggs did not want company. There would be no quiet conversation. He could see Twiggs up front, tall in the saddle, staring ahead, and Lee thought, What goes through his mind? What must it be like for the veterans, the men who have seen so much of this? We march behind him, and have no idea what is up there beyond those mountains. He knows as little as we do, but he stares ahead like it's all been done before, as though there are no surprises. Even General Scott believes this is simple, just march to the capital and show them the strength, the guns, and the war is over. He thought of Worth now, back in the square drilling his troops. He was nervous, that was obvious. But . . . he's always nervous, and General Scott has no patience for it. Maybe this is a good time to be nervous.

He felt a sudden chill, a sharp breeze blowing right into his coat. He looked out toward a tall ragged hill, then beyond, great pointed mountains, their peaks covered in snow. *August,* he thought. They call these mountains the *Rio Frio,* Cold River. The snow never completely melts. These hills look the same as they did when Cortez came through here, maybe that same patch of snow. He looked at Twiggs again, thought, Was Cortez like that, matter-of-fact, march straight into the fight? He had to be, I suppose. He knew far less than we do about what's up ahead. He had to believe God was with him, protecting his men. We're not so different after all.

THE AIR WAS MUCH COOLER NOW, AND LEE PULLED HIS COAT tightly around him. He kept his head down and stared at the mane of the horse, rocking with the slow rhythm of the march. They had moved uphill all day, still twisting around the sharp hills, the road even worse as the climb took them higher. The green of the farms was gone now, the land barren, gray, the vegetation in small clumps, short thick brush that hugged the cold rocks. There were few civilians now as well, a handful on horseback, men leading mules packed high with supplies, some for trade, some for survival, all standing aside patiently while this foreign army marched through their rugged and angry terrain.

Behind him the division had begun to spread out, and so the march had to slow, allow the men on foot to keep pace, prevent anyone from falling out. Even in the tall hills there would be bandits or guerrillas, following the army at a distance. But the sergeants were quiet, and even the men with the sorest feet, the weakest legs, did not have to be told that there could be no stragglers. Far out in front, Harney's cavalry patrol slipped around and through the ragged rocks, ready for the sudden assault, prepared for some attempt from Santa Anna to slow down the march. Lee had listened for it, the sudden flurry of muskets, but the only sounds were soft, the great rocks swept by the faint howl of cold wind, and the rhythmic clatter of tin cups and boot steps from the silent march of three thousand men.

There was a sudden calm, a brief respite from the chilling breeze. He sat up straight, flexed his shoulders to ease his tense muscles. He turned slowly to one side, when he heard a voice. He turned toward the front and saw Twiggs holding up his arm. The staff seemed to jump to attention, some men clearly waking up in the saddle, and from others a murmur of low voices. Lee kept watching Twiggs, saw him turn around, the first time all day he had seen his face. Twiggs glanced back at Lee, then looked at the men close behind him, said, "Order the march to halt. Only a moment."

A bugle sounded beside Lee, and behind he could hear another, and another farther away down the line. He still looked at Twiggs, thought, What is it, why stop? Twiggs stared to the front again, spurred his horse, began to move forward , and Lee thought, Where's he going? He's alone. He moved up beside the staff officers, stopped next to an aide, a young man with a short red beard.

Lee quietly asked, "What's he doing?"

The young man shook his head, said, "No idea. Looks like the road curves around that hill, then maybe falls away." Lee saw Twiggs ride into the curve of the road before he stopped. He seemed to stare ahead, sitting motionless for a long minute. Lee wanted to say something to the aide, but the man seemed to understand and said, "Captain, if you want to go up there and ask him, it's fine by me."

Lee moved the horse forward, stopped near the front of the column, beside the man with the flag. Twiggs turned, looked back at the men, said, "At ease. Take a moment, gentlemen."

The staff began to spread along the side of the road, some dismounting, briefly expressing their relief. Other men already started looking for someplace to stretch out on the cold ground. Lee still looked at Twiggs, thought, This is odd, there's plenty of light left. Surely this is no place to make camp. He spurred the horse, moved away from the staff, thought, If he doesn't want company . . . he can tell me. I have to see. He moved up close to Twiggs, moved around the curve in the road, came out of the shadows, and suddenly stopped the horse, stared out to the west, looked up toward the sudden glare of the setting sun.

Beyond the last of the great mountains the ground fell away in a wide sweep, the road snaking away below into a vast plain. Lee could see patches of all shades of green, a scattering of farms and open fields dotted with brown and black, great herds of cattle and horses. Beyond them wide splashes of silver, reflecting the sunlight, a patchwork of shallow lakes, surrounded by grassy marshes. He tried to focus through the sharp sunlight, put his hand up to his brow. He could see strange shapes now, far across the wide valley, more mountains, great conical shapes and jagged points far in the distance, cutting into the harsh glare of the sun. The shadows were already beginning to spread across the valley, and now, beyond the farms, the fields and lakes, he could see a mass of darkness.

He remembered his field glasses and reached into the saddlebag, felt blindly through the cold leather, still staring out into the valley. When the glasses were in his hand, he raised them up and looked at the dark mass. The shapes came into focus, first the tall steeples riding on a vast sea of churches. He scanned, thought, Dozens . . . no, hundreds. Now he could make out the larger buildings, and around it all, a solid line of gray, a wall, like Vera Cruz, another fat stone wall. He stared for a long moment, felt his heart beating furiously in his chest. His excitement rising, he felt suddenly like laughing. He glanced at Twiggs, saw the stern face staring out across the amazing sight, the sunlight reflected on the old man's ragged skin. Lee saw now there were tears on Twiggs's cheeks. The old man did not look at him as he said quietly, "I have waited for this moment. I shall never forget this sight, Captain. The valley of Mexico. *Anahuac.* Out there, that gray mass. That is Mexico City."

Lee felt something turn in his chest, looked again through the glasses, felt uncomfortable, thought, This is strange, an intrusion into some very private place. Maybe I shouldn't be here. He was right to be out here alone. This means something to him, and it's not for me to ask.

"Forgive me, sir. I didn't mean to intrude."

Twiggs stared ahead, said, "There are a few places on this earth a man was meant to see. One reason I became a soldier. Always thought the army gave you a chance to travel. Until now, didn't work out that way. Nothing like this in Georgia." He glanced at Lee now, said, "My home."

Lee didn't know what to say, had never heard Twiggs talk about anything but the fight. "Yes, sir. I'm from Virginia."

Twiggs sat silently for a moment, and Lee shook his head, thought, He could certainly not care about that. Twiggs said, "The Shenandoah Valley?"

"Uh, no, sir. East."

"The Shenandoah Valley, Captain. That's another place you should see. Maybe not quite like this."

"Yes, sir. The Shenandoah is a wonderful place."

He still felt awkward, knew no one would believe him, especially not Johnston. Joe, he thought, you should be here, listening to General Twiggs. He could imagine the junior officers making their jokes, commenting rudely about the commanders, making fun of the odd traits,

even Scott's bluster and profanity, the nickname "Old Fuss and Feathers." Lee stared out ahead, watched the sun moving lower into the far
distant mountains, thought, No, let this be. There is no need for you to
speak of a moment like this, no matter how people talk of General
Twiggs. They have their jokes. Judge a man by more than that.

Twiggs sat silently for a moment, then said quietly, "You have
something to do, Captain?"

Lee thought, No, not really . . . well, yes, of course. Time to
move away, leave him alone. "Yes, sir. Forgive the intrusion, I'll move
back to the men."

"I mean your *duty*, Captain. Reconnaissance, scouting the enemy's position. General Scott will rely on *you* to tell him what we need
to know. Our success may hinge on what you observe."

Lee looked again toward the wide shadows spreading over the valley, said, "Yes, sir. Thank you, sir."

"Don't thank me, thank Santa Anna. He let us march this far
without doing anything to stop us. It was either a clever strategy or a
stupid mistake. The farther we are from our base of supply on the
coast, the more vulnerable we are. That could be his plan. If he doesn't
have sufficient defense to protect the city, then allowing us to advance
could be his mistake. General Scott has no patience for the unknown. I
suggest you find out what Santa Anna has in mind."

Lee felt his throat tighten, said quietly, "Yes, sir. Of course."

His mind began churning, thoughts of the new plan, the reconnaissance. Lee thought, He's right. General Scott has said it. He will
rely on me. The scouting will have to be complete and thorough and
there can be no mistakes. We must find out what is truly in front of us.
He gazed across the vast valley and thought of Cortez again. Yes, he
must have seen this. And if he did not pause, did not admire this, it was
a mistake. Lee put the glasses down, saw the sun settling low into the
great faraway mountains. General Twiggs is right, this is a glorious
place. And we must find out if they intend to fight for it.

PART THREE
INTO THE
VALLEY

ANTONIO LOPEZ DE SANTA ANNA.

15. LEE

AUGUST TWELFTH

H̲E SLIPPED THROUGH TALL GRASS, THE GROUND SOFT UNDER HIS feet, his boots already coated with the mud of the boggy marsh. Behind him the horse soldiers, his escort and protection, were pushing up close, waiting for him to point the way.

There was no need to maintain the kind of stealth they had employed at Cerro Gordo. Santa Anna knew where Scott's army had camped, and Scott had suspected that the scouting parties might be attacked by Santa Anna's cavalry, still a strong and dangerous force. But Lee could not just stand in the open, ride his horse straight up to the positions he was to observe. Here, the roads were high and straight and exposed to any kind of fire the Mexicans might offer. The land had once simply been a vast lake, drained of water by nature, and then by man. There were smaller lakes still, serving as a natural barrier to the city, and where the roads crossed, the ground beside them was deep in grass and mud. It was a difficult place to advance an army, and Lee understood the scouting would have to be precise, knew he would have to move up as close as the enemy would allow.

Lee's escort was led by one of Harney's men, a gruff and profane major named Thorsby. Thorsby had insisted the horsemen stay up on the road, in formation, clearly visible to the outposts that Lee was trying to observe. But Lee was in command, and the horses had been left behind, and despite Thorsby's grumbling, his men had followed Lee down into the marsh.

Turning and peering through the tops of the reeds, Lee looked for Thorsby, thinking, He does not seem to understand. We do not want a confrontation, not here. We don't need to have a squad of their cavalry riding down our throats.

He saw the faces of Thorsby's men, watching him with simmering disgust, their feet as wet and muddy as his. He nodded to them, thought, Sorry, gentlemen. The cavalry does not get *all* the good jobs. He also saw Thorsby, pushing through a tall patch of grass, slapping at insects with his hat. Thorsby pushed aside a man, who stumbled and fell to his knees.

Thorsby ignored him, moved up close to Lee, spoke in an angry hiss, "How much farther, Captain? You comfortable down here in this damned swamp?"

Lee stared at the man, ignored his dark anger for the moment, said nothing. Orders, Major, he thought, you have orders. I shouldn't have to argue with you.

"Major Thorsby, we will proceed below the road until I can observe that village up ahead. We might be very close to the enemy, and I need to determine what kind of enemy we are facing. Do you understand that General Scott might very well use this route to make his assault on the city?"

"Captain, General Scott will not march his men through the mud. It would take them until Christmas to even find the enemy in this mess."

Lee turned, looked out over the grass in front of him and a distant line of low adobe houses. He raised his field glasses, looked for a moment, then said, "Major, we will advance as ordered. Have your men follow me."

Thorsby said nothing, and Lee could hear the men spreading out behind him, moving up on either side. Good, he thought, he may not like this, but he does remember his orders. He looked back, saw Thorsby pushing his way to one side, heard a low mumble, some comment about West Point. Lee took a deep breath, thought, Let's keep moving. We have work to do.

T HE MOST DIRECT ROUTE TO THE CITY WOULD TAKE SCOTT'S army straight into the eastern gates, and Lee had been assigned the job of feeling out the route and the Mexican strength that might occupy it.

Below, on the roads leading to the south of the city, other scouting parties were at work as well, slipping discreetly beside the raised roadways as he was, the only way to make a close observation without coming under fire from the cannon that Lee still expected to find.

The grass was still wet, taller now, and he could hear curses as the

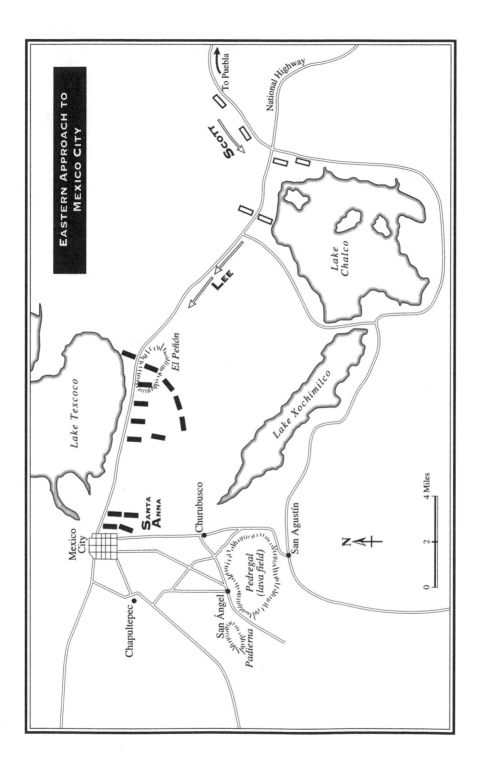

EASTERN APPROACH TO
MEXICO CITY

To Puebla

National Highway

SCOTT

LEE

Lake Chalco

El Peñón

Lake Texcoco

Lake Xochimilco

SANTA
ANNA

Mexico City

Churubusco

San Agustín

Chapultepec

San Ángel

Pedregal
(lava field)

Padierna

N

0   2   4 Miles

soldiers fought the thorns of some new tormentor, a thick vine that wound its way out of the mud. Then the water was deeper and he stopped, straining to see farther ahead, but even the village in front of him was gone from view. He tried to move to one side, but his foot was held tight. He pulled hard to free himself, felt his boot sliding off his foot. Major Thorsby may be right, he thought. This may be as far as we can go. He worked his foot around, slowly pulled it free. He looked behind him at the soldiers, who had stopped again. He motioned toward the road, and the grass seemed to come alive with the surge of men, all making their way quickly to the comfort of hard ground. He pushed clear of the grass and climbed the soft dirt embankment at the side of the road. Pulling himself up to the hard surface, he saw Thorsby, smiling, waiting for him.

"Well, Captain, you come to your senses? Look here."

Thorsby pointed out toward the village, and Lee was surprised how close the huts were. He felt a stab of anxiety, but the village was quiet, seemed deserted.

Thorsby said, "Looks like we were expected. Don't appear to be anyone home, Captain. Let's walk up here on dry ground, if you don't mind."

The rest of the men had climbed up to the road, and Thorsby spread them out in formation, a small column in the shape of an H. He pointed to the village, said, "It's all yours, Captain."

The men began to move beside him, and Lee felt the water in his boots, the wetness in his socks, thought, It was the right way. He doesn't think so, but there could have been soldiers here. We could have walked right into a problem.

The lead troops reached the first huts, and the men pushed open the crude wood doors, slipped inside, then quickly came back out, moving to the next hut. Lee glanced to both sides of the road, saw motion, a window, a flap of cloth moving in the breeze. He moved up behind one soldier, followed the man to the low doorway of a tiny home, looked inside, curious. Dishes and pans hung on a dark wall; beneath them stood a small wood table, three small chairs. The soldier looked at him, shrugged, said, "No one home, Captain."

Lee nodded, backed out into the light, and suddenly Thorsby said aloud, "Halt!"

The men all froze, and Thorsby lifted his field glasses. "There you go, Captain. That what you came to see?"

Lee moved out into the road, could see how it stretched beyond the village, leading straight toward a wide, flat hill. He detected some motion, a flag, then something else, and raised his glasses.

Thorsby said, "I reckon we'll not want to get too much closer to *that*."

The man's voice was different, serious now, and Lee scanned the hill, saw a row of uneven shapes, man-made, some logs, piles of rock. He stared hard, could see the glint of gold, the sun reflecting on the polished brass cannon.

He said quietly, "Yes, Major, that's what I came to see. I need to make a count . . . how many guns . . ."

Thorsby laughed. "More than I want to walk into, Captain. If you intend us to get any closer, I'm for slipping back down into that damned mud. Up on this road, we're an easy target."

Lee tried to count the guns, gazed slowly along the ridge of the hill, thought, We're an easy target right now. But they don't seem to care.

Thorsby said, "Looks like a couple dozen pieces at least, Captain."

Lee moved the glasses down to the left, where he saw another built-up road rising above the swampy ground, a cluster of fortifications lining both sides. He saw more movement, flashes of color, thought, Troops . . . a *lot* of troops. There were more guns as well, positioned along the road curving away in a perfect arc of defense, the guns all pointing out toward the east, where Santa Anna expected Scott's army to advance.

He lowered the glasses. "Major, you may order your men to withdraw. Our job here is done."

The men filed into line, and Thorsby moved them back the way they came. Lee glanced inside another of the huts, caught a glimpse of motion. His heart leaping in his throat, he backed away and felt for the pistol in his belt. He stared at something moving slowly in the shadows. It was small, and as it emerged into the light, he could see that it was a rooster. He glanced back at the soldiers, saw no one watching him, and allowed himself a small laugh. Looking inside another hut, he saw a chicken and another rooster, thought, This is, after all, a place where people live. These people are waiting somewhere, maybe behind the walls of the city, and they expect to return here.

Lee looked at the wide hill again, thought of Scott's prediction; we might just walk in and take the city. This time, these people did not welcome us, they've offered no gifts, no smiling women are here to greet us. That's an army over there, and they have guns and fortifications, and they are ready for whatever we are prepared to do. He thought of Santa Anna, the snide remarks, the jokes the American officers made, even Scott himself: He is through, he is disgraced. No, Lee thought, no matter what has happened so far, this time he is defending their capital, the soul of their nation. No matter what we have done to him in battle, no matter how superior we think we are, these people have pride and a sense of honor, and a man who knows how to lead them. And we have our hands full of a fight.

16. SCOTT

H E STUDIED LEE'S MAP, FOCUSED ON THE WIDE HILL, NOTED
Lee's label, El Piñón. "How many guns?"
Lee stood in front of the wide desk, leaned forward before replying, "At least thirty on the hill. More spread along the causeway. A full division of troops, perhaps more."

Scott glanced up at the others, looked briefly at each one, Pillow and Worth, then the old face of Quitman. He stopped at Twiggs, saw him leaning over, trying to see the details of Lee's map. "A formidable position, even for you, General Twiggs. The enemy appears to be waiting for us."

He looked at Lee again, said, "That about your take on it, Captain? We'd be walking into a trap?"

Lee stood straight. "Not exactly, sir. There is no deception here. They fully expect us to march right at them. It has been their way from the beginning, just as it was at Cerro Gordo. It is possible, sir, that a frontal assault could succeed. But it would be . . . costly."

"That is your opinion, Captain."

Lee stiffened, nodded slowly. "Yes, sir. Forgive me. My opinion."

"Mine too."

Scott pointed to a chair behind Lee, said, "Be seated, Captain. I believe what we have here is an opportunity. The enemy has committed a sizable force of his defense to this one approach to the city. He expects us to oblige him by assaulting him where he hopes we will assault him. I have no intention of doing so. General Worth, have your people given us a report on the southern road?"

Worth seemed to jump to his feet, said, "Yes, sir. My scouts report the road that runs below Lake Chalco is suitable, and would carry us easily to a major roadway south of the city. From there we could strike due north and catch Santa Anna napping. We could very well push right over those walls before he knew we were there."

Scott stared at Worth, thought, What is wrong with this man? He sees the ghosts of an army where none exists, and now he sees no army at all, when the enemy sits behind fat walls in great strength.

"General Worth, your enthusiasm is noted. However, I would ask you to consider the scouting reports we already have. The enemy may have as many as thirty thousand troops between us and the center of the capital. My mathematics skills are somewhat rusty but I believe that is about three times what we have. I do not expect we will be allowed the luxury of simply marching straight into anyplace around here without some serious opposition. We must even the odds. Surprise is our ally. We must move quickly to the places he does not expect us to move. General Twiggs, your division is already in place on the road to El Piñon."

Twiggs grunted softly, said, "We're ready to proceed."

"Yes, I'm sure. However, you will proceed only to make a demonstration, make a big show for the troops Captain Lee has observed. Hold them in place, while the rest of the army moves around below that big lake . . . Chalco. Once the bulk of the army has reached the north-south roads, only then will you withdraw, and follow." He looked at Lee's map again, set it aside, slid another paper across his desk, another map, scanned it slowly, said, "I never saw a city that could be defended as easily as this one. Swamps, lakes, marsh, God knows what else. The only approaches are on these built-up roads, these, uh . . . well, not bridges exactly . . ."

He glanced at Lee, who said, "Causeways, sir."

"Causeways. Right. You probably needed a straight-edge to draw them, Mr. Lee. Every one of them a nice straight line running right into some fortification." He glanced at Worth. "Once we fight our way through the fortifications, then we still have the city gates and that big damned wall to deal with. I don't expect there to be a welcoming committee."

Scott picked up another map, studied it a moment, then asked, "What's this? Another lake?"

Lee stood, moved to the desk, said, "I don't know, sir. That one's not mine."

Worth approached and nodded. "Yes, that's from my end, sir. There appears to be a large lava bed spread out to the southwest of the city. It's impassable. It's as far as the scouts could go. We focused our attention north from that point. Not much to be gained trying to go around it, sir."

Scott looked at Worth for a long moment, said, "What's on the other side?"

Worth moved back to his chair, said, "I . . . don't know, sir. It's impassable."

Scott looked at the map again, thought, What are scouts *for*? He handed the map to Lee, said, "You agree, Captain?"

Lee glanced at Worth, said, "I can't say, sir. I haven't seen it."

"*Go* see it, Captain. Find out what's on the other side. General Worth, with all respect to your scouts, nothing is impassable. It is likely that once we move the army into position south of the city, Santa Anna will have moved as well. There is little chance of complete secrecy, even if we move after dark. He has cavalry just like we do, a great deal more than we do. Before we simply charge like hell into his guns, we should explore other possibilities. Captain Lee, you will report to General Worth and proceed to that damned lava field. You will then tell me something I don't already know. You are dismissed, Captain."

Lee saluted, moved out of the office. Scott saw his son-in-law holding the door open, and the young man seemed to hesitate, then moved into the office, circling around behind his desk. Scott waited, said, "What?"

The young man leaned close, said quietly, "Excuse me, sir. Mr. Trist is here. I told him he would have to wait."

Scott glanced up at the young man. "No, Major, send him in. Let everyone hear what he has to say."

The young man moved away quickly, and Scott saw curiosity in the faces of the others.

"This could be interesting." He looked at Pillow and smiled, but said nothing. Pillow seemed to twist slightly in the chair. Yes, he thought, squirm a bit. Nothing seems to concern you unless it's political. Bet you wonder what I'm up to.

Trist stood in the doorway and looked quickly at the commanders, then at Scott. Scott saw Trist's expression and thought, Oh, God, he looks like he's going to cry again.

"Come in, Mr. Trist. Don't be alarmed. They bite even less than I do. I thought we should all hear your report. So, the war over?"

Pillow suddenly stood, said to Trist, "My word! Please, sir, tell us!

Have you been successful?" Pillow looked at Scott then, and Scott raised a finger, pointed slowly to the chair in silent command.

Pillow sat down, his eyes fixed on Trist, who said, "Forgive me for interrupting. I must report, sir, uh, no, actually it seems the war is not over. Not on my account, anyway."

Trist still seemed uneasy as he moved slowly up to the desk. He said quietly, "Sir, is this appropriate?"

Scott pointed to Lee's empty chair, said, "Entirely appropriate, Mr. Trist. Have a seat. I certainly want my commanders to know what is going on. These gentlemen have all been informed of your mission. No intrigue here." He glanced at Pillow again. "No intrigue at all. So, may I assume you have heard from our friends the British?"

Trist glanced again at the faces watching him, looked at Scott with a confident nod. "I have had a continuous dialogue with the British representatives, yes, sir. They are still expressing optimism that the Mexican Congress will be persuaded to accept our peaceful solution." He paused, and Scott saw Trist's confidence fade. The clerk glanced self-consciously toward the others, his cheeks flushing.

"Uh, sir, the first payment was made without incident."

Twiggs now sat up straight, said, "First payment of what?"

Trist looked at Scott, and Scott nodded. "Proceed, Mr. Trist."

"We, um, made a transfer of funds totaling ten thousand dollars."

Twiggs looked at Scott now, said, "You know my feelings about this, sir. I have no taste for politics, and I did not agree with this policy of bribery. If we are making payments, may I know what it is we are paying *for*?"

Scott nodded, said, "Mr. Trist?"

"Yes, um, General Twiggs, we made the payment at the request of the Mexican authorities. It was considered a deposit of . . . good faith, sir."

Pillow stood and addressed Twiggs. "My dear general, these negotiations are delicate. We must give when they take, and take when they give. It is quite proper."

Scott pointed again at Pillow's chair, and Pillow sat down, nodded to Scott with a satisfied smile.

Twiggs ignored Pillow, said to Scott, "Good faith? We have ten thousand muskets and a hundred cannon pointed at their capital. What other kind of faith do they need?"

Scott held up his hands. "All right. Let Mr. Trist complete his report. I authorized the payment, and it was no great secret. Obviously,

General Pillow was aware of it. But you raise a good question, General Twiggs. Well, Mr. Trist? What did ten thousand dollars buy us?"

Trist's eyes rapidly scanned the room. He looked down at his lap and tugged at his shirt cuffs, then said quietly, "As of yet . . . nothing, sir."

Twiggs spat out a loud grunt, and Pillow said, "Well, not yet. But surely, results are—will be forthcoming, yes?"

Trist looked at Scott, the younger man's confidence gone now, and Scott saw Trist's hand quivering. The general thought, Maybe this was a bad idea. Should have had him here alone.

Trist cleared his throat before speaking. "Sir, the British believe the funds were in fact given to General Santa Anna personally. That is the last information we have."

Surprised, Scott said, "Excuse me, Mr. Trist? We have given payment directly to Santa Anna? I was not aware you were going that far." His voice began to rise. "Were there conditions attached to the funds? Didn't we expect some document, some show of *their* good faith that a truce might be forthcoming? That was the idea, was it not?"

"The Mexican representatives did not offer anything in return. We were told there was still disagreement whether they should accept our proposal—whether the three million dollars would be enough to convince them to bring the matter before their general meeting. However, it is my feeling, sir, that if General Santa Anna is the final authority . . . it could be a mistake making payments without hearing directly from him. We were assured that if this first payment was made, the avenues of communication might open up. It doesn't seem to have worked."

Scott felt his face redden, his fists tightening on the desk. He saw Twiggs was looking at him now, his mouth open, his face a grim black mask of outrage. Finally Twiggs shook his head and said quietly, his voice thick with disgust, *"Three million . . ."*

Scott said quietly, "Yes, General Twiggs, I agree with you."

He looked at Pillow now, the man's glib confidence replaced by a small frown.

Scott said, "Mr. Trist, you are to be commended at least for performing the job you were sent here to perform. The only direct avenues we have open to Santa Anna are those damned causeways. The President may still believe we should purchase our way into Mexico City, but it is apparent that we will not conclude this affair with currency. So, we will conclude it with the gun. This is still a war." He paused, looked at Pillow. "The President certainly should be notified that his plan was a failure, however, *our* avenues of communication are a long way behind us. Some of you may still believe bribery is a productive policy. Certainly the Mexicans appreciate it. But I will not be played for a fool. The only gift Santa Anna will receive from us now will come at the point of a bayonet."

17. LEE

AUGUST SIXTEENTH

THE GUNFIRE HAD BEEN BRIEF, A QUICK RAID BY MEXICAN CAV-
alry, a harassment of Twiggs's flank. Lee could hear it from a
distance. Having climbed one of the great pointed rocks, he
stared out to the east, but by now there was nothing to see. The Mexicans had ridden away as quickly as the raid had begun, and now there
was the quiet again, the only sound a faint calling from the big black
birds that seemed to own the landscape.

He had seen signs of cavalry himself, had thought, Of course they
will watch us, might even try to slow us down. But the army had made
the march around the big lake, Chalco, and now was firmly in place
south of the city. And Scott had been right; it was no surprise after all.
Even if Twiggs's demonstration had held the El Piñon forces in place,
Santa Anna still had a great deal of strength around the city. By now
most of it was facing south, a vast show of force blocking the roadways
that would lead Scott into the city.

By late morning the sun was already reflecting sharply off the
edge of the lava field—the gray rocks a jumble of shapes and sizes, ta-
pering off toward the road where the troops waited for Lee to give the
first command.

Worth had given Lee a squad of infantry, commanded by a
huge sergeant, a gruff dark man named Calhoun. Lee watched Calhoun spread his men to the front, fanning them out in a protective
arc in the ragged rocks. Calhoun pointed and barked his orders in a
harsh whisper, pushed his men into position. He looked at Lee with
grim black eyes, and Lee nodded in return. Lee had insisted on absolute quiet.

Lee moved carefully off the big rock, jumped down onto soft

gray sand, was completely hidden from the others. He climbed again to a flat space between more of the strange formations. He nodded to Calhoun, and the soldiers began to move away in front. There was a muffled sound behind him, a low voice, and Lee turned, saw Beauregard scrambling over the rocks, waving, and now Beauregard shouted out, "Ho, there, Captain!"

The sound punched through the quiet, and Lee winced, closed his eyes, thought, He should know the value of quiet. He held up his hands, saw Beauregard's face flushed red, the young man puffing hard, and Lee said quietly, "Lieutenant, I should have informed you. We must maintain silence. As you know, sound will carry over these rocks. As the locals have told us, it's nearly three miles across, maybe more. We don't know what we might encounter."

Beauregard looked past Lee, saw the big sergeant, smiled, waved, and Calhoun nodded slightly, did not smile. Beauregard said quietly, "Yes, of course, Captain. Quite right. That's old Calhoun out there. You know him? Believe he's one of your people, a Virginian. Good man. Pity any Mexicans we run into."

Lee glanced at the sergeant, saw Calhoun moving away, and Lee said, "Please, Lieutenant, we need not run into *any* Mexicans out here. If we are to accomplish something today, it will be to provide a route for the troops that could greatly disadvantage the enemy. The fewer enemy we run into, the better. Let's move."

Lee stepped down between two sharply pointed rocks that rose nearly chest high, and Beauregard moved close behind him. He could hear the soldiers moving in front, heard the muffled sound of a man falling, one low voice, cursing, followed by a quiet hiss from Calhoun. This may not be so simple, he thought, and recalled Worth's word, *impassable*. We'll see about that. But it is difficult.

He reached out, gripped a jagged edge of gray rock, pushed himself up to a small ledge, and then his hand gave way, the rock crumbling into small pieces. His hand scraped painfully across the ragged surface, and he pulled his arm close, flexed his fingers, thought, You too, Captain. *Carefully.* He looked at the broken stone, picked up the smaller crumbled rock, examined it closely with the eye of the engineer. He squeezed, and the rock was crushed easily to a thick powder. He grabbed another rock, heard Beauregard behind him, and Beauregard said, "Soft. Never seen anything like it. It's nothing but ash and lava. Amazing."

Lee nodded, let the powder slip away from his hand, said, "Let's spread out. We should find out if it's all like . . . like this."

Beauregard moved away, climbed up a small ledge. He looked back at Lee and smiled. "No place to build a fort. This stuff wouldn't support anything."

Lee watched him drop down out of sight, and thought of the forts, his tours of duty along the Atlantic coast. The biggest problem was always the foundation, finding something firm enough so the fort didn't simply sink into the water. He climbed up, slid his leg over the next rock, saw Calhoun waiting for him.

Calhoun seemed impatient, said quietly, "We'll lead the way, Captain. You stay behind us. I want to know where you are all the time. You want me to change direction, you just point."

Lee nodded, stopped himself from saying "Yes, sir," smiled now, thought, All right, we're clear on one thing. I may be the engineer, but *he's* in command.

Calhoun turned away, motioned silently to his men to advance, and Lee moved up quickly behind him.

The rocks were smaller, scattered in a thick uneven carpet, and Lee thought, It's like someone just tossed them out here, all shapes, every direction. Some of the rocks seemed to shine in the direct sunlight, the glare blinding, while others were a darker dull gray. He could step over most of them now, most no larger than cannon balls, while out to the side there was a thick ridge of taller rocks, as large as a man, some with sharp peaks, others rounded, weathered, or eroded by time.

Lee studied the ground, pointed to a gap in the larger rocks, a space wide enough for a man to walk, and Calhoun led him that way. He could feel the rocks crumbling under his boots, thought, The lieutenant's right. Too soft to build anything out of this material. He stopped again and saw Calhoun motion with his hand, and Lee saw it as well, a smooth trail through the smaller rocks. He moved forward, studied the ground, saw no footprints, no tracks. Someone has done this, he thought, Indians perhaps, maybe even the Aztecs, someone had a reason to make this trail. He looked ahead, saw the trail leading into a gap between more of the larger rocks, said to Calhoun, "We'll follow this. As long as it leads west, it could make our job much simpler."

Calhoun moved again, waved his men forward, and Lee followed. The trail wound past the larger rocks, straightened out into a wide flat plain of more widely scattered stones. He bent down, picked up a rock the size of his hand, one of thousands around him, thought, How long has it been? Centuries, longer? This was all just, what? Blown here?

Spewed out from an ancient volcano long dead? Or, no, maybe it will happen again. The local farmers seem to believe it could.

He saw Calhoun waiting for him. He tried to locate the trail again, the small rocks closer together at that point, blending into a ragged sharp plain. Calhoun pointed ahead, and Lee saw beyond, another space between larger rocks. He followed again, saw another segment of the trail, the soft rocks cleared aside again, placed along the trail in a low row. He felt excited, seeing a long stretch of mostly clear, flat ground. The trail led straight across, disappearing again into larger rocks. He stopped. He could not help a smile, thought of Worth's word, *impassable*. No, not quite.

He thought of the locals, the men Worth had brought into the camp, the hostile interrogations they endured. The Mexicans would say nothing about soldiers, remained silent about Santa Anna's whereabouts, and Worth had grown angrier, threatened them with harsher measures. Lee was uncomfortable with Worth's methods, the bullying of civilians. In the end even Worth had to admit that forcing the simple farmers to cooperate with the *yanquis* might give them more incentive to serve as Santa Anna's eyes.

Lee had been relieved to see the captives finally released, had seen the faces of people who had no part in this war, no concept of its dangers. But he had learned one thing, something the farmers talked about with no hesitation. The lava field, this strange place, had a name, and though some of the locals called it the Pedregal, there were others who spoke of this great field of lava as though some awful misfortune would come to anyone who dared to cross it. To them, it was the home of the Devil.

But someone had cut this trail, he thought, some brave soul who must have defied the legends, probably a long time ago, someone who found a way past superstition and fear. He was probably guided by the sun, probably moved slowly, one rock at a time, through this frightening place. Someone who, for whatever reason, *needed* to find a way through this place. Whoever you were . . . God bless you. Now, with the pickax and a little muscle, we can widen your trail, cut through the narrow gorges, fill the holes so that even the wagons can cross. Now, we can build a *road*.

THEY HAD MOVED FOR NEARLY FOUR HOURS, AND LEE HAD PUT away the compass, followed the sun, shrouded in orange haze, settling closer to the tops of the great mountains to the west.

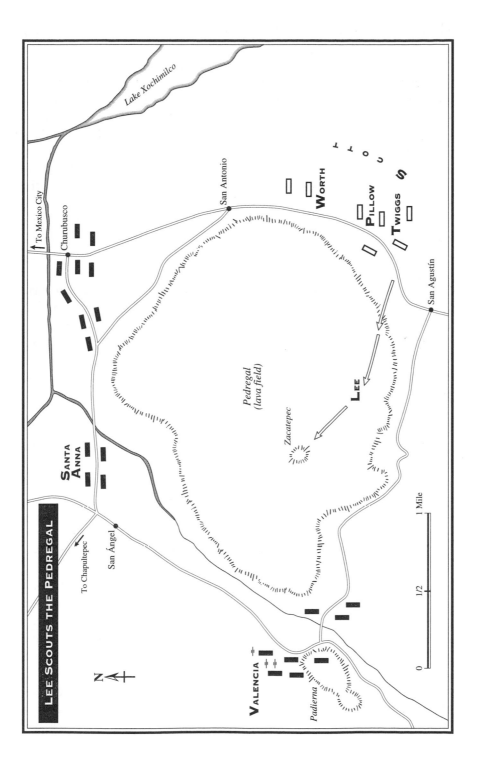

LEE SCOUTS THE PEDREGAL

Lake Xochimilco

To Mexico City

Churubusco

To Chapultepec

San Ángel

SANTA ANNA

San Antonio

WORTH

PILLOW

TWIGGS

SCOTT

San Agustín

LEE

Zacatepec

Pedregal
(lava field)

VALENCIA

Padierna

N

0   1/2   1 Mile

The escort was still close in front, and he could see the soldiers bobbing up and down, men climbing up and then disappearing into the small cuts and crevasses between the larger rocks. Deep into the lava, the trail had mostly faded away, and the soldiers knew to study the ground, search for any sign of human labor. They had found small traces, even some mule tracks, but what remained of the straight path west was now twisted and wound in all directions.

He pulled himself onto a wide flat stone and gazed through his field glasses in a wide circle. It was even hotter now, the lava around him reflecting the heat in a shimmer of silver. The dust clung to the sweat on his hands, and he had smeared the lenses of the field glasses. He wiped the dark glass with his sleeve. The sweat was soaking him, and his uniform was coated with the lava dust as well. He had blinked away the rough dust all day, but as he wiped with his handkerchief, he realized his face had been a mask of gray.

The rocks were spread again in an uneven carpet, more uniform in size, smaller, easier to step over, flat hard ground between them, but all of it the same dreary gray. He looked for some landmark, anything that stood out, something to help guide the troops. If we cannot use the old trail, he thought, we must find something else. But there are no trees, no brush, nothing at all. There's not even color, no brown, no green. If we are to be guided by anything, it will have to be a trail of our own making.

In front of him the soldiers had grown used to the conditions, seemed more adept at moving around the larger rocks. The men were still quiet, still laboring under the angry glare of Calhoun. A Virginian, Lee thought. He felt a comfort in that. We're a long way from home. A bit of familiarity is a good thing. I should ask him about his home, probably in the mountains. He doesn't look like an easterner. Lee could see the big man look back, waiting for him again, and Lee stepped quickly forward, felt like a child being scolded by a stern parent. Perhaps we can talk . . . later.

The flat gentle plain had ended, replaced by larger rocks, their jagged points stabbing out in all directions. Some of the rocks were taller than the troops who moved between them. He dropped into a small cut between two of the larger rocks, his boots kicking up a cloud of thick dust as he landed. Momentarily drained, he blew out a sharp breath before quickly climbing a small rise from where he could see through a small opening to where the ground flattened out again, another small section of the narrow trail. He moved toward it, feeling even more of the effects of the labor, his legs stiffening, the sweat tormenting his eyes, his soaked uniform clinging to him, weighing him down. He thought, It's time to take a break. He walked along flat ground and through another gap, caught glimpses of blue, the soldiers marching on. Quickening his step, he thought, Catch up to Calhoun, tell him to halt for a moment. Suddenly the rock beside him splattered, small pieces spraying in his face. A shout came from in front, and he could hear more sounds now, above it all Calhoun's voice, shouting, "Down!"

Lee blinked hard, shook his head, brushed at the powder on his face. He heard more sounds, the crack of muskets, the slap of the lead ball on the rocks. A shot was fired from close by, a response from one of his men, and he heard Calhoun yell something profane, then another command, "No firing!"

Lee raised his head slowly above the edge of the rock, saw Beauregard tumbling toward him, his face wild with excitement. Beauregard saw him, slid along the edge of the rocks and moved close.

"Mexicans, sir! We've run into the Mexicans!"

Lee saw that the young man's hat was missing and a trickle of blood wandered like a thin stream across his scalp. Lee said, "Are you all right, Lieutenant? Are you wounded?"

Beauregard saw Lee's look, felt his head, saw the blood on his fingers, said, "Oh, God. Uh, no sir. I slipped down a ways back. Uh . . . where's my hat?"

Lee watched him for a moment, thought, Easy, young man. We'll get through this. Beauregard pulled out a handkerchief, wiped at the blood and looked at Lee sheepishly. Lee turned away, thought, Don't embarrass him. We have bigger problems.

More shots rang out, but the sounds were distant, and Lee looked again over the tops of the rocks, saw Calhoun moving back toward him.

Calhoun said, "Just a few. They weren't looking for a fight. They hightailed it back the way they came." He looked at Beauregard. "Nothing to be afraid of, sirs. Probably just some scouts, more surprised than we were."

Lee looked past Calhoun, up and over the rocks. "Scouts from where, Sergeant? Scouting for whom?"

Lee moved higher up on the rocks, found a flat ledge and stared out to the west. The sun was settling behind the mountains, and Lee looked again through the field glasses. The ground was darkened by shadows, the reflections dimming. He could see a round hill, a fat bulge in the lava bed. A vantage point, he thought. We must reach that hill. Surely, we will be able to see the far side.

He scanned the hill, thought, They could be waiting for us there, watching us, an ambush. But there was no motion, no color, nothing to interrupt the dead gray of the rocks. Perhaps Mr. Calhoun is correct, he thought. They believe we're no threat, nothing to be concerned about, just a scouting party as well. Thank God.

He saw something moving above the hill, watched the arcing flight of the big black birds, drifting slowly up and over the hill, then moving out of sight. He thought of Calhoun's description, *scouts*. Perhaps not, perhaps they were something else . . . a skirmish line. If those men are out here in these rocks, they probably didn't come far. That means . . . we're close . . . and there's a way out the other side. I have to see. I have to climb that hill.

He looked back into the silent stare, the expressionless face of the big man. "Let's get moving, Sergeant. I believe we're near the end."

T HE BIG HILL WAS JUST INSIDE THE WESTERN BOUNDARY OF THE lava field, and there was no one waiting for the slow advance of the Americans. He had climbed up, moving carefully over the ragged ground, could see out now to the west, the ground beyond bathed in the last golden light of the setting sun. Beauregard was beside him, while Calhoun stood quietly to one side, still scouting the rocks below for any sign of movement. Lee scanned with the glasses, could hear Beauregard breathing heavily.

Beauregard said, "The rocks look smaller . . . and there's a wide ravine."

Lee nodded, said, "It will be a difficult crossing, but we still have the advantage. They're still not expecting us to be here."

Beauregard scanned out beyond the rocks. "Don't know about that, sir. They're expecting somebody. Those buildings . . . a village or something, I can see artillery."

Lee looked to where Beauregard was pointing, saw a road running beyond the edge of the ravine that ended the Pedregal. To one side there were several small buildings, a few larger ones, and spread in front, a row of mounds in the earth, dotted with the black muzzles of cannon.

Lee felt a stab of excitement. "Now we know where the scouts came from. But the important thing, Lieutenant, is not the enemy. It is the road. That road runs north. Surely it will take us toward the western gates of the city."

Beauregard looked at him. "How do you know that? Is there a map? I was not aware we had the details."

Lee smiled while still scanning through the glasses. "All the roads here eventually reach the same place. They all go to Mexico City. This is certainly another spoke in the wheel. Can you count the guns? I see fifteen, perhaps a few more. Below, down there, that low hill, appears to be a camp, probably where their troops are positioned. It's a formidable obstacle but not an impossible one. If we can move the enemy out of there, this road could be a serious advantage."

Beauregard sniffed, said nothing, and Lee thought, He doesn't see it. The guns are all facing this way. Whoever is in command there has been told to keep an eye out for us, but he isn't prepared for a major assault. Whatever troops he has are concentrated in one place. They don't really believe we will move this way in force. And if we come at all, he expects us to come straight at him.

He glanced at the rocks to the north, the lava spreading far out to the right of the big hill. This is all good cover, natural cover.

"Lieutenant, that ravine will be a difficult crossing in the face of those guns. The enemy is aware of that. He's probably counting on it. I will report to General Scott that it might be in our interests to convince the enemy we intend to do exactly as they want. We should make a demonstration here, while a strong force moves out above us, crosses farther up the road. If the demonstration is successful, those guns will stay where they are."

Beauregard scanned out again, said, "We don't know how many troops are there, what kind of strength."

"We will when the fight begins. With enough of a surprise, it may not matter." He glanced back, saw Calhoun watching him with a puzzled look.

In a moment, Calhoun nodded, smiled for the first time, said quietly, "Very good, sir. Very good."

Lee looked away, embarrassed, still felt like a child under the gaze of this gruff soldier. No, there is nothing to be praised for, he thought. It should be plain to anyone. The lieutenant will see it. He just doesn't have the experience yet. He stared back down the hill, could see the soldiers, some perched up on the side of the hill, peering up and over the rocks, some just sitting, holding canteens, nursing sore feet. Calhoun looked at Beauregard now without expression, and Lee saw the young lieutenant still glassing the enemy. He felt a stab of impatience. All right, tell me something I do not know. He thought of Scott's instructions, how the commander used the same words, *tell me something I do not know.* He shook his head. No Captain, focus on your own job. Do not judge this young man. It has been a long day, and we still have a long walk back.

He looked out toward the enemy, thought, Now we must give General Scott what he requested. What he does not yet know is that there *is* a way through this Pedregal. It is not impassable after all.

He looked out toward the last faint glow of the sun, the great mountains now deep in violet shadows. He glanced up, saw the first stars, took a long breath, said to Calhoun, "I believe we're through here for today, Sergeant. Best head back."

Calhoun nodded silently, began to climb down through the rocks. Quickly, his men moved into line, waiting for Lee's command. Lee looked east into the darkness, ran his hand across his pocket, feeling for his compass. He looked at Beauregard. The young man was already staring at a compass of his own. Lee moved down, picked his way carefully to the base of the hill, saw the troops watching him, some faces looking nervously up to a dark sky. He said to Calhoun, "Let's move out, Sergeant."

Calhoun glanced out toward the darkness in the east, looked at the compass in Beauregard's hand. He smiled again, a broad toothy grin, said to Lee, "After *you*, sir."

18. LEE

AUGUST SEVENTEENTH

NEARLY ALL THE ENGINEERS WERE PRESENT, AND MOST OF THE scouts, and the reports from the junior officers had all been made. Lee had listened with curiosity, thought it unusual that the meeting would be so large, making sensitive information available to so many ears. But as the reports were read and the maps laid out, he began to feel the importance, the necessity, of so much input. The position of the army and of the enemy had to be clear. There was no longer the threat of some surprise assault, and the ghosts that had plagued Worth were replaced by an enemy that was now very real, and very much in control of their own ground.

It was a forum for many of the lower ranking engineers to make a favorable impression on the senior commanders. Each man had his own recommendation, some plan of action, and nearly all proposed that the first grand assault should of course proceed in the direction of their own observation. Some of the reports drew a quick response from Scott, a curt thank-you, and Lee had felt a growing impatience, a sense of annoyance, thought, This is not the time for young men to strut their vanity.

Lee was listening now to James Mason, an engineer who was Lee's senior. Mason had given Scott his own map, spoke in a low, serious tone.

"Sir, I can confirm many of the reports you have already heard. The enemy is . . . there. Their position includes a long fortification above the Churubusco River. It is a position of great strength, but can be carried, I believe, by a strong and coordinated assault."

The men were silent while Scott studied the map, and Lee

considered the simplicity of the plan that Mason was laying out. Now he began to feel uneasy, looked at Mason's cool confidence with growing astonishment, thought, He cannot be serious. He looked over at Twiggs, saw him looking at a copy of Mason's map, his face registering quiet approval. No, this is not Captain Mason's plan, he thought. It comes from General Twiggs. Why do they always want to employ the same strategy, a straight-ahead, all-out bayonets-to-the-front assault? How can he believe it is the best way? Twiggs glanced at him, looked right past him, and Lee saw the general's grim determination. God forgive me, but . . . God help us if he is ever in command.

Mason had completed his report, and Scott stared down at the table, a silent pause, looked up slowly at Twiggs, said, "You propose to move straight up the road through San Antonio, assault the enemy at his strongest point?" Scott sat back in the chair, and Lee saw his pained look, expressing the familiar frustration. Scott said to Mason, "Surely, Captain, you observed that while you were scouting that position you were directly under the guns of the enemy. If I am not mistaken, that route would be swept by a great deal of artillery the entire way. There is no place to hide, no place to form troops that cannot be shelled. We have seen this before, gentlemen, is that not clear? Once again, Santa Anna is expecting *us* to accommodate *him*."

Scott leaned forward, glared angrily at Mason, said, "Captain, one day soon I hope to finally make the *generalissimo*'s acquaintance. I'm sure he will be greatly entertained when I tell him how so many of my officers were so anxious to play this game by *his* rules."

Twiggs sat back in the chair, crossed his arms, stared past Lee, holding silently to his response. Scott ignored him, looked at Mason's map again, studied it for another moment. "This road that runs out of San Antonio, to the northwest. We know where it ends up?"

Mason took a deep breath, glanced at Twiggs, said, "Yes, sir. It intersects another road that comes up west of the big lava field."

Scott glanced at Lee, and Lee felt his heart jump, thought of the road he had seen. Yes, Captain, you were correct.

Scott said, "If we can advance to that point, reach the intersection from the southwest, we can assault the strength of Churubusco from the flank. Might that be a damned sight better idea than hitting them head-on?"

Mason looked at the map, nodded slowly, said, "Yes, sir."

Scott looked at Lee now, and Lee felt the old man's impatient anger, the hard eyes pushing him back in the chair. "I believe it's time for Captain Lee's report."

Mason moved away, sat quietly behind Twiggs. Lee stood slowly, unrolled his map, laid it on Scott's desk, and waited while Scott examined it. He felt the eyes on him from behind, was suddenly very nervous. He had watched all the faces, heard it in all the voices, the seriousness, the grim reality, and it settled into him now as though it were a hard fist in his chest. He had made a mental note as each man spoke, thought it was just chance that his report would be heard near the end. But when Mason went up before him, he had felt a sudden uncomfortable awareness. It was not chance at all. Scott had wanted him to be the last one. All through the reports, Scott had glanced at him, as though holding him in one spot, a silent command Lee did not understand. He had seen it from the others as well, Twiggs, Worth, and the other engineers, even from Joe Johnston. There was weight to what he would say, and it was not just Scott who felt that way.

He tried not to listen to the talk in the camps, the brief comments about the heroic Captain Lee. He had accepted that his name, even his face, was recognized now all through the army, but he tried to explain it away. Of course, you are on the general staff. And it is a small army. But more recently the comments, the quiet compliments, came even from the men Lee had believed had a deep dislike for him, Twiggs certainly, Worth, even Pillow. The engineers below him, Beauregard, Meade, George McClellan, their talk, their descriptions of him, sometimes carried that uncomfortable edge of jealousy, and even Johnston would tease him relentlessly about his special relationship with General Scott.

He continued to watch Scott studying the map, waited for the questions, held his fists clenched tightly at his side. I have heard none of this from *him*, none of the compliments, little mention in his reports, certainly nothing official. Perhaps that is how it should be.

He had gone through this before. No, you should not do this, you should not be concerned with what the others think or say. The orders come from General Scott, the duty comes from God. God does not speak behind your back, and General Scott does not issue praise as some would expect, like passing out candy to children. Every man here knows in his own heart if he is doing his job. The rest of it is just gossip, speculation. And no, none of the talk matters. You do what General Scott expects you to do. There is nothing heroic or even special about performing your duty. I am fortunate to have the opportunity. I wish I could understand why there is such a . . . commotion.

Scott now pointed to a circle Lee had drawn in the Pedregal, said, "What's this?"

"Sir, it's a fairly distinctive hill. From this spot . . . we observed the enemy's position. It is an excellent vantage point, sir, and I believe it could be the best rendezvous point for us to coordinate and deploy the advance."

Scott nodded. "If you made it through that damned lava field that far, Captain, then with all due respect to General Worth, you believe the lava field is not . . . impassable?"

Lee glanced at Worth, who closed his eyes as though he was in pain, and Lee said, "General Worth may not have had the best information, sir. However . . . yes, sir, we did observe the far side."

Scott did not look at Worth, sat back in the chair, and Lee saw a smile now, and Scott said, "I had no doubt. All right, Captain, sounds like you had quite a day. Why don't you give us the rest of the story."

AUGUST NINETEENTH

They pushed out into the Pedregal like a thick blue snake, pushing aside the smaller rocks, widening the old trail. The day had begun early, before the sun could heat the gray dust, and the work went quickly at first, the men using shovels and picks and their bare hands. Where the trail faded into jagged rock, they cut and hauled, and where there were no obstacles, they quickly created a wide flat path that even the field guns could follow. Lee led the way, and they kept him moving, pressing him from behind, working quickly and efficiently. There were nearly five hundred men, Pillow's troops, all following Lee's direction, and even Pillow himself understood Lee's responsibility and would not interfere, riding far to the rear while his men cut their way forward.

Lee climbed a low flat rock, looked back at the men working through the ragged lava field, a great mass of blue spread behind them, the rest of Pillow's division, joined by Twiggs's men as well. This was not like Cerro Gordo, when his workers had plenty of time to complete their task, while the rest of the army simply sat in their camps and waited. This time the workers were followed closely by the fighting men, and once Pillow's muskets reached Lee's big hill, Twiggs would be close behind, adding to their strength with his own troops.

Lee had discovered that the hill had a name, had spoken of it to one of the farmers who was still selling grain to the army. The man had looked at Lee with surprise, his eyes grown wide. He bowed respect-fully, said the hill was called Zacatepec, and though the farmer did not know the origin of the name, he made it clear to Lee that the fat round hill was believed to be the eye of the Devil himself. Lee glassed that way now, could barely see the top of the hill, rising above the vast shimmering gray, and above everything the big black birds again, slowly circling, the only movement in the perfect blue of the sky.

THE SUN WAS HIGH OVERHEAD WHILE THE MEN MOVED QUICKLY to their tools, back to work after a brief rest and a brief meal from the cooked food they had stuffed into their packs. Lee was still out front, listening to the sounds again, the voices of the sergeants, the dull ringing of metal against soft rock, the pickaxes cut-ting into the taller rocks, widening the narrow gaps, lengthening the usable trail. They began to move closer to him, their progress steady again, and he did not have to look at them to recognize that the sounds he heard were of men working with their backs. He watched the skirmishers out in front, some still sitting quietly, waiting for the workers to allow them to press forward as well. They began to look expectantly toward Lee, waiting for his command, Up, move out. He raised the glasses, scanned out beyond the thin line of riflemen, looked across the dull gray expanse of rock and compacted dust. He focused far ahead, getting his first glimpse of color beyond the ragged gray. He focused closer in, on the last stretch of rough ground they still had to cross. He could still see segments of the old trail, leading out past the big hill. They were close now, and the hill was a clear landmark for the men with the tools. Far back along the fresh pathway, the column of blue followed, the men knowing that as the sun began to reach the far hills, they would be closer still to an enemy most of them had not yet seen.

Lee moved quickly, the big hill looming in front of him. A sweat-ing officer, the man in command of the skirmish line, his face covered with the gray dust of the trail, approached him.

Lee pointed, said quietly, "Up there, Lieutenant. Have your men spread out just beyond the hill, with a squad accompanying me to the top. I must see if the enemy has changed his position."

The man saluted without speaking and moved away. Lee looked to the ragged path he had used before, and, taking a deep breath, be-gan to climb the hill.

Across its face the soldiers moved with him, some watching him, others with their eyes focused on the crest. He climbed quickly, stepped over smaller rocks, scrambling up on large ones, taking a moment to steady himself. Even the large rocks were uneven, rocked and tilted with the weight of a man's step, and the climb had to be slow, careful. He tried to avoid the rocks altogether, leery of taking a fall, the twisted ankle that would result. Around him the riflemen bounded past, climbed ahead of him, displaying their youthful energy, their recklessness. He stopped nearly halfway up the hill, his chest pounding, his breath coming in short hard gasps. The soldiers began to stop with him, and he saw their smiles, and he nodded, held up his hand, as if to say, Yes, fine, you're young. But we will wait just one moment. He felt for the blessed canteen, took a drink of warm water, swirled the canteen in his hand, measuring. Half empty. Pay attention to that. No water out here, that's for sure. He looked up the hill again, his breathing still labored, thought, I don't remember this being so much . . . work. He tried not to look at the young faces watching him, not think of their young legs as they patiently waited for him to find the strength. Nothing to be ashamed of. You are after all . . . older. No, wrong word. You're not an old man. This army has its share of old men. You're simply a . . . senior officer. Well, senior, let's move up this hill.

He nodded to the men nearest him, said, "Let's go."

He began to climb again, reached out, pulled himself up between two large rocks, saw only smaller rocks, an easier climb now leading up to the crest. Suddenly, there was a burst of sound, an uneven chatter of musket fire. He dropped down, but the shots came from beyond the far side of the hill, from the enemy. The men around him were scrambling up the hill, some already at the crest, their muskets held tightly, waiting for some command, the sharp order from their lieutenant.

Lee looked behind the hill, saw the workers disappearing from the trail, spreading out into the rocks, looking for cover. Down below, the skirmishers were settling behind their own cover, muskets pointing out, looking for a target. The lieutenant was moving forward as the sound of scattered, uneven firing from the men in blue echoed off the rocks.

Lee felt a rush of frustration, thought, I have to see. We must know what is happening. He climbed quickly, pulled himself up to the crest of the hill, crawled up close beside a man with a musket. "Do you see anything?"

The man shook his head. "Just a little smoke, sir. Down there, maybe two hundred yards."

Lee lifted himself up, peered over the top of the rock. The soldier said, "Uh, sir. Your hat. I'd take off your hat. It's a good target, sir."

Lee reached up, touched the tall black felt and pulled it from his head. He nodded, said nothing, thought, Of course, a man who has done this before. He raised his glasses, scanned the rocks close to the base of the hill then out, farther away. There were more sounds now, the musket fire coming in scattered bursts, a few shots from alongside the hill, from the skirmishers. He could see movement among the rocks, thought, Two hundred yards . . . no, more, farther. He heard a dull smack of lead on a rock beside him, dropped down again, felt his heart pounding cold in his chest, thought, I have to know how many . . . if they have moved out here into the lava. If they are in force . . . we are in serious trouble.

He looked back behind the hill, could see a heavy flow of blue moving forward, a column of Pillow's troops marching in quick step past the workmen who still crouched low in the rocks. He also saw officers, men with swords pointing forward, heard their quick shouts as the flow of blue spread through the rocks on both sides of the hill. His chest was still pounding, and he watched the troops filling the spaces, their muskets pointing up and over the rocks. More men were climbing the hill, and he turned and saw another officer, his higher rank made obvious by the gold eagles on his shoulder straps, pulling himself up through the rocks. He moved with the quick precise moves of an athlete. Lee was glad there was someone to take command, and he put his hat back on and crawled back from the crest of the hill. When he tried to stand, his stiff knees protested with a sharp creaking pain.

The officer stopped and regarded Lee for a moment before looking past him to the crest of the hill. The man was older, but his face did not fit the rest of his appearance. He was tall, muscular, wide-shouldered, and Lee could see his breathing was not labored, apparently unaffected by the climb. Lee recognized him now, Bennett Riley, the man who had helped him at Cerro Gordo. Riley was another of the old veterans, the experience of 1812, a commander even the troops respected, something rare in Scott's army.

Lee saluted, said, "Colonel Riley."

Riley looked at him, shook his head, laughed briefly. "Captain Lee. You're always in the middle of the excitement. What have we run into?"

"It's not heavy fire, sir. I could see enemy troops, but hard to tell the strength. It's similar to what we found out here before, a picket line most likely."

Riley peered up over a rock, stared for a moment, and Lee moved up beside him, removed his hat again. He glanced at Riley, the man raising field glasses, and Lee saw Riley's hat still in place. He felt foolish now, thought, Combat officers don't think about hats.

Riley said, "The shooting has stopped." He looked behind him, and Lee saw more officers moving up the hill toward them.

Riley shouted, "Cease fire. Hold the brigade where they are. Get word to General Pillow that he should move up here, if he can bring himself to climb this hill. Captain Lee has found us a good vantage point."

Lee felt a sudden rush of pride, thought, Yes, a good vantage point. I had thought so myself. He felt odd receiving Riley's compliment, felt the weight of that, thought, He's one of the good ones. General Scott knows it, the men know it. How different that is when a real soldier sees the ground, understands. Instinct, I suppose, experience certainly. He shook his head, tried to push the thought away. No time for this, for vanity. You're not a schoolboy. Learn from him. Bennett Riley is doing his job. Do yours.

He looked again over the crest, could see the Mexican troops backing away. He raised his glasses, looked now to the far side of the lava field, saw the ravine, and beyond, the low mounds of earth, the artillery batteries still in place. He thought, Thank God. It was just as before, only light opposition, only a skirmish line.

He turned to Riley. "Colonel, I believe we can proceed with the work on the trail. It seems our show of force has scared the opposition away."

The air above him suddenly screamed, a high sharp shriek, a hard breath of wind that knocked him flat against the rocks. Then there was a blast, down behind the hill, shattering the gray rock. There were more sounds, the air coming alive with streaks of gold and blue, more great blasts of fire and black smoke in the rocks all around the hill. He pulled himself up, saw Riley still glassing out at the crest, and Riley said, "Don't think we scared anybody, Captain."

He could hear the shouts and screams of the men in the rocks, the cries of the wounded echoing. More of the shells impacted all through the lava. He moved up beside Riley, focused on the enemy again, but there was nothing to see; the ground beyond the ravine was hidden now in a gray cloud. The horrible sounds stopped, and he

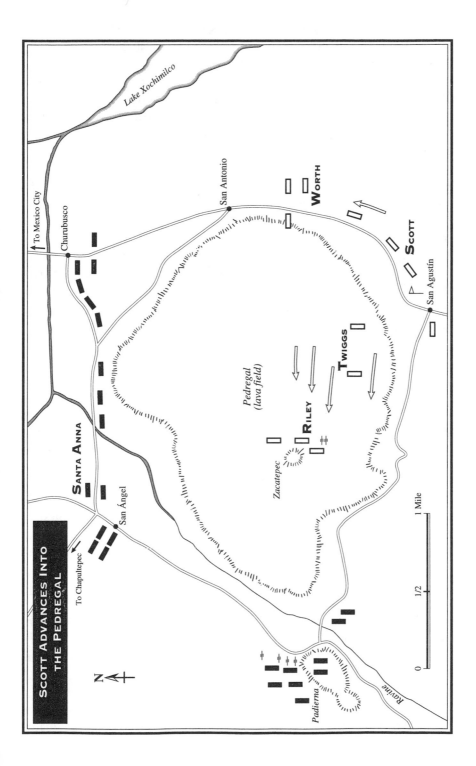

SCOTT ADVANCES INTO
THE PEDREGAL

N

Lake Xochimilco

To Mexico City

Churubusco

San Antonio

WORTH

SCOTT

San Agustín

To Chapultepec

SANTA ANNA

San Ángel

Zacatepec

RILEY

Pedregal
(lava field)

TWIGGS

Padierna

Ravine

0   1/2   1 Mile

heard a roll of low thunder, the first sounds of the Mexican cannon fire rolling toward the hill. He could see the flashes of fire through the drifting smoke, and the streaks of color came again, some passing overhead, some dropping below their position or off to the side. The rocks began to shatter, more men screaming, and he backed away, sat slowly down behind the rocks, heard Riley shouting orders: "Find Captain Magruder! We need his guns! Where the hell is General Pillow?"

The ground shook with the impact of the incoming shells. Lee watched as more troops moved up the trail his men had made, the workers still crouching low in the rocks. Far back on the trail he saw horses trotting past the troops, and rolling and bouncing behind them, the field guns, the smaller cannon that had been sent along with Pillow's troops. He could still feel his heart pounding his chest, his breath coming now in fast sharp gasps. He pulled himself up, peered out over the rocks, and the ground under him jumped again. He thought of General Scott, the maps, the strategy, *his* strategy, thought, my God . . . it has begun.

AUGUST NINETEENTH, LATE AFTERNOON

The troops continued to come forward, Pillow's division spreading out on either side of the big hill, some of Twiggs's units joining them, forming a strong line of muskets. But there was no enemy to fire at, no advance of troops from the Mexican position, but still the shelling from the Mexican guns continued.

Lee stood with Riley again, near the base of the big hill, protected by a small rock pile. He watched Pillow glancing about anxiously, looking quickly up over the taller rocks, flinching with each blast of the incoming shells. More officers were gathering, and Lee thought, Not too close. Probably not the best place for a meeting. One shell could do some serious damage to the command.

Pillow looked past Lee, toward the east, said, "Is General Twiggs on the field? Have we heard from General Twiggs?"

There were glances, officers understanding now that Pillow might not be the best commander to have in this situation. Riley said, "Sir, with all respect, my orders from General Twiggs were clear. Find the enemy and engage him."

There were nods, a few muttered comments, and Lee watched the others, thought, They support General Pillow, they want him to do the right thing. He felt an odd sympathy for Pillow. He probably never thought . . . had no idea what a division commander might have to do. But he has good men under him. Lee saw a flag as another of Pillow's brigades moved forward through the rocks. The flagstaff was held high by a compact man with glasses, and he stepped up beyond the small clearing, moved to the base of the hill, while the troops filed past. Another officer appeared, climbing into the clearing, and Pillow seemed to jump in that direction, said, "General Cadwalader, thank God . . . you made it. We were just considering our situation."

Cadwalader glanced at the others, looked curiously at Lee, said, "Captain, did General Scott instruct you what to do once the shooting started?"

It was a strange question, and Lee tried to read the man's face, saw only the grim stare of another veteran. "No, sir. I was able to scout the forward position; however, we could only go so far as the ravine. It is not likely we can cross straight in front of us, sir. The Mexican artillery commands the ground."

Cadwalader stepped forward, moved past Pillow, looked up over the rocks. A shattering blast just behind the officers showered them with rock. Lee put his hands on his eyes, felt the fragments of rock, blinked hard, wiped at his face.

Cadwalader waved his arms toward his staff, shouted, "The flag, you idiot! Lower the flag! You're giving them a target!"

Lee heard a faint apology, saw the brigade flag disappear behind the rocks.

Cadwalader said, "This is not a damned parade."

Lee tried to focus his watery eyes. The others brushed off the dust, hats slapping pant legs. All along the line the incoming shells were still thundering, blowing gaps in the larger rocks, showering the crouching troops with gray dust. He could hear another strange sound, a hollow *clang*, the solid shot bouncing and careening through the rocks. They had always been able to see the shells as they came toward them, the slower flight of the Mexican copper, but there had never been cover like this. The shells impacted and then bounced up at odd angles, ricocheting through the jagged lava, some finding the man who sat behind a fat rock he believed was protecting him.

He could see the wounded being carried back now, still heard the screams of the men when the shells found their target. Pillow was staring toward the rear, and Lee looked that way, saw a man carried past with no legs. He felt his stomach turn and looked away, heard Pillow say, "My God . . ."

There was a new sound now, a sharp clatter of wheels, erasing the horrible image, and Lee saw a horse pulling a field gun, the gun crew riding close behind on more horses, a small caisson. The men quickly dismounted, unhitched the gun, spun it around. Lee saw an officer, a tall thick man, bearing red stripes on a perfect uniform.

The man yelled, "Here, behind these rocks! Aim between them!" The gun rattled into place, the men digging furiously to level the wheels.

The commanders were all watching, and Pillow said, "Thank God. Now, we'll make a fight."

Riley moved up behind Lee, said, "Captain, I would suggest you supervise the gun positions. You're the engineer. Make sure they are in the right location."

Lee saluted Riley, said, "Yes, sir. Right away."

Lee moved slowly toward the gun, admiring how the men's training was coming to life, the precise efficiency of their movements. An officer quickly came toward him, glanced at Lee's rank, moved past, obviously looking for someone with greater authority. Lee watched him climb toward the group of commanders, saw him look briefly at each one, appraising, then he saluted toward Pillow, said, "Captain John Magruder, at your service, sir. We have three more guns moving up. And I believe, two more batteries are coming forward as well. With your permission, sir, we will begin firing at will."

Pillow returned the salute, and Lee watched him focus, holding himself together before speaking. "Proceed, Captain. Knock those fellows out over there."

Magruder's smile was wide. "Count on it, sir. We'll give 'em hell!"

Magruder moved quickly past Lee, who followed, thinking, Observe, Captain. He knows his job as well as anyone in the army. He followed Magruder back to the gun, and now other horses were moving up, the other guns rolling forward. Lee saw another officer leading the way, younger, familiar, the face of Johnston's nephew. The young man saw Lee, nodded quickly, his expression stern. Lee thought, Let him be. It is his time.

Magruder barked a command, pointed down below the trail toward another small flat space, and the young lieutenant turned the horse, his crew following closely, pulling the gun that way.

Lee moved through the rocks until he reached Magruder's gun. The barrel was positioned just behind a shelf of rock. Yes, he thought, they do know what they're doing. Magruder barked a new command,

and the gun crew backed away, one man holding a lanyard, and the gun burst into life in a roar of flame and smoke. Lee felt a sharp pain stab his ears, put his hands up to cover them, thought, Pay attention, Captain. No surprises. He saw Magruder staring out with glasses now, observing, and Magruder yelled something again, and quickly the gun crew swarmed over the gun, then moved away, and the gun fired again.

Lee shook his head, tried to clear his ears of the fierce ringing. He moved toward the other guns. They were already unlimbered, rolling up close to the larger rocks, the men again scrambling to place them in good cover. He saw the young lieutenant again, giving the commands to his men, placing one gun behind another gap in the rocks. Lee moved close, stayed well behind the gun, could see the angle, the line of fire, looked straight down the barrel, thought, Fine, good elevation. The young man did not see him, and Lee moved away to the next gun, where he saw another officer, another familiar face. The man stood stiffly behind his gun, and Lee paused, thought, Yes, too familiar.

He moved up behind the young man, said, "Excuse me, Lieutenant. We have met before?"

The man spun around, seemed hard at attention, saluted Lee, said, "Lieutenant Jackson, sir. I served with Captain Taylor's battery at Vera Cruz."

The accent was unmistakable, the Virginia mountains, and Lee remembered now, the awkward man with the sharp blue eyes.

"Yes, of course, Lieutenant." Lee wanted to say something more, something about the good work at Vera Cruz, but Jackson was already far away, seemed impatient standing in one place. Lee said "Please, do not let me interfere. . . ."

Jackson turned quickly, and the crew seemed to wait for the moment, and suddenly the gun fired, and again Lee was late putting his hands on his ears.

Now all of Magruder's battery was in place, and the men began to find a rhythm, the four guns opening in a rapid sequence. Lee backed away, moved through the thick lines of men in blue, all down low in the rocks. He stopped beside one man, and could see the streak of blue coming overhead. He covered his ears, the movement nearly instinctive now. The shell exploded a few yards behind them. The man seemed to moan, and Lee said, "Don't worry soldier. Stay low." He looked up to where the officers had gathered, thought, We cannot stay here. We don't have the firepower. We cannot duel the enemy like this.

He waited for a pause in the screaming of the shells before moving quickly out of the rocks. He saw the gruff Magruder again, moved up behind him, covered his ears again as the guns fired another volley.

"Captain Magruder, can you tell . . . have you inflicted any damage?"

Magruder stared at Lee with black fire, said nothing, turned again to his guns. Lee was suddenly angry, had no patience for stubborn commanders, shouted, "Captain Magruder, you will cease fire! By order of Captain Lee!"

The crews looked at him curiously, and Lee saw Magruder's face darken, thought, He's going to explode. Keep your tongue, Mr. Magruder. This job is too important for one man's pride. The guns fell silent, and Lee moved between the two closest to Magruder. He climbed up and raised his glasses. He stared out at the wide field of smoke, could still see the flashes of light from the Mexican guns, new streaks of fire coming toward the rocks.

He looked back at Magruder, said, "No, Captain, there is little damage. With all respect, these guns are not big enough. This is not going to work."

Lee backed away, and Magruder moved close to him, said angrily, "I have been ordered to eliminate the enemy's artillery! These guns will perform as I tell them to perform! Give us time, Captain. We will find the range."

"The enemy will find the range as well. And they have two dozen guns. With respect, Captain, this is not a fight we can win."

Magruder stared at him, tried to say something, and Lee still felt the other man's anger, thought, There is no time for an argument. The crews were watching them still, and Magruder turned abruptly, shouted, "Resume firing!"

There was no delay, and Lee covered his ears again, thought, I cannot tell them to stop. He's right, he has his orders. There is nothing for me to say. But it will not take the enemy long to find the range.

He heard the odd metallic thud again, turned, saw a streak of blue light, the ball now bouncing straight up in the air, bounding high above Magruder's gun, a strange twirl of round blue fire. He could see it begin to come down, falling toward the next gun, right into the gun crew, spinning to the side, bouncing off toward the troops behind him. Next there came a scream, the awful sound, and Lee saw one man on the ground, the crew moving low around him, pulling him away from the gun. One of the man's legs was gone, the ball cutting it clean away. Lee felt his gut turn cold, moved beside the soldiers as they carried the wounded gunner behind the lines. The man was still screaming, staring up wide-eyed. He looked straight at Lee, and Lee felt his throat tighten into a hard knot, saw the face of the young lieutenant. It was Preston Johnston.

Lee said, "My God . . . Lieutenant . . . no . . ."

The young man stared at him, but his eyes were empty now, and the screaming had stopped. Lee could not look away, stared through rising nausea. The young man's mouth still hung open, but no sounds came out. The mouth twitched once, making the final faint utterance no one would hear. Lee wanted to move close to him, felt a desperate wave of panic. For a brief moment he could not move, his legs seemingly paralyzed, locking him in place. Then the young man was taken away, the other men quickly disappearing behind the rocks. Lee stared in the direction the litter bearers had gone for a long moment, but he could only see the face of his friend, what this would do to him. I will have to tell him, he thought. He will want to know I was here. Oh, God, Joe. I am so sorry. The crew was already moving forward again, returning to their gun, and he still looked to the rear, said in a quiet voice, "God bless you, young man."

He felt a sudden blast of wind, another shattering explosion, the rain of dirt and small rock pelting him. He tried to concentrate, brushed the dirt away, and Magruder's guns fired. The sound jolted Lee, and he fought now to bring himself back, thought, *Your job,* Captain. There is not time for this.

He moved back toward the gun, thought, They do not have an officer to lead them. Perhaps I should—

He stopped, saw the crew swarming around their gun, while another officer rushed past a pile of rock, moving toward the gun, and Lee saw it was Jackson, the young man taking command. The men did not even look at their new officer, but heard his words, worked the gun as they had before, and now the rhythm was complete again, the guns firing in perfect sequence. Lee moved away, thought, Of course, it has to be that way. Fill the gap, plug the hole. A good officer knows that. That young man is a good officer.

He worked his way back toward the big hill, thought, Back to work, Captain. Find the commanders, find General Pillow.

They seemed to be waiting for him, having moved to another flat open area, farther behind the big hill, a place safe from the enemy guns. Most of the men were seated now, scattered around on the smaller rocks.

Pillow suddenly stood and said, "Captain Lee. You have seen the ravine. Is it possible to advance in that direction?"

Lee saluted absently, still felt a cold sickness in his gut. "It is better than just sitting here."

The other men all looked at him, and a moment of silence passed. Lee pulled himself up straight, thought, Get hold of yourself, Captain.

"My apologies, sir. The ravine is in fact a deep streambed. It is very thick with underbrush. From what I could see, and hear, the stream itself is swift, possibly deep." He glanced at Cadwalader. "A crossing straight into the enemy's guns would be inadvisable. Their artillery controls the ground. As they control it . . . *here*."

Pillow looked at Riley, said, "Captain Lee agrees with your assessment, Colonel. I cannot find fault with the logic. And since Captain Lee possesses the eyes of General Scott, I would ask his endorsement of the plan."

Lee felt uneasy, could feel the stain of Pillow's politics.

Riley stood and said, "Very well, Captain. Since you have scouted this lava field, would you agree that it is possible to move up to the north, and cross the ravine far beyond the enemy's left flank? I propose we send at least two brigades. If we occupy the ground across that road, the enemy forces will be cut off from Mexico City, and if we make enough noise, they most likely will abandon their ground."

Lee looked at Pillow, saw that the general was as nervous as a schoolboy. Cadwalader said, "Captain Lee may be impertinent, but he is correct. We cannot remain where we are. It will be dark very soon. My men are ready to make the move."

Lee felt awkward, thought, It cannot be decided by . . . *me*. I have no authority to order an advance. General Scott would . . . what? Attack? We don't know what's over there, across that road. If reinforcements should come down from the city, we could be trapped. He thought of Twiggs, knew the old commander was advancing behind them, probably close by now, bringing more of his men forward. If Twiggs were here there would be no waiting. And this time, he might be right.

"Sirs, I believe General Scott's instructions were for me to locate a means of assaulting the enemy from this direction. Since we have found the enemy, I believe the general would disapprove of . . . inaction."

Pillow exhaled loudly, and Riley said, "General Pillow, with your permission, my men will file out to the north, followed by General Cadwalader's brigade. We can cross the ravine at a safe distance above the enemy's position. By tomorrow morning . . ."

He paused, and Cadwalader said, "By tomorrow morning, General Scott will be *pleased*."

19. LEE

NO ONE HAD NOTICED THE HEAVY CLOUDS THAT ROLLED toward them, blocking out the usual sunset, the last great glow of orange from behind the tall mountains. As the early darkness put a blessed stop to the artillery fire, the once heavy line of blue that faced the Mexican position was a small part of what it had been. The two brigades under the command of Riley and Cadwalader were away to the north, had marched quickly and quietly out of the lava field, then cut and pushed their way across the wet ravine. As the darkness pressed hard on the field, nearly two thousand men had moved across the valuable road and settled into a quiet camp a half mile north of the Mexican position.

The scouts and the commanders had hoped to see the stars, some piece of a bright moon to guide them into the best position for the morning assault. But the clouds had brought the wind, and soon after, a hard, steady rain.

Lee was still in the small clearing behind the big hill. He had tried to find something in the rocks he could use for shelter, but finally gave up. Every part of him was wet. He discovered that standing was more comfortable than sitting on wet rock. The muffled sound of horses moving through the gloom made him feel no less miserable. A small speck of light appeared ahead of him, one man on foot, walking in front of the horses, holding an oil lamp low to the ground. Lee wiped at his face, blew water through his mustache, saw the wide dark form, the shadow of General Scott.

Scott dismounted, said, "Kill the light."

The lantern went dark, and Scott moved up toward Lee's clearing, said, "Here, if this is the place, put the damned tent here. Quickly."

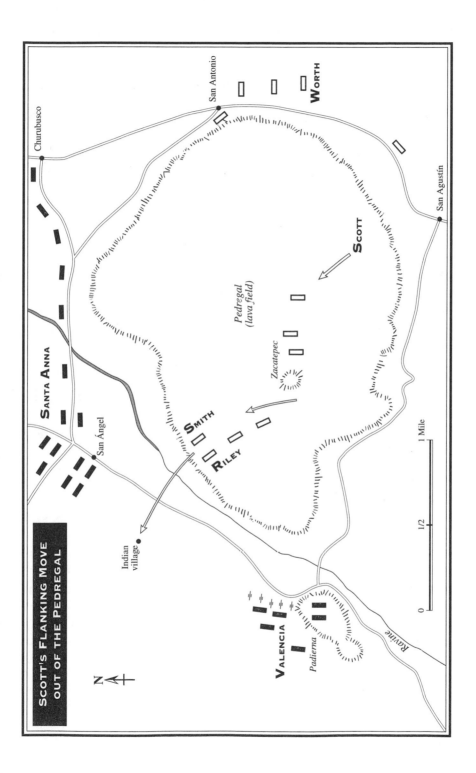

SCOTT'S FLANKING MOVE
OUT OF THE PEDREGAL

N

Churubusco

San Antonio

WORTH

San Agustín

SANTA ANNA

San Ángel

SMITH

RILEY

SCOTT

Pedregal
(lava field)

Zacatepec

Indian
village

VALENCIA

Padierna

Ravine

0   1/2   1 Mile

The men behind him moved forward, scrambled to unroll the dull canvas. Men began to gather, Pillow's officers, and Scott said, "Anyone here seen Captain Lee?"

Lee, who had only been a few feet away, stepped forward. "Right here, sir."

"Fine place you picked out here. You choose it because of the beauty or the fine accommodations?"

Lee wasn't sure if there was humor in the question or not. "This hill is an excellent vantage point, sir. Back here, we're safely hidden from the enemy position."

The tent was up now, men pulling hard on ropes, the stakes hammered down into soft rock. Scott waited a moment, said nothing, then moved to the tent. "Give me a moment, Captain."

Scott turned to the gathering staff, said, "Find some shelter if you can. We may be here awhile. Where's the man with the lamp? Can't see a damned thing." There was movement around the tent, and Scott said, "A safe location, Mr. Lee? You sure about that?"

"Yes, sir. There's a large hill . . . you can't see it now, but the enemy is far—"

"Light the damned lamp. Hope you're right, Mr. Lee. I left a warm dry office to come out here."

Scott moved into the tent, and the tent was suddenly alive with light. Lee glanced back toward the big hill, thinking, I am . . . certain this is a safe location. He strained to hear, fought the sound of the rain, thought, Any sign of artillery, any sound, put out that light.

Inside the tent, Scott was struggling with a huge rubber raincoat, his son-in-law assisting. The coat came free, and Scott sat in a small chair. The general saw Lee and said, "In here, Mr. Lee."

He moved inside, could feel the feeble warmth of the lamp, said, "Thank you, sir. I'm sorry about the rain."

"The joy of war, Mr. Lee. You can't plan everything. Just shows us, God is watching, giving us a challenge. I draw my inspiration by re-membering I have a soft bed in a nice comfortable house not more than three miles from here."

Lee smiled, thought, I did not expect him to be in good humor.

Scott said, "So tell me, Mr. Lee, what the hell have you gotten us into out here?"

AUGUST NINETEENTH, LATE NIGHT

He had stayed with Scott for over an hour, reviewing another map, providing another detailed report. There was no sign of Pillow or Twiggs, and the junior officers reported only what they knew, that Riley and Cadwalader were probably across the road now. Reports began to come in from Twiggs's division, and Lee had been surprised to learn that two more brigades were moving up to the right as well, more of Twiggs's men, under Persifor Smith and a brigade of Quitman's volunteers, commanded now by James Shields. If they had all reached secure ground, and put themselves into position in the awful weather, by morning the enemy would have a force of four thousand men on his flank. Being inside the tent was a relief, but Lee had not stayed long enough to dry his wet socks and soaked shirt.

Scott had to know the position, had to know where the four brigades had stopped. Persifor Smith was the ranking officer of the four brigade commanders, and now Lee was moving slowly out through the lava, to the north and west, on Scott's instructions to find Smith, to find out what the plan would be. When the blessed daylight came, there could be no mistakes.

He stayed close to the trail the troops had used, visible even in the rain, the lava dust now so thick and clotted it held the boot prints of the soldiers. Beyond the lava he slipped through short dense brush, found the ravine. Here the trail was easier. Thousands of boots had trampled the brush into a flat soft road, and the tall thickets that fed down into the ravine itself had been cut away by the men with machetes. The stream was faster now than before the rain, an angry tumble of muddy water. He stayed close to the rocks, where the mass of footprints spread out along the stream, knowing that the men would have found the easiest crossing. He moved quickly across, pulling himself carefully, supported by branches of brush, thorny vines. On the far side he climbed up the sharp muddy rise, pulled himself up to the flat ground, more flattened brush. The hardest part of the journey was past, but in front of him there was no sign yet of the men, of the four brigades, of anything at all.

HE MOVED QUICKLY TOWARD THE ROAD, HOLDING HIS HANDS up to let the rain wash the mud away. Stopping in the middle of the road, he listened hard, tried to hear any sound through the rain's dull roar. He stared up to the north, toward the big city, hoping to see some sign, the telltale glow of light, any light at all, but there was only thick, miserable darkness. He searched the ground beyond the road, thought, Keep moving, Captain.

The trail in the low brush was still plain, and he moved to the west, studied the dark, tried to see something of the horizon. He could finally see shapes, small buildings, huts. The ground hardened beneath him and he knew that he'd reached a small road. He felt for his pistol. He told himself to be careful, but when he glanced down at his side, he thought, Don't count on your powder being dry.

Hearing voices in the distance engaged in conversation, Lee moved toward the sound, could see the outlines of the huts more clearly now. He heard the soft shuffling sound of movement, then saw a man suddenly step close to him. He felt a sharp stab in his stomach, heard the man say, "Easy there, amigo. No sound."

Lee held his hands out to the side, said, "Captain Lee . . . of General Scott's staff."

More men stood around him now, and a man struck at a match, cursed under his breath, struck again, and there was a sudden burst of light in Lee's face. He blinked, heard another man say, "Let him pass. Sorry, Captain. You'd be wanting General Smith, I suppose."

Lee rubbed his stomach, felt the stab of the bayonet still at his coat, said, "Thank you. Yes, General Smith."

"Right this way, Captain. I'll take you."

The man moved past more of the buildings, and Lee followed silently. The huts were all filled with men, some lingering outside, standing under whatever cover they could find. Behind the huts men were spread out all along a wide hill, small clusters of raincoats. Other men were grouping together, forming low flat tents, still others sitting quietly, finding no cover at all.

"Right here, Captain."

The man had stopped, and Lee saw a larger house, heard the rain echoing off its metal roof. He moved up, felt hard stone steps, and the man behind him said, "It's Captain Lee."

He heard boots on the porch, detected faint movement and several dark shapes. There was a burst of light as the door opened. He saw the faces of the men beside him, their bayonets, the guards squinting in the light. He looked toward the open door, moved through, heard a sharp voice, "Close the damned door!"

Then he was inside, his eyes not yet adjusted to the light. He could see blankets hung up to cover the windows, the room filled with a black haze of cigar smoke, the smell of tobacco. There were men sitting, some standing in front of a fireplace, then the faces were familiar, some men laughing.

"You're a sight, Captain. How about some coffee?"

Lee wiped away the water dripping into his eyes, said, "General Smith, thank you. Coffee . . . would be wonderful."

He saw Cadwalader watching him, shaking his head, and Riley was laughing as he said, "Don't imagine you ever thought being an engineer meant walking all night in the rain. Probably didn't teach you that at West Point."

There was more laughter, and Lee nodded, smiled, looked down at the spreading puddle at his feet. "No, sir. I rarely had to do anything like this at Fort Monroe."

The coffee came forward, and Lee took the small earthen cup, felt the steam on his face, smelled the dark richness, the marvelous Indian coffee.

Smith said, "We got lucky, Captain. This is an old Indian village. What folks were here when we arrived took off pretty quick. Didn't seem to care much which side we were on. The coffee is compliments of whoever our hosts are. Didn't catch their names."

Lee sipped the coffee, said, "Thank you, sir. General Scott sends his compliments. I am to find out your dispositions." He glanced at the covered windows, said, "How close . . . are we?"

There was a small laugh, and Cadwalader said, "Right to business. Good. Short meetings. I'd like to get at least a *few* minutes sleep before we resume this war. We're about a half mile north, maybe a little northwest of the enemy's artillery position. Close enough that we don't want him to see anything that looks like a campfire."

Smith said, "Captain, General Scott needs to be informed that our situation here is somewhat . . . precarious. We captured a few stragglers wandering up the road, a few of those boys lonely for their *señoritas* in the city. From what we can tell, there's maybe five, six thousand men down there, under General Valencia. They're situated around a big ranch called Padierna. From our position here we should have a clean shot at rolling up their flank, and possibly getting in behind them. It's pretty rough ground, but that means there's cover. And, according to our prisoners, it seems they have no idea how many of us there are."

Lee was feeling the excitement again, said, "General Scott was hoping you had not been detected. If their artillery is still facing east—"

"Hold on, Captain," Smith interrupted. "We were detected, all right. They sent a squad of cavalry to chase us off, probably figured we were some scouting party. Once they ran into a whole brigade of muskets, those fellows didn't waste any time hightailing it back to where they came from. Just before the rain started, we scouted up to the north. The Mexicans are moving reinforcements this way. A whole *lot* of reinforcements."

Smith stopped, held a handkerchief to his face, coughed roughly, then said, "Not more than a mile or so above us are maybe ten, twelve thousand troops. They didn't seem to be in any hurry, but when they learn how strong we are, that will change. If they come marching down that road, they'll be right in our backside. We are in a very advantageous position, for the moment. Only for the moment."

He stopped, and Lee contemplated the report, thought, twelve thousand men . . . these troops could be cut off, surrounded.

Smith said, "Obviously, I need you to get word to General Scott, Captain. Tell him I intend to attack Padierna at dawn. We will keep one eye on those fellows up north, but my guess is that we can make short work of the forces below us. The Mexicans have yet to stand up to any kind of serious offensive. If we hit them hard enough, quickly enough, we could scatter Valencia's forces all over the countryside. Probably make those fellows above us think twice."

Lee nodded slowly, and Cadwalader said, "Captain, this plan can't succeed if those cannon down there turn this way. We can't respond to artillery, and they'll bust us up good. We need some help from the lava field, a good demonstration, maybe even a full-scale assault straight at their position. General Twiggs has been itching for one, this could be his chance. All respect to General Twiggs."

There was muted laughter, and Smith said, "We need that support, Captain. We need those fellows in the lava field to advance, put pressure on those guns, draw their fire. If we're successful, and the enemy position breaks, General Twiggs can march right on across."

Lee felt the water still flowing down his entire body, moved his toes in the wet boots. He glanced up, listened to the rain, the dull roar unchanged.

"I understand, sir. I will inform General Scott. He should still be at Zacatepec, in the lava field."

Smith coughed again and nodded. "Understand, Captain, that our attack will begin at first light whether we receive support or not. We cannot just sit here and wait to be hammered from two sides. Am I clear, Captain?"

"Quite clear, sir."

Riley leaned forward, placed hands on his knees, said, "General, he should have an escort, some guards. Too dangerous going it alone."

Smith said, "Of course." He turned, pointed to an aide standing behind him, and the man slipped quickly outside.

Lee took a deep breath, backed toward the door, looked at the fireplace, his body greedy for the blessed heat.

Riley stood, moved close to him, said, "Be careful, Captain." He held out a hand, and Lee felt the firm grip.

"Thank you, sir."

Riley backed away, and Smith added, "Good luck. God be with you, Captain. You are dismissed."

The door was opened, and Lee stepped onto the porch, the door closing quickly behind him. The darkness was complete now and he blinked, stood perfectly still, waiting for his eyes to adjust. He felt the guards moving close to him, and a voice said, "Take a minute, Captain. Hard enough to see anything. We'll have a few volunteers here in a moment."

There was a laugh from a man Lee could not see, then shapes appeared on the road, and Lee tried to count, saw six men.

One man stepped up on the porch, said, "Captain Lee, is it? Good, name's Huckabee. Corporal Reavis Huckabee. Appears I'll be leading your escort. At least as long as we can find each other in this damned mess. This is some dangerous work, sir. I'd be mighty beholdin' to you if we survive this mission, you might see fit to find me a promotion."

There was laughter from the others, and Lee heard another voice, "Enough of that, Corporal."

Another man climbed the steps and said, "Lieutenant Ames, sir. These men will accompany you as far as you require."

Lee looked at the six faceless figures. "Thank you, Lieutenant. I'll get them back home safely."

It was a small joke, but no one responded, and Lee thought, No, well, it's not the most pleasant assignment they could find. "We should be under way. Gentlemen?"

He moved to the edge of the porch, shivered slightly and stepped down into the hard rain again. He pulled his coat around him, began to move through the small village, the silent escort falling in behind him.

He passed by more guards, heard their quiet voices, the sound of men moving out of their shelters to watch them as the odd parade moved past. There was a burst of light, a glow above him, and a second later a sharp crack of thunder, but the sound faded quickly, drowned by the relentless rain. There was a small comment behind him, something he could not hear, and Lee thought, An escort is a good idea, I suppose. But if I get lost . . . they will all be lost. That won't help anyone.

The wetness was already soaking him completely, and he focused to the front, tried to see the road, moved through wet grass and short brush. Another flash of lightning came, this one longer, reflecting on the low clouds, and he could see the wide hillside for a brief second and the dark patches where the men waited. In his mind, Lee could hear their prayers and curses, the men enduring the awful minutes until the dawn would come. He did not watch the troops behind him, but he could hear their footsteps in the mud. He moved quickly across the road, tried to find the ravine. He focused on the trail, what tracks he could see, the path now a river of mud from the boots of many men. The ground fell away and he nearly tumbled over the edge of the embankment. He fought for his balance, slid down, his feet giving way in the mud. He slid on his back, rolled over once, felt the brush punching his side. Reaching out, he grabbed a handful of something sharp, the thorns cutting him, but the fall was stopped. He fought his way upright, stood on the sharp slope, flexing his fingers. He could see nothing, the rain and mud disguising the blood from the cuts on his hand. Above him, the men slid down, following him with grim silence.

Lee tried to see through the rain to the far side of the ravine, where the lava would begin. He felt a cold twist in his chest, thought, The trail, don't lose the trail, move straight across. He stepped carefully down, still slid in the mud, but kept control, his hands feeling for the rocks. The sound of the running water was close in front of him now, and there was another sharp flash of light, enough to show him where the stream lay and beyond the dull white of the rocks. He paused, stared at black nothing, moved close to the rush of water. Turning to face the men gathered close behind him, he reached out, felt a man's arm, the hand, held it tightly, said quietly, "Take the hand of the man beside you. One line, all together across the water. No one lets go. Understood?"

The men stepped into place, each one holding to another. He turned, tried to see the water again, stared only at sound, took a deep breath and began to push across.

G UARD STATIONS HAD BEEN SPREAD ALONG THE TRAIL, AND LEE led the men toward each one carefully, calling out through the incessant thumping of the rain, surprising even the most alert guard, the men who stayed close to their muskets. From each station he was given a fresh direction, but little else. There were no fires, no coffee, so there could be no rest, no relief from the rain.

The men were slipping and stumbling behind him, and all of them had fallen more than once. He could feel the raw skin on his knee, the sharp pain scraping inside his pants leg. He had tripped over a sharp stone that he had not seen at all. Do not think on that, he thought, just . . . focus, move in straight lines. He passed between two large rocks, tried to see something familiar, some landmark. He fought against the frustration, the mounting anxiety. You have been here before, he thought, you are moving in the right direction. There was lightning again, a new burst of hard rain, and he stopped, leaned against a tall rock, felt himself breathing in short gasps. Easy, Captain, he thought, slow and steady. It cannot be much farther. He glanced up, the rain washing his face again. There was another flash of lightning, and he waited for the thunder's dull rumble. The lightning came again, and now he saw something new, a wide reflection swelling up in front of him. He stepped away from the rock, waited for more lightning, thought, Please, God, one glimpse, let me see. He waited a few seconds, began to move again, and the lightning burst over him, close this time, lighting up the rocks all around. The reflection was clear now, and close. It was Zacatepec, the great fat hill.

He pointed, said, "There . . . this way."

He moved quickly, stumbled again, caught himself, thought, All right, slow. It's all right. You're here. He moved around the base of the hill, called out, "Hello! Guards! Captain Lee here!"

There was commotion in front of him, and now on both sides men moved out of the rocks. The lightning came again, and the faces were ghostly, the muskets all pointed at him, and he said, "Captain Lee . . . I am Captain Robert E. Lee. . . ."

The voices rose around him in surprise. Their questions and the sounds of their movement flowed together, blending with the rain. He closed his eyes, thought, Thank you, God, for delivering me . . . thank you. He saw light now, the faint yellow of the lamp, felt a rush of shivering excitement. Behind him, Huckabee said, "Well, bless my bones, Captain. I'd a never thought . . . you done brung us home after all."

Lee could not help a small laugh, said to the guards, "Would you gentlemen please see to my escorts, here. They have done exceptional work." He turned, tried to see the faces, caught a glimpse of the corporal's stripes.

"Corporal Huckabee, if it's in my power, I'll get you that promotion. Right now, I have to see General Scott. Excuse me."

He moved toward the light, saw movement around the tent, stopped, straightened himself, stepped calmly toward the tent. Seeing an officer, he said, "Excuse me, can you tell General Scott I have returned?"

The man looked at him, an unfamiliar face, said, "I'm sorry, Captain. The general is not here." The man pointed a dripping sleeve toward the east, toward the far side of the lava field. "General Scott has returned to his headquarters."

AUGUST TWENTIETH, AFTER MIDNIGHT

It had been an easier walk, following the trail cut by his men. He could see their lights, a small sea of campfires, stubborn against the downpour. He moved through the last of the big rocks, out of the lava field. He still had a small escort, growing larger as he moved toward Scott's camp, guards falling in beside him, leading him.

He did not notice the men watching him, the staff moving slowly in behind him, the guards catching glimpses of his uniform, the torn pants, the raincoat ripped down one side. He felt the rain still, his mind numb from the cold, the water that seemed to flood over him in slow waves. He stepped toward the house, heard voices beside him, but he did not understand the words, knew only that he was being asked questions. He still stared up at the lights, felt a hand under his arm, felt the hard pull, more hands, his mind pushing him through the rain, his brain saying, No, do not stop me, I'm almost there, almost . . . home.

"YOU ALL RIGHT, CAPTAIN?"
He could see the lights above him, felt the wetness on his back and realized he was lying down. He sat up, felt the swirling in his brain, his hands pushing against soft cloth. Then there were hands on his arms, helping him to sit. He fought to clear his mind, saw the young Scott sitting behind a desk, saw the walls of a small den, pictures in frames, dark wooden shelves. He tried to see the men holding him, felt the dizziness pull him, heard the young man say, "Dismissed. He'll be all right now."

There were footsteps, the men moving away, and Lee looked at the yellow light, the small flame, then saw a steaming cup, china this time, on the desk, said, "May I?"

The young Scott nodded. "It's for you, Captain. Coffee. Help yourself. Make you feel better."

Lee could see that he was on a small couch, his eyes focused on the fabric's floral pattern. He stood and moved to a chair in front of the young man's desk, where he sat down and wrapped stiff fingers slowly around the cup. He took a slow drink, his mouth and throat burning him awake. He looked around, saw more oil lamps, but the guards were gone. "How did I get . . . here?"

"Are you feeling better, Captain?"

Lee felt the fog in his brain clearing, the warmth returning to his hands. He looked at the coffee. "Yes . . . I'm all right. Tired."

"You fainted, Captain. Outside."

"Fainted?" Lee shook his head, the dizziness fading now, and he sat back slowly. "My apologies, Major. It has been a long night." He felt a sudden stab of alarm. "What time . . . is it?"

The young man looked at a watch, said, "Nearly two o'clock."

Lee sat straight, felt a jolt in his brain, said, "I have to see the general. It is important."

The young man pointed to a door, said, "He's waiting for you."

Lee set the coffee cup down. He stood and steadied himself against the back of the chair. He looked at the young man, saw papers, the man writing something.

"Thank you, Major."

The young man said nothing, motioned with the pen toward the door. "He's waiting for you, Captain."

Lee wanted to say something, but they were never familiar with one another, nothing like friendship passed between them. I don't understand that, he thought, not really. I suppose, for whatever reason, he just . . . doesn't like me.

He moved wearily toward the door, pulled it open and stepped into a sickly yellow glow. He stared up at a great dark shadow on one wall, the exaggerated image of Scott sitting at his desk.

The general looked up, said, "Yes, what—" He stopped writing and let the pen fall out of his hand. "You're alive. And a godforsaken sight, that's for sure."

Lee nodded, felt a smile growing, but could not stop it. He could feel the weariness in every part of his body, the cold chill spreading across his skin. "Yes, sir."

"Get lost, did you? Lord knows, nobody could find their way in that damned place. Don't feel bad, Captain, there's been a whole flock of scouts come sulking through here tonight. We sent people out all over the place, trying to find out what the hell is going on. Nothing to be ashamed of."

Lee nodded at Scott's words, said, "Sir . . . um . . . with your permission, sir. I have a message from General Smith. . . ."

IT WAS AFTER THREE O'CLOCK NOW, AND LEE HAD EVENTUALLY been offered a towel, given another pair of pants, and was finally beginning to feel comfortable. Scott stood beside him, completing the map, filling in details from Lee as needed. Scott leaned back now, said, "This has been one long damned day, Mr. Lee."

Lee nodded, felt the weariness rolling over him, and Scott said, "Coffee, where's the damned coffee?" He shouted past the open door of the small room. "Major! You got any more of that damned coffee? There's an engineer in here about to fall off his chair!"

Lee sat up straight, thought, No, not just on my account, and there was the sound of boots, voices, and Lee turned, saw Twiggs and Pillow limping slowly into the room, water dripping from both men. Scott asked, "Where the hell have you been?"

Twiggs looked toward the only other chair in the room, sat down heavily, and Pillow stood at loose attention, said, "Sir, we attempted to follow our commands . . . we attempted to maintain contact with the troops who advanced—"

Twiggs interrupted, "We got lost. Sir."

Pillow nodded hesitantly, seemed embarrassed, and Lee stood, pointed to his chair. "General Pillow, please . . ."

Pillow smiled weakly. "Thank you, Captain. It has been a long day."

Lee stood back against the far wall, felt himself sagging, tried to stand upright, and Twiggs said, "We have no idea what happened to the brigades, whether or not they made it across to the enemy's position. This has been one big damned mess."

"Your report is noted, General Twiggs. Please take a look at this." Scott held his map out.

Twiggs reached over, took the paper, held it in the lamplight. His eyes grew wide, then Twiggs looked at Lee, said, "This is your work, Captain?"

Lee was too tired to feel embarrassed, nodded slowly.

Pillow slid his chair close to Twiggs, looked at the map, said, "They . . . all made it? They're together? All four brigades?"

Lee said, "Yes, sir. They will be launching an assault against the Mexican position at daybreak. General Smith is in command of the situation, sir."

Twiggs sat back, looked at Lee again. "I'll be damned."

Scott leaned across the desk, said, "General Twiggs, I would prefer you to return to that big hill . . . Zatapata . . ."

He looked at Lee, who said, "Zacatepec, sir."

"Yes, that big damned hill in the lava field. General Smith has requested with some urgency that we provide him with assistance in the form of a large-scale demonstration from that position. We need the enemy's artillery to stay aimed at us, and not him. If you see an opportunity to cross over to the enemy's position, you may do so."

Twiggs stood slowly, and Lee saw the tall man grimace, lean slightly to one side. Twiggs said, "Yes, sir. I will return there immediately."

"Good. General Pillow, you may remain here."

Pillow seemed to jump, startled by the general's words. He composed himself enough to say, "Thank you, sir. Yes, thank you."

The room fell silent. Scott looked at Twiggs's legs and asked, "Are you fit, General?"

"I'm a bit sore, sir. That's all. When we were turned around in the lava field, I took a couple of falls. I'll manage."

Scott rubbed his temples with his fingertips and leaned back. He looked at Lee. "Captain, do you understand the importance of General Twiggs's presence on that ground out there?"

Lee felt as though Scott were talking to him from the end of a long corridor. He tried to stand straight. "Certainly, sir. Someone must be in overall command."

Scott still looked at him, said nothing, and Lee felt the black haze in his mind begin to clear. He looked at Twiggs, who was watching him with a soft, pained look.

Lee said, "Sir, may I be allowed to escort General Twiggs to our position at Zacatepec?"

Scott stood now, said, "You should get started immediately, Captain. Time is crucial."

Lee saluted and stepped toward the door, heard Twiggs moving unsteadily behind him. They walked out of the small house, and Lee nearly stumbled down the steps, catching himself on the railing, but his foot found the deep puddle below, his boot filling with water. He raised his foot and bent his knee, letting the water pour out of the boot. Get hold of yourself, Captain, he thought. He turned, saw Twiggs moving up beside him, still limping.

"I'm right behind you, Captain," Twiggs said vacantly.

Lee moved away from the house, aware of a faint shadow, *his* shadow. He scanned the sky. The rain had stopped. The thin clouds reflected the moon's pale white glow. He moved toward the first big rocks of the Pedregal, marking the opening to the trail. Men fell in behind him, Twiggs's staff and more, the guards who had accompanied Lee, his personal escort. The faces were strange, new, and he thought, Of course, it's the first time I've actually *seen* them. One man was watching him with a ragged toothy grin, and Lee noticed the stripes on his sleeve.

"Onward again, Mr. Huckabee."

He stepped into the rocks, felt a stab of pain in his foot, his knee, still raw, rubbing against the rough wool of his pants. He ignored the irritation, stared ahead, glad that the trail lay lit by blessed moonlight. He heard Twiggs behind him, grunting in pain. Lee slowed a bit, thought, Easy, he's an old man. He settled into a comfortable rhythm then, the march slow and steady. Twiggs fell into step, and Lee did not have to look back. He moved past the tall rocks, through the long rows of small ones, the trail, *his* trail, now smooth under his soggy boots. He stared ahead, looked for the big hill, knew it would be a while yet, that there would still be time to reach the troops, to allow Twiggs to organize and order the details. When the first light drifted across the lava field, the men would be ready, eager for the good fight. The words hit him like a shock—the good fight. He thought of the young man, Johnston's nephew, the image of the horrible wound sitting hard in his mind, a fleshy stump, the bit of exposed bone as white as the moon. The man's leg completely . . . gone.

He did not know where Johnston was, thought, I will have to tell you. I want you to hear it from me. He died doing his duty.

Lee shook his head, as though the motion would clear his mind. He thought of the energy of so much youth, the men who would carry the muskets, who would charge the guns. All our good work, all our pride in a duty performed, and it will still come down to that, to the good fight, the death of so many. He felt awake now, his mind alive. He thought, I do not have the luxury of rest, of sleep, not when those young men are waiting out there for the command that says, *You* go now, *you* face the guns. He glanced again at the moon, thinking of all that remained to be done. A long day indeed.

20. SANTA ANNA

H E SAT IN THE GREAT FAT CHAIR, STARED OUT PAST THE CAMP-fires that covered the hillside. It will be light very soon, he thought, and down there the enemy is waiting, sitting in the dark, planning their evil. But surely some among them already have the feeling, the horrible premonition, and they will not sleep, they will stare up into the black because they know I am here. They already know what will happen to them. And I want them to think about it, obsess about it, know the paralyzing fear of it. To know what a man feels when he stares at death. The fear will spread, and soon all of them will feel it, all the *yanquis* will know they have come here to die.

The idea gave him chills, delicious anticipation. There is no one in Mexico who can do this, he thought. The army, the peasants, they always come to me, they always seek me out in times like this.

He looked across the field, the men sleeping on the wet ground clustered around their small fires, thought, I do not understand that, why they come to me when the crisis unfolds. And there is always a crisis, a country that cannot seem to find its way. I suppose we are still a primitive people, depending on others, still looking to the old customs, the Spanish, the European ways.

He had spent the previous afternoon on the San Ángel road, riding among the troops, riding in the grand carriage as it moved slowly through the camps. He had felt in need of the cheers, the salutes from his men. At one point, deciding to exercise his leg, he climbed down from the carriage, moving among them, even spoke to the officers, surprising them all, especially his personal bodyguards. The soldiers had been kept at a distance, the bodyguards forming a barrier in case they would try to get *too* close. But the cheering came anyway, the hats waving, his name echoing across the field. When he climbed back into the carriage, it was with the buoyant satisfaction that this was not just an army fighting for its home, for some political cause. This was *his* army, and after all, they would still fight for *him*.

He had eaten his evening meal very late, ordered the chefs to prepare something special, a late night feast, a great roast of beef, fresh fruit soaked in a glorious liqueur. It was a unique occasion, a grand prelude to the destruction of the invaders. If his army was to be ready at the first light, there would be no sleep, and so it would be a night he wanted to remember. The feast had seemed entirely appropriate.

As the food disappeared, reports came in of the cavalry assault near San Agustín, where their General Scott had his headquarters. It had been a weak, mindless ride into the muskets of the *yanquis*, nothing gained. Once, the lancers used to be the elite, the most feared part of any army, the men on horses who would ride hard into the enemy, ripping the heart out of any assault. He thought of Buena Vista, that awful day months ago, the battle against that horrible sloth of a man, Zachary Taylor. He, Santa Anna, had formed the lancers himself, sent them at the enemy in a grand parade, even the horses covered in the glorious spectacle, adorned with the symbols of glorious might, the same ribbons and banners their ancestors had carried into battle for centuries. The *yanquis* had waited for them to march in close, and he had thought it was a fatal mistake, allowing his horsemen to begin their final charge so close. He had even led a cheer for them, his foot soldiers coming out of their cover, cheering with him, and they had all thought, Yes, even the *yanquis* are stunned by the sight. Now they will understand something of tradition, of history, of where we draw our strength.

He had thought that Taylor had finally grown weak, lost the necessary resolve for this criminal war, but then the *yanquis* began to shoot, concentrated volleys, and he stared in horror as the lancers had simply come apart, their grand assault collapsing in complete disaster. Now there is no heart in them, he thought, none of the old spirit, none of the traditions. The horses were our strength, but this war has changed that. They cannot stand up to the new cannon. And the *yanquis*, despite everything, shoot straight.

It was difficult for him to walk over the slick, wet ground. He pulled himself out of the chair, stretched the soreness in his back and blinked hard to push away his exhaustion. He saw the silver goblet at one end of the table, thought, More wine, perhaps. But no, not now. If there is to be any sleep, it will come soon. He was still wearing his grand uniform, always kept it on when his men were close by, would not even allow his personal guard to see him in bedclothes. He flexed the leg, took a few steps, put his weight on the wooden leg, anticipating the jolt of pain. There was only the dull ache, and he massaged the top of the thigh, thought, If I am awake, then the army is awake. We must always be prepared, ready to make war when the opportunity strikes.

He stared out at the quiet beauty of the camp, relishing the silence, thought, At least, this late, there are no annoying visitors, no meetings, no one begging for my attention. I do not have patience for government, for dignitaries, for the weak-minded men who still believe they control this country. When they heard that the devil Scott was coming, when the *yanquis* approached the capital, the Congress just disappeared, showed no stomach for running a nation when there was a serious challenge at hand. Even my enemies came on their knees, begging me to save them. It has always been that way. Bureaucrats, men who know nothing of honor or combat, and certainly nothing about power. They cannot lead. There is only one power, and it does not come from pieces of paper or committees arguing endlessly.

He thought of the British and their fawning diplomats. They bring me papers and more papers, begging me to change my *manner* of government. He laughed again, thinking of the official, whose name he could not remember. You dared to sit in my office, a foreigner, using those words, lecturing me about my *illegal dictatorship*, treating me like some criminal. And then you quivered like a frightened child when I pulled my sword. I showed you where the power comes from, what your *papers* were worth, and you ran away like a little girl.

He reached for the silver goblet, swallowed the last remnant in one quick motion. You come here with your titles and your fine suits, describe Mexico in that superior tone, insult me with your absurd suggestions that this war would have ended quickly, just faded away, if *I* had not taken control of the army. A dictatorship is simply control of the country by the will of one man, and it is never illegal when that man is supported by the will of the people. What do the British know of the people? All they know is meetings and committees. What of their own dictatorship, their queen? Did the British people have a voice in her ascension? And the *yanquis*, with their elections and their democracy, look what it has produced, look at the political intrigue. What is *legal* about what they are doing here? What is legal about this war?

He was suddenly feeling lonely, missing the cheers of the people.

I will do that very soon, he thought, ride through the great plaza, surprising them. Victorious. They will gather, come out of their homes and shops, and I will see their smiles, hear their love. That will never change. It is a gift they are only too happy to offer. Even . . . when there is defeat. He could not help thinking of that day, the panicked retreat from Cerro Gordo, returning to the city feeling the shame of that. But the people still cheered, and he thought, It was God who turned against this army. He infected these men with shame, turned us into children, running from shadows in the dark. We had the ground, the guns, and it all just collapsed.

I marched back here to all that talk, so much chatter from the fat politicians, drunk with courage because my army endured one shameful defeat. How quickly the talk was silenced. Their voices were drowned out, not all by my hand, but by the cheers of the people. They understand that I will not win every fight. The *yanquis* are determined to carry out the work of the Devil. It will take more than simply good ground and troops. It will require spirit, pride, patriotism. I showed them that.

There is no one in the capital who dares to speak out against me. They only reveal their treachery. The people still came to *me*, the men still lined up, and now we have an army even greater than before. This time I will be smarter, I will not wait for the *yanquis* to decide our fate. They march to Mexico City, full of confidence. They believe I am weak, beaten, that my people have turned away. They believe the Mexican people will *welcome* their invasion. He felt a burst of fury, shouted, *"The arrogance!"* the sound exploding over the quiet of the camp.

He smiled suddenly, brought his outstretched hand toward his chest. Yes, General Scott, come closer. Now I have brought you right into my trap. You have tied your own noose. Now, God will *see* your arrogance. This time God will understand, and my enemies will be swept away. The people are loyal, they understand strength, they welcome my power.

He looked at his hand, rolled it into a fist. It is so simple, after all. *Here* is the power. If you don't control with a fist, you don't control. Even the Church understands that. It's why there is no threat to me here, no one who can take that from me, not even the priests. They have been controlling their people for centuries. But they do not control me, and that makes them nervous. He smiled again. Yes, I enjoy that. As long as they keep their distance, do not try to interfere with my order, do not preach of some ridiculous new revolution to their flock, then I will respect their desire to stay out of this war. If they do interfere, they will make a mistake. The people will have to choose between their priest, and life under my hand. The people will know what is best. But, no, I do not want that fight. We do not need another revolt. In this country, one spark can set aflame a revolution, and it is always the power, the *fist* that brings it under control.

He was feeling impatient now, began to pace, staring to the annoying darkness in the east. Where is the sun? This day must begin. I am ready. Surely, God is ready. He stopped beside the table now, reached for the empty goblet, suddenly threw it out toward the camp, watched a guard quickly retrieve it. He looked again for the first break in the darkness, the first of the dawn. I am through with meetings and diplomats and peacemakers. It is time to end this madness, time for the enemies of our people to face their deaths, to choke on their own blood. And it is not just the *yanquis*, sleeping in their camps, but those bureaucrats in the city, sleeping as well, with their soft beds and warm women. I will force them all to breathe the fires of hell.

I T WAS STILL DARK WHEN THE COURIER ARRIVED. THE MAN HAD been gone since before the rain came, had gone to General Valencia with Santa Anna's order to withdraw. Valencia had laughed when he heard the reports of *yanquis* moving toward him across the Pedregal. But the reports proved real, and despite Valencia's boast that his cannon would send them back in pieces, it was soon clear that a strong body of *yanquis* had moved out between him and the rest of the army. There was great risk in Valencia remaining isolated, and the order was clear and direct: pull back, move your men north and rejoin the main force. But Valencia had not responded, and once the rains came, and the roads were dangerous, Santa Anna knew that Valencia would disobey.

He did not trust any of his subordinates, could never trust a man who had ambition to command. It was a short jump from command of an army to command of a nation, and many of the generals mistook the devotion and loyalty of their own troops as a mandate from the civilians as well.

Gabriel Valencia was one of the few who had the courage to be vocal, who openly questioned Santa Anna's authority, and Santa Anna had understood for months that he could be a threat. Valencia had skill in the art of politics, had begun to find loyal allies, men who would back him when Santa Anna showed any weakness.

Santa Anna's plan had been deliberate, ordering Valencia to hold the right flank, to prevent access to the city from west of the Pedregal. He had thought Valencia would be out of the way, still assuming that Scott's assault would come from the south, through San Agustín. But when Scott moved his army farther west, and somehow found a way to cross the lava field, Santa Anna understood that fate had played a trick. The one man Santa Anna wanted out of the way was suddenly the one man who was in a position of glory, the man who would meet Scott's assault head-on.

He saw a horseman now, moving quickly up the long rise, watched him move past the fires. He waited impatiently, was already angry at the response he expected to hear. The man jumped down, saluted the guard, and Santa Anna shouted, "Let him through!"

The man moved close, seemed to cower, removed his hat, said, "Excellency, I have word from General Valencia."

Santa Anna crossed his arms. "Why did it take you so long to return?"

The man looked down, said, "Excellency, the position of the *yanquis* made the ride long. . . . I had to go around them. It was raining heavily, I could not see. The route was unfamiliar. I did not want to be captured."

Santa Anna stared at the man, said slowly, "You are an expert in excuses. Did you enjoy the warmth of Valencia's camp? Did he make you comfortable?"

The man looked up now, shook his head. "Oh, no, Excellency, I only saw General Valencia when it was very late. He would not see me when I arrived. I had to wait with his soldiers."

Santa Anna looked up past the man, staring toward the south, thought, He would not see a messenger from the commanding general? What kind of treason is he planning that he would keep me so uninformed?

"Did you give General Valencia my orders?"

"Oh, yes, Excellency. I gave him your papers, and I saw him break the seal. He read the orders, and then he . . ." The man paused, looked again at the ground. "He threw the orders into the fire."

Santa Anna felt the fury boiling up inside, but still he merely stared into the darkness. "Did he respond in any other way?"

The man reached into his coat, withdrew a coil of paper, slowly held it out. "Excellency . . . his response."

He reached for the paper, slid his thumb under the seal, unrolled the dispatch. He turned to the firelight, read the words, the message short, the language blunt. His anger was building again, his eyes skimming the words, *I will remain where the enemy can find me.* He looked at the courier, who flinched, expecting to be struck. Santa Anna shouted at him, "Leave my sight! If you were loyal, you would have informed me sooner. Now there is no time to prepare!"

The man slipped away quickly, climbed his horse, rode away across the camp. Santa Anna turned, stared again toward the east, thought, Valencia disobeys my order because he knows there will be glory in the victory, glory for him alone. God has played a trick on me, has put a traitor in the path of the enemy. My orders were not just about glory. It is strategy as well. If our troops are united, we hold all the advantages, we have the numbers, the strength. Yet, Valencia believes his five thousand men can triumph alone. If he is right, he gains power. If he is wrong, this army is weakened and the *yanquis* will gain confidence. He is foolish and arrogant.

He balled the paper in his hand, thought, I can see him now, strutting in his camp like some grand rooster. What arrogance, making a good show of burning my orders. He walked toward the fire, and his staff moved away, giving him a wide berth. He stopped close to the fire, squeezed Valencia's message hard in his hand, thought, Now I will have to rescue him, save his army. I must send support to a traitor. He tossed the wad of paper into the fire, said aloud, "How dare you burn *my* orders!"

THE TROOPS WERE UP AND MOVING, THE DAYLIGHT FINALLY spreading across the wide hill. He rode in the carriage, the horses at a trot, moving quickly into the road, past the men who were already on the march, the escort riding close beside him. He sat straight in the seat, stared hard to the front, thought, We might still reach Valencia, combine the army. If the *yanquis* stay in their camps, if there is any delay . . .

The carriage rolled up a short rise, reached the top of the hill, and he shouted, "Halt here!"

The driver pulled the carriage to one side, and Santa Anna climbed out, the guards extending their hands to him, helping him to the ground. He stepped away from the carriage, stood in the center of the road, stared in the direction of the sounds now rolling up toward him. There was thunder, a series of low thumps. He had heard the same sounds the day before, Valencia's artillery barrage. But now there were more sounds, something new, and he thought of the weather the night before, glanced at the sky. This is odd, he thought, it sounds like rain, the sound of rain on the hard ground. The sky was clear, and he looked again to the front, knew then it was not rain, it was musket fire, the sounds growing louder, the assault of the *yanquis* already pouring hard into Valencia's army.

HIS COMMANDERS ADVANCED THE TROOPS FARTHER ALONG THE road, spread them out in the open ground above a small Indian village, mud huts and ragged wooden houses. The fight was all down below, spread out all over Padierna. He could see very little, a low flat cloud of smoke hanging tight to the low ground, drifting slowly east. There were familiar flashes of light, the sounds from Valencia's cannon, but the new sounds were louder, more big guns, different, the sharp hollow sounds he had only heard when he faced the *yanquis*.

The commanders had gathered behind him, and he moved toward them now, asked, "The troops are in formation?"

There were nods, one man stepped forward. "Yes, Excellency. We are prepared to advance on your order."

Santa Anna stared at the man, said, "Did I instruct anyone to prepare an advance?"

The man seemed confused, said, "We thought, Excellency . . . the fight is there. The troops are ready to attack."

Santa Anna turned away, looked again to the south, where he could see his scouts moving toward him, the advance skirmish line climbing the hill, a few men waving to the officers, signaling something.

He said aloud, "What are they doing? What does that mean?"

Now a man was running up the hill toward him, still waving, called out, "Excellency, they are coming! The enemy is coming!"

He stepped forward, tried to see past the man, the smoke still rising, said, "This is madness! I will see what is happening!" He turned, the guard rushing forward to help him, and Santa Anna pushed the man to the side, said, "Out of my way! I will see what is happening!"

He climbed awkwardly into the carriage, shouted to the driver, "Move!"

The man slapped the horse with the leather straps, and the carriage jerked forward. Santa Anna leaned out the window but could see nothing, so he sat back in the carriage, began to pound his fists together, asking aloud, "What is that traitor doing?"

The carriage moved down the long rise, past the small village,

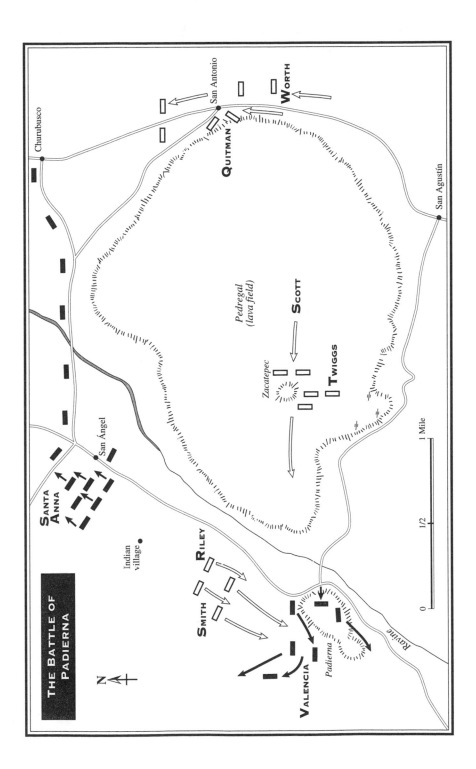

THE BATTLE OF
PADIERNA

N

Churubusco

San Antonio

WORTH

QUITMAN

San Agustín

Pedregal
(lava field)

SCOTT

TWIGGS

Zacatepec

San Ángel

SANTA
ANNA

Indian
village

SMITH

RILEY

VALENCIA

Padierna

Ravine

0   1/2   1 Mile

where the guards swarmed past him, pushing their horses in front of the carriage. They climbed another small rise, and the smoke was above him now, and he could smell the powder, the thick odor of sulfur. The carriage jerked to one side, and the driver shouted something to the horse, stopped the carriage, then said, "Excellency . . . look!"

Through the window, he saw a soldier running past, the man looking at him with dead, hollow eyes. He yelled at the man, "What is happening? Who is your commander?"

The man said nothing, merely stood beside the carriage gasping for breath. Santa Anna opened the door and pushed the man away hard, stepped down onto the road, a dense choking cloud of smoke blowing around him. He could hear horses behind him, the officers, and heard shouting, orders, could see a flood of men suddenly in front of him, running toward him, and it was not the enemy, not the blue of the *yanquis*. It was Valencia's men, *his* men, some with wounds, some stumbling, falling. He felt for his sword, stepped into the center of the road, the flood of chaos now swarming all around him, and he began to shout, "Stop! Have you no shame?"

The horde was passing by him, the men in a panicked retreat, and his fury boiled over. He waved the sword, striking the men as they passed by, still yelling at them, "Stop! Cowards!"

There were hands on him now, and he felt himself pulled to one side, close to the carriage. Turning, he saw the face of an officer, the man saying, "Excellency, it is too dangerous here! We must go!"

He stared at the man, thought, You will die for this, and he raised the sword, but there was a flash of light, a thunderous crash, then screams from the retreating troops. He saw the fresh crater in the road, a bloody mass, a piece of a man's body, headless, spilling itself into the road. He felt himself lifted up into the carriage, hands pulling him roughly. The carriage lurched forward, spun in a tight circle, and he fell against the seat, the sword still in his hand. There were shouts all around him, men on horses, and he pulled himself up, could still see men running, but the carriage was moving with them. The carriage reached the crest of a hill, and Santa Anna shouted, "Stop here! This is far enough! I have to see!"

The driver obeyed, and he eased out of the carriage again. All across the open ground, a steady flood of troops, wagons, horses flowed away from the battle lines, as though moving on a powerful current. He still held the sword in his hand, felt his rage building, thought, I will hang Valencia. I will see that man burn in hell for this. Disobey my order . . .

The sounds of the fight were moving toward him now, a wave of musket fire flowing up from Padierna. There were more impacts of the enemy shells, some coming close, the ground shaking under him. He could see horses moving toward him, his own men, officers. One man rode close, dismounted, and Santa Anna saw the face of Colonel Cardozo, the efficient man, always calm.

Cardozo said, "Your troops are waiting for the order, Excellency. The enemy has broken General Valencia's position. It has been a disaster. There is no order, on either side. If we move in now, we can still save Padierna, still assist General Valencia. May I order the charge, Excellency?"

Santa Anna looked at him, thought, They should all be like this one. They should all be as loyal. There is a price for disobedience, for not showing the proper respect. He thought of the word, disaster. It has been Valencia's disaster. This will be a lesson, this will be the traitor's price.

"There will be no assault. Prepare to retreat back to San Ángel."

Cardozo stared at him, looked down the broad hill, said, "Excellency . . . retreat? The troops are ready to advance. We are very strong here."

Santa Anna looked at the young man but did not answer. Your loyalty saves you from a lashing this time, he thought. I do not give my orders twice. He turned, moved to the carriage, climbed up slowly, settled into the seat. Cardozo was still watching him, his face full of questions. Santa Anna thought, He is too young, he does not yet understand.

"Colonel Cardozo, there will be no saving General Valencia. His defeat will be his alone. That will be his shame, his reward for disloyalty. It is beyond my control. Come, move the men into position. We will prepare for another day."

21. SCOTT

THERE WAS NO ORGANIZED FIGHT NOW, THE FLOOD OF TROOPS and guns moving in all directions, a confusing sea of assault and retreat. The Mexican forces around Padierna were simply gone, had left behind all of their guns and nearly fifteen hundred men either dead or captured, including four generals. Because they had expected the Americans to come straight at them from the lava field, most of Valencia's troops had never been a part of the fight. When the first rush of sounds came from above and behind their position, there was no order that could hold them in place. Even Valencia himself had fled, scattering his men all over the countryside as they tried to find a safe route north, a route that would take them to the safety of the defenses close to the city.

Scott had climbed Zacatepec early, stayed high on the crest of the big hill while Pillow and Twiggs tightened the circle, clearing Padierna of any defenses in less than an hour of fighting. Now, what fight was left was flowing rapidly north, and Scott had followed, had come across the ravine, moving out of the lava field with the last wave of troops. They splashed through the wide creek, the men surging out hard and fast into the fields of Padierna, troops who would only see the enemy if they could catch up to their rapid retreat.

He pushed the horse up the wide road, was moving north himself behind the hard advance of Twiggs's troops. He stopped, the staff gathering close behind him, following his gaze out across the confusion of the vast hillside, scattered signs of the fight, the debris of a panicked retreat, swarming with men in blue. From the long ravine above Padierna the wave of men was slowly pulling together, their momentum and the orders pushing them all in one direction, focusing on the enemy they were pursuing.

The troops began to move toward the road, officers guiding them into position, units organizing again, and they could see him now, no mistaking the sight, the huge man in the grand old uniform perched high on the big horse. Even the officers were gathering, leading the cheers, the pace of the fight slowing again, the distraction coming from the glorious sight of their commander staking his claim to the field of battle.

He always absorbed the sounds of the men, bathed himself in their loyalty and the demonstration of their affection. But the moment was passing quickly, and he began to feel impatient, frustrated. He looked back to the staff, shouted, "Do we know where Twiggs is?"

Expressionless faces stared at him. He scanned across the field again, over the heads of the mass of men who were still moving into ragged lines, and he said aloud, "Where the hell are my generals?"

There was a sound behind him, and he turned to see an aide pointing up ahead, the man saying something Scott could not hear. He turned back as an officer moved toward him, pushing past the flow of troops. He smiled when he recognized the weary stagger of Captain Lee.

"Well, now, here's a friendly face. Tell me, Mr. Lee, does anyone know what the hell is going on up there?"

Lee was breathing heavily, and Scott sat back in the saddle, thought, Give him a moment.

"Take your time, Captain."

Lee fought for air, took one long breath, looked up at Scott, said, "Yes, sir. Colonel Riley's brigade is close to the retreat of the enemy. There has been some resistance near the main intersection, but the enemy is moving north, toward the Churubusco River. It is believed that the retreat has been complete, sir. I heard that Santa Anna himself was observed making his way toward the city."

Scott looked to the north, the troops around him now filing past with some sign of order. He climbed down from the horse, said to his aide, "The map . . . bring me the damned map."

Lee moved with him, pulled his own map out of his coat, began to unroll it, and Scott looked at the crumpled paper, the scribbles of pencil, turned to his son-in-law, said, "Never mind."

Lee spread the map on the ground, and Scott bent over, said, "I assume this is a damned sight more up-to-date than what *we* have. Tell me a story, Captain."

Lee ran his finger along the road beside them, pointed now to the intersection above the town of San Ángel. "We have the option of going north, sir, which will lead straight to the city, or we can move east, and push through the village of Churubusco. There is a bridge . . . here, that crosses the river."

Scott straightened, groaned, put his hands behind him, massaged the stiffness in his back.

"Next time, Captain, bring a table. So, we can cross the river, push that much closer to the city, just like that. I doubt it. There was too much of an army up there for them to just have . . . vanished. Santa Anna is still in command. The question is, *where* is he in command? If we move on the north road, we could extend ourselves, divide the army, and that will leave General Worth too isolated. He will be the first to scream like hell about that, whether his troops are close to the enemy or not. With our limited strength, it's best we link up with him, move north together. I will have his people advance up the St. Agustín road and link up just below Churubusco . . . here. We will move against that bridge together."

Lee was still looking at the map. "Sir, excuse me, but this road north . . . if it's open, we could move past Churubusco without being bottled up at that bridge. We should scout that ground."

There were horses moving back through the tide of troops, and Scott said, "Hold on a moment, Captain." He stepped up on the road, saw Twiggs now, the old man covered in gray dust, riding tall in the saddle. Twiggs stopped the horse, looked at Scott, paused dramatically then slowly lifted his hand in salute. Scott watched the spectacle, thought, All right, you gray-haired peacock, strut a bit. You earned it.

The moment quickly passed, and Scott said, "We're having a good day, General. What's going on up there?"

"Sir, General Pillow and I have conferred at the intersection up ahead. We are of the opinion that at the speed we are advancing, we can storm the gates of the city before dark. I speak for General Pillow when I recommend the troops be ordered to continue their pursuit."

There were cheers now, men moving past Twiggs, reacting to his words, but he stared hard at Scott, refusing to acknowledge the salutes, would not let on that there was anything of a performance to his words.

Scott glanced at the passing troops, thought, Enough of this.

"General, walk with me. I would prefer this discussion be private. Captain Lee has a map."

Twiggs climbed down from the horse, and Scott waited for him, watched as his expression changed, the smugness of a man feeling his popularity now slipping away, replaced by a sullen frown. Scott thought, Don't take it so hard, General. You'll have your share of glory after all. But for now it's good to remember who is in command.

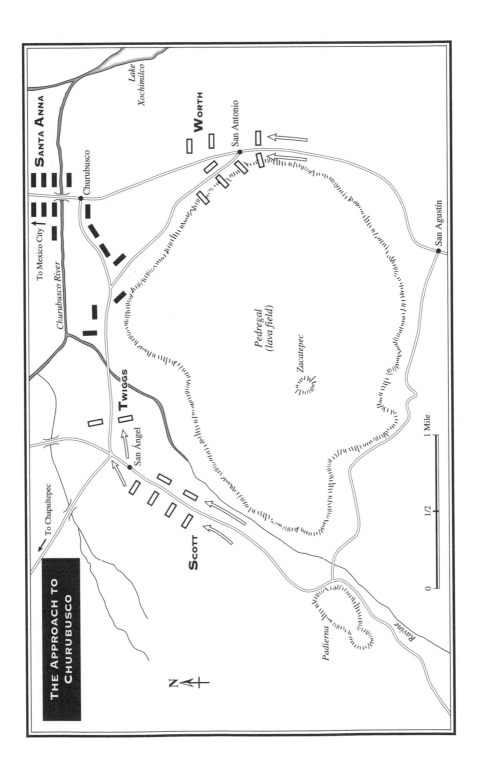

THE APPROACH TO CHURUBUSCO

N

SANTA ANNA

Lake Xochimilco

WORTH

San Antonio

Churubusco

To Mexico City

Churubusco River

San Agustín

Pedregal
(lava field)

Zacatepec

TWIGGS

San Ángel

To Chapultepec

SCOTT

Padierna

Ravine

0   1/2   1 Mile

Twiggs was beside him, and they moved out into the grass. Scott stopped, stared out across the open ground, could still see small groups of men in blue flowing toward him, the last of the disorganized units finally coming together. "Where is Santa Anna, General?"

Twiggs was silent for a moment, and Scott turned to him, saying, "It's a good question, don't you think?"

"I don't know for sure, sir. The Mexican retreat was a mass of confusion. You couldn't tell troops from civilians."

"Been meaning to ask you about that, General. I heard reports that there were as many as twelve thousand Mexican troops up on this hill in front of us. I know what happened to the people who were with Valencia. That's what's making that big damned cloud of dust up there. But where did the rest of them go?"

Twiggs rubbed his chin, said, "Best we could tell, when Valencia's defense collapsed, the rest of the Mexican troops withdrew. Valencia's retreat probably panicked them too. From what we could see, they were hell-bent on getting across the Churubusco River. We saw some of that. It was a mob . . . didn't look like much of an army at all. Can't say how much farther they've run by now."

Scott was feeling a new frustration, thought, He is still the same man, I cannot escape that. He seems to forget there's actually an enemy out there at all, like this war is all about a one-way fight, the only direction is forward. Sometimes . . . that is dangerous. He glanced at the map in Lee's hand, said, "General, I hope these instructions are clear. You will move your men on the east fork of the road, hold to a position below Churubusco. General Worth will advance from his position and hook up with your right flank. Until we know what Santa Anna is up to, I want this army concentrated."

Twiggs seemed wounded, and Scott said, "General, for God's sake, Mexico City isn't going anywhere. If we don't get inside those gates today, maybe we can do it tomorrow. I have to think of the safety of this army. I shouldn't have to explain that. In fact, General, I have no intention of explaining it again."

Twiggs straightened, said, "I understand, sir. If you wish, I will convey your orders to General Pillow. He is forming the troops at the intersection. He . . . expects to send them northward."

"What he expects is to follow my instructions. You have my instructions, General?"

Twiggs saluted, said, "Yes, sir." He walked slowly to his horse, climbed up, said nothing. Scott watched him, thought, Good, no argu-

ment. It's wise to let me have the last word. At least they are learning
how to do *that*.

Twiggs moved the horse away, and Scott glanced at Lee, saw the
map still in his hand, said, "Probably wish you hadn't heard all that,
eh, Mr. Lee? Sometimes you have to be a damned parent. You sure as
hell can't assume they will do the right thing."

Lee said quietly, "I assure you, sir, nothing said will be repeated."

"No, I'm sure of that, Mr. Lee." He watched Twiggs moving
away, cheered by his men, said, "I must admit, I'm intrigued by that
open road north. Let me see the map. . . ."

Lee unrolled the map again, held it out, and Scott studied the
roads and Lee's drawings. "If Twiggs's wishful thinking is accurate, and
there is no opposition, we *could* be in the city by tonight. Hate to let a
good opportunity get away."

He turned, walked slowly toward the road, Lee moving behind
him. I wish I knew, he thought. I wish I knew where Santa Anna went.
He's not ready to hide behind walls, not yet. He's too strong. He had
twelve thousand men right near this spot yesterday, and they simply . . .
backed away? We swept Valencia from the field, rolled up this entire
flank, and I cannot accept that a force larger than ours decided that
was just fine, no problem at all. We'll fight you again some other day.
We are too close to the capital, too close to *ending* this. It cannot all be
this easy.

"Captain, I want some people to try that northern road. If Santa
Anna is putting up any kind of defense along that river, we can get up
behind him. Seems to be the best strategy we have. Take two brigades,
try to use fresh troops."

Lee moved beside him, said, "Sir? Are you ordering me to lead
two brigades?"

Scott looked at him, saw wide eyes, a fog of weariness on Lee's
face. He smiled, said, "Mr. Lee, I don't expect you to lead the damned
charge. But you're the best guide we have. I need to know they're
heading in the right direction. You drew the map, for God's sake." Lee
seemed stunned, and Scott said, "Problem, Captain?"

Lee shook his head, blinked hard. "None, sir. Should I begin . . . ?"

"*Now*, Captain."

22. LEE

AUGUST TWENTIETH, EARLY AFTERNOON

THE MARCH HAD ALREADY BEGUN EAST OF THE INTERSECTION, and Lee watched as Twiggs led his troops toward the first of the Mexican defenses. Pillow had already gone, moving farther east, and word had been given to Worth to move up to connect with Pillow's flank. The two brigades that would go with Lee were a mixed lot, the veterans under James Shields, men whom Lee had helped put into position at Cerro Gordo, and the new brigade under Franklin Pierce, part of the blessed reinforcements that had reached the army in July.

Pierce would march first, and his men were forming quickly. Lee had not yet spoken to Shields, understood that Shields was the senior commander, and that by now Twiggs had sent him the order to follow Lee's guidance.

Lee rode back along the line of troops, the horse bouncing under him, the footing uncertain in the loose gravel at the edge of the road. Lee focused on the reins, held on tight, had not been on horseback in several days. The weariness was now blossoming into a complete fog of exhaustion, and he fought against his mind drifting away. It had been two days, and it most certainly would be one more. He held himself upright, stared ahead, his mind repeating the same words, Find General Shields.

He saw a group of horses carrying officers, more riding up, gathering. He spurred the horse, thought, There, surely. He must be there. The horse slipped, stumbled on the edge of the road, a slope of soft dirt, and Lee slid sideways. He nearly lost his grip, pulled hard on the reins, reached out with one hand and grabbed the horse's mane. He was back upright, looked at the faces of the men still watching him qui-

238

etly, respectfully. The officers were moving toward him, and one spoke, "Captain, you look a fright."

He saw the face of Joe Johnston now, the man trying to smile, but Lee could see the shattering grief, Johnston's own exhaustion showing through tired red eyes.

Their horses moved close together, and Lee said, "Joe, you have heard. I am so very sorry."

Johnston nodded, said nothing, and Lee continued, "I was there. I saw him. There was nothing anyone could do."

Johnston looked down and said, "He was too young, too young to fight a war." He paused for a moment. Lee tried to speak, to say something to fill the quiet, but Johnston looked at him with tear-filled eyes, said, "You couldn't tell him that, you know. So many of them . . . come out of West Point thinking they're men, mighty warriors. They have no idea what a war really is, what . . . death really is." He paused again, said quietly, "He could have been my son."

Lee could see the struggle in Johnston's face, grief and anger, the pure awful sadness. It is another wound, this one so much worse. He felt helpless now, tried to think of words, something to comfort. "He is with God now."

Johnston nodded slowly. Lee saw the tears on his face, the man's control gone. Johnston's shoulders shook from the short sobs. Lee put a hand on his friend's shoulder, and Johnston took a deep breath, fought for control. "God has a great deal of company these days."

Lee still fought for words, but there was nothing he could say. He thought, This will stay with him for a long time. But it cannot affect him like this. Men will die, but we still have our duty. He started to speak, held it back. No, I cannot say that to him, not now.

There was a rumble of thunder from the east, and all the faces turned toward it, the troops in the road coming alive, the hum of their voices growing. Lee looked past Johnston, saw the faces of the officers, mostly unfamiliar, and beyond them were more horses, moving forward. Lee saw the flag. It was Shields. Lee leaned close to Johnston, said, "We will talk later, Joe."

Johnston put a hand on his friend's shoulder, said, "Thank you, Robert. I'll be all right. It just takes time."

Lee moved the horse toward the gathering horsemen, and Shields saw him now, said, "Well, Captain Lee. You are our guide once more."

The sounds rumbled again, and Shields looked that way, said, "Worth's division. They should be close to the bridge by now. Sounds like a few Mexicans hung around to give them a reception. All right, Captain, let's move. For a while at least . . . this is your show."

Lee saluted. "Sir, General Pierce's men are already in column at the intersection. Your men should stay up close. We will march north, until we are past the river. After that, we will see what opportunity presents itself."

"Whatever you say, Captain."

The sounds from the east had grown steadier, and Lee turned his horse and moved quickly alongside the troops. Up ahead he could see more flags. He slapped at the horse, said aloud, "Come on. Let's go."

The troops began to cheer as he passed, a chorus of *hoorahs*, the voices blending together with the hard sounds of the growing fight. He focused on the horse, thought, Stay up, easy now, stay up. No time to fall. He heard his name, the officers calling out to him, and he looked for the source of the voices, saw only a blur of faces. He tried to ignore it, thought, This is not happening . . . it is some odd dream. He tried to sort through the sounds, focused on the growing thunder, but he saw the faces of the men again, and they were not staring out toward the east, toward the low rumble, as the troops always did. They were looking toward *him*. He saw a young officer holding his hat high, saluting him, a quick bow, and Lee stared through a fog of confusion, thought, No, I am not your commander. . . .

He spurred the horse. The road wider now, the horse's steps became more solid, steady. He felt the rhythm of the ride holding him in the saddle, and he looked again to the flags, saw Pierce, more officers, all watching him. There was laughter, men pointing at him, and he glanced back to the troops, the cheering now falling away.

He moved the horse close to Pierce, who said, "They're giving you a hero's welcome, Captain. Must make you very proud. Some fine work, I must say."

Lee nodded, didn't know what to say. Pierce looked away, then said, "All right, Captain, whenever you're ready."

Pierce moved his horse slowly, waiting for Lee to move in front. The officers and the column of troops began to march behind him. Lee felt the fog in his brain lifting, his energy returning. Out front, the skirmish line was moving ahead of the column, the men spreading out on both sides of the road. To the east the sounds were louder still, closer. He thought, It must be Twiggs, the left flank is engaged as well. The entire army is engaged. Except for . . . us. He pushed the horse again, moved faster, could see smoke rising to the east, the fight growing around Churubusco. Pierce was close beside him, and he thought

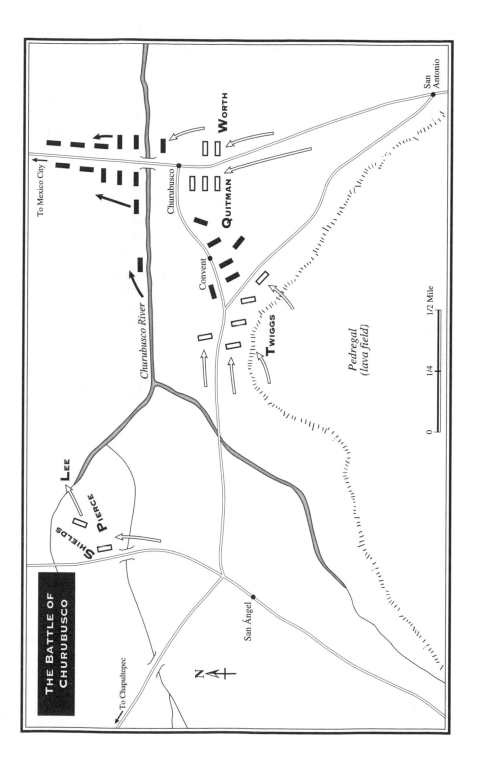

THE BATTLE OF CHURUBUSCO

San Antonio

WORTH

QUITMAN

Churubusco

To Mexico City

Churubusco River

Convent

TWIGGS

Pedregal
(lava field)

LEE

PIERCE

SHIELDS

San Ángel

To Chapultepec

N

0   1/4   1/2 Mile

of his words, hero's welcome. Surely, he thought, he cannot mean . . . me. The troops were cheering their own, cheering the sounds of the fight. They know it will be their turn very soon.

THEY HAD STAYED ON THE ROAD WELL BEYOND THE RIVER, THE northerly road crossing far to the west of the fighting. The bridge was small and there was no defense, and if there were Mexican troops at all close by, their focus was to the east, to the fierce fighting at Churubusco. Lee had scanned the river itself, a straight line, saw that it was hardly a river at all, more like a drainage ditch carved into soft marsh, pulling water from the low wet ground. They were close enough to see the fighting now, a mass of Mexican troops defending the main bridge. The Mexicans held a fortified position, and many of the sharp sounds of cannon were not from the American side.

Above the river, Lee led the troops into the fields, moved through soft mud in the cornfields. It was not long before they could see another road in front of them, and Lee did not have to look at his map. It was the road that led north from the bridge at Churubusco, straight to the gates of Mexico City.

Pierce's troops were spread into battle lines now, and Shields was close behind. Lee still moved alongside Pierce, the horses fighting their way through the difficult ground. He focused up to the left, could see small buildings, a fence row, livestock pens.

"General Pierce, there's some sort of outpost or ranch. We should move to occupy those buildings. That would give us an anchor on the road. We could be in position to cut off the enemy's retreat."

Pierce looked through his field glasses. "We better hurry, Captain. Look toward the bridge."

Lee raised his glasses, focused toward the sounds of the fighting, saw movement on the road behind the bridge, a flow of troops moving north.

Pierce turned, said to an aide, "Get General Shields. He must see this."

A voice called out from behind, "Sir, he is coming forward now."

Lee still glassed the road, said, "They are pulling away . . . it looks like a retreat!"

Shields led his staff, pushed his horse through the stalks of corn. He moved up beside them.

Lee said, "General Shields, we have observed enemy troops moving north, away from their position at the bridge. If they are in retreat, they will certainly be vulnerable, in some disorder. We may have an opportunity to cut them off."

Shields rode past them, gazed out toward the small buildings, said, "Double quick, gentlemen. Let's cut that road. General Pierce, you may take the left flank. My men will move up on your right." He looked at Lee now, said, "Good work, Captain."

Shields spun his horse, moved quickly back toward his men. Pierce was already giving the orders to his aides, the officers pulling their men forward.

Lee felt the rising excitement, thought, It could be over very soon. If we cut them off, there might be nothing for them to do but . . . surrender.

He rode forward, moved up close behind the advance of the troops. There was no sound beyond the steady roar from the right, from around the bridge, and beyond, below the river. The troops in front of him seemed suddenly to rise up in one long line, and he saw they were climbing a small causeway, a dry ridge rising up from the marshy ground. They began to disappear, dropping down the far side, and he pushed the horse, climbed the ridge as well. He stopped. He could see the road clearly. He glassed again, observed a thick column of troops, thought, They're not moving very quickly for a retreat.

He watched Pierce ride up beside him. Pierce said, "We'll be in those farm buildings in a few minutes. That will anchor our left flank on the road. General Shields's men should be alongside us soon. I doubt anyone will be retreating past *this* position."

Lee said nothing, heard the word in his mind, *retreating,* still studied the road, saw several flashes of light, small puffs of gray smoke. He lowered the glasses, felt his stomach slowly turn, said quietly, "My God . . . down . . . get down."

Now he could see the streaks of blue light arcing toward them, the artillery shells ripping the air, and he shouted, "Get down!"

He pulled the horse back off the ridge, and the shells began to burst just in front of the ridge, then out to the left, where Pierce's men were still moving into position. He jumped off the horse, heard yelling, officers ordering their men to take cover, but the orders weren't needed. The men quickly hugged the soft ground, already finding any cover they could.

Lee moved slowly up the side of the causeway, heard a sharp

scream, then men began to shout, and he saw a horse bolt past him, galloping away in a panic through the tall grass. He pulled himself to the top of the ridge, saw Pierce on the ground, his staff gathering close.

Lee moved quickly beside Pierce, said, "Sir! Are you wounded?"

Pierce did not answer, his eyes staring in a daze. Lee felt a hand on his shoulder, and Pierce's aide said, "We have him, Captain. Knocked his head. He'll be all right."

Pierce was carried back into the taller grass, and Lee was alone now, standing high on the dry ground and looking toward the road. Shields's men were moving up in line beside Pierce's brigade, the low blue mass spreading to the left, disappearing into the cluster of wooden buildings. They had begun to answer the Mexican assault, and Lee could hear the growing chatter of musket fire, smoke now flowing across the open ground near the road. He raised the glasses again, scanned the Mexican position, saw a burst of smoke from a volley of Mexican muskets. Behind him, Shields had moved close to the protection of the dry ridge, and Lee heard his voice, "Captain, get back here! Get down!"

Lee moved back, slid down behind the small ridge, saw Shields now on the ground, the horses being led away by an aide. Shields said, "Pierce is wounded, but they don't think it's serious."

Lee nodded, said, "Yes, I was with him."

"What kind of strength we facing, Captain?"

Lee stood now, brushed the dirt from his coat, thought of Shields's compliment, said, "You may have been premature, sir. My work here was not especially good. We did not anticipate the enemy might have prepared for us. They just waited for us, held their fire until we were in close range. It was a poor job of scouting. They are on the road in strength, sir, a good deal of strength."

"We're in the rear of their bridgehead, Captain. They are protecting their position. It's simply good tactics. We had to anticipate that. Too easy to believe they were running away."

A staff officer moved close, said something to Shields, and he turned to Lee, said, "You're on your own, Captain. I have to move forward, stay close to the men, keep them together. I've ordered some field guns moved up, Lieutenant Reno's battery, if they can make it through all this mud. Keep your eyes open for them, Captain, send them where they can do the most good."

The fight was growing in front of them now, and Lee watched Shields move away, slip beyond the ridge. Alone again, he sat for a moment, thought, I should have moved forward, scouted close to the

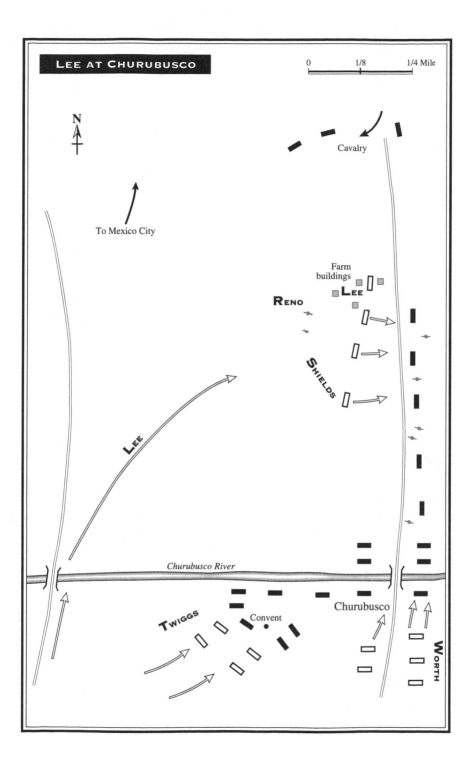

LEE AT CHURUBUSCO

0   1/8   1/4 Mile

N

To Mexico City

Cavalry

Farm
buildings

RENO

LEE

SHIELDS

LEE

Churubusco River

TWIGGS

Convent

Churubusco

WORTH

road. I thought . . . they were in retreat. This is the price for arrogance, for ever believing it will be easy. General Scott understands, even if some of the others . . . even if *I* do not. They are still an army. They will still make a fight.

S HIELDS HAD KEPT HIS MEN IN LINE FOR NEARLY AN HOUR, ABSORB-
ing a steady barrage of musket fire from the Mexican position.
When Lee led Reno's battery into line, the added power from the American cannon began to take effect on the Mexican strength, and the volleys finally began to slow.

Lee was keeping close contact with Shields, and Shields had sent him out to the left flank, behind the safe cover of the ranch buildings. The troops in the small house were facing south and east, the men firing steadily at the Mexican position on the road. He sat close to an open window, facing north toward the city. There had been skirmishers sent up that way, guarding against anyone slipping past the flank. While the fight was steady to the right, the road above had been quiet. Word had come back to the officers, and to him: there was something moving toward them, a column on the road to the north, coming down from the city. He could see the front of the column, a scattering of bright colors, flags held high. The skirmishers did not give him any detail, but they did not have to. He knew what it was, could see clearly a heavy column of Mexican cavalry. His eyes began to water, and he lowered the glasses, blinked through the weariness, tried to focus. We are too close to the city, he thought. It is easy for them to get support. If the lancers keep coming, keep to the road, they will hit us right here, right on the flank.

He focused on the sounds nearest to him, looked at the men sharing the small wooden hut with him, firing muskets through the win-
dows on the far side. There was an officer watching him, a short major with a thick black beard. The man had followed Lee's gaze, had seen the new threat for himself, said, "Captain, keep me informed. We have to pull back from here if they advance much closer."

Lee nodded, said, "Certainly, sir."

He wiped at his eyes, raised the glasses again, saw the column mo-
tionless, the flags still, thought, All right, what happens now? They know we're here, certainly. Maybe they won't get too close . . . just observe. Maybe there's only a few of them, hard to tell from this angle. But even if there's not much strength, for cavalry to just . . . sit there. That would be a mistake.

He had two aides with him, two nervous couriers from Shields's staff. They had moved hay bales into the center of the hut and settled down behind their blessed protection, teased by the men with the muskets. Lee looked around now, saw only the tops of two hats, said nothing, thought, The army's finest. They're in no hurry to leave here. That may have to change.

He stared through the field glasses again, saw a change in the column. He could see many flags, thought, A dozen, more. Do they mean anything? Is that some sign of strength, the flags of individual units, or just . . . ceremony? He could see all the colors of the decorations now, red and green and gold, the bright ribbons streaming from the horses, blending with the extravagant uniforms of the officers. The army had become accustomed to the Mexican lancers as a nuisance, a presence generally out of the way, off to one side, observers more than any kind of threat. Rarely did Santa Anna's horsemen bring an assault, rarely had there been any kind of full-scale attack.

It had been several minutes now, and the horsemen had still not changed their position. He heard sharp sounds behind the farm buildings, a new round of volleys from Reno's cannon. They've changed positions, he thought, kept in motion. His mind turned to Magruder and his young lieutenant, Jackson, and some of the others. That is our advantage. If we have no other superiority, we have better artillery. Those lancers know that too, learned that pretty quickly. Don't charge into our guns. *That's* why they're just sitting there. He lowered the glasses and looked back toward the hiding places of the aides, then out the far window, past more wooden huts, where the smoke spiraled in the air from the steady fire of muskets. Their fire was being answered by the sharp whistle and dull smack of musket balls against the wooden walls. We cannot just stay here, he thought. If it gets dark, we will have to withdraw, or surely they will try to get behind us, cut us off. We cannot afford to lose two brigades.

He looked south, toward the road in front of the men, could see very little through the solid cloud of smoke. Far in the distance the sounds of the fight at the bridge were still rolling toward him, and he thought, What is happening back there? It has been a long time . . . hours, and the sounds have not changed. This time the enemy did not run. But this time we came right at them, hit their defenses the way they expected us to. If we could somehow push these people off the road and come at the bridge from the rear . . .

He raised the glasses again, looked toward the Mexican troops on the road, saw the flash of cannon through the haze of smoke. There may be too many . . .too strong. He swung around, glassed the cavalry again, saw motion now, something new. He felt his heart jump. He raised himself up slightly, focusing the glasses again. The horsemen were spreading out, moving off the road, out to the left. He looked around, said, "Major!"

The man was beside him quickly, and Lee said, "They're moving off the road. They may be trying to flank us, get behind us."

The man spat something on the hard ground, said, "We better get word to General Shields pretty quick."

Lee looked toward the hay bales. "Sergeant Johnson!"

A hat rose slowly from behind the hay, and then the eyes appeared.

Lee had no patience for the man's caution, said, "On your feet, Sergeant. The danger is out *there*." Lee motioned toward the distant cavalry, said, "They are moving to turn our flank. If they advance, we will have a serious problem. Go to General Shields. Tell him our position must be watched. We could be in some danger. He may wish to place part of a battery to cover our position."

The man stood, seemed to find strength, a new seriousness. He focused on Lee's words, said, "Yes, sir, I understand. I'll go right away."

Lee glassed out again, studied the movement of the horsemen, the line extending farther into the field above them. We have time, he thought, at least there is some warning. They don't seem to appreciate the power of speed, of surprise. It's all about *show*, as though the threat itself should be enough. He studied the flags again, the flow of horses still extending, stretching far back on the road. He tried to count, but the distance was too great, and he thought, It has to be over a thousand men . . . more.

He put the glasses down, said to the major, "I should speak to General Shields myself. This is too important."

The major patted him on the shoulder, said, "Godspeed, Captain. It's a dangerous trip. Should probably take your friend there."

He motioned toward the hay bales, and Lee looked for the second aide, saw no sign, felt a stab of irritation, said aloud, "Mr. Spence, it's time to go. If you're still here, I suggest you follow me."

The man suddenly appeared, a skinny corporal, strands of hay protruding from his uniform. He said, "Right here, sir. At your service."

"Our service now is to General Shields. You know how to locate him, I assume?"

"Yes, sir. We'll find him, sir."

"Let's do that."

Lee followed the man outside, and he could see the line of troops below the buildings, settled hard along the ground, spreading out at an angle from the road. The line was much thinner than it had been, and Lee could see scattered mounds of blue, the dead and wounded spread behind the men who were still firing forward.

He looked at the young corporal, said, "You ready?"

The young man was looking past him. "Uh, sir. Look, it's Red . . . it's Sergeant Johnson, sir."

Lee turned, saw the man running low to the ground. Then the sergeant was before them. He saluted, leaned forward, breathing heavily, his hands on his knees, said, "Captain, orders from General Shields. I reported the cavalry as you said, and he said, sir . . . uh, he said it probably ain't nothing to worry about. He told me to tell you, sir, we been watching Mexican cavalry all over the place, and they don't seem to ever do anything but just sit there. But the general did say it's a chance we can't take. He said we ought not stay here."

Lee glanced up at the road. "Yes, I assumed that. Did the general advise me how soon the withdrawal would begin?"

Johnson blinked, said, "Uh, no sir. We aren't withdrawing. We're . . . charging."

Lee heard bugles now, saw officers scrambling along the lines of men, and quickly the blue mass rose up from their cover.

Johnson said, "Captain, if you don't need us now, we should get back to General Shields. I expect he'll be needing us."

Lee was confused, thought, A charge? Where? He moved to the far window again, glassed out, saw the cavalry still in motion. He stared for a long moment. But, now . . . they're moving the other way, back to the road.

He watched for a moment longer, shook his head, said aloud, "General Shields is right. They're not coming. They're moving off." He lowered the glasses, was still confused. Why send them out here at all? Are we supposed to be . . . afraid?

He turned, saw the couriers moving outside, said, "I'm coming, gentlemen."

Lee followed the two men as they moved quickly out into the open field. He hopped over a short fence into tall grass, saw the two men were staying low, moving quickly away from him. Lee felt his chest pounding. He slowed, then stopped, thought, Yes, they've done this work before. All right, Captain, easy. You're not twenty.

He could hear the new sounds now, the musket fire replaced by the sound of the men, a long low cheer all along the line. He felt a chill, his skin tingling with the sound, his heart still pounding, and he watched the lines surge forward, the two brigades pouring their strength together in one sudden burst of power. He glanced toward the two couriers, saw only the tall grass. He looked again at the blue mass, moving in a heavy line across the open ground, said aloud, "You two go on. I think I'll go . . . with *them*.

THE CHARGE HAD REACHED THE ROADWAY, AND HE HAD MOVED up close behind the last line of Shields's men, climbed with them up into the road itself. The fight was sharp and quick, pushed hard by the men who had endured the enemy fire protected only by the muddy grass of the open ground. The Mexicans were moving away, a swarm of gray flowing out across the swampy fields above the road. He stood up high now on the Mexican fortifications, empty except for the debris of their retreat, muskets, broken guns, hats. It was the same debris Lee had seen before, mixed with the bodies of the men who could not run, some killed by musket fire, some by the bayonets of Shields's charging men.

The sounds of the fight were fading, and he could see to the south, toward the bridgehead at Churubusco, realized now the sounds were slowing there as well. He moved behind the works, past groups of men picking through the Mexican guns, appraising, some already gathering muskets that would be burned. Officers were shouting orders, assembling the men into line again, the swords pointing out toward the Mexican retreat. Lee stared out toward the escape of the Mexicans, heard scattered musket fire, men trying to find a target, a final shot at the army they had swept away. The orders still came, but different now, and he heard one man shout, "Cease fire. By order of General Shields! Cease fire!"

He saw Shields, on his horse again, moving along the road, staring toward the Mexican retreat. Shields waved his hat, yelled, "Run! Go back to Santa Anna! We have whipped you again!"

Around Shields, his men—their muskets pointing in the air, some still holding the bayonet—whooped and shouted their joyous salutes. Lee watched Shields, saw the pure joy, the man reining the horse back hard, waving his hat high in the air, absorbing the calls from his troops, the grand moment. Lee tried to shout with the men, but his energy had faded, the exhaustion crawling over him again. He backed away, stood in the road, stared down toward the bridgehead.

Shields saw him, moved closer, said, "Captain, you lose your horse?" Shields was still laughing, and Lee was about to speak, then saw a wave of motion coming from the bridgehead.

He pointed, said, "Sir . . ."

Shields turned, began to move toward the bridgehead, and now Shields began to yell, to wave his hat again. Lee climbed up again on the Mexican works, watched Shields, moving down, leading another charge, his men trying to follow, moving south on the wide road.

Lee pulled out the field glasses, looked past Shields to another flood of gray, moving out to the left, away from the bridgehead. The musket fire was scattered there as well, brief, intermittent pops, the flow of the Mexican retreat moving quickly away. He focused on the road again, saw a wave of motion, a thick blue mass, coming forward, moving up past the bridgehead. He lowered the glasses, jumped down, tried to run, to follow Shields's horse. He saw Shields stopping, heard more cheers, the blue mass rolling up around him, men embracing, shouting hoarsely, bayonets punching the air.

Lee stopped running, his breath coming in short gasps. He moved slowly toward the cluster of troops. The men's faces and uniforms were covered with signs of the fight, black grime and torn coats. The men were smiling, some crying, and as Lee moved forward, through the growing chaos of the victory, he saw new flags, officers, familiar faces. He realized that they had met up with Worth's division, and he smiled, his exhaustion clearing for a moment, and he began to understand. They had broken through the bridgehead, had finally pushed through the toughest fight the Mexicans had given them. He raised his hat again, too tired to shout with the men around him, let the sounds wash over him, the hurrahs, the salutes, the sounds of victory.

23. SCOTT

H E HAD MOVED ALONG THE LINES ALL DAY, FROM TWIGGS'S hard fight on the left at a convent that Santa Anna had forti-fied into a powerful, solid defense, to the middle and right, where Pillow and Worth led the assault at the bridgehead. He had waited impatiently for the final word, the breakthrough, had expected it soon, expected another quick result like the marvelous success at Padierna. He had sat high on the big horse as the orders were carried forward, making himself visible to the troops. He knew that the men always responded to the dress uniform, always seemed to draw some inspiration from the extra show, the gold braid and glorious medals, the great wide plume in his hat.

He had been with Twiggs when he heard the first great roar of musket fire, but then he saw the retreat, men falling away from the Mexican defenses, chaos erupting in the thick cornfields as men trapped in open ground with no cover from the Mexican guns sought refuge behind the bodies of their own men. The sounds and the chaos of battle had lasted for long hours, through another advance, another retreat, the commanders sending in everything they had. But the Mexi-cans had the good ground, the strong defenses, and the fight only turned when the Americans could not be kept away after all. They ad-vanced still, broken and shattered lines of men coming forward, mov-ing closer each time, until finally the men in blue could climb past the logs and dirt, face their enemy hand-to-hand. If the guns of the Ameri-cans had not been enough to drive the victory, it had finally been the spirit of the men themselves. In the end the Mexican resistance had given way only to the raw brutal energy of the men who took the fight straight to them, put the bayonet straight into their hearts.

S COTT CROSSED THE BRIDGE, OBSERVING SIGNS OF THE FIGHT ALL around, shattered timbers, pieces of guns, scraps of clothing. He moved slowly up the road where the men now watched him, falling into line along the edge. There were cheers, but not as many, more subdued, and he waited for them to pick up the call, the same salutes they always gave him. He scanned their faces, looked into their eyes, something he rarely did, saw some of them staring back at him, some just staring at nothing at all. A few were calling out, but their enthusiasm did not spread. He began to feel angry, thought, They behave as if they lost the fight. This should be a . . . celebration!

He stopped the horse, the staff moving up behind him, and he said aloud, "It has been a glorious day! This army has much to celebrate!"

He watched the faces again, and they were all looking at him, and he saw a few hands raised, saw a few hats go up, but still the cheers did not spread.

He glanced back at the staff, said quietly, "What the hell is wrong with these people?"

No one responded, the aides well aware he was not expecting an answer. He spurred the horse, moved again on the road, the last daylight nearly gone, the lamplight filling the small houses and huts along the road. He felt like speaking to them again, thought, They should understand. They are just . . . tired. It was a tough fight. But it was *our* fight. I should remind them of that. He felt like stopping the horse again, saw men moving toward him on the road, marching slowly in single file, following a young officer. They drew near and he saw the officer glancing up at him, wide-eyed surprise on the man's face. But the men behind him did not look at all, moved with reflex, slow and plodding, the uniforms ragged, filthy.

Scott leaned over, tipped his hat, said, "I congratulate you, gentlemen! A glorious victory!"

The officer saluted him, said quietly, "Thank you, sir."

But the column moved past him, the men not stopping, most still not seeing him. The anger came back now, and he looked back to the staff, said to his son-in-law, "Where the hell is that house? We close yet?"

Major Scott moved up beside him, said, "There, up ahead, sir. Horses in the yard. I'm certain that's it."

Scott looked down the road, where more troops were crossing in front of him, walking slowly, another officer guiding men to their unit. He moved the horse again, said quietly, "Is *everyone* lost?"

He could see the horses now, tied up in front of one small house. Its low gray walls, fat stones, broken by small uneven windows lit by the glow of lamplight, held up a low flat roof. Guards, a dozen or more, lined up on both sides of the house, more men on the small porch, all with bayonets. He climbed down from the horse, the men all coming to stiff attention, snapping their bayonets tightly to their sides. An officer stepped forward, a young captain. He saluted, said, "General Scott, welcome, sir. This way, please."

Scott followed the man up the short steps, and beside the door he saw four more guards, more bayonets, thought, What the hell is all this for? There's no threat here. It must be Worth, seeing ghosts again.

The officer held the door open and Scott moved inside, could hear the small talk of the commanders, and the officer beside him suddenly shouted, "Atten . . . hut!"

The voice startled him, and he glared at the man until the men backed quickly out the door, pleased with his good work. Scott looked into the single large room, the voices quiet now, the officers all standing straight. He let out a breath, said, "At ease. For God's sake."

There was still no sound, and Pillow stepped forward, said, "General Scott, this was a day to remember. My division, the glorious soldiers under this command, distinguished themselves as never before." Scott looked at him wearily, said nothing. Pillow waited for the response, seemed disappointed, said, "As they all did, I'm sure, sir. The entire army, I mean."

Scott moved toward a chair, sat, looked around the room, saw the younger faces, Pillow's staff standing back quietly. There were a few older men, some he knew, and he nodded to a familiar face. "Colonel Riley, glad to see you made it through this day."

Riley bowed quickly and said, "It was a day I would like to remember, sir. And then, forget."

Pillow threw a quick frowning glance at Riley, said, "Sir, I'm sure Colonel Riley would care to rephrase his comment. We are all tired. But this is a day for celebrating heroes. There's already quite a bit of talk. The war might well be over! The Mexicans are in complete chaos, their army no longer exists!"

Scott said nothing, watched Pillow standing in the silence, could see him slowly deflate, the response from the room not what he was expecting. Scott looked at the others, saw Worth now, sitting back in the shadows. "General Worth, your men did fine work today. They have much to be proud of. This *is* a day that made heroes. I must say, not much of a celebration out there."

Worth looked at him, said quietly, "Celebrate what, General? Do you know how many heroes are not coming home?"

Scott was still feeling the frustration, thought, It comes from him, from the command. His mood has infected his men. He felt angry again, said, "What the hell is the matter with you? This was a tough fight, a difficult day. But consider the day the enemy had. We completely routed their defenses, *twice,* at Padierna and here. Pillow's right, their army *is* in chaos, if there's an army at all."

Pillow stepped forward, said, "I've told him this already, sir. I don't understand why some in this army do not understand how glorious this day was, for all of us, for our country, for our cause. The loss of soldiers is a price we accept."

Worth stood now, moved into the light, and Scott was surprised to see his red-faced anger. Worth looked hard at Pillow, said, "How much loss, General?"

Pillow glanced at Scott, backed away to a chair. Scott looked at the others, saw a few younger faces, staff officers, thought, This might be a time for privacy. He said, "Junior officers, aides, dismissed. Now."

The men moved slowly out, until only the four senior officers remained. Scott asked Worth, "Do you have casualty figures, General?"

Worth sat slowly, said, "I have conferred with General Pillow, and Colonel Riley here has given me some accounting from General Twiggs. I've been to some of the hospitals myself. For now, a close estimate . . . is that we took over a thousand casualties."

Scott sat back heavily, the chair rocking under his weight. He felt the wind punched from his chest, the shock of the number. "Are you certain of that?"

Worth nodded slowly, and Riley said, "Reasonably certain, sir."

Pillow stood again, said, "Sir, I am aware we took some heavy losses. It was a costly fight. But, I thought the important thing was the victory."

Scott felt the energy flowing away, and there was silence in the room, the men looking at him. He turned to Pillow and said, "Sit down."

Pillow obeyed, shook his head. "We won. We destroyed their army. . . ."

Scott looked at his hands, flexed his stiff fingers, said, "We thought we destroyed it at Cerro Gordo."

He looked down at his uniform now, felt suddenly ridiculous, the spread of medals on his chest, the grand show for the men seeming inappropriate, hollow. No wonder the men didn't react. They had more important things on their minds.

"If that number is confirmed . . . then we cannot afford any more victories like this one."

There was silence again, and Scott leaned forward, put his hands together, rested his arms on his knees, said, "I am to blame. I truly expected an easy fight. Why shouldn't we believe that after all? We begged for the opportunity, just to bring them out to face us, to stand up before all our strength, all our arrogance. We swept them away at Cerro Gordo, we swept them away just this morning, at Padierna. I heard it from the men, Santa Anna cannot stand up to us, we are after all victorious! All we need do now is march in some great stupid parade in front of Mexico City, and they will fall to their knees, beg us not to destroy them!"

He was shouting now, saw the faces watching him, and even Pillow seemed subdued, sitting back in his chair like a scolded child.

"We have never understood these people. We sure as hell have never understood Santa Anna. How does he do it? How can he keep them following him, inspire them to fight? Is it simply charisma? His charm? Good speeches? Or does he touch something in these people that maybe they *need*. Whatever it is, we have failed to see it, failed to understand. This is a *foreign* place."

He saw a short dark bottle resting on a small table. He leaned out, wrapped his fingers around the neck, held it up to the lamplight, the bottle nearly empty. He looked at the label, all in Spanish, the one word standing out, *Brandy*. He uncorked the bottle, sniffed the fragrance, took a short drink, the sharp heat cutting his throat. His face twisted, and he set the bottle aside.

"They sure as hell need to work on *that*." He sat quietly for a moment, tried to work the awful taste from his mouth, saw the others still watching him, waiting for him to speak. He glanced down at the medals again. Why the hell did I put this on?

He looked at Worth. "*Now* I understand the mood of the men. None of us have been through a day like this. None of us ever expected a day like this. We will learn from this."

He looked at Pillow. "Tell me, General, do you imagine the President would be pleased by today's result?"

"Certainly, sir. Forgive me, sir, but I do not understand the attitude here. Our losses were tragic, yes, but the enemy lost a great deal more. Is that not the point here? From what I hear, this might be the end. My men tell me there is no resistance preventing us from marching to the city tomorrow. Would the President be pleased with that? Most certainly. We have prevailed. Our mission—our cause—has prevailed."

Scott stared at him, watched Pillow retreat back into the chair, saw Worth put his head down in his hands. Worth said quietly, "Our *cause—*"

Scott cut him off. "Let's not speak on this anymore tonight. I don't want anyone saying something here that could become a problem later. The bottom line, gentlemen, is that we learned a valuable lesson today. I was beginning to believe all the talk about Santa Anna, that he was nothing more than a strutting martinet. Our best officers were convinced the Mexican army would never stand up to us. Well, they stood up to us today. General Pillow, despite what your people tell you, I am not at all certain that Santa Anna has yet crawled away, nor that Mexico City awaits us with brass bands."

Riley cleared his throat. "Forgive me, General, but a while ago I saw some of the prisoners. We captured a number of officers, and several generals. To a man, they're still in the fight, they are saying almost nothing but his name."

Scott said, "We have pushed up close to something we don't yet understand. We have come too close to their heart. This city is more than government, it's a symbol, it defines this whole country. Reverse the situation. How would *we* fight if an enemy sent an army at Washington? Washington is a symbol too, something much greater than just white buildings filled with fat bureaucrats. It's our identity, it represents where we came from, and what we stand for. And it sure as hell is something worth fighting for, and the American people would damned well respond to that. We've ignored that, but Santa Anna hasn't. He's used patriotism to inspire his people, and he draws power from it. And today that power cost this army a thousand men."

There were sounds outside, hoofbeats, and the horse stopped close to the house. Scott heard voices, then saw a tall man filling the doorway. The man wiped his eyes and knocked the dust from his hat. Riley stood, saluted, said, "General Twiggs."

Twiggs answered the salute, stepped into the room, and Scott said, "Welcome, General. Your men fought with distinction today."

Twiggs nodded quietly to Worth, seemed to ignore Pillow, said, "We have good men. Today, they found that out. Today they had a *fight.*"

He shouted the word, punching the air, and Scott said nothing, did not want the same discussion again. Riley stepped toward Twiggs, said, "Do you have orders, sir?"

Twiggs put his hands on his hips, seemed to sway, looked at Scott now, said, "As a matter of fact, Colonel Riley, I do. I would like you to escort General Scott to see our prisoners. With his permission, of course."

There was a strange tone in Twiggs's voice, and Scott, curious, said, "Why is that, General?"

Twiggs glanced at the others. "These are very special prisoners, sir."

"No mood for mysteries, General. What are you talking about?"

"We have the deserters, sir, around eighty men. We captured the whole damned bunch of 'em. We captured the San Patricios."

THE PRISONERS STOOD STIFFLY, STARED SILENTLY AHEAD. THE grim-faced guards stood to one side, bayonets held high. Scott turned to the captain of the guard, said quietly, "The bayonets are dangerous, Captain. Could prove tempting. Do you believe it's necessary?"

The man spoke aloud, aware of his audience, "The bayonets are useful, sir. They know what will happen if anyone steps out of line."

Scott looked at the faces of the guards, thought, Yes, that's what worries me.

He looked behind him, the staff curiously eyeing the deserters, and he said, "Major Scott, I want more officers here. No offense, Captain, but this is too important. I want a colonel in command here."

The captain seemed wounded, said, "Yes, sir. Certainly, sir."

Scott stepped forward, moved close to the first man, but the man did not look at him. "Where you from, soldier?"

The man did not reply, and the captain said, "They won't talk, sir. Once the fighting stopped, they clamped up good. They know what's waiting for 'em."

Scott looked down the line of cold stares, looked back across the rows of men. He saw the wounded now, men with bandages, one man's head wrapped in bloody white cloth. So, you *did* fight, he thought, you did join the enemy after all.

He turned, moved back toward the captain, said, "No accidents, Captain. Keep control of your men. This is a dangerous situation."

"I'll do what I can, sir."

Scott looked at him, saw a slight smile. He felt his annoyance growing. "It could be a dangerous situation for you, Captain. Do you understand?"

The smile faded, and the man stared ahead, said, "Yes, sir."

Scott moved toward the door, held open now by two guards. Stepping outside, he saw Twiggs waiting for him.

Twiggs said, "Wasn't that extraordinary?"

Scott asked, "What do you mean?"

"They didn't say a word, right? They know . . . they're already dead. Every one of them knows what will happen next."

Scott began to walk, Twiggs moving beside him. Scott said, "General, *I* don't know what happens next. I have to give this considerable thought. The whole country, hell, the whole world will know about this eventually. It had better be handled correctly."

Twiggs stopped. "Excuse me, sir, but there is little discretion here. The rules of war are plain and simple on this point. Those men must be executed. *They* know that, they accepted that the moment they made the decision to cross the line, to slip away from their own men and join the enemy. They picked up arms, they put up a hell of a fight. They were only captured when they ran out of ammunition. What else do you need? *Sir?*"

Scott stared out into the dark, trying to prevent Twiggs's sarcasm from penetrating. "There will be a hearing. This will be handled by military law. We must control our emotions about this. Any guard who abuses his position, anyone who causes injury to any prisoner, will be arrested." He looked at Twiggs, endured his grim stare. "This will be handled in the manner I decide, General."

Twiggs nodded slowly.

Scott looked away again, said, "I hope we can find out *why*. I can understand a man just breaking, coming apart under fire. But to turn against your own, to kill the men you served with . . ."

"They are not our own, sir. Most of them are barely even Americans. There's quite a few Irish. You see their flag? Has the Irish harp, even the name was Irish, St. Patrick."

Scott shook his head. "That isn't a good enough answer. Being Irish doesn't make a man a traitor. What about the others? Not all of them were Irish."

"Catholics, then. It has to be the religion. When the shooting started, they decided it was the Mexicans who were their own kind, not the Americans."

Scott thought of the church service he attended, the old priest who ignored him. Is this what that old man was hoping for, is the Church the only loyalty that matters? Angry again, he thought, Now I have to decide whether they should be executed for it. There was not enough loss today, now there must be death on top of death. He looked up, saw the stars and a tall white steeple. He realized suddenly he was standing beside a church, thought, I had not even noticed. The

San Patricios are confined inside a church. I suppose there is some justice in that.

He began to move away, said to Twiggs, "Good night, General.
We'll talk tomorrow."

Twiggs said something Scott didn't hear, and he was already moving out in the dark, saw the staff waiting for him. He could still see the
cold faces of the deserters, heard the voice of Pillow, the words of
the politician, victory, *our cause*. Words, he thought, ridiculous words.
The *cause* lies out there on that awful ground. *Those* men did not fight
for a Church, or some boundary dispute, and they aren't dying for a
President. They fought for the men beside them. *Those* are the heroes.
And today we lost too many of them.

24. SCOTT

AUGUST TWENTY-FIRST

E HAD MOVED INTO THE HOME OF THE LOCAL BISHOP, A grand estate above Churubusco. He was not sure how the invitation had come, whether his staff had arranged it or the offer had come from a man with enough political awareness to offer some kindness to the power of the *yanquis*. Scott had only met the bishop once, early that morning. Both men had extended strained cordiality. Their exchange was brief, Scott's impatience and discomfort obvious, and it was plain to both men that there would be no point in additional pleasantries, no need for social conversation.

He sat now at the massive mahogany desk, ornately trimmed with gold. He had become used to this style of decor, of grand excess that he had seen in the homes of the upper class or the prominent politicians. He shifted himself in the deep leather chair, thought, How many servants did it take to load this thing in here? And how many of them are now carrying muskets for Santa Anna?

He was still exploring the desk, poking his hands into each drawer, all empty, the preparations thorough for the occupation of the conqueror. He thought of the bishop. What does he use this for? Is he so busy with earthly matters that he must have this grand office, all these drawers? The bishop was gone now, had left the house immediately as the staff moved Scott's baggage inside, and Scott thought, He probably won't stay here at all until we're gone. If he did, he might have to answer for that eventually, explain his disloyalty. By now he's probably in the city, telling his archbishop how we kicked him out. They do like their martyrs.

He had barely slept. Instead he had paced for long hours near the small huts the men had secured for sleeping quarters. The faces of the San Patricios still haunted him, but there had been something unsettling in the quiet darkness that overshadowed the image of the deserters. He could not hide from Pillow's words, *It might be over.* All night there had only been silence, no skirmishes, no cavalry raids, only the glow in the north from the lights of Mexico City, and he had thought, Yes, Pillow could be right. The Mexicans are not sleeping either. They know what we did to their army, and Santa Anna could be in very deep trouble. That's all it usually takes for those people. Their history is full of revolutions that seem to happen when the strong man shows he is not so strong after all.

Damn it. Pillow could be right about that too. I don't like believing he's right about anything. Santa Anna cannot stand up in front of his people this close to the city and not give them a victory. He might be gone already, some other strong man telling their Congress that *he* knows a better way. Right now the better way may be to save face the only way they can. If they cannot win on the battlefield, then they must settle this thing by keeping their honor intact, even if they admit military defeat. At least they have their scapegoat. Santa Anna has filled that role before, after they lost Texas. He can sure as hell fill it again.

Scott had not ordered a new assault, made no plans for the new dawn. Instead he had given the commanders instructions only to get the men in shape, close up the lines, bring the units together. The only change in position would be the artillery; he'd already arranged the heavier batteries in a wide arc, in preparation for a siege, the same strategy they had used at Vera Cruz. If the troops were to be sent in against the walls of the city, it would be very helpful if the walls were broken up first.

The casualty reports were more accurate now, and Worth had been right, the army had lost over a thousand men. We still don't know what strength the Mexicans have, he thought, and we will probably never know just how many we faced yesterday. But our numbers have never been good, and after yesterday they are worse. It would be damned convenient if somebody out there decided this should end without us having to break down the doors.

He closed the drawers, ran his hand over the smooth black desktop, looked to one side, where he saw the wooden boxes filled with his papers, books, the growing pile of reports that would eventually go to Washington. He leaned down, pulled one box toward him, then stopped, sat up straight, said aloud, "I'm not in the mood for paperwork."

He saw a face now, Sergeant Dunnigan peering around the huge doorway, and Dunnigan said, "You called, sir?"

"No, dammit!" His voice echoed in the large room, seemed to push the small sergeant back into the hallway.

Dunnigan hesitated, came forward again, said, "Sorry, sir. I thought I heard you say something."

"Tell me something, Sergeant. Do you spend your whole day perched just outside my door, waiting to pounce on every peep I make?"

Dunnigan pondered the question, said, "Um, no, sir. But Major Scott was very clear, sir, when I was assigned to this duty. If the major was unavailable, it was my responsibility . . . your needs were very particular, and you expect only the most rapid response. Major Scott said that you don't like to be kept waiting, sir."

"Major Scott said that?"

"Yes, sir."

"Is that the *fuss* part of *Old Fuss and Feathers?*"

Dunnigan seemed to shake. "No . . . uh, I don't know what you mean . . . oh God."

"At ease, Sergeant. I don't mind it. I know the men have to call me something. It's a tradition of every army that ever marched. Actually, has a bit of flair to it. Better than simply calling me *the old man.*"

Dunnigan seemed able to breathe again. "The men have nothing but respect, sir."

"Yes, well, I appreciate hearing that. But there's perhaps a bit less respect today than there was yesterday. It was not this command's best performance." He paused, rubbed his hand across the desk again. "We lost . . . a *lot* of people yesterday, Sergeant."

Dunnigan said nothing at first, then stepped closer, said, "Is there anything I can get you, sir?"

"Not much anybody can get me right now. Unless it's an open route to Washington. I have to tell them, you know. It will be official, black and white, for everyone to see. Men are dying down here in astounding numbers, both sides. Mexico's had their share of wars, but they've never had an enemy like us, never this efficient." He paused, his finger tracing the gold trim on the desk, his mind beginning to wander. He looked up at Dunnigan again, saw patience in the small man's face, thought, He's a good listener. Maybe I need that right now.

"We're killing more of them than they are of us, I'm certain of that, Sergeant. As a military commander, that is supposed to make me happy. It makes General Pillow positively giddy. And that's a strange thing, because he's not a soldier anyway, he's a politician. The only reason a politician is happy about bad news is when he can blame it on somebody else. Pillow knows that his friend James Polk is too far removed, too far away to be blamed. But someone has to answer for this, someone has to be responsible. When we get back home, the news of what happened down here will already be there, the people will already have read the newspaper stories, seen the numbers. There will have to be some answer, a damned good answer about why their husbands, sons, brothers, and neighbors died." He stopped again, tried to see the President's face in his mind, thought, Good God, I've forgotten what he looks like.

He shook his head and continued, "Polk handed us a war, a nasty little fight about land, all about boundaries and territory. My job was to end it, simple enough. Conquer the peace. All right, we're winning. But it won't be Polk who will hear it from the people who lost family today. It won't be Polk who will send those damned San Patricios to the gallows. It will be me."

He looked up at Dunnigan now, saw something different in the small man's expression, the nervousness gone. Dunnigan said, "Sir, I don't know much about politics and the like. I learned when I joined this army to do what I was told and don't say nothing about it. Forgive me for saying this, sir, but there's not a man I know in this army, not an enlisted man anyways, that doesn't believe in what we're doing here." The nervousness began to overtake him, and Dunnigan hesitated.

Scott intervened, "Go on, Sergeant."

Dunnigan thought for a moment before going on. "Sir, I never knew much about the fight in Texas or about Santa Anna, but when my unit was told to march south, when we got on the boats at New Orleans, didn't none of us ask why. It was our duty. That's what being a soldier is all about. If there's a problem for you when we get back home, you got a whole army here that's gonna stick up for you. You can depend on that, sir."

Scott was stunned. He stared at Dunnigan, felt something tighten in his throat. He fought it, blinked hard, wanted to say something, but saw his son-in-law now, standing at the door, a look of horror on the major's face, staring at Dunnigan's back. The young Scott said, "General, I'm sorry. I was out for a moment. Is there a problem? Has the Sergeant done something . . . ?"

Dunnigan stood aside, seemed to shrink again, and Scott said,

"Calm down, Major. I asked Sergeant Dunnigan to come in. Nothing of concern."

The young Scott glared darkly at Dunnigan, said, "Sergeant, you may return to your work. I will handle things now."

Scott watched the scene play out, thought, My daughter loves this man. I have no idea why.

Dunnigan headed out the door, and Scott said, "Sergeant. Thank you."

Dunnigan looked back, nodded quietly, and was gone. The young Scott grunted, said, "Any insolence should not be tolerated, sir. My job—"

"Your job, Major, is to do what I require. I requested that Sergeant Dunnigan come in here. You will not think any more about the matter."

The young man's face tightened into a sulk, and he said, "No, sir, of course not."

"Is there anything else, Major?"

The young man's eyes widened and he said, "Oh, yes, sir. Forgive me. Mr. Trist is outside."

TRIST BROUGHT WORD FROM THE BRITISH DIPLOMATS THAT HE should expect a visitor, some official from the city. But Scott did not want to stay in the office, decided instead to ride forward, move through the men. If there was to be some delegation, he would not sit and wait in the bishop's house, but would meet it on the road, surrounded by the energy of the troops.

They rode out near the artillery batteries, and Scott watched the men moving the larger guns into position, Duncan's battery, and he could not help but become involved, had asked politely if he could sight one of the guns himself. He estimated the arc, turned the small wheel to raise the barrel of the first gun that would carry the deadly shell straight at the old castle, Chapultepec, the strong fortress that had always dominated the defense of the city and might do so again.

He backed away from the gun, stepped up into the road, looked out toward the fat walls of the castle, said aloud, "That should have some good effect. You men carry on. And, thank you." He walked back to his horse and climbed up.

Scott looked at Trist now, who had sat quietly while he worked with the gun, and he said, "I rather enjoy that, you know. Don't have much chance to help the men. There's always been something appealing about artillery, the power of that."

He looked toward the gun crew, could see the officer nervously waiting. "Best get moving. They need to correct my aim, repair whatever damage I might have done, and they won't do it while I'm watching them."

Trist laughed, and Scott turned the horse, moved away. He saw Trist glance back, and Trist smiled again, said quietly, "It seems you're correct. They're climbing all over the gun."

Scott smiled, said nothing, stared straight up the road to where a squad of cavalry moved slowly toward him, and behind, a black wagon.

"It seems, Mr. Trist, we have a visitor."

The troops stood aside, watched the wagon roll slowly through the lines, following the escort of Harney's cavalry. The word had passed quickly, the soldiers already beginning to speculate, the rumors beginning to flow. The men who actually caught a glimpse of the well-dressed Mexican passenger were the first authority, spreading the word of something very official, certainly an envoy to see General Scott. One word began to find a voice all along the lines: *surrender*.

Scott watched the cavalry move close, and the horsemen moved to the edge of the road, the wagon slowing. Scott waited, thought, Protocol, stay on the horse. The first move comes from them. Well, hurry up. Damned politics.

Trist leaned close, said, "It's General Mora. I met him with Mr. Bankhead, back in the spring."

Scott heard the excitement in Trist's voice, said quietly, "At ease, Mr. Trist. Let's hear what he has to say."

Mora stepped from the carriage, glanced briefly at the gathering soldiers, then turned to face Scott. The Mexican general bowed slightly from the waist. He eyed Trist for a moment, seemed to study the two men, his face locked in a somber seriousness. Then he slowly drew a folded paper from his pocket, held it out toward Trist.

Trist said quietly, "Uh, sir, may I? I believe this is my position here."

Scott stared at the paper in Mora's hand, said, "Go."

Trist climbed down from the horse, said something in Spanish Scott did not understand, then took the paper and glanced back at Scott. "Allow me, sir?"

"Go on, Mr. Trist, read it."

Trist unfolded the papers, turned slightly so Scott could see the pages. Trist read slowly, and Scott saw more than one document, thought, Whatever it is, it's complicated. We're not invited to a party.

Trist said something to Mora again, and Mora moved back to the carriage, climbed in, and Scott said, "That's it? He's leaving?"

"Oh, no, sir. He'll wait out of earshot while I explain this. Diplomacy, sir."

Scott felt suddenly out of place, like a child at an adult gathering. "Well, can I get off the damned horse?"

Trist moved closer, said, "Oh, certainly, sir. He will wait while you and I discuss . . . this."

Trist handed the papers to Scott, and Scott saw the crown, the British seal, thought, At least this is in English. He read the short letter, said, "Bankhead. You've mentioned this one before. Friend of yours?"

Trist nodded. "Yes, quite so, sir. I spent some time with him after I arrived here. He's been on the side of peace from the beginning. The British have spent a considerable amount of energy trying to bring the Mexican officials to the peace table, with no success. It seems that may have changed."

Scott sniffed. "Yes, having an army outside the gates of your capital will do that."

"I know from personal conversation that Mr. Bankhead's frustration has been extreme. This is all the more reason, sir, to take this seriously. Mr. Bankhead is endorsing this letter from the Mexicans. He would not do so if it was, um . . . a waste of time."

Scott scanned the Spanish words, said, "You understand this?"

Trist hesitated, said, "Yes, sir. Should I read it to you, sir?"

Scott scanned the papers, said, "Just tell me what it says. Are they surrendering?"

"No. This is a first step, though. Mostly they are demanding concessions, terms that I suspect you would find, um, unacceptable. They are certainly under a great deal of pressure to save face, and this letter reflects that. It is not very constructive, though . . . it is a first step. They are open to your point of view."

Scott handed the letters to Trist, said, "My point of view is that we're about to reduce their capital city to rubble. Your friend Bankhead endorses their demands? Frankly, Mr. Trist, I'm confused. The Mexican authorities should be asking for peace, not making demands. I believe we're holding the cards here. The Mexicans aren't in any position to demand anything."

"No, sir. But they have to start somewhere, they have to put on the good show for their people. Then they can blame . . . the enemy, if the terms are not generous."

Scott laughed, shook his head. "They can blame *me*. Fine, whatever

it takes, Mr. Trist. But surely they understand we are prepared to assault the city. If we march into the city square, there won't be much to
talk about."

"Sir, consider who we're dealing with. If General Santa Anna is
captured, or if he flees, there is no government in Mexico City, in the
whole country for that matter. The chaos would not be helpful to us.
Mexico has difficulty governing itself in the best of times. Unless we
can deal with officials who claim to be in charge of the capital, who are
still authorized to sign documents or treaties representing the power of
their country, the negotiations won't mean anything. If we march into
the city and simply take over, we would not only be an army of occupation, we would *become* the government. That is not a situation of
which the President would approve."

Scott looked toward the carriage, saw the grim face of the driver,
a small dark man who nervously glanced in all directions, appraising
the strength of his enemy. Scott said, "He's waiting . . . for what? What
am I supposed to do?"

"Give them your own terms, sir. Give General Mora something
to take back."

"You mean, something like, Surrender, or I will destroy your city?"

Trist moved behind him, and Scott could see the impatience
building in the man's face. Trist said, "Sir, please. We have an opportunity to end this war. They are opening the door to a diplomatic solution.
They are proposing an armistice, a truce, to allow official discussions to
begin. Forgive me, sir, but I must insist you accept this possibility. This
is why I was sent down here in the first place. Please allow me to do
my job. Do you really want to attack the city? Is that your preference?"

Scott saw Trist let out a long breath. Well done, Mr. Trist, he
thought. You are a diplomat after all.

"Mr. Trist, if we truly have an opportunity here to end this war
without further loss of life, then I place myself at your disposal. What
would you have me do?"

Scott's words had a calming effect on Trist. He thought a moment, said, "Propose a truce of our own. Their letter demands . . . requests a full year."

"*A year!*"

The sound boomed past the troops, and Scott looked hard at
Trist, who seemed to wilt, said, "Please, sir, no—"

"You told me this wasn't a waste of time, Mr. Trist. So far I'm
not convinced."

"The demand is ridiculous, sir, certainly. But they have to say something to make themselves look good. Now you can tell them something more appropriate. They expect that, sir."

Scott looked around now, saw his son-in-law waiting with the rest of the staff, said, "Major, come here."

The young Scott dismounted, moved quickly forward, and Scott said, "Get a pen and paper."

The young man backed away, and Scott said, "I don't have the patience for walking on eggshells, Mr. Trist. I understand diplomacy, and I understand negotiation. But I am not going to tiptoe around their pride." He saw Trist frown, said, "Don't worry, Mr. Trist, no threats, nothing to make them puff up. I'm willing to give you time to negotiate a peace, but this cannot drag on. They have to show some good faith, cut through all the face-saving."

"Yes, sir, I believe that can be accomplished. The reality is quite clear. I would suggest . . . if you don't mind, sir, I would suggest you continue to move your artillery into some visible position. It is a good point of . . . negotiation."

Scott laughed, said, "A little visual reminder. Not *all* negotiations are subtle. Very good, Mr. Trist. I'm learning to appreciate your skills."

Trist seemed to blush, looked down, said, "Um, sir, how much time do I have? Would you offer them an armistice?"

"On very specific terms. Neither side may strengthen or reinforce their armies. No new fortifications may be constructed." He paused, thought, Supplies, we can't sit in one place indefinitely without food. "We be allowed to send wagons into the city to purchase food. In return, they be allowed to send communications out, and bring their own supplies into the city, without our molesting them. This should make your British friends happy."

"Yes, sir, that will. There has been concern. . . ."

The young Scott moved close now, held a pad of paper in his hand, said, "Ready to write, sir."

Scott moved back behind the horses, and the two men followed. Scott said to Trist, "If this works, you will be as much of a hero as anyone here. You'll certainly get more credit for ending this war than the President will give me. Doubt you'll have to go back to your old job."

Trist seemed concerned, said, "Oh, no, sir. The credit will go where it deserves to go. I will not accept praise for what you have accomplished."

Scott glanced at his son-in-law, the words forming in his mind, thought of Washington now, the dark suits and fat buildings. He looked at Trist again. "Thank you. But do not underestimate the power of that place. Good intentions are easily corrupted."

He stared out past the soldiers, all the faces watching him, looked toward the silhouette of Chapultepec.

"Let me think on this a moment, I always have difficulty with the first words."

He scanned the wide fields that spread toward the city, could see the narrow roads, the causeways, the deadly ground his army would have to cross. He saw the camp of the troops, Worth's men, scattered across a trampled cornfield, small campfires fueled by corn stalks. This is not just for the honor of Mexican dignitaries, he thought. We don't create a quiet pause in the war so the politicians can strut about and play with words. He thought of the letters, the ornate seal of the British monarchy, and the other, the absurd demands written in the language he didn't understand. Words and more words, he thought. That's not what this is about, who is right, who saves their honor. That's how wars *begin*, the angry words, misunderstood words, lines drawn on maps. We are beyond that now. Those men . . . my men understand that. They know that after all, the war was given to *them*. If this is to end now, it is because of what *they* have given up. If I did not understand that yesterday, I understand it now.

"Major, we shall write a letter to General Santa Anna. You may begin. . . . 'Too much blood has already been shed . . .' "

25. SCOTT

SEPTEMBER THIRD

THE TRUCE HAD BEEN SIGNED, MEN APPOINTED BY BOTH COM-
manders to sit face-to-face, hash out the small annoying details,
but the message on both sides was plain. There would be a
pause in the fighting, and if neither side would admit it openly, both
armies needed the time to recover from the fight at Churubusco. There
were protests in the American camp, officers who had watched the retreat of a beaten enemy, who did not understand why they should
stop, wait, while the enemy healed themselves and grew strong again.
But the senior commanders did not object, and even Davy Twiggs
agreed that it was time to stop, to take a breath, and if the Mexicans did
not surrender after all, there would be a new strategy, another full-scale
assault on the city.

The truce provided an arrangement for both armies to have access
to supplies, some relief from the stale monotony of the dwindling rations. Almost immediately great stores of meat and grain, accumulating
in the farms and ranches far beyond the city, had begun to move into
the capital. Their passage was uncontested by the Americans, and in return, Scott's men would be allowed to travel unmolested into the city
to make their own arrangements. The first train of wagons Scott had
authorized carried men from the quartermaster's staff, sent to negotiate
the purchase of grain and bread. But while Santa Anna's official ministers had promised a peaceful and cooperative welcome, it was apparent
that the citizens did not share the sentiment so carefully worded in the
diplomatic papers. The wagon train had been attacked by a mob of
civilians, men with clubs and axes, their frustration exploding into a
riot of anger and hatred that no one expected or was prepared for.
There were casualties, several of the American drivers, the men who

would load the supplies, and it was clear that if the Americans would not retaliate, the Mexican soldiers were helpless as well. Even the Americans who spoke little Spanish sensed the mob's anger, could hear clearly that the civilians were not just assaulting the men in blue, but were striking out in words and violence at their own soldiers. It was, after all, the only access they had to their leader, the man who had allowed the *yanquis* to come so close to their city. There was outrage from the Americans, of course, a clear violation of the truce, and Santa Anna himself sent an apology to Scott, and a promise that no such incident would occur again.

The wagons moved at night now, led through the gates of the city by an escort of Mexican lancers. They had made the trip several times, loading their cargo quietly, each man doing his job while casting nervous glances into the dark.

The gates were opened, providing a discreet entry into the city one more time, men nodding to their enemy, a strange show of civility, some faces now familiar, both sides understanding that this was a war that came from somewhere else, the orders and strategy far beyond what these few men would ever control.

The supplies waited, great piles of cloth bags, wooden boxes, and when the wagons reached the square, the officers from both sides met and exchanged papers, receipts, authorizations. Quickly, the wagons were loaded, while the lancers spread out down the side streets, keeping the citizens in their homes, keeping anyone away who might not understand or respect the fragile agreement.

Piled high, the wagons began to move again, the drivers slapping the mules impatiently, each man staring ahead into the dark, the route familiar now, counting the blocks, the intersections, knowing just when the gate would finally appear. But the lancers suddenly held them up. The drivers heard hushed shouts and looked questioningly at their commanders, the American officers riding ahead. In front, moving through a dark intersection, was another train, horses and men, but not wagons and supplies. The Americans could not be held away, would see for themselves, moved up beside the lancers, who watched in helpless frustration as the street was blocked, the intersection clogged. It was one commander's mistake, the man not knowing or not remembering that the Americans would be there, would have come into the city again to draw supplies.

The Americans stared in nervous surprise, saw Mexican soldiers leading horses, each horse in the long line strapped to a brass gun, the guns all pitching and bouncing noisily over the uneven cobblestones of the street. The American drivers sat in blind confusion, knew only that their progress out of the hostile city was delayed, but their officers watched carefully, counted in the dark, made a mental note of each gun, the numbers, the size. Each man could see that the guns were moving forward, were moving southward to line the walls, to face Scott's army.

The lancers realized that these few Americans would know what the darkness could hide, each side understanding that this truce, this moment of peace, would not last after all. When the column finally passed, the Mexicans were still looking at each other with quiet urgency, each one already conjuring up his own excuse for how the mistake had happened, some speaking in low voices the Americans could not understand. The excuses mounted, the men already protecting themselves from Santa Anna's wrath by conspiring that perhaps no one would ever hear of this quiet incident, that perhaps the Americans would not understand, would not report what they had seen.

The wagon train began to move again, and the drivers stared ahead, waiting for the first glimpse of the gate, but their anxiety had spread now to the officers, who did not speak to their escorts. Each man focused ahead, counting the desperate seconds until the lancers would fall away and the wagons would reach the security of their own cavalry.

S COTT STOOD BY THE BIG WINDOW, LET THE SUNLIGHT WASH OVER the pages of the report, turned now, said to Trist, "This what you were after? This is what we spent two weeks waiting for?"

Trist sat at the bishop's desk, his head in his hands, said nothing. Scott stepped away from the window, tossed the documents on the desk, the papers scattering around Trist's arms. Scott felt the heat boiling up inside him, a full blast of fury, said, "We should give them back Texas? We should pay them gold for all the damage we caused? We should release the San Patricios? We should get the hell out of their country and be grateful we didn't all receive fifty lashes with a whip?"

He moved to the larger chair, pulled it away from the desk, sat down heavily, said, "What kind of a fool . . . what kind of simpleminded buffoon does he take me for? They ask for a truce, we give them a truce. They ask for supplies for the city, we let their people pass by unmolested. *We* ask for supplies, they attack our teamsters. *We* agree not to fortify, and *they* rebuild their damned army! Mr. Trist, is it reasonable to assume that this truce has been a one-sided affair? Am I out of line when I say that we should have shelled that city into a pile of rubble?"

Trist leaned back, and Scott saw the man's thin face, the tired eyes staring past him. Trist shook his head. "I am sorry, sir. I truly believed . . . I was encouraged to believe that we were negotiating a real peace." He reached out, gathered the papers together, stopped, stared at the documents in his hand, said, "There is nothing more for me to do here. I should advise the Secretary that my mission has been a failure, and request recall."

Scott saw the pain in the man's face, thought, We all believed it, we all *had* to believe it. He leaned forward, laid his arms on the desk.

"We're still at war, Mr. Trist. Wars end, even this one. If not this week, or next week, then it will be later. But it will end, and we will require a treaty. You have not yet finished your job."

Trist nodded slowly, said, "How can they believe we will just walk away? They know, certainly they know, that their proposal is not only unacceptable, but it does not leave room for further negotiation."

Scott thought of the discussions, all of Trist's optimism, and he tried to picture Santa Anna. So you sit at your big damned desk and make up these terms, so then, what? We reject them? He blinked, focused on the sunlight in the window, the thought suddenly clear in his mind. He made a fist, pounded the desk, startling Trist. Yes, so we reject them. You *want* us to reject them!

"I'm surprised at you, Mr. Trist. You have given me so much insight into the Mexican way of thinking, and you don't see it? This is not a negotiation, it is a delay. Santa Anna certainly told his people to negotiate in good faith, push these meetings along, always hinting at some progress, some possible break. Now, he's pulled the rug out from under the whole ceremony."

Trist seemed puzzled, said, "Why? Why bother to go through all of this? To what end?"

Scott looked at his fist, felt excited, glanced around the room, looked for something soft, something he could hit, the energy rolling up inside of him. Breathing heavily, he looked at Trist, who leaned back in the chair, eyes wide. Scott abruptly leaned forward.

"Manipulation! I won't stand for it, not from Washington, not from my commanders, not even from my wife! But, Santa Anna . . . damn him! Mr. Trist, the man's a master manipulator. He has played me like some simple parlor game. I suppose it's a talent necessary to every dictator. Even his own people believed they were negotiating in good faith, and so you believed it as well. But, after all, they will only do what he tells them, and so today their demands suddenly leap into the ridiculous. Why? So it will end, all the talk. He's had enough time. He's ready for us again. His army has come together, his guns are ready. End the talks. Game over."

Trist seemed surprised, said, "If you thought . . . if you knew he was doing this, why didn't you stop it?"

"I didn't know, Mr. Trist. I believed just as you did. He gave us what we wanted, a way out of this war, no more bloodshed, only a few pieces of paper holding us away from victory, home, *peace.* Powerful stuff, Mr. Trist."

Scott stood again, his fists still clenched, his breathing still sharp. Still he searched for something to punch, saw a small pillow, picked it up, tossed it aside. Damn him! We are so arrogant. And he has used that against us. He moved to the window, stared out toward the old castle, tried to calm himself, get control.

"We have won every fight. Had to, or we wouldn't be here now, wouldn't have come this far. He only has to win once, one big fight, and we're in serious trouble. I knew that when we left Vera Cruz, but I had confidence in this army. He *let* us come this close, he staked everything on a fight right here, because if *he* wins, it's over. This army could be in such a mess that we'd have to give in to anything he wants. We can't have our people scattered all over the countryside, it's *his* countryside. We can't handle another two or three thousand casualties, we can't continue to feed this army so close to his power. This is what he wants. And we have no choice now. We have to fight, we have to take the offensive again. We have to go after that big damned castle out there."

He turned, saw Trist watching him, said, "All he needs is one victory. This whole thing was engineered to give his army one more chance, one good shot at busting us up. And damned if I didn't give it to him."

26. WORTH

THE MEETING THE NIGHT BEFORE HAD BEEN BRIEF, AND THERE had been little doubt where the first strike should take place. A half mile west of the great castle of Chapultepec there was a compound of low, thick buildings, an elaborate millworks called Molino del Rey. The reports from the scouts had come during the truce; the Mexicans had begun to use the facilities there to manufacture cannon, were melting old church bells from the city, quickly restoring the artillery the *yanquis* had so effectively destroyed. Scott believed the reports, but to Worth there was nothing to *dis*believe. He had been quiet in his objections to the truce, knew he would not have swayed Scott from his course, but he had felt instinctively that Santa Anna could never be trusted, would violate whatever terms Scott naively granted. If Santa Anna was using the quiet time to begin making cannon, that was not only believable, it was inevitable.

With the presentation of the scouting reports, Scott had suggested the assault begin at night, a quick surprise, pushing hard into the Molino before Santa Anna could react. Worth had objected, would not have his division sent into an assault without the support of the artillery. He knew that in the dark, once the troops began to move, once the assault closed in on the enemy, the big guns could do nothing at all. In the end, Scott had to agree, had unexpectedly deferred to Worth's judgment. Worth was accustomed by now to Scott's disregard of him as a serious commander, still did not understand what he had done, what small act had somehow blossomed into Scott's total dislike of him.

Worth had taken great offense at being assigned to guard the army's rear at Vera Cruz, while Twiggs and Patterson pushed inland. There was in fact nothing there to guard, no threat at all from a Mexican army that was already scattered farther inland. He perceived the assignment as a post for troops who could not be trusted. Worth had been insulted, but finally took a stand with Scott, strongly wording a request to join the rest of the army that Scott could not ignore. When Worth's division was finally ordered to leave Vera Cruz, he marched his men inland with as much speed as they could endure. They reached the fight at Cerro Gordo barely in time to participate. He viewed Scott's actions as another insult. If his men did not seem to share his sense that the commanding general's orders were unfair, these slights only added to Worth's festering dislike of Winfield Scott.

Scott did not realize how deeply Worth disliked him, and Worth's own commanders did not fully understand his distaste for the commanding general. They knew that Worth's overcaution was legendary. The division endured the summer months at Puebla, growing more accustomed to Worth's fits of sudden panic, his bizarre routine of pulling the regiments together on short notice, lining up the tired troops into formation, only to receive the all clear, the word that the threat had passed, that the enemy was not waiting for them in hordes, ready to spring some surprise attack from just beyond the horizon. The jokes flowed quietly around the campfires, and the officers were tolerant, knowing they had to let their men blow off steam, release the small frustrations of a division commanded by an odd old bird, a man who saw ghosts. No real harm had come from the strange orders, the sudden defensive reaction to an assault that was never there. None of Worth's troops believed their commander had become some kind of target for Scott, none believed the division had ever been singled out for punishment in the form of some obscure or humiliating assignment. That dark label was held tightly inside the mind of William Worth.

Now, the assault was to be his, his alone, a stroke of fate that had placed his division the closest to the Molino. This time he would receive no slight, no insult. Worth knew Scott could not avoid giving his men their opportunity. When the dawn broke, thirty-two hundred men would strike out hard at the cluster of low flat buildings. If the truce was truly over, the truce that Santa Anna had so brazenly used for his own benefit, he would know that the *yanquis* still had the fire, were still determined to bring the fight straight to his army.

THE MEN HAD FALLEN INTO LINE BY THREE A.M., WOULD WAIT for the artillery barrage to break up the stone walls of the front buildings, opening the paths for the first wave of the assault. Worth chose five hundred men, handpicked from each of the regiments. He had named Major George Wright, an efficient and energetic man who would never be found anywhere but in front of his troops, to command them. There was no sign of daylight yet, but the troops were standing ready. If they had done this before, standing in line in quiet darkness, they knew that this time there were no ghosts. When the order came, it would be *Forward*.

Worth stood high on a mound of dirt, stared to the east, waiting for the sun. Soldiers murmured around him, the nervous sounds of men who must wait, small bits of meaningless conversation, quiet prayers, the whispered commands of officers, *Keep in line, muskets front*.

He looked again toward the white stuccoed buildings of Molino del Rey, squat shapes in the dark, thought of the scouts, the engineers, the latest reports he should have had hours ago, thought, Where are they? The engineers had performed the dangerous mission several times, and tonight it was the same, crawling close to the low stone walls, noting the openings, verifying the position of the enemy cannon. He strained to see in the dark, men shifting their position, more voices, now heard his name, an aide moving up behind him.

"General Worth. The engineers have returned, sir."

He stepped back off the mound, saw a small lantern held by the aide, saw now the face of Major Mason, smeared in black ash, smiling at him, his head bobbing up and down like some odd toy. Mason said, "Sir, I wish to report. . . . We believe there has been a development. Lieutenant Foster and I crawled up within seventy-five yards of the gun positions we had mapped during the truce. It seems, sir, that the Mexicans have pulled out. The guns are gone. I suspect, sir, that they have pulled out of the compound altogether."

Worth looked at the other man, the younger lieutenant, saw him nodding as well, said, "You saw . . . none of the enemy? No guns?"

"That's right, sir. It was all quiet."

Worth made a fist, pounded it into his open hand, thought, If they have pulled away, they must have seen us moving into position. They have scouts too. He looked to the east, saw the first faint glow of low gray light on the horizon.

"Have you told anyone about this?"

Mason seemed puzzled. "Um, no sir. We came straight here. My apologies for being late, but we took the most circuitous route to be safe."

Worth moved back up the mound of dirt, looked past the patch-work of cultivated fields toward the compound, could see the dark shapes changing, coming alive under a faint white glow. There were officers in front of him now, looking at him, all the men knowing what the daylight would mean. Worth glanced behind him, back toward the south, thought, Watch us now, General Scott. We will flow past this Molino place like a wave the enemy has never seen, and there will be nothing to prevent us from reaching Chapultepec itself. By noon this division, *Worth's* division, might very well have captured Santa Anna himself! He looked down, scanned the faces, saw Captain Huger, said, "You may commence firing, Captain. But make it brief."

The artillery officer stepped forward, said, "Excuse me, sir? Brief?"

"Make it quick, Captain, a dozen shells, no more. That's all we need. We don't need to drag this out, spend half the morning shelling empty buildings. When you cease fire, the men will advance."

Huger moved away, the officers speaking in a low hum now, questioning. Worth put his hands on his hips, stared at the awakening glow from the Molino.

"This is wonderful, gentlemen. This is the opportunity this division has needed! We'll see what Old Fuss and Feathers has to say when this day is done!"

THE OPENING BARRAGE CAME FROM ONLY TWO BIG GUNS, Huger's twenty-four pounders. When the first rounds were fired, the deep thunder rolled the ground under the feet of the troops. The men gave out a small cheer, knowing that as long as the steady, hard bursts split the air overhead, across the deadly space, the enemy was held low, might even be moving away. The word began to spread, the men close to the officers hearing the reports, and it was a rumor the men picked up with great energy. The enemy wasn't even there anymore, had fled in the night, fled from the sheer spectacle of this strong presence. The big guns added to the spreading energy. Across the way they could see the impact of the shells, the solid shot first, great smashing blows against soft stone, then the exploding rounds, the flashes of fire throwing debris high in the air. The cheering settled into one voice, low and steady, erupting again as another shell struck the stone walls. Then, as abruptly as it had begun, the deep roar of the guns suddenly stopped.

They still expected more, and the men looked down the line, looked to the officers, who stared back expectantly toward the battery.

There had been less than a dozen rounds from each gun, and the men waited for the guns to fire again, no one believing the artillery assault would be this brief. Now a different order came, a short blast from a bugle, and the officers moved quickly, swords high, the men rolling forward. The cheer began again, the men moving down into the open ground, all faces focused forward to the row of white stone. The officers stayed to the front, waved them on, and behind, the sergeants moved close, straightened the line. But there would be no stragglers, not from these men, the handpicked, the best men Worth's division could send to the fight.

Worth stood high on the mound again, raised his field glasses, but his hands were unsteady, shaking from the raw excitement, the thrill of watching the first wave move out in line. He saw the small flag waving, saw Major Wright holding his sword forward, pointing at the first building, the men now beginning to break line, the anticipation of being the first one to cross into the compound driving them forward.

The line disappeared, moving down across a cornfield, the tall stalks rolling forward with the footsteps of the troops. Worth raised the glasses again, held his hands as steady as he could, finding Wright's sword, pushing ahead through the corn. He lowered the glasses, saw the faces below watching him. "Send the next wave . . . send them!"

The call went out, and now far down to the left the next line began to move. McIntosh's brigade moved more to the west, sweeping around another smaller compound, then rolled ahead to link with Wright's men in the Molino. Worth looked out to the right, saw Garland's brigade waiting, the men who would move straight into the Molino from the south, and he thought, Not yet, soon. We should all converge together. Once the first wave is in, once Wright sweeps away any resistance . . .

He glassed again toward the compound, saw Wright's men coming up out of the corn, crossing a small road, still moving forward in one great mass of blue. He lowered the glasses, could not help but smile, thought, It has never felt this good. The eyes of the army—of the entire *nation*—are on these men.

The troops were within a hundred yards of the first buildings, and Worth thought again of the scouts, Mason's report, seventy-five yards away. Right about . . . there, he thought. But they could have gone closer. If the enemy was gone, they could have walked right in. Perhaps they should have.

There was a sudden flash of fire from all along the Molino, and he felt his chest turn cold, the smoke already blowing out, covering the

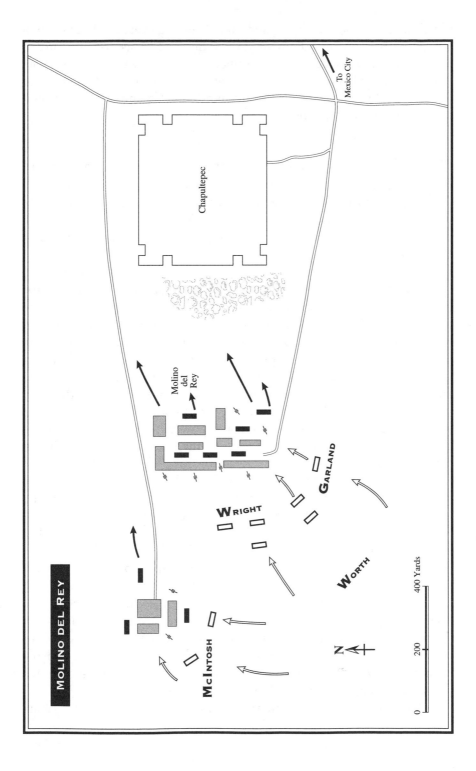

MOLINO DEL REY

McINTOSH

WORTH

WRIGHT

GARLAND

Molino
del
Rey

Chapultepec

To
Mexico City

N

0   200   400 Yards

blue line. Now the sound reached him, one long roar, a rolling echo of black thunder. Raising the field glasses, he tried to see, but his fingers numb, he could not focus. He dropped the glasses, saw only the thick cloud engulfing his men, heard the continuous roar of gunfire, watched flashes of light from inside the compound, the big guns throwing their deadly charges into his men.

THE FIRST WAVE HAD COLLAPSED, AND THE MEN WERE STREAM-ing back to the safety of their own lines, pushing their way in a panic through the advance of the second wave. The guns were still firing all through the buildings of the Molino, and the troops who did not run could only lie low, hugging the soft dirt and the trampled cornstalks in the fields.

He moved forward, saw men climbing the low rise toward him, emerging from the smoke, ghostly, men who had seen enough of the fight, who had been too close to the faces of the enemy, their confidence shattered. He looked for officers, saw men being carried toward him, the first wounded, and the screams finally reached him, the awful sound of broken men. He stopped, his aides scrambling up behind him, speaking in voices he did not hear, men touching his coat, pulling him away from the danger. The hands began to move him back, the aides herding him up the long rise, but the troops still flowed up from the smoke, the sounds still filled him, overpowering. His mind began to clear, bloodied officers began to gather, men who had seen their soldiers swept away.

Worth looked at them, the faces all speaking to him, their voices a confusion of noise, and he focused on one man, an older face, a captain, said, "They were not supposed to be there! The scouts reported—"

The man's expression curled into dark anger and he said, "The scouts were wrong, sir! The enemy moved their guns, pulled their artillery in close to the buildings. We're pretty shot up, sir. We lost . . . most of the officers are down. Major Wright is down."

Worth turned, stared at the rising wave of smoke, saw more men now moving toward him, couriers, and he stepped toward them, saw them salute. One man stepped forward. "General Worth, Colonel Garland reports heavy fighting in his front, a heavy concentration of the enemy. We were repulsed . . . but the colonel is re-forming the men and requests your orders, sir. Do we send them in again, sir?"

He felt an explosion bursting in his chest, shouted at the man,

"Of course, send them in! Colonel Garland knows the plan! No one is to retreat! Our objective is to capture the Molino! Hold back nothing, no reserves! We must take those buildings! All of you, go back to your commands!"

The couriers moved quickly away, and he looked around, and walked toward the tall mound of dirt. There was a new sound now, from up toward the smaller compound, where McIntosh's men had found their own fight. It was cannon, the sound different, distinctive, *American*. He climbed the hill, stared out, could see nothing but another thick cloud of smoke spreading out through the fields, hiding the small buildings. Yes, he thought, *our* guns, take it to them. We have better artillery. It will decide the day!

The smoke began to drift away out to the east, and for a moment he saw the great fat castle, rising up beyond the Molino. It should be ours, he thought. That place . . . it should belong to us . . . to this division. He saw Scott's face now, tried to push the image away, but it was firmly fixed in his mind. You knew, you must have known, he thought. The enemy was waiting for us, knew our plan. There is no glory here today.

M OST OF THE MEXICANS HAD BEGUN TO PULL OUT OF THE Molino, and Worth's men fought their way into the buildings in small groups, firing at close range into pockets of Mexican soldiers who did not hear the order to withdraw, or would not obey it if they had.

When the Americans came face-to-face with their enemy, the fighting changed, became something new, a different kind of horror for the men on both sides. When the muskets were empty, the soldiers attacked with their hands, grabbed and pulled and tore at the men who faced them. As more of the men in blue pushed inside the walls of the Molino, the Mexican defense could not hold them away, and finally the resistance collapsed.

Prisoners were gathered up, the officers sending them back across the ground where so many of the men in blue lay scattered. The few officers who survived the assault led small squads of men into the buildings one by one, and each time, they pushed hard through a thick doorway, expecting to find the smelting pots, the barrels of the new cannon the Mexicans would not after all be able to use. But the buildings of the Molino were empty, and the reports of the cannon, of the melting of church bells, proved to be only rumor, another sad mistake. If the massing of Mexican troops had been for some assault of their own, then Worth's attack had been successful, driving the Mexicans back to the gates of the city, back to the thick walls of Chapultepec. But the cost was another disaster. In a fight that lasted barely two hours, Worth's division lost a quarter of its strength, left nearly eight hundred men behind.

27. LEE

H
E MOVED SLOWLY FORWARD, STEPPING CAREFULLY BELOW THE edge of the causeway, staying off the high open road. He stopped, listened, but there was nothing to hear. The sounds had faded completely from around the Molino. He had been out early, heard the sounds of Worth's fight, a steady rumble of cannon and musket fire, still had no idea what had happened. He could only guess that if the Molino was quiet, Worth was inside, had occupied the compound that could provide the army with a starting point for another push, closer again, this time from the west. If Scott made the decision to begin the final push to the city's gates from that point, it would mean they first would have to overcome the enormous difficulty of assaulting the old fortress, Chapultepec.

He was scouting the southern gates of the city, easing along the Piedad causeway, moving as close to the Belén gate as the Mexican sentries would allow. They had paid no attention to him thus far, no patrol had been sent to interfere, no sporadic crack of musket fire from bored lookouts. The attention had all been to the west, and the movement he had seen, wagons, guns rolling both ways on the causeway to the Molino, had stayed well to the northwest, above his position.

At first light Beauregard had begun his own mission, scouting a parallel course to the east, using another of the high roads that led straight into the southern gates. Lee was surprised to see him now, scrambling up behind him, his uniform muddy at the knees.

Lee squatted down, waited for Beauregard to move close, said, "What happened? Couldn't you get close to the gate?"

Beauregard took a moment to catch his breath. "The sentries . . . they caught sight of me pretty quick, fired a few rounds down the road.

I got close enough to see they blocked the road, earthworks, a pretty good stack of timbers. I could make out two batteries, back close to the city. They have the whole area covered by artillery."

Lee was impressed, thought, A good report, he's getting better at this job. "Sounds like they expect us to advance that way. That's important. We must make sure General Scott is aware."

Beauregard seemed to inflate. He smiled, rubbed his brow with a handkerchief. "What about here? They see you?"

Lee looked up the embankment toward the roadway. "If they have, they haven't made any move. I think they're more concerned with what happened at the Molino. If General Worth was successful, the Mexicans would have to protect the road that runs west, toward Chapultepec. We're no threat here."

Beauregard crawled halfway up the embankment and stood, his head nearly level with the road. Lee thought, Careful, Lieutenant. No easy targets.

Beauregard looked down at him. "You want to keep going?"

Lee stood, straightened stiff knees, nodded, pointed toward the base of the embankment. "Down here, Lieutenant. Keep low. No point in attracting any more attention than we have to. I don't care for facing a squad of cavalry."

Beauregard jumped and slid down beside him, and Lee moved ahead, stepping carefully through soft dirt, rocks, keeping close to the side of the causeway. The ground out to the left was thick with grass, tall weeds, black patches of muddy water. There was a sharp sound of cracking brush now, and Lee raised his hand, *Halt,* could hear heavy movement in the weeds. Beauregard was silent behind him, and both men listened, staring into dense brush. There were more sounds, branches cracking, quick footsteps in water, and Beauregard pulled his pistol, pointed at the sound.

Lee reached out, put a hand on his arm, whispered, "Easy. It's probably a pig. I've already scared a few this morning. So far, they seem more inclined to run away than make a stand. Best to leave them be."

Beauregard didn't seem convinced, hesitated, and Lee pointed to the holster, issuing a quiet command. The pistol disappeared. "Keep in mind, Lieutenant, that's the escape route. It's all we can do if they send somebody down this road. Follow the pig. I'd rather stay dry, if it's the same to you."

He began to move again, pushed through a clump of bushes, then stopped, raised his field glasses, scanned a moment, heard Beauregard breathing heavily behind him.

"There. That ravine. We can make it that far, then move away from the causeway. It's clear ground on the far side. We have to get closer, see what's happening up near the gate."

He stepped forward again, more brush, saw a low pile of rocks, extending out from the causeway, climbed up, saw a wide ditch filled with black water on the other side. He heard Beauregard make a small groan behind him. Lee stepped over the rocks, looked down at his dry boots, the soft mud, said, "Leave them on. Can't chance what might be . . . down there. Better to have wet boots than bloody feet."

Beauregard sat on the rocks, shook his head, said with a frown, "I used to love to play in mud. When I was a kid, you couldn't keep me in dry shoes. But I swear, Captain, there's more mud around this city than the whole state of Louisiana."

Lee smiled, but had no patience for reminiscing, knew there was too much yet to be done. "Let's go."

He stepped one foot into the black, his boot sinking down, quickly took a second step, the water now flowing over the top of his boot. He looked at the far side of the ditch, thought, Fast . . . do it now.

He lunged ahead, taking long strides as he splashed his way to the far side. He moved up to another row of rocks, turned, watched as Beauregard struggled across. The young lieutenant reached the rocks, and Lee turned, began to climb up, and Beauregard said, "My boot! I lost my boot!"

Lee turned back, saw Beauregard's one bare foot, even the sock pulled away, the skin pale white. Lee turned away, self-conscious, not wanting to stare at the man's embarrassment. Beauregard looked back at the swirling mud, stared for a moment, and Lee thought, No, don't go back, let it go.

"Lieutenant, you'll have to manage. You'll never find it."

Beauregard seemed wounded, moved away from the ditch, climbed the row of rocks, said, "I like these boots. Expensive."

Lee began to move again, heard small grunts behind him, the young man picking his way slowly. Lee turned, saw the young man stepping tenderly, felt his impatience rising again. "Lieutenant, I'm going up to that ravine, then I'll try to move out to the right until I can see the gates. I suggest you . . . go back and get your boot. Join me when you can."

Beauregard saluted him. "Thank you. Thank you, sir. I'll be along directly."

Lee moved away, still close to the edge of the causeway. He could see the ravine a few yards ahead, more thick grass, thorny brush. He felt his foot grabbed tightly, caught in a tangle of vines. He tried to twist free, then reached down to slide a thick ropelike plant off his boot, felt a sharp sting in his hand. He jerked his hand back, saw a spot of blood on his palm, saw the long thorns on the vine. His patience was gone now, and he felt his anger suddenly wash over him. Jerking hard, he ripped his boot through the vines, thought, What kind of unholy place is this? Is this some kind of message from God, go home, go back to green grass? He stood still for a moment, took a deep breath, said aloud, "Calm down, Captain."

Lee stepped more carefully as he eased down into the ravine, picking his way through the vines, more thorns, before moving across the bottom and climbing the far side. He could see movement, a long low line of brown, raised the field glasses. There was a fresh row of logs, cut trees, men moving around them, shovels, dirt flying. He scanned down the line. More men were dragging clumps of brush out of the ravine he was in, and beyond, a reflection off a brass cannon caught his eye. He spotted two more, a full battery. He looked back along the cut trees, saw a different color uniform, an officer, the man directing the workers. More officers, several standing together, stood and watched. The men in charge, he thought.

He lowered the glasses, slid down the hill slightly and settled into the soft grass behind the edge of the ravine. He heard sounds coming up behind him now, brush cracking, saw Beauregard, the young man soaking wet, every part of him covered with a dark ooze. Beauregard climbed up close to him, said, "Found it, sir. Thank God! You see those thorns?"

Lee felt the weariness flooding over him, did not look at Beauregard. "Take a look . . . carefully, Lieutenant. They're building a defensive line."

Beauregard climbed up, wiped at his field glasses with a dirty hand, looked at Lee, his face a silent question. Lee already had pulled the clean handkerchief from his pocket, held it out. Beauregard wiped the glasses, scanned out, said, "My God. They're expecting a fight."

Lee nodded, said, "It's a very strong position, high ground, looks like a solid line of works running between the two causeways, supported by artillery. If anyone in this army believes the Mexicans are ready to turn tail, he should come here. They intend to make a stand."

Beauregard sat beside him now, held out the muddy handkerchief, and Lee glanced at it, saw the young man withdraw it, discreetly tuck it away. "Um, sorry, sir. I shall replace it."

Lee did not respond to the apology, was thinking of the artillery. "We must count the guns, we must report the number of cannon."

Beauregard raised himself up to the edge of the grass. "It's just like this to the east, sir. Same way on the other causeway. They're going to an awful lot of trouble unless they believe we're coming this way."

Lee stared back toward the south, toward the position of the army, Scott's headquarters. He sat up straight now, thought, Of course, nothing has changed. Even after all the fights, it's the same strategy. They still expect us to come at them in a straight line. These gates . . . they're the closest point, the closest to the center of our position, good solid roads running in a straight line right at the city. They still believe we will do this by their rules. But this time . . . they may be right.

He turned, crawled up, saw Beauregard glassing out to the left, the west, and Lee looked the other way, toward the San Antonio gate. It is the closest . . . the straightest line, he thought. The ground is difficult, and their artillery will make the causeways nearly impassable. But with our strength, with quickness, we can push through.

Beauregard still glassed to the west, said, "It's impressive, isn't it? *The Halls of Montezuma . . .*"

Lee looked in that direction. He had grown used to seeing the massive stone hill, the thick walls of Chapultepec emerging straight up from the rocks, a part of the hill itself. Lee said, "Remember Vera Cruz. We do not have to attack their strongest point. Our goal is the city. Chapultepec dominates the ground. It would be a difficult place to make an assault. The cost could be very high."

Beauregard lowered the glasses, looked at him, said, "Sorry, but I don't agree, Captain. The enemy is preparing a strong defense of these gates, the southern gates. They don't expect us to attack the fortress itself. That's why we should."

Lee slid back down the hill, put the glasses in his coat, said, "That fortress has dominated this place since before Cortez. If we try to hit them there, it could make Santa Anna very happy. These gates . . . the southern gates are vulnerable, much harder to defend. If we move quickly enough . . ."

Beauregard was beside him again. "Sir, with all respect, my report to General Scott will include a recommendation that we make the first assault from the west, toward Chapultepec. If we are successful, there may be very little fight left in the Mexicans, and the city will certainly fall. We might not even have to fight to get through the gates."

"If we are *not* successful, Lieutenant, then the city will *never* fall. We will lose too much."

Beauregard moved down to the bottom of the ravine. "Sorry if I'm out of line, Captain. But I have a responsibility to report the situation here as I see it. General Scott will give your report more weight than he will mine. But I cannot see how we can just . . . ignore that big fort. Half the Mexican army could be in that place."

Lee felt the weariness clouding his brain, thought, This is no different from Vera Cruz. I will not argue this, not now.

"We better get moving, Lieutenant. General Scott will be anxious to know what we saw out here."

Lee moved down past Beauregard, stepped through the vines, heard the young man close behind him. He was very tired now, felt the soreness stiffening his knees again, the soggy wetness in his boots. I do not make the decisions, he thought. Thank God for that. I could not weigh it all, decide this right now. We're just engineers, we have no right to choose the fate of this army, to throw our reports in the general's face as though we have the experience, the wisdom, to know what is best. That is the job of the commander. He stopped, glanced back at Beauregard, saw the young man moving up close, curious, waiting for Lee to say something. Lee saw the defiance still on Beauregard's face, wanted to make his argument, but he needed all his energy for the march back. His mind was already far ahead, moving him through the mud and brush. He turned away, began to move, could see the low rocks again, the awful muddy water, looked up toward the roadway, pointed, said, "This way."

He climbed up to the road, reached back, pulled Beauregard up, and the two men moved quickly on the open roadway, crossed a small bridge over the wide ditch. Lee stopped to look back, stared at the city walls. He could still see the motion of the workers on the defensive line. The sun was falling low now, and he looked toward Chapultepec, the dull white walls reflecting a soft glow of sunlight, thought, No, not there. He is wrong. Surely he is wrong.

28. LEE

SCOTT HAD MOVED OUT OF THE BISHOP'S GRAND ESTATE. AS A result, the meeting was held in a church, the only large building in the small village of Piedad. The meeting had been Scott's way of getting all the input he could, listening to all the arguments, the opinions, about what strategy the army might use to assault the city. It had been awkward at first, and they all knew it was because of General Worth. He had entered alone, and the talk grew quiet, the faces of the staff watching him, the other senior commanders attempting not to. Worth had tried not to notice, moved self-consciously to a seat behind even the junior staff. Lee could not help watching Worth suffer in quiet pain. It led him to think of words, something to say to help. But on a deeper level, even Lee understood that Worth himself would have to find some way past the awful cost of the fight at the Molino.

As the meeting began, Scott did not speak directly to Worth at all. Lee wondered if the two men had engaged in quiet conversation before, words from the commanding general to heal Worth's wounded pride, to soften the strange hostility between them. All through the meeting Lee had glanced back, trying to read the man's face, but Worth barely spoke at all, spent most of his time staring down between the pews, lost in his own depression.

The focus of the meeting was strategy, and Lee had spoken his mind about attacking the southern gates, still believed the cost in casualties would be far less than sending waves of troops up the sloping approaches to the big fortress. The other engineers had agreed with him, but Beauregard had made his case as well, and now the engineers were silent, having given as much as Scott would allow.

Scott sat back in the chair, faced the others, spread out in the rows of pews. He looked at Twiggs, said, "General, you've been fairly quiet tonight. I would like to hear from you."

Twiggs shifted his weight on the hard wood, slowly stood and leaned forward, laying his hands on the back of the pew in front of him. Staring down, he spoke very quietly, matching his tone to the meeting's somber setting.

"My views are well-known, sir. It has been difficult for me to accept that what I have often considered to be the best strategy is usually disregarded by the commanding general."

Twiggs paused, seemed to be forming his thoughts, but he spoke no more. Lee studied Twiggs's face, saw his strange sadness, quiet frustration. He glanced around, saw the others looking down or glancing away self-consciously, and Lee thought, He seems defeated, as though he expects no one to listen to him.

Scott said, "I would like your views, General."

Twiggs looked at Scott now, leaned forward again, exhaled loudly. "If we are to beat these people . . . if we are to win this war . . . we must beat them completely. This is a big country. General Santa Anna can make war against us forever unless we take him out, eliminate his command. It accomplishes very little if all we do is rush into the city and put up a flag."

Twiggs sat down, still showed the frustration, and Lee looked at Scott, who stood up slowly, said, "Beginning tomorrow, I want the engineers to coordinate with Captain Lee. I want sites chosen for the placement of batteries. The artillery will be our most important asset. When the guns are in place, I will direct the placement of the troops. I can tell you now that the southern gates to the city are critically important. . . ."

Lee felt his heart jump, thought, Thank God, he agrees with me. I had so hoped . . .

"They are critically important," Scott continued, "because Santa Anna believes they are important. We must convince him we agree. We will make a significant demonstration in that area, a full brigade at least. The rest of the army will focus their attack . . . on Chapultepec. This meeting is over. You are dismissed."

Lee felt a shock, sat still while the others began to move away, sliding across the polished wood, standing in the aisle. He looked to the side, saw Twiggs still sitting as well. Twiggs slowly stood, his eyes on Scott. Twiggs's sadness was gone now, replaced by something Lee could not name. Scott glanced at Twiggs, and Lee saw the quick nod, the acknowledgment, two old commanders sharing something the young officers could not understand.

Twiggs moved away, glanced quickly at Lee. His expression was different now, softer, and he made a brief nod toward Lee, then turned and walked slowly down the aisle. Lee still sat, waited for the aisle to clear, saw Scott stand, stretching his back. When Scott saw Lee, he asked, "You decide to hang around for a bit of religion, Mr. Lee? It's a Catholic church. If you do any praying, best keep it to yourself."

Lee nodded, didn't know what to say, felt a tumble of words rolling through his mind.

"Something bothering you, Mr. Lee?"

Lee felt a low burn on his neck, thought, Stop this, this is not your place. He shook his head slowly. "No, sir."

"*Bull.* What's on your mind?"

Scott moved to the aisle, slid into the pew, sat heavily. "Damn these hard seats. Makes it hard to spend much time in these places."

Scott shifted his weight, tried to get comfortable. "We have a hell of a fight in front of us, Mr. Lee. I believe it is the last fight. This war could have ended any time we sent their army packing. But there was always some negotiation, some piece of paper signed by Mr. Trist. But Davy Twiggs is right. Unless we defeat Santa Anna, unless we remove him from power, there will still be a war."

Lee glanced to the rear of the church, saw the young Scott watching, waiting impatiently. Scott followed Lee's gaze. "Dismissed, Major. I'll call you if I need you. Mind the door, no visitors."

The young man disappeared outside, the large wood doors swinging shut quietly. Scott looked at Lee, said, "My son-in-law needs to be in some office, locked away in some damned big building in Washington." Scott paused, seemed to clear his mind.

"Maybe you need to know this, Mr. Lee. Maybe you need to hear this before you feel comfortable talking to me. I've been in a uniform a long time, a damned long time. My friends consider me an outstanding commander. Hell, so do I. My enemies, and there's a few, they think I'm a foolish old peacock. Davy Twiggs thinks I'm soft. Gideon Pillow thinks I'm dangerous. Worth . . . God knows what Worth thinks. I'm his personal tormentor. Point is, Mr. Lee, command is all about the minds of the people around you, understanding how they think, how they see you, and how they see themselves. Am I making sense, Mr. Lee?"

Lee nodded. "I believe so, sir." He studied the old face, tried to see

Scott's eyes, the old fire, but Scott was looking away, seemed to study the small statue behind the pulpit, pale yellow marble, the Virgin Mary.

Scott shook his head. "It's a hell of a thing we do here. We sit in a house of God and plan the conquest of our enemies." He turned to Lee.

"War is not a natural state, Mr. Lee. It is not a fact of nature, something man must adapt to or accept, like floods, or smallpox. We create it. We perpetuate it. And it is incumbent on us to do the best job we can, or we suffer the consequences. The worst consequence of fighting a war is not if you lose, Mr. Lee. The worst thing you can do is win badly. The losers go back to their people and endure the shame, or the humiliation, and the politicians make excuses, we were outgunned, outfought, but still they hold on to their cause, create their martyrs. The winner, he has proven his cause is the stronger perhaps. Might makes right. The glory, all the celebrations, the parades are his. But if the winner has not won completely, efficiently, the loser will not respect him, will never accept that the defeat was just. They will begin to find strength. The cause, the martyrs, will come back to life, and before you know it, there is *another* war, and if the winner isn't careful, all his boasting and bluster may make him blind to history." He stopped, looked up, scanned the walls of the church, the artifacts, seemed lost for a moment.

Lee started to speak, but Scott continued.

"There are generals in this army who remember Cerro Gordo, and say, 'Well, see, they ran away. They won't fight. All we have to do is ride up to the gates of Mexico City, and we will win.' That kind of thinking has cost this army a quarter of its strength." Scott leaned back in the pew, took a long breath, said, "My fault. Ultimately, I am accountable." He looked at Lee. "Remember that, Mr. Lee. The commander is always responsible. If your subordinates are incompetent, you had better remove them quickly. It is not them who will suffer for it, it is you."

"I don't believe I will face that predicament, sir."

"Bull. You are born to it, Mr. Lee. Your heritage, your upbringing, your training. And frankly, Mr. Lee, I will admit to you, knowing full well this will embarrass the hell out of you . . . you are the best damned officer I've ever served with. You know that?"

Lee looked down, said, "Surely not, sir."

"Ha! Told you it would embarrass you. Be honest with me, Captain. You don't agree with my strategy, do you?"

Lee felt the burn coming back again, said, "My apologies, sir. But, you asked for our judgment . . ."

"Doesn't mean I have to listen to it. It's still my decision. I understand why you think the southern gates are the best route. It's cleaner, more likely to be a quick fight, put us into the city with fewer casualties. But Davy Twiggs is right. Putting our flag in their city square may give President Polk a case of the giggles, but it doesn't mean the war is over. We could be here for years, keeping the guerrillas away. And who do you think will command the guerrillas? Our friend, Mr. Santa Anna. There's more to this war than good tactics. Remember what I said. We have to win, completely, utterly. Victory means conquest. *Think* like your enemy, understand how *he* sees things. That damned castle out there *means* something to those people, to all of them, the army, the civilians, the politicians. It's a symbol of who they are. If we just skip around it because it's inconvenient, the symbol will have survived. They will not *respect* our victory. Santa Anna would use that, you can bet your life. He can draw power from that. We have no choice, Mr. Lee. We *have* to defeat Chapultepec. It is the only defeat they will accept."

Lee looked toward the front of the church, looked to the statue, the ivory face staring upward. "There is more to command than I expected. My apologies, sir."

"For what? You did your job. No one could do it better. You're still learning, Mr. Lee. That's the important thing. Learn. I'm still learning, for God's sake. A year ago I thought Davy Twiggs was nothing but a thick-headed old mule. But he's also a combat officer, and with a stern hand guiding him, he's a damned fine leader of troops. A year ago I thought Pillow would collapse under the strain, crawl back to Washington the first time he saw combat. But he proved me wrong. He's not perfect, but he's a fairly competent commander. You, you're what, forty years old? You have a long career in front of you. And a hell of a lot to learn. When I'm put out to pasture, when some new pink-eared President decides my time is past, I'll wager *you'll* be ready. And the country will be better for it."

Lee was feeling overwhelmed, said, "Thank you, sir. I try not to think about the future. God will decide what course I follow."

"Whatever you say, Mr. Lee. But sooner or later I'll have a little chat with God, if you don't mind. Bring a few things to His attention."

Scott stood now, stretched his back again, groaned softly. Lee stood, faced him, waited for the final word, the formal end to the meeting.

"Tomorrow, you will begin placing the batteries. You're in charge, I'll make sure they know that. Hell, they know it now. But keep one thing clear when you set those guns. I want that damned castle blown to hell. If we can break up those walls, our job will be a great deal easier."

He looked Lee squarely in the eyes. "We have one chance, Mr. Lee, one last chance. If we don't take that place, there won't be enough of us left to try again. If we don't take that place, we will lose this war. There is more at stake here than where the hell Texans can graze their cattle. If we lose, it means we are weak. It means anyone who has enough ambition and enough strength can come after our land, *our* boundaries. The English, the French . . . we could have a generation of war on our hands. We *have* to win, Mr. Lee. We have to go home from here with the whole world understanding that you cannot conquer us, that our resolve and our borders are absolute. We have to win this war so completely that the whole world believes *God* said so." Scott moved into the aisle, said quietly, "Good night, Captain. Get some sleep."

Lee watched as Scott made his way slowly toward the door, and he thought, I can never speak of this, can repeat none of this. It was not appropriate for him to share this with me. He still felt embarrassed, his mind racing with Scott's words. He is right about one thing. You have a lot to learn. Perhaps he is right about . . . all of it. He thought of his father now. Would this have been the same? Would the lessons have come from him as well? He heard Scott's words again, *your heritage.* Does that matter after all? Is that what destiny is about, what brought me here? He felt a wave of frustration. No, I am not supposed to know the answers. I may never know.

He looked up, scanned the darkened glass of the windows, focused on the small paintings on the ceiling, angels and cherubs. His eye caught motion, and he realized now Scott was still there, standing by the door, watching him, and Scott said, "If you're going to stay here awhile, Captain, it couldn't hurt if you'd put a good word in for the rest of us."

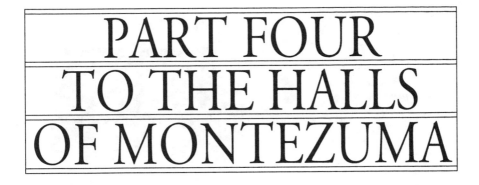

PART FOUR
TO THE HALLS
OF MONTEZUMA

The battle for Chapultepec

29. LONGSTREET

September thirteenth, predawn

H E LAY ON HIS BACK, THE BLANKET FOLDED UNDER HIM, AND stared up at a sky filled with stars. The moon had set, falling away to the west, and he knew the sun would come soon and that around him the sleeping army would begin to stir. But there were always these few moments, the quiet time when he would come awake, listen to the silence, and stare up at the sky.

He saw the quick dart of a meteor, the streak of light fading away, and he smiled. He had always enjoyed this, the feeling of floating in the endless dark, the small thrill of catching the glimpse, the piece of burning rock, the last fiery gasp on the long voyage. He turned to one side, felt a dull pain in the shoulder, flexed the arm, thought, Not too bad, still stiff. It won't bother me today. There will be other concerns.

The men of the Eighth Infantry had already seen the hardest fighting of the war, had been part of Worth's bloody awful day at the Molino. The regiment was gathered close now, the units reorganized, the wounded long taken away, to a hospital a mile behind them, a small village with a name few of them could pronounce. To the men who slept under the stars, there would be little time for missing the men who were not there, and over the last two days all conversation had been about the great fortress. Even the men who had been stubborn about learning a few words of Spanish, whose crude pronunciation twisted the name of every town, knew the name Chapultepec.

The regiment had accepted this blessed rest, stayed quiet, and for the most part the commanders left them alone. Longstreet had spent the day before playing cards, but there was no spirit in the game, no bawdy jokes, none of the quiet tales of the strangeness of William Worth. One by one the players had moved away, thoughts of poker overshadowed by thoughts of what would happen tomorrow, how early the orders might come, how few men they had left. And if anyone had sought the quiet space, to be alone with his thoughts or his prayers, those moments had been swept away by the steady thunder of the artillery barrage.

The shelling had lasted nearly all day, the batteries relentless, pouring their shot into Chapultepec until it was too dark to find the target. A few of the men had gone forward, moving up through Pillow's camp, seeking a better view. They cheered, as did Pillow's men, when the good aim found the tender spot and a piece of the fat stone wall came apart, shattering under the impact of a twenty-four-pound shell.

Longstreet rolled over on his back again, knew the dark would give way soon. He let his eyes relax, waited to catch the next quick flash of another meteor. He heard sounds coming from the hills far to the south, a long low howl, then higher, the short quick yelps of a coyote, protesting this large intrusion into its domain. He thought of Texas then, the coyotes everywhere, darting across the flat grassland, filling the dark with the strange, frightening sound many of the soldiers had never heard before. Here, the coyotes stayed far away. Back then there had been contests, the men who knew how to hunt claiming some prize for actually shooting one, but they were rarely successful. He smiled, thinking of his friend, Sam Grant, trying to shoot the shotgun. His target was far out of range, and the smoky blast from the fat gun knocked Grant off his frightened horse. They had plenty of time for such things then. They were in wild country, a place of adventure for the men from the cities, sometimes experiencing wide-eyed fears, snakes, spiders, the scorpion. The officers had fished, hunted, played poker, but then it was time to move south, begin the march with Zachary Taylor, and the good times had ended. He knew Grant was close by, the Fourth Infantry, another piece of Worth's division, and he thought, Sam's still sleeping. He won't wake up until he has to, the last man out of his blanket. Stay low, Sam. This could be a difficult day.

Longstreet had been out of the Point now for five years, had risen to the title of adjutant for the Eighth, the title a simple reward from Worth for good service in the field. But with the experience had come something new, something disturbing. He still worried about the men, as he worried about his friend Grant. But he felt little concern for the enemy, for what these men and their guns would do to those men across the way. He thought of the strange feeling, the cold numbness, stepping across the bodies at Resaca de la Palma, and then the first glimpse of one of his own, a young corporal from Tennessee, the man shot dead right in front of him. He had cried, had to pull hard at his own discipline, keep going, move forward. But the face of the boy had stayed with him, even as he fired his pistol into the chest of a young Mexican soldier.

At Cerro Gordo he had stepped over the twisted bodies of more Mexican soldiers, ignoring the horror of their bayonet wounds. He focused instead on the enemy who could still run, chased the panicked Mexicans as far as his lungs would allow. His sword raised high, his throat hoarse with the high screams that came from someplace inside him he had not known was there, he raced headlong and outran his fear and reached that place that was inside all of them. It gave him a chill even now, and he thought, It is so easy to do that, to become a killer. What is it that makes them the *enemy*? He had asked himself the same question after every fight, and he settled for the vague notion that it was, of course, the duty, the soldier's duty. And the commanders seemed to understand that the unexplainable quality was clearly in this man Longstreet, and had pointed him out, recognized him in the reports. Lieutenant Longstreet was a *good soldier*.

He began to feel restless, knew he was fully awake now and there would be no more sleep. He did not have a watch, had no idea what time it was. Maybe you should get up, he thought, find the coffee. There was always coffee, somewhere, a small fire still glowing red. But he was suddenly anxious, felt the nervous twist in his stomach, thought of the dawn, the first light, when the hard sounds from the big guns would begin again.

No, there is no hurry. Think good thoughts, something pleasant. He saw her face now, the wonderful Louise, the devilish smile, a hint of mischief. He thought of Grant again, this time at Fort Jefferson, near St. Louis. Sam, you chased that poor Julia, that *teenager*, all over the countryside. Finally she chased you back, served you right, and even *you* knew it was love, mad, stupid, childlike love. But Louise . . . very different, something very adult. He could remember the first time she winked at him, *winked,* and he smiled again, thought, It scared me. Women don't *do* those kinds of things. But it became their secret code, the forbidden signal in the crowd of her family, always embarrassing him. He thought of her father, the unfortunate coincidence.

Colonel John Garland, the old soldier, the crusty veteran of 1812, was one of Worth's two brigade commanders. He's right here, Longstreet thought, probably a few yards away, and he certainly hates *you*, probably hates anyone who looks that way at his daughter. Good thing my orders come from Colonel Clarke. I'd probably be in front of every assault. He remembered the argument, Garland putting a finger in his face, the only argument a father has left: *She is too young, Mr. Longstreet.* But he knew there was more left unsaid, thought, Colonel Garland is a veteran. He knows what the orders mean, what can happen when soldiers march away. No matter how much some young man loves your daughter, there is always the chance that he might not come back. But I will. God help me, I will.

The stars were fading now, and he heard a bugle, far in the distance, then closer. Around him, men began to move, muttering the small curses that greet every bugler. He sat up, rolled to one side, felt the soreness in the shoulder again, pushed himself up. The faint daylight was growing in the east, and he looked out across the camp at a dozen campfires, men moving to stir the ashes, the clanking coffeepots ending what remained of the silence.

Most of the men were up and moving about. Longstreet reached under the blanket for the tin coffee cup, blew the dirt out, ran his finger along the scratches, the initials. He had picked the cup up in the cornfield, the horrible ground near the Molino. The fight was by then over, the sounds of musket fire scattered, and he moved among the bodies, counting, looking for the men who had marched in his command. The cup had been dropped, kicked away. The initials, L.L.S., had been scratched with great care, probably with the point of a bayonet. He had looked over the roster, tried to find the name, but the initials made no match, and so he wondered if it was not those of a soldier, but someone else, a remembrance, a girl.

No one had claimed the cup, and he could not just hand it over to the cook, had thought, It was important to—one of them. If we are to leave so many behind, bury so many in foreign soil, there should be something, some memory, some symbols we bring home. Maybe someday I will find out who L.L.S. might be.

The losses were staggering, and among the officers a strange feeling of dread began to grow as they watched the strong units dwindle away. It had been sickness at first, from the first landing at Vera Cruz, and even before, in south Texas, the tormenting misery of heat and strange food, insect bites and water that carried some odd odor. There were always long lists of men on sick call, and a horrifying number of men did not return at all, would be buried in this hostile land a victim of some unknown plague. As the fighting grew bloodier, the beds were filled with the wounded, and the men with knotted stomachs would have to find some other place to endure their misery. As the numbers continued to fall away, the officers could not keep the question to themselves: Are we, after all, enough of an army?

Longstreet thought of the low conversations, the quiet fears, the young lieutenants watching their small commands grow smaller still. The commanders still believe, he thought, they know how many of *them* we will face today. If we are so many fewer, they are as well. Thank God for General Scott.

He had no patience for jokes about Scott, would not tolerate the nicknames, had given many of his men a good dressing down for their loose comments. If Taylor were still in command, he thought, we might still be up there near the Rio Grande, in some godforsaken desert, waiting for Santa Anna to make the next move. Yes, thank God for Winfield Scott.

He moved toward a fire, saw a coffeepot hanging, felt the sudden need. A few officers had begun to gather, some sitting close to the coals, and he stayed a step back since he could feel the dampness in his shirt, was already beginning to sweat. The heads began to turn, drawn by the smell of frying bacon, and he saw men already forming a line, waiting for food. He shook his head, thought, Too early. How can anyone come out of sleep just to eat? He looked again at the coffeepot, saw a corporal move close, the man's uniform barely evident, the blue cloth stained black with soot and grease. The corporal saw Longstreet watching him, picked up the pot with a gloved hand, said, "Sir? Might not be too good, same grounds I been using for a week."

The corporal poured, and Longstreet watched the steam, nodded, and the man moved away, the other cups rising now. Longstreet blew at the steam, tasted carefully. His tongue curled, and he made a small grunt, thought, *God-awful.* He stared into the dark liquid, and the corporal said, "There's sugar there on the wagon, sir. Can I get you some?"

Longstreet nodded quietly, and the man retrieved a small brown bag, came back to the fire, held it toward Longstreet. He felt inside, his finger wrapping around a hard lump, and he tried to ease it into the cup, but let it drop, hot coffee splashing his hand. He thought of Colonel Garland again, the old veteran. Did he ever enjoy this?

There was a voice now, the first loud sound of the morning, a brief explosion of profanity. The faces all turned, and Longstreet saw George Pickett moving past the wagon, up to the fire, wrestling with a button on his coat, saying, "By damned, if I ever find the scoundrel . . ."

There were quiet laughs, shaking heads, then Pickett saw Longstreet, said, "Well, Pete! A good morning to you, sir!"

"Morning, George. What's the trouble?"

Pickett smiled, seemed for a moment to forget he had been angry, then remembered his temper, frowned again, said, "Oh, well, I am in some distress, Pete! Last night I had been graciously rewarded with the presence of a truly fine lady, who was sympathetic to the pain and suffering endured by us fine American soldiers. She was kind enough to offer up this fine local brew, a bottle of this fine *tequila*, and . . ."

He watched Pickett probing his stomach, in obvious discomfort, as he seemed to drift away, shaking his head sharply, a mess of ruffled curls.

"Hmmph. Well, anyway, we had this bottle of fine brew, and naturally, not being gluttonous, I determined to save a good portion of it for . . . a future encounter. And now, some soldier has taken it! And I'll find it, by damned!"

He looked at the faces around the fire watching him, glared a menacing frown, as if to confront the thief.

Longstreet smiled, said, "Now, George, don't you think it's possible the young lady decided to keep the bottle for herself? There's plenty of, um . . . *brew* around here as it is. Your half-empty bottle is hardly enough cause to convene a court-martial."

Pickett looked at him, and the anger seemed to slip away. He shrugged, said, "If you say so, Pete." Pickett rubbed his stomach again. "That brew went down a good bit smoother last night. There seems to be a protest this morning."

Pickett rubbed his hands together. "That coffee any good? Anybody got a cup they aren't using?"

Pickett stepped closer to the fire and a cup was offered, the routine from the officers who knew that Lieutenant Pickett was rarely carrying anything useful. Longstreet saw his uniform now, thought, My God, he's a disaster.

"George, your coat's on inside out."

Pickett looked down, the men around him laughing out loud now, and he stepped back, tossed the full cup aside, pulled at the coat.

Longstreet smiled still, said, "At least it's your own uniform."

Pickett straightened, wearing a wounded look. "Enough of this, gentlemen. I shall not be your source of amusement. I must go to my men, prepare them for battle."

Longstreet watched him move away with a slight waver in his step. He sipped at the coffee, thought, How did you ever make it through West Point? At least I know where you'll be when I need you.

The quiet returned to the campfire, low conversations resumed, and he backed away, moved toward his rumpled blanket gathered on the soft ground. He knelt down, rolled the blanket into a neat coil, wrapped it around his pack. Catching more of the food smells, the lines at the wagons growing now, he moved that way, thought, Something to eat. Probably a good idea. He felt a soft grumble, the familiar spasm low in his gut. No, please, not today. He waited, and the feeling passed. He filled a tin plate with steaming meat, bacon, some black bread, put the bread in his pocket, thought, This could be a good thing later. It could be a long day. He moved to a low, flat rock, sat, ate everything in fast bites, the food gone before he noticed the taste. He stood then, a hand on his belt, probing. No more problems. Thank God.

Looking to the east, he could see the jagged horizon, the sky a dull gray behind the mountains, and now there was a bugle, the familiar call to *Fall in*. He put his hand on his pistol, an old habit, and moved past the wagon, tossing the plate into a pile. He could see the men flowing together, moving into line, the sergeants already beginning the angry ritual, shouting into the faces of their men. Longstreet moved past the formation, saw the flag lashed to a small tree. He untied the rope, wrapped his fingers around the wood of the staff, heard a new sound now, turned as they all turned, looking back, the batteries well behind, the bright flashes of the artillery opening the dawn.

THEY FACED A THICK GROVE OF CYPRESS TREES, THE REGIMENT standing in battle line while in front of them the smoke from a thousand muskets was already beginning to rise. He stood alone, holding the regimental flag upright in front of him. Behind him the three lieutenants were spread out in formation, each in front of their own company of troops. He had guided them into place, paying special attention to Pickett, could not help a smile, a small break in the awful tension. Pickett's uniform was perfect.

He stared down into the trees, at a drained swamp, the sounds of the fight rolling back toward him. It was Pillow's division, the first wave of the assault, pushing straight into the grove of ancient trees, to sweep aside the resistance, the Mexican soldiers who had been sent forward as the first line of defense. Behind the grove was the final hurdle, the walls of Chapultepec.

His mind was filled with sounds, the pop of a single musket, the shouts of an officer, the sudden zip of the stray musket ball above his head. He focused on the trees, the ground, made himself think about the details, what they would do first, what he would have to *make* them

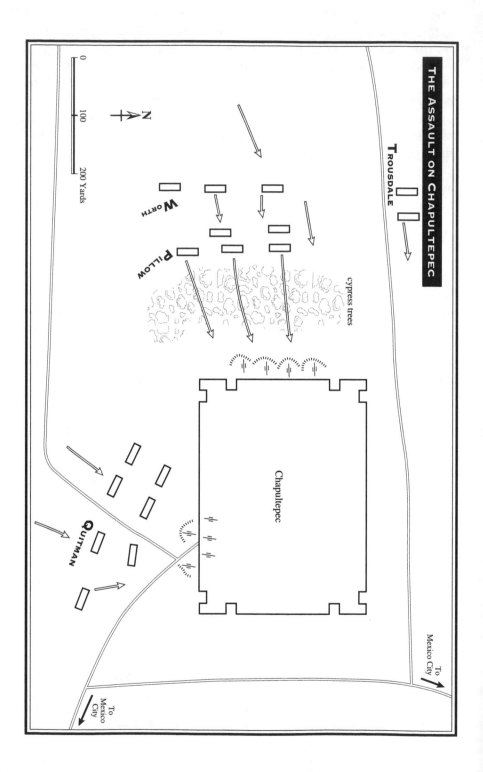

THE ASSAULT ON CHAPULTEPEC

TROUSDALE

WORTH

PILLOW

cypress trees

Chapultepec

QUITMAN

N

0
100
200 Yards

To
Mexico City

To
Mexico
City

do after that. He looked at the ground, the first of the trees, thought, A swamp, it could be muddy. Please, no mud. Hard ground.

He glanced to the side, saw more units, more troops with flags, waiting, as he was. He thought of the talk, the nervous chatter as the men moved into line. There were no jokes this morning, none of the catcalls toward the enemy, the careless boasts, the loud voices of men who were trying to mask their own fear. Since Churubusco, the mood had been different all through the army, and even the fear had been replaced by something else, the grim clarity of veterans. The fear came from the unknown, the unexpected, the sudden panic, the worst of it before the first guns began to fire. But they were all veterans now, the men on both sides, and those who were left would not run from the fear. Longstreet thought of the men who had gone down beside him, in front of him.

Now, when a man dies by your side, you don't expect the man who replaces him to survive either, you don't even want to learn his name. And now, when you march into the guns, you accept that this time it might be you, as if it's already decided, God has made his mark on those who will not come back. If it is not your time to die, then there is only one other choice, one other duty. You do everything in your power, bring all the energy and hate and fire you can to those fellows over there. You make sure it is *their* time to die.

Men were pulling back out of the trees now, some wounded, some carrying men who could not move themselves. The men behind Longstreet began to make a sound, and he knew what it meant. Their instincts were taking hold, the call inside each man to rush forward to help, each man watching the worst that could happen. He turned, said aloud, "Hold the line!" The call was repeated, the sergeants moving behind the men, prodding them with mild curses.

He saw a horseman now, the man ducking low as he rode along the line of troops. He reined the horse close to Longstreet, said, "Lieutenant, are your men prepared for battle?"

Longstreet felt the punch of annoyance, the staff officer who questions the obvious. Leave it alone, he thought, he's more scared than anyone here. "We are prepared, Captain."

The man looked down the line, and Longstreet could see his freckles, his youth. The young man flinched, ducking from the sound of the musket ball. "Colonel Clarke advises that you will advance with the brigade at the sound of the bugle. General Pillow is down. The field is now commanded by General Worth."

Longstreet nodded. "The Eighth is ready, Captain."

The young man looked around, anxious to leave. "Colonel Clarke instructs you to press through those trees and assist General Pillow's efforts. The ladders will be waiting for you at the wall."

Longstreet saw the man flinching again, said, "Sir, you may tell Colonel Clarke that we will meet him inside those damned walls."

The young captain did not respond, spurred the horse, moved away down the line, pulling up close to the next flag. Longstreet watched him, thought, Pillow is down? Generals don't . . . fall. He began to feel the anxiety now, focused again on the musket fire in the trees. What is happening up there? Ladders? That was to be Pillow's job, some handpicked infantry. If we don't have anybody inside that fort by the time we get there, we'll be bunched up outside, a nice fat target. He gripped the flagstaff tightly. All right. Enough of this. They can blow that damned bugle anytime now. We need to be . . . *out there.*

The smoke hung over the trees in one low thick cloud, and the smell of the fight, sulfur, drifted back toward them on the light breeze. He felt his heart beating, his hand sweating against the wood of the flagstaff. From behind the line came the sound of the bugle, a short quick blast, the familiar notes they all recognized.

He turned, looked at the lieutenants, saw Pickett staring to the front, and Longstreet shouted, "Route step! Forward . . . *march!*"

He raised the flag slightly, held the staff close to his belt, began to walk forward. He did not look back, knew what was happening, the line advancing in a slow wave, the men finding the rhythm, the sergeants keeping them tightly together. He heard other shouts, officers down the long line, pulling the entire division down the slope, straight into the trees. He stepped around a group of wounded men, saw more coming up toward him, staring at the fresh troops with wide-eyed shock, the line opening up in small gaps to pass them by.

The smell was filling him now, and he blew hard to clear the smoke from his lungs, felt his eyes beginning to water. He blinked it away, looked at the first of the trees, picked out the path he would take, moved in steady rhythm into the smoky darkness.

There was no underbrush, the ground soft, giving way beneath his steps. He could see more trees to the front, flashes of light and motion, could hear the musket balls flying close now. He saw a man lying flat, and he stepped over the blue uniform without looking down, looked into the fog in front of him, heard the voices, screams, blending with the sounds of the muskets. He saw more uniforms, men kneeling to fire, others in a small group huddled behind a massive tree. There was a shout close by, and he saw an officer, his face bloody, a stain growing on his shirt. The man was yelling to his troops, a raw, hoarse scream, pulling them out into line, driving them forward.

Longstreet shouted, "Here! We're here!" but his voice was drowned by the noise. He waved the flagstaff until the officer saw him and the line of fresh troops coming up behind him. The officer yelled something Longstreet could not hear, pointed to the front. Longstreet looked back for the first time, saw the men tightly together, slipping between the trees, still one line, one good strong mass. He waved the flag again, saw Pickett looking at him, and Pickett smiled before he turned to his men, waved his sword, pulling them deeper into the trees.

Longstreet still moved forward, stared to the front, thought, Yes, he knows. They all know. They are damned fine soldiers.

He tried to see beyond the scattered men in front, the smoke now low to the ground, drifting in small clouds between the trees. He could see the officer again, the man's back a few yards in front of him. He was still collecting scattered troops, pulling them into line, moving them forward. Longstreet turned, looked back to his men, saw them still together, no one firing, and he said aloud, "Good, hold your fire, stay together! Get closer!"

He stepped over more bodies, passed another huge tree. A great flash erupted in front of him, men in blue kneeling, a volley of fire going forward. He moved through the smoke again, felt his heart jump, saw the officer again, pointing his sword, calling the men to advance. The musket fire was all around them now. Men stood behind trees, firing and reloading on their own. He looked back, saw Pickett watching him, waiting for the order, and Longstreet shook his head. *Not yet.* He pointed toward the officer in front. *Keep moving.*

He saw the officer still waving him forward, the troops around him stopping to fire again. Then another flash of light scattered across the dark trees in front of him, and he heard the lead balls smacking the tree beside him, whistling past him into the lines of his men. Longstreet turned and yelled, saw his men falling away, the line breaking up in the trees, some of the men firing on their own.

He shouted, "No! Move forward! No firing!" There was no order as men caught sight of the enemy, began to find their own target. Longstreet looked to the front again, saw the officer moving his men into a ragged line, frantically cutting the air with his sword. The officer spun around, his bloody face turned toward Longstreet then away. He was down. Longstreet stared at the empty place for one frozen moment, then yelled again, a new sound, fury. He waved the flag over his head, knew his men could see, thought, There, we need to be . . . *up there.*

He moved quickly, stepping over another body, this one wearing gray and white, looked down into the face of a dead young Mexican. He stepped forward again, saw more bodies, colors of both sides scrambled together, some men locked arm in arm in the last good fight, face-to-face, struck down together by a shower of musket fire.

More blue troops had taken positions in front, men in some kind of line behind a fallen tree led by another officer. Suddenly they were up again, moving forward in pursuit of a retreating enemy. Longstreet looked back, waved the flag again, shouted, "Advance! Don't fire! Advance!"

He hopped over the tree, could see motion in front, a glimpse of gray, men moving away, blue troops pursuing them, bayonets, muskets swinging wildly, clubs, hands reaching out to grab any piece of the enemy.

The sounds seemed to slow, and he coughed through the smoke. In front, light came through the thinning trees. A swarm of blue still moved ahead of him, more men emerging from their cover as the Mexicans pulled back. He still moved forward, saw how the Americans had poured into a small earthwork, a shallow trench, just beyond the trees, an abandoned Mexican defensive line. The men lay low to the ground, firing at will at the enemy, who still scrambled away.

Longstreet's men were all around him now, and he waved the flag, shouted, "Hold up here! Form a line. . . ."

His voice faded, and he looked out beyond the trees, to where the last of the Mexicans climbed over some low timbers, a long row of cut trees and brush. He saw that the defensive line was backed up against the great white stone wall. A row of muskets pointed out from the top of the wall, firing intermittently, each man picking his target from the mass of blue gathering below. He felt a sudden rush of dread, thought, My God . . . the wall . . . it's huge.

He turned, looked for the lieutenants, saw a sword pointing forward, the man holding his troops together, order returning in the lull. He moved along the line of troops, saw more coming up behind, the line strengthening. The musket fire from the works in front of him was slow and scattered. The men in blue aimed carefully, choosing their targets on the wall with deadly accuracy.

There was a sharp explosion from the base of the wall, and he turned to see a mass of his men blown aside, creating a sudden gap in the line. The deadly pieces of scrap metal from the Mexican canister ripped the bark from the trees behind them. He dropped down, felt his heart in his throat, thought, You are not hit, but ... we can't just stay *here*. Men in blue were crouching low all around him, some still firing their muskets, the enemy behind the brush. He looked over the heads of the men in the shallow trench, saw a broad flat space, and beyond, a wide ditch in front of the works, below the mouth of the cannon. *We must get there*. If we drop down low, we can take out the gun.

He heard an order coming from an officer he could not see, but the men in front of him suddenly surged forward, rising from the trench, running hard across the open ground toward the ditch. The cannon fired again, and he crouched low until he heard the screams. He looked up and saw a horrible carpet of twisted men, but beyond, many others who had reached the ditch were dropping down, some already firing up into the brush.

He held the flag upright, shouted, "On my signal! Advance to the ditch!" He waited, took a long hard breath, pulled himself up to his feet, said, *"Forward!"*

He jumped over the small trench, heard the roar coming from his men, swarming out of the trees behind him. He stopped, waved them forward, watched them move past him across the final few yards of the open ground, closer to the wide ditch. The cannon fired again, but the men were too close, the deadly storm of canister blowing past them. They began to drop down behind blessed cover, a thick blue mass filling the wide ditch, waiting for the next order. He looked back to the trees, saw more of his men still moving into the clearing, but now there was a new line of troops, men filling the trench again, already firing up over his head, toward the muskets on the wall. Across the strip of open ground, a mass of blue came out of the trees above him, more strength rolling straight up to the fat wall. Men began to crawl up out of the ditch, still moving forward, some going up and over the thick line of brush, throwing themselves straight into the Mexican defense. The cannon fell silent, the quick work of the bayonet. More men in blue filled the Mexican works, safe for the moment, too close to the base of the wall for the enemy above to take aim.

Longstreet waited beside the ditch, waved the slower men forward, saw more officers holding their men together, the woods behind them alive with thick lines of blue. Then he began to hear one word, carried by the shouts of the officers, and each man picked up the cry. *"Ladders!"*

He saw them now, brought forward all along the clearing. He had not thought of this moment before, what would happen next, had kept it from his mind. The men pulled the ladders across the ditch, swung them up until they slapped hard against the stone. The Mexican muskets reached out over the wall, firing straight down. The first man on the ladder drew their fire, while behind him a dozen muskets fired at the enemy on the wall, sweeping him away. He felt his throat tighten, thought, This is . . . utterly foolish. How can this work?

More men began to climb up, the first man reaching the top of the wall, vulnerable to the bayonet, falling away, more musket fire from both sides. There were ladders close by now, more coming up out of the woods, and he saw them pass over the wide ditch, saw an officer shouting, pointing to the wall, and another ladder swung upright, then two more down to one side. Now it was time for his men, and he waved the flag in a tight circle, shouted, "Up! To the ladders! *Go!*"

They surged up out of the ditch, and he watched the first man climb up, the musket fire coming from behind him, keeping the Mexicans back. The man went over the wall, disappeared, followed by another man, and he wanted to shout again, *Faster,* but the progress was agonizing, one man at a time.

He looked out along the wall, could see the ladders full of men in blue, a steady stream reaching the top, pouring over to the other side. He looked at the ditch, thought, Get across, you have to go up . . . and he felt a sharp stab, a hard jolt punching his right leg. He fell forward on his knees, felt the biting pain in his thigh, the wetness, was amazed at the sight of the dark blood, the hole in his pants, thought, Not there . . . I never expected it . . . there. Then he was falling, rolling to one side. He tried to balance himself, leaned his weight on the flagstaff, felt a strong hand under his arm, heard the voice, saw that it was Pickett.

"Got you, Pete. You just lie down there, easy now."

He rocked back, sat, felt more hands behind him, supporting him, felt the flagstaff slip from his hand, saw the flag tilting, beginning to fall. He tried to grab it, missed, and then it was straight again, and he saw the hand, saw . . . Pickett.

"George . . . damn . . . they shot me."

"Don't you worry, Pete. You'll be all right. You rest a bit. We'll be back for you."

Pickett turned away, and Longstreet saw the flag go with him.

Pickett jumped down into the ditch, then up the other side. The men moved aside, letting him through to the ladder.

He felt more hands on him, something hard wrapping his leg, a voice saying something, *Lie back, rest.* He would not listen, not yet, kept his eyes focused on the ladder. He had to see, yes, there, the flag moving up the ladder, and Pickett, full of fire, raising the flag high, going over the wall.

30. JACKSON

THE SOUNDS FROM THE FIGHT IN THE GREAT FORTRESS WERE fading, and on the north side of Chapultepec a fresh column of troops was already in line, waiting for the order to advance.

In front, Magruder's battery was assigned to push forward, clearing the way, supporting the march of two regiments from the combined mass of Pillow's and Worth's divisions. The mission was simple at first: move beyond the walls of the great fort, cut off any escape route for the Mexican defenders. But now, as the defense of Chapultepec collapsed and a mass of prisoners was gathered by the men who had swarmed over the wall, there was no escape, no great surge of Mexican troops either toward or away from the fortress. The road was open, and farther to the east it made a turn northward, then back again to the east, a path that led straight to the gate of San Cosme, and a direct route into the heart of the city.

Jackson had been with the guns, watched the sunrise while he sat on a spoked wheel of his six-pounder, the light field piece he had rolled into several fights now. While the rest of the army had moved, the infantry massing into the heavy lines, the officers scrambling to pull the slowest men to formation, Jackson watched, waiting impatiently, wiping the dampness of the dawn from the barrel of the gun with his hand.

Magruder had sent him the word early—Lieutenant Jackson and his two guns would ride in front, would lead the support wherever Colonel Trousdale required it. The assignment was an honor, and Jackson would not believe it was for him, not a result of anything he had done. It was for these two pieces of artillery, a reward for the good work *they* could do, the accuracy they had already shown. Jackson had begun to feel an odd connection to both guns, as though, when the fight began, when the crews were working in good rhythm, he could feel the energy of the powder, and the sharp blast of shot would come from *him*, sent to the target by *his* hand. It gave him a raw spirit for the fight, a frightening enthusiasm that brought him a hesitant respect from his crews and outright admiration from Magruder.

At Cerro Gordo the enemy had run too quickly, not allowing enough time for the field artillery to find the range. And Jackson had still been under the command of Francis Taylor, and Taylor would not let him pursue. He had great respect for Taylor, admired the man's decency, the strength of his religious faith, and he knew that Taylor relied on the hand of God for guidance. Jackson had been curious about that, had sat beside many campfires while Taylor explained the fascinating complexity of God's work, the destiny that had been given to all of them. To Jackson it had been a revelation. He had never considered that God would pay any attention at all to *him*, to one young officer from the hills of Virginia. It always seemed that God had greater priorities, managing the heavens, sending floods and plagues to punish the guilty, all the obvious jobs that God *should* have. But Taylor had a talent for clarity, for the profound explanation, and Jackson had begun to look skyward, seeking some hint, some evidence to support the growing feeling that Francis Taylor was right, that God was indeed watching him.

When the army had spent long weeks at Puebla, his curiosity pushed him to investigate even further, seek some guidance beyond Captain Taylor. He had agonized over the language, spent hours in camp coaching himself, practicing Spanish. He was never very good at expressing himself, even in English, but the few words of Spanish became sentences, and then conversation, enough to seek out the priests, to find out what they might offer him, to explain just what it was God expected him to do.

There had been no answers, but he began to feel uncomfortable with Taylor, impatient that something was missing. There was opportunity in this war, a chance to explore some piece of himself that always seemed to be . . . out there, somewhere. Taylor was his friend, his teacher. But Jackson was beginning to see that Taylor was not the best commander.

When the vacancy opened in Magruder's battery, Jackson leapt at it, had expected resistance from Taylor, but Taylor understood, allowed Jackson to move to the command of the man they all said would find the hottest part of any fight.

At Padierna, Magruder led Jackson and his guns across the big ravine, and just as they had seen at Cerro Gordo, the Mexicans were running again. But they were not as fast this time, and there had even been a defense, Mexican gunners trying to hold a weak line against the strong American tide. Jackson had burst into the fight with a fire that amazed even Magruder, had driven his crews straight at the Mexican defenses, and the defenses did not hold. If the senior commanders did not yet see what Jackson carried to the fight, the soldiers around him, the swarms of Americans who swept over Padierna, had seen it clearly. There was something strange, something oddly dangerous, about this quiet young lieutenant. After Padierna, Magruder knew it as well. And when the fight was over and the guns were quiet, Jackson had stayed close to the hard brass, the exhausted crews watching him from a respectful distance as he sighted down the barrel, moving around the gun, still absorbed in some private fight of his own.

Even Magruder did not understand what was driving him, but the hard energy of the fight, the smoke and the sounds, the faces of the enemy, had opened something in Jackson, had given him answers that Taylor and the priests could not. In the quiet of the darkness, as the army came together and the camps were loud with talk of victory, Jackson still sat quietly alone, still carried the powder on his face, in his clothes. He had come to understand what God expected him to do.

H E LED THE GUNS FORWARD, TRAILING MAGRUDER AND OTHER officers, but stayed close to his crews, thought, If he needs me, he'll give me . . . that look. Those are infantry officers, probably Colonel Trousdale. He could see a flag now, a gold *II*, nodded, knew the Eleventh Regiment was one of the units the guns would support.

Magruder looked at him now, the black fire in his eyes, the look that intimidated even the superior officers, but Jackson knew the meaning, turned, said to the crews, "Hold here."

He rode forward, saw the other officers watching him, but he ignored them, looked straight into the grim stare of Magruder, who said, "Time for work, Lieutenant. Pull your guns up this road. We will take a position on the right flank of the column. Your job is to eliminate anything that might get in their way."

Jackson saluted, saw the other officers still looking at him, and he said to Magruder, "Is there . . . anything else, sir?"

Magruder glanced at the others, saw their expression. "Colonel Trousdale has heard about your fine work."

One of the officers moved his horse closer to Jackson. "We have not had the pleasure, Lieutenant. Colonel William Trousdale. Your captain tells me we can expect more than adequate support from those two field pieces of yours. I look forward to seeing your men in action."

Embarrassed, Jackson nodded and saluted Trousdale. "Um . . . yes, thank you, sir."

He looked at Magruder again, who said, "Lieutenant Tom Jackson is not a man for polite conversation, Colonel."

Trousdale said, "I have no intention of being polite myself, Lieutenant. Let's move, shall we?"

The officers rode back to the column of troops, the men cheering for their commander. Magruder leaned close to Jackson. "Bring up the guns. We need to move out a ways, find a good location. You ready, Lieutenant?"

Jackson nodded, surprised at the question. "Certainly, sir." His men were watching him, waiting for the silent signal, and now he turned, motioned with an arm, and immediately the guns came forward. Behind him a bugle sounded, and the column of infantry began to move. Magruder spurred his horse, and Jackson moved alongside. "Once the column moves past the castle, Mr. Jackson, I expect we'll run into some kind of resistance. That's your job, bust 'em up. Clear the road. I'll be moving out to the left, protecting the column from the north. Until we see what's waiting for us, the battery will be spread out."

Jackson did not respond, knew that Magruder's orders did not require any input from a lieutenant. He looked to the right toward the thick grove of cypress trees, still holding the gray smoke of the first assault. There were faint pops now, scattered musket fire from inside the fortress itself. He could see the ladders, most still up against the thick walls, a few men still climbing up. He watched as small pieces of blue disappeared over the top of the wall, thought, Climbing up into the face of the enemy . . . that close, close enough to see the look in their eyes, to see their fear. That would be . . . magnificent.

He stood staring at the specks of blue high along the wall, until he heard a cheer behind him. Turning toward the sound, he saw an officer pointing, looked again, caught the motion, the Mexican flag suddenly dropping, sliding down the flagstaff high in the center of the fort. The column had halted, and now all eyes were on the flagpole. He saw the first flicker of motion, could hear the roar building in the men behind him, heard Magruder say something, watched now as the Stars and Stripes was pulled up the pole. The cheering echoed all down the road, answered by the cheers and waves of the men up on the wall. Jackson moved the horse again, suddenly impatient, looked back to his gun

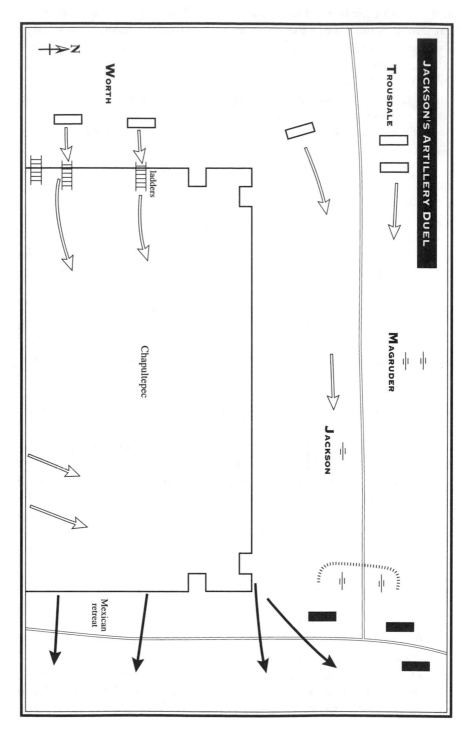

JACKSON'S ARTILLERY DUEL

Trousdale

Worth

ladders

Chapultepec

Magruder

Jackson

Mexican
retreat

N

crews, who were cheering as well. But when they saw his look, their brief cheer grew quiet and they moved forward again. He moved away from Magruder, led them farther out on the road, said quietly, "We are not yet done."

H E WAS BEYOND THE WALLS OF CHAPULTEPEC NOW, COULD SEE the intersection to the east, and beyond, the low walls of the city. Gripping the reins tightly, he focused on motion near the intersection, a low mound of brown, a long row of cut trees spreading to one side. He was alone with his gun crews now, the infantry spreading out into battle lines far behind him. His men were holding his guns at the side of the road, glancing out over the open ground, anticipating, looking for the good placement. Out front he could see the advance skirmishers pushing out ahead of the infantry in a wide thin line, and he thought, We should move up there, get closer. If they're not shooting at anything, I should be able to move at least that far. He turned, motioned for the guns to advance, heard a strange sound, louder now, ripping the air in front of him. A bright streak whistled overhead. The shell hit behind his guns, a dull blast of dirt and rock, and he stared out to the front, saw the small cloud of smoke rising from the low mound. He saw the flash, another shell streaking over him, exploding back close to the column of infantry, and he saw men swept down by the shattered metal, could hear their shouts, the first screams. He pushed the sounds out of his mind, turned, looked again at the small rising cloud, felt the blade of the knife rising in his chest, the cold steel of the fight beginning to grow inside of him.

Magruder rode up beside him. "Protect your guns, Lieutenant!"

"Sir. There is one gun directly in our front, in that defensive position." He pointed, and the gun fired again. Magruder watched with him as the shell streaked toward them, then dropped low, impacting to the side of the road, a quick blast of fire blossoming in the dry brush.

Jackson said, "Sir, we need to remove that gun."

"Hold here, Lieutenant. I have to check with Colonel Trousdale, see how he wants to advance his troops."

Still looking toward the Mexican works, Jackson said, "Sir, we must take that gun out before the infantry moves up."

Magruder's voice rose into his familiar growl. "Lieutenant, that's not our decision. Our orders are to move up in support of the infantry. When you wear the stars, you can do what you damned well please. But this time you follow orders."

Jackson stared hard at the Mexican gun, saw another burst of smoke, felt the knife blade slowly turning in his chest. The shell arced toward them, dropping quickly. It landed close behind them, shattering into pieces on the surface of the road. They both looked back, and Jackson could hear the sputtering of the fuse, the broken pieces of copper bouncing away, and now Magruder's horse surged and he fought the reins.

"Whoa, dammit!" The horse calmed a bit, still turned slow circles in the road, and Magruder cursed again.

"Sir, they have found the range." He waited for the next shell, thought, If we stay here, we are a fine target. The knife blade was turning hard now, working down through his whole body, and he felt the burn beginning in his brain. He looked at Magruder again, stared at him with cold blue fire, said, "Captain, it is time to *go*."

Magruder held his gaze. A brief quiet moment passed between them. "Lieutenant, I'm going to ask Colonel Trousdale if he plans to join us today. Why don't you see if you can do something about that damned gun?"

Jackson heard another shell pass overhead, followed by the blast close behind, but he did not see it, was staring at the cloud of smoke far in front of him. The smell of the explosion drifted past him now, and the knife blade made one quick twist in his chest, and he turned to the men at his guns and shouted, "Forward!"

With a single surge, wagons and horses and the two small guns were in motion. He spurred his horse, led them straight down the road. Another shell streaked overhead, but he did not look back. He moved at the familiar speed, knew the crews were close behind. He stared at the Mexican works, still too far for him to detect movement, but another puff of smoke drifted skyward. He looked for the blue arc, but the sound came straight toward him, a sharp whine. The shell burst close beside him, throwing him in the air, clear of the horse. He hit the hard dirt in a roll, on his back, then over, on his knees. He saw the horse lying next to him, jerking violently, kicking at the air. Jackson stood, saw the deep gash in the horse's neck, felt the pain in his ankle. He flexed it, thought, No time for that now. He leaned close to the horse, wanted to shout, Get up, but the blood still poured from the neck of the quivering animal. He felt suddenly helpless, angry, but he saw one of his men pulling another horse forward. He grabbed the reins, pulled himself up, the wounded animal already gone from his mind. He did not look at the crews behind him, spurred the fresh horse forward.

He still focused on the low mound, could see a flicker of motion, a small flag, thought, Almost . . . almost close enough. There was a new sound now, a different kind of shell, smaller pieces ripping the air above him. He heard the splatter of impact and the sound of a wagon coming apart. He slowed the horse, turned to see one of the caissons rolling into pieces in the road, men falling, shattered by the blast. He shouted, "Keep moving! Forward!"

The men on the ground scrambled to the horses, some climbing up on the second caisson. He saw two men still on the ground, felt a burst of anger, wanted to shout at them, *Up, let's go* . . . but now the blood was spreading on the hard ground, and he turned away, would not look at it, spurred the horse again. He glanced back to check on the guns, saw them both moving with him. He looked to the side for cover, a small hill, some good place to position the guns. There was another blast, right behind the horse, and he felt a shower of rock hitting his back, knocking him forward. He pulled the reins tightly, the horse pitching wildly, carrying him off the road. His mind screamed at him, *Jump,* and he swung a leg over and hit the ground hard, felt the pain in the ankle again, looked back at his men, pulling another horse toward him.

He looked out off the road, saw a small rise, shouted, "There! Move there!"

The crews moved off the road, the guns bouncing awkwardly. He grabbed for the horse, but there was another blast, more dirt and fire. He felt the hot wind knocking him back, saw the red streaks above him, the shower of canister, the horses going down, men falling, bloody horror, the second wagon shattered into pieces. He tried to run, saw the guns still rolling toward the small rise, thought, Yes, move to cover, go! He ran past them, pointing.

Suddenly he was falling, tumbling, dirt and dust in his mouth. He came to a stop and sat coughing, blowing dust from his mouth. He wiped his eyes, tried to see, thought, A ditch, we're in a ditch. He looked along the flat bottom, said aloud, "Dry . . . thank God."

He saw the guns, both lying on their sides, his men still following him into the blessed cover. They began to line up, holding low to the side closest to the Mexican position, and he looked for the horses.

"Where are the mounts? We must position the guns!" The men were looking at him in wide-eyed shock. He ignored them, crawled close to the brass six-pounder, said, "Get this gun up! Pull it up! Prepare to fire!"

He stood straight and peered up over the edge of the ditch. He could see the small flag clearly, thought, They will come. They will take these guns! He looked at the faces watching him, shouted, "Do you want to die by the bayonet?"

No one moved, the men holding tight to the safe ground. He looked up toward the Mexican works again, then back at the small brass gun, grabbed the wheel, shouted, "Help me roll this up! Move! We must fire!"

The gun moved under his grip, rolled over, sat upright. He pulled it around, began to drag it toward the sloping side of the ditch, the men watching him, paralyzed. He moved up the side, put one foot up, began to pull at the gun, making slow progress, his feet digging into soft sand. He felt a fury blowing in his brain, looked at the man closest to him, the sergeant, said, "You! Up . . ." There was a sudden rush of wind, and behind the ditch the ground burst into flame, the shell blowing dirt and rock on top of them, showering the men who crouched low. Jackson grabbed the spoke of one wheel, turned hard, and the gun rolled out of the ditch. He jumped back down, saw broken boxes, grabbed a shell, saw a cloth sack of powder. He carried them both out of the ditch again. He focused on the gun, turned it to face the Mexican works, sighted quickly down the barrel, his mind burning, the knife spinning in his chest.

Another blast of air knocked him back, but the shot did not explode. It burrowed into the side of the ditch, behind the men. Now the faces began to move, and he could see them coming closer, thought, Yes! Up here! Let's go to work! He bent low, picked up the powder charge, moved to the front of the barrel, slid the charge into the muzzle, reached down for the small ramrod, saw the hooks empty. He shouted harshly, moved toward the ditch again. There was a sudden strange sound, a rumble underneath him. He looked down, saw the unexploded shell furrowing the dirt between his feet, then pushing out through the soft sand into the ditch, rolling slowly into the bottom. He looked at the hot glow of the copper ball, thought, God is here! God is watching! That one was meant for me! He looked again at the sergeant, the others, the men staring at the blessed misfire. Laughing softly, he said, "You see, soldier? They can't hurt me! There's no danger here! Come on, get up! Help me fire the gun!"

The sergeant turned, looked at Jackson, who saw the man's eyes clearing, his soul opening up, the strength returning. The sergeant scrambled up beside him, and Jackson shouted, "Yes! Come on! Bring up the other gun! Let's go to work!"

The men climbed out of the ditch, and Jackson saw the ramrod now, the gunner bringing it up, moving quickly to the muzzle, ramming the powder charge in place. Another man had the shell, and quickly the gun was loaded. Jackson stared out to the Mexican works, shouted, "Fire!"

The gun bounced high, the smoke covering them all. Jackson waved the smoke away, saw the shell drop far in front of the works.

"No! Increase . . ." He looked to the gun, saw the crew doing their jobs, working quickly, and he backed away. Two men were gathering the shells, more powder charges from the ditch. Now the second gun was up, began to fire, and Jackson stared at the Mexican defense, saw a blast of brush and logs, the shell finding the mark. He smiled, nodded quietly. Yes. Now we shall see.

The Mexican gun fired again, the burst of smoke showing him the position, and he pointed, shouted, "See? There! That's the target!" The guns were both working now, quickly responding. The smoke flowed over him, the shells from the Mexican gun bursting behind, then out to one side. He turned, thought, Horses, if we had some horses, we could get closer. . . . He saw a rider, one man, followed by two more. It was Magruder. He saluted, smiled, and Magruder jumped off the horse, hopped down into the ditch.

"Well, Lieutenant, you've started your own private war. How is it going?"

Jackson wiped his eyes, turned toward the enemy, saw nothing but smoke, said, "I believe, sir, if you give me a few more veterans, we could take the city!"

Magruder, beside him now, was looking through field glasses. "Might not be necessary. They're pulling out."

Jackson moved forward, strained to see, thought, No, it cannot be . . . not yet.

Magruder shouted to Jackson's crew, "Cease fire!"

Jackson moved past the hot muzzle of the gun, saw motion, the flag moving away, thought, But . . . we're not through here.

Magruder put a hand on his shoulder, said, "It's all right, Lieutenant. You won."

There were more sounds now, coming up the road, more guns, Magruder's field pieces, and behind, the quick march of Trousdale's infantry. Jackson stared at the Mexican works, silent now, and his men began to cheer, tossing hats in the air. He glanced at the men, smiled, stepped closer to the one gun, the gun he had dragged out of the ditch.

He put a hand out, touched the hot barrel, thought of Magruder's words . . . *You won.* He glanced up, thought, Yes, I know You were here, I know You were watching this. I can feel it, I know this was a gift, this is Your hand. He looked at Magruder, saw a smile, Magruder shaking his head, and Jackson said, "Sir, I believe this is . . . the most fun I have ever had."

31. GRANT

SEPTEMBER THIRTEENTH, MIDDAY

WORTH'S MEN HAD ROLLED IN A THICK COLUMN PAST THE intersection where Jackson's guns had broken up the Mexican defense. Next the move had been north, along a wide, hard road that paralleled the western walls of the city. To the south, Quitman's volunteers were moving east, fighting the last remnants of the troops from Chapultepec, pushing closer to the Belén gate.

Grant had grown to dislike his commander, had no respect for the way Worth had exercised his discretion. He knew only fragments of the quiet conflict between Worth and Scott, things he learned from the indiscreet comments from senior officers. He had endured, as the entire division had endured, the comical ghost-chasing in Puebla, but when the comedy had turned to deadly seriousness, when Worth had his opportunity to command the fight at the Molino, it was difficult for any of them to feel good about the victory. There were too many friends, too many good soldiers, left behind.

He had a good feeling about Scott, had sensed it from the earliest days before the invasion of Vera Cruz. Scott brought something very different to the command, some ingredient of discipline and formality that was the complete opposite of Zachary Taylor. Grant had taken his West Point training seriously, had come to enjoy the rituals, the dress parades, the perfect order of the drill. Taylor had made it clear from the first days in Texas that there would be none of that in his camp, that the white glove formality of command didn't exist in his world. He was a crude, friendly man, who could engage in conversation with the private or the general, and neither would feel intimidated by the presence of their commander. Taylor rarely wore any kind of uniform, would wander through the camps in a straw hat, denim pants, seemingly more interested in stories from home than tomorrow's strategy. It made him popular with the troops, but to Grant, and to many of the younger officers fresh from the strict training of West Point, it was a difficult collapse of discipline.

Scott changed that, and Grant had been much more comfortable with "Old Fuss and Feathers" in command. The formality returned, and Scott was very clear about protocol, about dress, about all those things that the younger officers had expected from life in the army. The senior commanders were there because of age, experience. But without Winfield Scott to control them, Grant knew that this war would already have been a crushing disaster. If he had doubted that, if he had still believed any of them could have sent Santa Anna packing, after Molino there was no doubt at all.

G RANT MARCHED QUICKLY, FOLLOWED BY A MIXED CREW OF troops, men gathered from units scattered by the quick decisions that came with the assault. Part of Worth's division was now inside Chapultepec, and Grant knew Longstreet had gone that way. He had watched the flag go up with the same cheer that rolled over the fort itself. We will talk about this, he had thought, we will tell our children what this day was like. I hope to God you are safe, Pete.

They pushed on through the intersection that turned their march eastward, the final push toward the San Cosme gate. There was no defense here, no earthworks or cannon to slow the American advance, and Grant waved his men forward, the column spreading out, feeling its way through houses, small buildings. The city had spread outside the walls here, and along the last causeway were the outskirts of the city itself—shops, churches. The residents were mostly gone, had seen the American flag rise on their great fortress. They had moved into the city itself, seeking the safety of the last great barrier, huddling in the open squares, gathering in marketplaces behind the last stand of their soldiers.

The roadway was divided at that point, an aqueduct splitting the center, supported by great stone arches. The men moved more slowly, picked their way carefully, avoiding the musket fire from Mexican snipers. The sharp whistles of the lead balls had been scattered at first, but were heavier now, coming from the last concentration of Mexican troops still outside the city walls.

Grant slid in behind a fat column of stone, peered out, watched for motion. The shooting was slow and steady now, lacking any rhythm, the lead smacking and splintering the stone. Behind him, men were easing along, finding their way with no formal orders, no massed column of assault. He looked back, saw men behind each wall, each pile of stone, men peering from doorways, some emerging onto rooftops. There was the answering shot now, one man finding a target, a quick shout, success, or silence, the man reloading, moving closer, to try again.

He stared to the front again, caught a brief flicker of motion, men scampering away, dropping down from the roof of a small house, while behind him several muskets cracked, his men seeing the opportunity. He made a quick wave, thought, *Now,* slid quickly out from the cover, crossed the road, flattened up against the white wall of a house. He waited, heard nothing, thought, Keep going. You cannot give them time, not offer yourself as a target. He looked back, saw faces watching him, and now several men followed his lead, scampered across the road, blending into the cover behind him. There was a burst of musket fire coming from another rooftop somewhere in front, and he heard laughter behind him, a man's voice, "Not this time . . . !"

He heard more comments, the men enjoying the pure thrill of the chase, the slow and steady pursuit of the hidden enemy. This is very different, he thought, this is nothing like Molino, or any other fight we've had. This requires something besides pure mindless power, sending your troops straight into a blaze of fire, killing your own men in great numbers just so you can claim a victory. Here each man is on his own.

Shots came from the left of the road, across the aqueduct, and he peeked out, could see nothing, thought, Good, move up. He could see no sign of the men behind him, and he knew they were huddled tightly behind cover just as he was. He had never experienced a fight like this before, and for one brief second he felt suddenly alone, felt a small cold chill, thought, Have faith, Lieutenant. They're back there. No one's pulling out of here without telling you. He waited, no musket fire in the road, peeked around the side of the house, thought, All right . . . let's go!

He ran into the road, past the house, keeping low, looking for another gap between walls, but the house connected hard to the next one, a long low stone building providing no opening, no cover at all. He felt the cold rush again, thought, Nothing to do but run. He moved faster, farther down the roadway, heard the crack of the musket now, the high zip of the lead ball, then more, the sound of muskets coming alive in front of him. He saw a break in the wall to the left, a wide crack, thought, Finally, thank God, and leaped into the gap, pushed hard against the cold stone. The musket balls smashed the rock beside him, and he saw a flash of light, the smoke flowing down from a rooftop across the road. Oh, God . . . too close.

He saw a space between the houses across the road, thought, Go, *there,* and burst out of the cover, a quick dash, collapsed against the stone again. He could hear voices, high, excited, speaking *Spanish.* He put his hand on his heaving chest, his breathing hard and quick. He found his pistol, thought, Now . . . you *are* alone. He looked back down the road, saw brief glimpses of faces, the men looking for him, for where he had stopped. Good, he thought, very good. Just . . . wait there a second.

He moved farther into the dark gap between the houses, could see a small green yard now, bordering the aqueduct. He listened, heard the voices still, held the pistol close to his chest, faced the wall, cold stone on his face. He eased slowly toward the edge, one eye close to the wall, then a quick glimpse. The yard was empty, and he let out a breath, listened for the voices again, could hear quick shouts, thought, It sounds like orders . . . *officers.* He moved past the back of the house, close to a short rock wall bordering a small garden, a scattered mass of bright flowers. He stepped over them, the soft dirt yielding under his feet, making no sound. Crossing into another small yard, he stepped over flower pots. He glanced behind him, breathing in short hot bursts, thought, Keep a count how far . . . this is not the place to get lost. The voices were quiet now, and he thought, They must think they got me. They don't know I'm here. This is not . . . the best place for me to be. But if there are a lot of them, I have to see. . . . We could be moving into a trap.

He reached the far end of another house, flattened himself against the wall again, the dampness in his uniform pressing into his chest. He eased his head out, then pulled back, felt his chest pound, felt a cold burst of anxiety. The voices had come from a barricade along the road, a low pile of wood, scraps from the houses, furniture, and lined up behind was a squad of Mexican soldiers. He held himself still for a moment, his hands shaking, could hear his own breathing, his heart pounding in his ears. Easy, he thought, calm . . . slow down. Think what you have to do. How many are there? He looked again, could see the uniforms, one officer, counted small clusters of men, muskets all pointed out. He heard voices above him, pulled back, flattened himself again against the rough wall, thought, The roof . . . they're all over the place. He eased his face along the stone, took another look at the barricade, and the officer stepped aside, pointing to something out in front

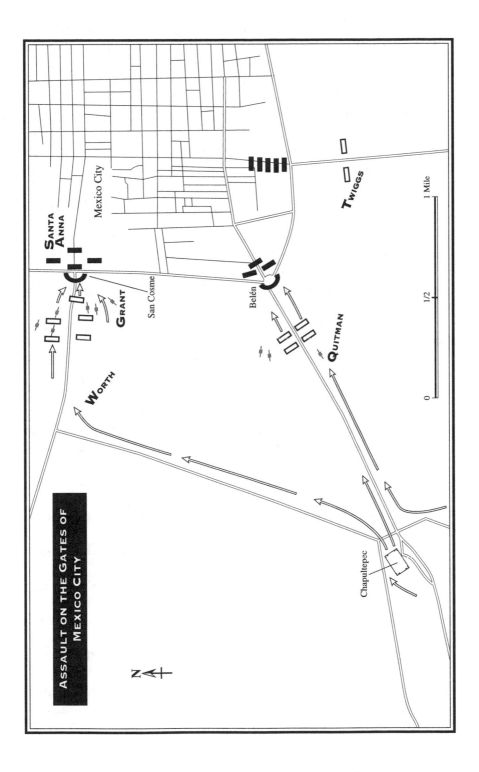

ASSAULT ON THE GATES OF MEXICO CITY

N

Mexico City

SANTA ANNA

San Cosme

GRANT

WORTH

Belén

TWIGGS

QUITMAN

Chapultepec

0   1/2   1 Mile

of the muskets. Grant saw it now, the bright glint of brass. It was a cannon. He pulled back again, thought, All right, get out of here. He eased back across the yards, slipped between the garden walls, watched for his gap between the houses. He slipped into the darkness again, felt his breathing, smiled, thought, Never guessed I'd be a guerrilla.

He moved out to the front of the house, peered out toward the barricade, but could not see it, thought, It's concealed, somehow. If we advance . . . they'll blow us to pieces. He looked back down the road, could see faces again, his own men, some closer now, some men still moving forward in quick dashes. He saw something new, a body dressed in a blue uniform, a pool of blood spreading out on hard stone. Damn, he thought, careful. He waited, listened for the voices, heard only quiet now. Yes, they're waiting for us. I have to get back. . . .

He jumped into the road, ran hard toward a stone arch, slipped behind it. He'd drawn no musket fire, and he looked across the road, where a larger group of men, huddled low, were watching him. He waited, took a breath, crossed the road in a dash, the men pulling back to make a space. He saw an officer now, Lieutenant Gore, and Gore said, "Lieutenant, where did you go? Awfully risky . . ."

Grant nodded, said, "Yes, sir. I flanked them, sir. They're in force up ahead, just beyond those buildings, at least one artillery piece. But I found out how we can get behind them."

Gore glanced back, and Grant saw another officer, wearing a marine uniform. The man moved close and Gore said, "Lieutenant Ulysses Grant, this is Lieutenant Raphael Semmes. He is observing our activity today. I do not think he expected to be fighting house-to-house."

Semmes nodded to Grant, said, "You believe we can get behind them?"

"I was there, sir. I moved to within a few yards. They did not detect my presence."

Semmes looked at Gore. "It's your decision. You're the ranking officer."

Gore glanced back down the road. "I thought . . . we should wait for the rest of the brigade. This is risky."

Grant saw the look in Gore's eyes, thought, He will not make the decision.

Semmes looked at him, seemed to read him, said, "Lieutenant Grant, would you prefer to wait for the rest of the brigade?"

Grant took a breath, thought, Careful. You're the junior man here. "Sir, the brigade will take considerable loss if they move against that barricade. No doubt there are more just like it, and the closer we get to San Cosme, there will certainly be more artillery. This requires . . . finesse."

Semmes smiled, nodded, and Gore said, "All right, Mr. Grant, until we hear from Colonel Clarke, this is your show. What would you suggest?"

"A dozen men can slip back beyond the barricade. Your men here can wait for the first assault, then move up in front."

Semmes said, "I suggest you take out the gunners first. Take the cannon out of action. Not likely the Mexicans will hold their ground if their gun goes down."

Grant nodded, and Gore motioned behind him, said in a hoarse shout, "Volunteers. A dozen men . . . go with Lieutenant Grant, follow his commands."

The men moved up, and Grant saw their eagerness, their confidence, thought, Take good care, Lieutenant. They seem to . . . believe in you.

H E LED THEM UP CLOSE, SLIPPING OUT QUICKLY INTO THE ROAD, sliding up into the cover as the enemy muskets tried to find the aim. He could see the gap between the two houses, knew it would be the last dangerous crossing, held up his hand, the silent command, *wait*. He peered out around the house, saw nothing moving, no sign of the enemy. Looking across to the space between the houses, he pointed, saw the heads nodding, and he whispered, "No firing. No talking. We are very close."

He peered out again, raised his hand, *Wait,* then glanced back at them, dropped his hand, whispered, "Let's go."

He ran out into the road, slid quickly into the dark space, the men filing in behind him. There were smiles, wide eyes, and he shook his head, touched his lips, *No sound.* They could all hear the voices now, and he waited, thought, The talk is not . . . excited, they still don't know we're here. He moved farther between the houses, peered into the yard, heard a different sound, backed into the gap, could hear the splashing of water, footsteps. He put his hand up, *Stay here.* He slipped low into the yard, moved close to the aqueduct, then eased up slowly, saw hats, let out a breath, thought, American . . . thank God. He eased forward, held up a hand, and they saw him. He quickly motioned them to quiet, held a finger to his lips. He saw the officer now, recognized Captain Brooks, who said, "What . . . are you doing here? Not where I expected to see an American officer."

Grant slid into the aqueduct, said quietly, "There is a fortification, just past these buildings. I have a dozen men, in a flanking movement. Lieutenant Gore is preparing to advance on the road once we surprise the enemy from behind."

Brooks looked behind him, said, "Lieutenant Grant, I have about a hundred men here. Could they be of help?"

Grant looked down the aqueduct, saw a long row of bayonets. "If they're quiet, yes, sir."

Brooks looked back, said to the man at the front of the column, "Pass the word. Silence. The enemy is close." The man whispered behind him, and Brooks said to Grant, "You're in charge, Lieutenant."

Grant climbed out of the aqueduct, saw his own men now emerging from between the houses, frowning, concerned, and he moved close and whispered, "It's all right, gentlemen. This is still our mission. Don't ever be disappointed by reinforcements."

Brooks's men began to emerge from the aqueduct. Grant motioned them forward, past the garden walls, closer to the enemy's position.

They all heard the voices now, and Grant, fists clenching, could feel the energy behind him. He drew his pistol, waited for a brief moment. The men were staring at him, some hearing the sounds for the first time, the voices of Mexican soldiers. He raised his hand, all faces were watching now, and with one quick wave he shouted, *"Charge!"*

The men poured past him, and suddenly the shouts turned to sounds of a fight, muskets firing wildly, the voices of the Mexicans rising into shouts of alarm. He moved into the rush, followed the men up and over the rear of the barricade, could see Gore's men now, running hard, straight up the road. The Mexicans were scattering, leaping down from rooftops, filling the road behind the barricade. Grant saw the gun now, moved that way, saw a small cluster of men sitting, the gunners already subdued, captured by one man holding his bayonet high. Grant looked past, saw Gore climbing into the barricade, and Gore shouted, "Good work, Lieutenant! They're on the run!"

Grant said, "Sir, we should pursue! They're getting away!"

Gore seemed to hesitate, said, "The rest of the brigade should be up soon."

Grant felt a punch of anger, saw the last few Mexicans emerging from a house behind them. A quick burst of musket fire came from Brooks's men, but the Mexican soldiers were quickly away, dodging through the gaps of the houses.

Grant said, "Sir, with all respect, is this still my . . . show?"

Gore saw the soldiers gathering, the men beginning to shout, raising their muskets in salute, and said, "It seems . . . it is still your show, Lieutenant."

Grant smiled, jumped out the back of the barricade, moved into the road, the men following him, moving in pursuit of the enemy. Down the road, they could see men scrambling up onto the rooftops. A moment later the sound of musket fire rang out as the Mexican defense found a target. Grant waved the men out of the road. The men kicked doors in, and the houses began to fill with blue troops. Grant slipped between two houses again, looked toward the front, saw Mexican troops still in the road, scrambling away to safety, while above them more snipers covered their retreat. He felt hard anger, wanted to shout, to let out the frustration he felt at watching the enemy escape.

"Damn!"

He could still see men in blue slipping forward, moving house-to-house, firing toward the enemy on the rooftops. Yes, go, he thought. We are very close. The main gate has to be just ahead. He waved the men on, could see faces watching him from the houses, and he thought, We cannot just stop, not now. He jumped quickly into the road, waved again, shouted, "Go! Forward!"

The men followed him again, dodging in and out of cover. He stayed low against a waist-high rock wall. Across the aqueduct, through a wide opening between the houses, he could see the high stone wall of the city, and the massive archway. He stopped, thought, San Cosme. *Yes!* We can push straight through. . . .

He slipped past the last of the great stone arches, could see clearly across a wide plaza to where the Mexican troops were scrambling back into another barricade, this one larger, heavy timbers spread in line in front of the massive gate. He stopped, felt a sudden shock, could see flags now, many flags, saw the wall on both sides of the gate lined with a thick mass of muskets, the barricade dotted with a row of cannon. He felt a hand pulling him, grabbing his coat, and he moved back behind the low wall, slipped into the open doorway of a house. The hand released him, and he turned, saw Gore, Semmes, more men seeking the close shelter of the house. Gore said, "I believe, Mr. Grant, we should *now* wait for the brigade."

WORTH ORDERED HIS MEN TO PULL BACK FROM THE MEXICAN strength at San Cosme, and began concentrating them in heavy cover, bringing the larger guns forward, to throw the power and strength of the artillery against the Mexican position. The scouts had slipped forward, and now the reports were in, confirming what Grant had already seen. The houses along the wall were heavy with Mexican troops, and the barricades held a strong battery of cannon. There was a different kind of report as well, word from the Mexican prisoners, and now that word had spread. The Americans waited with grim impatience, a slow-growing enthusiasm for what surely could be the final fight. They had learned that the man commanding the Mexican defense at the gate was Santa Anna himself.

Behind the gathering infantry, the guns were put into the most effective locations, and many of the smaller field guns were carried up, placed carefully in elevated positions, some rolled right out onto rooftops. The Mexicans did not allow the work to proceed without a protest of their own, and the artillery quickly began to trade rounds, the Mexican cannon throwing a deadly shower of grapeshot and canister toward the open road, toward any clear route the Americans would have to cross.

Grant had not seen Colonel Clarke since early that morning, had wondered what the brigade commander's response might be to his independence. Grant still did not have a formal position leading troops, no specific command of the Fourth Regiment's combat units. Since well before Vera Cruz, he had served as regimental quartermaster, had proven to be so efficient at the job, it was assumed by the other officers that Clarke would keep him there. But Grant would not stay out of the line of fire, and by the time the army gathered at Puebla, he had learned that Clarke would look away, would not hold him back. If Clarke demonstrated lenience toward his quartermaster, Grant would take advantage, would always find some way to stay close to the guns. If Clarke admired Grant's skills with the valuable supplies, he could not deny the young lieutenant what Grant wanted most: the opportunity to fight.

As the brigade crowded tightly into the buildings and gardens, Clarke had sent word back to General Worth. The men were ready, the assault could begin. As the troops held low to their cover and the artillery dueled above their heads, Grant was again on his own.

THE MEXICAN MUSKETS WERE CONCENTRATED NOW, AND THE open ground was cut by a hail of deadly fire. The officers were still forming the men, doing last minute checks, but Grant could not simply sit and wait. He had thought of making the same approach as before—create some opportunity, get close, keep moving, the fast burst, no time for the enemy to find you. But there was no cover in front of the gate itself, and if there was another way, it could only come far down on the flank.

The houses were more plentiful here, many newer, freshly built stone walls, more gardens still spread with bright colors. The area was dotted with small churches, open air markets, an arm of the city spread out far to both sides of the gate. He had scouted on his own again, slipped down to the right, easing slowly between the older stone huts with low flat roofs and the larger houses, surrounded by wide porches under dark copper awnings. He could see the defense at the wall through every gap, but there were no snipers now, the Mexicans all pulling in to the walls of the city. He stood alone now, in the open, a small market-place, crude tables covered with the remains of yesterday's trade, scraps of vegetables, the hard smell of spoiled meat.

Along the main road the sound of cannon fire was growing, a hot duel between the artillery, accompanied by the steady shower of musket fire. The men were pushing forward, making slow progress, while the cannon threw a heavy charge into the Mexican batteries, holding the Mexican guns silent, but the quiet moments were brief, and soon the roadway was swept again by Mexican shells, and Clarke's men were back behind their cover.

Grant retreated from the Mexican position, slipped behind a low, flat house, heard voices, an officer shouting, saw now a small field gun, pulled by its crew. The officer pointed the way, and the men rolled the gun toward Grant, no one seeing him. When the officer spotted him, he looked at Grant, surprised, said, "Whoa, hold it! Who the hell are you?"

Grant saw the man's rank, a captain, saluted him, said, "Lieutenant Grant, sir. Fourth Regiment. Been doing some scouting, sir."

"Well, Grant, you much of a scout? You find someplace I can put this damned gun? I'm Captain Flannery, Second Artillery. Colonel Garland sent me down this way to find some good vantage point. Damned if I can see one."

Grant looked at the small gun, the four-man crew now catching their breath. The two men hauling thick cloth bags over their shoulders shifted their load. Grant felt suddenly excited, thought, This could be . . . an excellent opportunity. He saw the angry frustration on Flannery's face, thought, Careful now. But what could we do with this wonderful gun?

"Sir, I have discovered the Mexicans do not protect their flanks very well. If we move farther down this way, we will certainly find someplace to position the gun, and possibly enfilade their works at the gate. There is no opposition here, no sniper fire."

Flannery moved forward, peered around the closest house, looked back at Grant. "Don't care much for snipers, Grant. I'll take your word for it. You lead the way."

Grant waited for the crew to prepare themselves, two men now lifting the tongue of the gun carriage, watching him, and he pointed past the house. "That way."

He slipped past the house, could see the main wall again, from where the Mexican muskets were still firing. Thick clouds of smoke drifted overhead, and he heard the impact of a shell, close. Flannery said, "Dammit, not here. Over that way!"

Grant looked back, expected the man to be cursing him, but Flannery was looking back toward the walls, said now, "That's one of our guns. Probably that fool Lane. Couldn't hit a barn door if it was falling on him. We're in more danger from him than the damned Mexicans."

Grant saw the grim, weary faces of the crew, but knew they must press on. "This way. Quickly."

The gun rolled forward again, as Grant scanned the buildings, his anxiety growing. We can't just sit out here in the open, he thought. The rooftops are flat, no cover for the gun. The muskets will pick us apart.

He turned a corner, saw a column of smoke far to the south, could hear a low rumble, more guns, another fight down below, the other gate, Quitman's men.

Flannery said, "Hear that? Old Worth is gonna have a fit if Quitman and his volunteers get inside first. I heard it's some kind of damned race, who sets foot in the city first. Worth said our pride is at stake. I take more pride in staying alive. Damned generals."

Grant tried not to listen, avoided the looks from the sweating crew, the men straining now, the gun growing heavier by the minute, the work usually done by horses. He moved across a small intersection, past a narrow alleyway, where he looked in both directions. More low, flat rooftops, and now he heard a cracking sound from the wall closest to him and saw a spray of splintered rock falling away. Flannery said, "Hey! No snipers, eh? Don't think so, Grant. You sure you know where the hell we're going?"

Grant said nothing, waved them forward, moved past the alley, the road curving slowly, turning them straight toward the long wall again. He felt an angry twist in his gut, thought, There has to be . . . someplace. Find it! They are counting on you. He stopped, straight-

ened up, saw a dull white wall rising in front of him, beyond a wide
ditch. High above, he saw a stone archway holding a small brass bell.
It was a church. He smiled, felt a rush of relief, turned to Flannery,
pointed, said, "There."

Flannery moved up beside him, and Grant saw the crew lower
the gun, the heavy bags dropping to the ground. "Where?"

Grant pointed. "The church. Good cover up on the roof. They've
been mounting batteries on rooftops all day. We can just cross the
ditch—"

"Ditch?" Flannery said. "It's a damned river!"

Grant moved to the sloping edge of the waterway, his patience
gone. He began to wade out, the slope deeper now. He unhooked his
pistol belt, held it high, felt the warm water rising in his clothes, his
feet sliding down into soft mud. He stopped himself, turned, said, "If
you want to put that cannon to some use, Captain, you had better follow me."

He moved farther across the ditch, could feel the water seeping up
over his waist, higher now, his chest, and he thought, Please, no
deeper. Be mighty embarrassing to drown right here. I'm supposed to
be the scout.

Flannery barked to his men, "Well, dammit, we got nothing better to do. Take her apart, let's swim."

Grant ignored the activity behind him, was feeling the mud with
his boots, inched himself forward. The slope was gone, the bottom of
the ditch level, more solid, the water still up to his chest. He saw a mass
of green in front of him, reached out, pushed aside thick weeds, his
hand gripping a thick vine. Good, he thought, pull . . . easy . . .

The ground under his feet began to rise, and he climbed up, dug
his boots into the mud, and then he was clear of the water. He looked
back, saw the gun crew wading in, the heavy bags of powder held high.
The men were across quickly, and he reached out, took the precious
powder from them as they came up. They splashed quickly back across
the ditch, and he watched as the gun was broken down in pieces, two
men now cradling the barrel on their shoulders. Flannery watched
from across the ditch as Grant waited for the men to come out of the
water. Seeing a frown on Flannery's face, he said, "We're all set over
here, Captain. You coming?"

Flannery moved to the edge of the water, said, "Any snakes in
there? Anybody see anything moving around?"

The men laughed, and one of them said, "Aw, come on now,
Captain. Just be quick, won't hardly get your feet wet."

Flannery scowled at his men, looked at Grant. "Don't like snakes. Not one bit."

He eased slowly into the water, holding his own belt high, his angry frown changing to wide-eyed fear. He pushed quickly, made small grunting noises as he worked his way across. "They missed me. They were there, I know they were there."

Grant watched the men put the cannon back together, while Flannery wiped at the muddy slime on his uniform. "No more ditches, Lieutenant. I'd rather fight Santa Anna by myself than mess with a snake."

Grant said nothing, moved away, looked again at the belfry of the church. No more ditches, he thought. This ought to do just fine.

The crew was ready now and the gun was rolling again. They crossed a narrow street, moved into a small open yard in front of the church. Grant moved to the door, thought, Could be . . . someone here. He pulled his pistol, looked back, saw Flannery draw his as well, the crew spreading out to either side of the old wooden door. Grant took a breath, knocked on the splintered wood. There was a silent pause, then the door slowly began to open. Grant stepped back, held the pistol ready, saw the old face of a priest, stooped by age, smiling. *"Sí?"*

Grant glanced at Flannery, put the pistol away, said, "Uh, *señor.* We need to come in."

The priest nodded, still smiling, then looked at the cannon, seemed to understand, and began shaking his head, laughing quietly. *"No, no. Aquí? No."*

Flannery was beside him now, said, "Look, padre, we need to get these men off the street. This gun of mine is under orders. Now, I'm as respectful of the church as the next man—" He stopped, said, "Shoot, he don't understand a damned word."

The priest still smiled, and Grant stepped back, moved to the gun, reached down and grabbed the tongue of the carriage, tried to lift it, but the gun barely moved. He looked at the crew, and the men moved toward him, helpful hands. Grant said quietly, "Spin it around."

The priest watched the gun turning, still smiling pleasantly until the carriage was lowered and the mouth of the barrel came up, facing directly into the doorway, directly at the old man's face. The smile changed as the old man's wide eyes stared straight into the round black hole.

Grant stepped toward the door again. "Now he understands." The priest looked at him in silent anger, nodded slowly, backed away.

Grant moved inside, pointed up. "Stairway? The roof?" The priest pointed, and Grant saw it now, narrow winding steps. He looked at Flannery. "Can we get it up there?"

Flannery looked at the stairway, then back at the crew. "I think so, Grant. All right, boys. Take her apart again."

G RANT STEPPED ONTO THE ROOF, MOVED TOWARD THE STONE archway, the belfry enclosed by a low round wall. Behind him, Flannery directed his crew, and now the gun came up the stairway, the spoked wheels first, the hard wood of the carriage, and finally the brass barrel. Grant stood aside, watched in quiet amazement as the gun was reassembled. Then Flannery came up into the belfry, looked at the tight space, said, "Not much room."

Grant looked out toward the great rising clouds of smoke, the fight now swirling all along the wall, the sounds of muskets punched by the thunder of the big guns.

Flannery said, "Hell, Grant, we're not two hundred yards from the gate. Not likely they'll ignore us up here for long." He looked to the crew, the men hauling the cloth bags up on the stairway, and said, "Keep low, boys. We're in easy musket range. Chances are they'll send somebody out here to take this gun away from us. So, while we have the time . . . let's make the most of it."

Grant eased behind the gun, saw one man slide the powder charge down the barrel, the ramrod pushing it tight. Then came the small round shell, six pounds of lead, another man placing it in the barrel, the ramrod pushing tight again. Flannery was beside Grant, sighted down the barrel, adjusted a small elevation wheel.

"What's your pleasure, Grant?"

Grant could see the thick burst of smoke from in front of the Mexican battery, the thunder rolling out through the houses, could see the motion of the gun crews, the officers pointing, guiding the deadly shell.

Grant pointed, said, "I believe we should begin . . . there. How about we send the first one right into that battery?"

W ORTH GLASSED TOWARD THE MEXICAN BATTERY THROUGH small gaps in the smoke and chaos of the fight. From his vantage point on the rooftop, he could see his men very clearly, watched their artillery finding the mark, taking deadly aim at the strength of the Mexican defense. The troops were still advancing, and the muskets had been finding their targets, while the Mexican infantry pulled back off the wall, the troops in the houses, on the rooftops, backing away into the city. The reports were coming in all around him, and aides waited, some showing quiet impatience, especially the young couriers not yet accustomed to the rhythm of the senior commanders. Worth ignored the aides, their fast talk, the quick movement of officers, still glassed along the wall, focused now on a column of gray smoke rising from the belfry of a church. He saw the burst of fire, the impact of the shell close by, the Mexicans behind the barricade answering with muskets. The gun fired again, and there was a shattering blast in the barricade. Worth tried to see through the smoke, lowered the glasses, said, "Who is that? There's a cannon up in that church tower."

Clarke, beside him now, raised his glasses, stared for a moment, and Worth said, "He's got 'em running! Some good work there. Fine work. I'd like to know who it is."

Clarke shook his head, looked now to the far side of the rooftop, saw another officer glassing the church. "You see it, Captain Lee?"

Lee lowered the glasses. "Yes, I see him."

Worth said, "Send someone out there, find out who it is. Splendid idea. Put a gun in every steeple."

Clarke glassed again, said, "It's dangerous . . . risky. He's awfully close. He could lose the gun."

Worth moved away, said, "Then he's either a damned fool or one of the best soldiers we've got, eh?"

Lee still stared through the glasses, smiled. "He's winning the day, General. I think we need a few more just like him."

32. SCOTT

THE PRISONERS HAD MARCHED OUT AS THE FIRST SOUNDS OF MUS-
ket fire could be heard from the assault on Chapultepec. The
guards had led them, some prodding them from behind, with
their bayonets, some moving just that much closer, threatening, taunt-
ing, but the San Patricios did not respond, would not give the angry
men who led them an opportunity for revenge.

The march was slow, the men winding through narrow streets,
each man staring to the front, past each small curve in the road, beyond
each wall, the small houses. They expected to see the formal gathering
of troops, Colonel Harney's men, the cavalry serving as the final guard,
Harney himself commanding the ceremony. Finally, it appeared, and
some of them didn't believe it yet, had dreamt of this moment through
long fitful nights, the vision of this awful place, the horror of the last
few steps. Now the vision was real, and they moved into a small plaza,
each man staring up at the tall, sticklike gallows, long rows perched up
on narrow platforms. There was a low murmur from the throat of
each man as he saw the rope, the stiff coils, the narrow loop hanging
empty. The bayonets pressed closer now, but again there was no need,
the deserters moving in slow, automatic steps, climbing the short stairway, guided along the platform by the cavalry officers. Each man was
placed beneath his own rope, a silence settling over them, the faces
turning slowly, the men looking for the grim old man who would give
the order. Harney stepped out in front of them now, saying something
about loyalty, but few could hear him, focused instead on a new sight,
far to the north, the great fat fortress, the slow rise of smoke, the rumble of sounds from the fight they had missed.

Even Harney had turned to watch, the veteran officer knowing with absolute certainty what the assault on Chapultepec might mean for the troops, for the war. All through the army, all through the thoughts of men who had not yet begun their own part of the fight, the hard thunder of cannon, the rolling chatter of musket fire, echoed deep in some quiet place.

Harney saw it in the faces of the deserters, the men staring at the distant Mexican flag, some making low comments, and the officers were surprised, low voices telling Harney the men were praying for a victory, urging the army forward, the *American* army. The decision was his alone, and he ordered the ceremony delayed. The drums fell silent, the prisoners watching as they all watched, as the wide gray cloud drifted higher, beyond the great walls. When the sounds of the battle began to fade, Harney's men gathered, all staring north, nervous, expectant, waiting for the moment, some with field glasses, all focused on the motion above the dull white walls: the slow flutter of the Mexican flag. Their awareness that something important was happening dawned slowly, and men began to point, excitement growing in their voices. Even the deserters could see it clearly, the flag slowly dropping down, disappearing into the smoke. A silent moment passed, as each man held his breath, waiting. The men with the field glasses saw it first. They called out, waving, and quickly it was visible to them all, the smoke clearing away, the Stars and Stripes rising slowly, now fixed high over the walls of Chapultepec.

The troops, the cavalry officers, began to shout, the guards holding their bayonets high. The sound then passed through the rows of deserters, their voices muted by the tightness of the ropes around their necks. Some called out, experiencing a sudden rush of emotion, their voices blending with the voices of the men who held them firmly in line. Some were crying, some simply stared in mute acceptance, and when the flag was high on the staff, Harney turned, glanced down the rows of men who knew it was their time. Now the order was given, and the platform fell away, and the voices were suddenly silent.

SCOTT HAD MOVED EARLY THAT MORNING THROUGH THE SMALL plaza where the troops had constructed the gallows, stopped for a brief moment, even said a small prayer, something he rarely did. The artillery had already begun the assault on the thick walls, and he knew his place was forward, but he had to take some small amount of time to absorb this place, the spot where the men who had betrayed their country would die.

The place stayed with him, and he had watched as the Stars and Stripes rose over Chapultepec as well, had heard the cheering around him, the staff, the other commanders, reacting to the glory of the wonderful moment. He had raised his hat as they had, but his mind was already working, and he knew he should move again, closer still, guiding the new assaults that would follow, Quitman and Worth pushing at the two gates of the city. He thought of the plaza again, looked to the south, but there was nothing to see. The row of gallows was nearly a mile away. The word had come quickly, a short message signed by Harney, and he knew by the timing of the message that the old cavalry commander had waited for the Stars and Stripes, had given the deserters an image to carry with them to some other place, the image of victory from the army they had abandoned, the soldiers they had betrayed.

All that morning there had been rumors and whispers, and through all the excitement, the urgency of the great assault, there were comments, brief glances at Scott. He ignored it all, had always understood it would come down to his own responsibility. The deserters had been tried in two courts, and over fifty had been condemned to die, some immediately, the ringleaders, no opportunity for the most hardened among them to spread any more influence. There had been a firing squad, and now the leaders were gone. To the men who would find another fate, there had been two choices, and Scott had received the advice of the courts, agonized over the decision, but ultimately had to abide by military law, by what every man in the army knew was the appropriate sentence. At Harney's command, nearly fifty men had been hanged, and there was no surprise at that, but the law was obscure, and what many did not know was that Scott was not bound to execute them all. There was another punishment, some bit of leniency for the men who showed the most regret for the crime they had committed, and if the court did not believe it appropriate, Scott did. The decision, after all, was his, and so instead of death, nearly thirty men had been allowed to live, but would carry a punishment that dulled the anger of the troops they betrayed. Even the guards could not watch as the punishment was carried out, an unexpected horror. The men who would not die would be branded, a *D* carved into the cheek, a hard scar that would never fade. They would return home marked with the permanent sign of their betrayal, would have to find a life somehow in a country that would never forget that the *D* meant *Deserter*.

As he began to ride toward the new sounds of the fight, the great flow of strength moving past Chapultepec, Scott thought of those men, the men who would be reminded of their guilt every day. How many of them, he wondered, would rather have climbed those short steps, would rather have felt the rope?

H E WORE THE GRAND UNIFORM AGAIN, WAS NOT SELF-conscious about it now, the foolish spectacle he had seemed to be at Churubusco. This was already different from the horror of that bloody day, and even if the fight around the great castle was costly, all the momentum was forward. The army knew, as he knew, a victory here would be the most important day of the war. He spurred the huge white horse, moving up the long road from the south, along the route the Mexicans had thought protected, the one direct roadway into the great fortress. He was not smiling as he moved past the wounded and the men who helped them, and he did not wait for cheers. He fixed his eyes ahead, rode closer to the walls of the castle, pushed hard by the urgency of *being there*, moving inside, joining his men in their great triumph.

He could see the remains of the fortifications, now splintered away, the abandoned Mexican guns already hauled up into the fort it-self by the marines, throwing their fire into the enemy who had thought the *yanquis* would still be held away. He made the sharp turn in the road, the angle where the Mexicans had built a strong works, the place where the fight had been the most difficult. But the roadway was open now, cleared of the bodies of the men from both sides, the debris of the fight pulled aside. He moved uphill, the road climbing straight up through the walls of the fort, straight into the heart of Chapultepec.

The word had spread, and the men knew he was coming. The fight was still growing hot at the two gates of the city, but he would pass through this place, stop for a brief moment, see them, speak to them.

They had gathered in a ragged crowd, and he saw wounded men, men already in bandages, but they were lining up, and the officers did not have to guide them; the discipline, the order, came from him, from his grand presence. He waited, saw more of them emerging from in-side, from dark hallways and deep cavernous rooms. There were new sounds, growing now, the voices of the men who had conquered this magnificent fortress, and he waited awhile longer, let them come, let the numbers grow, let them all be a part of this.

He sat stiffly upright on the great horse as it stood quietly. He felt the sun reflecting on the uniform, the medals, all the symbols of his command. He glanced up at the flag, and they saw the look, and the

voices erupted into a vast cheer. He looked at them now, scanned their
faces, saw the fire, the tears, and he wanted to speak to them, say something, give them some important words. He fought for it, but his mind
was filled by them, by their exhausted joy, and he waved to them,
thought, There are no words. There are never words to explain this.
They know it already, they know what they have done here. They
came up over these walls. And they *won*. He waved again, said to
himself, a soft voice they could not hear, "God bless them. There are
none finer. . . ."

H E HAD RIDDEN OUT PAST THE NORTH WALL OF CHAPULTEPEC,
glanced again at the flag, could hear the men still, hats and
hands held high all across the top of the wall. He waved toward them, and the cheering grew louder again, and he smiled, shook
his head, cleared away the faces and the cheers, focused ahead.

The fight was in front of him now, a great tide flowing out from
Chapultepec to the east, Quitman's men already pressing the enemy
hard at the Belén gate. Farther east, on the causeways that led straight
up from the south, Twiggs had made the good show, Bennett Riley's
brigade giving the hard feint, the noisy demonstration along the southern gates of the city. From all reports it had worked, had held a great
number of Santa Anna's troops in place there, facing an enemy that
had no intention of making a fight. As a result, the Mexican troops at
the San Cosme and Belén gates did not have the strength of numbers
they could have had. Even with the powerful assault of Chapultepec,
Santa Anna had stayed back, kept a strong force still at the southern
gates, a force that would not see any part of the fight.

Couriers moved along the road, delivering a flow of messages
from Worth's commanders, who remained in the great fort, to the
troops fighting at San Cosme. Some moved past him, saluted nervously, surprised to see him, and he waved them past, would not hold
them to formality today. The messages were not for him.

He saw a rider coming up from the south now, from below the
big fort, the man waving at him, and Scott stopped his horse, could see
the manic excitement in the man's face. He felt a quick burst of cold in
his chest, thought, This one is for me. Something has happened, something . . . important.

The man reined up, saluted him, and Scott recognized him as a
young major from Quitman's staff. The man said, "General Scott . . .
with your permission, sir. General Quitman offers his respects and

wishes to inform the commanding general that, um . . . at . . . one-twenty this afternoon, our troops broke past the Belén gate. We have taken up a strong position . . . inside the city, sir."

Scott sat for a quiet moment, while the man watched him, waiting for a response. Scott stared again at the city, spread out all across the horizon, his mind suddenly blank, leaving him with no words, nothing to say. He wanted to shout, let out a cheer of his own, throw the wide hat straight in the air, felt his hands gripping hard to the reins. He smiled, a small betrayal of his real feelings, closed his eyes, nodded slowly, said, "Thank you, Major."

The man seemed disappointed, said, "Sir, excuse me . . . but . . . we are inside the city, sir!"

Scott opened his eyes, tried to see the young man, blinked through a blur. He felt the wetness on his cheeks, nodded again, and finally the man seemed to understand and moved slowly past the horse, back toward the staff. Scott tried to clear his mind, thought, This is ridiculous. You are in command, there is no time for . . . this sort of thing. He took a deep breath, said aloud, "I should move up."

He blinked again, his eyes clearing, and he looked back, saw the major beside his son-in-law, said, "You may return to General Quitman. This day is not yet over. Certainly he knows that. Tell him . . ." He paused, thought, There is only one message. "Tell him, fine work."

The young man rode up beside him, one last look, saluted, said, "General Scott, with your permission, sir."

Scott returned the salute, and the man spurred the horse, was quickly gone. Scott looked back, focused on the flag again, high above Chapultepec, thought, No, the day is not yet done. But my God . . . it has been a good one thus far.

He took another breath, felt the emotions passing, his mind sharpening, the sounds of the fight now reaching him again. He looked at the young Scott, said, "Major, let's find General Worth. I'd like to know what his people are doing up there."

33. LEE

E HAD PLACED THE LAST OF THE BATTERIES, GUIDING THE BIG guns close to San Cosme. The firing was now steady, a hard barrage at the Mexican defense, close over the heads of Worth's infantry, who were pressing hard at the best resistance Santa Anna's men could offer.

He climbed up on the roof again, saw Worth glassing the wall, could smell the thick sulfur from the guns mounted on the rooftops beside them. Worth pointed to the front. "There! We're pushing them back! We have men right up at the wall, on both sides of the gate. They're digging into the houses!"

Lee sensed Worth's excitement, could see only a cloud of smoke, hanging low all along the wall, flowing back through the rows of low buildings. Across the road, the bigger guns opened in a slow rhythm, the battery firing in sequence, the rooftop jumping under Lee's feet. He saw Worth raise the glasses again, said, "General, do you have orders, sir? I should report to General Scott."

Worth lowered the glasses, looked at him with a hard glare. "Captain, you will leave this command when I do not require you here. If General Scott is not aware what is happening here, what these men are doing here, there will be plenty of time for you to tell him. I want a full report, Captain. I want nothing left out. General Scott will know that this division has performed with heroism."

Worth had been shouting, and Lee felt himself backing away, could see the black fire in the general's eyes, thought, He's still fighting more than just the Mexicans.

Worth said, "I want you to see it, Captain, all of it! We're marching straight into this city by tonight. We will be the first troops to occupy the enemy's capital! Do you understand, Captain?"

"Certainly, sir."

Worth turned away, raised the glasses again, and Lee saw Worth's hands quiver, the hard anger still flowing. Lee moved away then, saw other officers watching him, and no one spoke. He could be right, he thought. I will make the report. General Scott ordered me up here. But . . . I am expected to stay in communication. He felt uncomfortable now, did not expect to find himself caught between the strange feud Worth insisted on creating with the commanding general.

There were couriers delivering reports from close to the front. Lee tried to listen over the roar of the big guns drowning out the voices. Worth turned toward him, pointed straight down, and Lee understood the silent message, *Come here,* and moved quickly that way. The last courier was already gone, jumping down the steep stairway.

Worth said, "Find a gun, Captain! A big gun. A twenty-four. Position it out front, close to the gate. We're ready, Captain! Do you understand? I want a hole . . . a big damned hole blasted right through that defense! Blow it to hell!"

Lee hesitated, thought, In front? "Sir, do you mean . . . out in the open?"

Worth seemed to explode, said, "Don't question me, Captain! Move! Get a big gun out there and make a hole! We're going in!"

Lee hurried down the steps, his mind racing with the heat of Worth's anger. He passed the horses, did not ride, knew there was a battery down a side street, more of the guns he had brought forward, waiting for their instructions. He turned the corner, saw the wagons, the caissons, saw the men unlashing the ropes that held one gun close behind the draft horses. Lee waved, shouted, "Prepare to move! General Worth's orders!"

The words left him, and he didn't know what else to say, thought, How do I order them out in front, with no cover, no protection? It is . . . suicide.

He saw the officer now, the man moving toward him with the tall dignity of a veteran, his expression full of questions.

"Lieutenant Hunt, I have orders from General Worth. Your twenty-four pounder is ordered to advance beyond the cover of the houses, to begin a short range assault at the gate itself." Lee hesitated, waited for a protest, but Hunt nodded, listening to every word. "The general is specific, Lieutenant. He wants a hole blasted in the enemy works. The infantry will follow behind you."

Hunt still said nothing, considered the order, then let a strange smile spread across his face. Lee moved to the side, watched Hunt climb his horse, his men scrambling up to the caisson. Hunt said, "We have a job! Let's go!"

The gun rattled past Lee, the crew hanging tight to their seats, and Lee followed on foot, watching the gun and the men roll out toward the gate, toward the thick smoke of the fight. He ran, moved to Worth's lookout position, climbed the steps, his breath coming in hard gasps. Worth did not look at him, was focused to the front, as were the others, watching as Henry Hunt's single gun rolled forward, out past the houses, the low stone walls, past the men who fired their muskets, past the last bit of cover, out into the flat open ground of the wide plaza. The Mexicans began to respond, and Lee saw the men on the caisson hunched low, one man falling away, sprawling out behind the gun, left behind by Hunt's charge.

Lee could hear Worth shouting, "Yes! That's it! Closer! Take it to them!"

Hunt was far in front of any support, and Lee began to lose sight of them in the thick smoke. He caught a glimpse, saw the gun spinning, the muzzle now facing the Mexican works, the crew jumping down, doing the good work, swarming in one rush over their precious gun. One horse fell, then another, swept away by the storm from the enemy muskets, and Lee felt a rising heat in his chest, thought, My God . . . they will never come back. This is . . . insanity. He could see Hunt now, behind the gun, saw more of the crew falling away. But then the gun fired, one sharp blast, followed by a bloom of smoke. Lee strained to see, the gun bathed in its own fog, a blur of motion from the men still working. The gun fired again, and Worth shouted, "That's it! One more . . . one more . . ."

Lee could not look at him, felt his stomach clench, but now he could see the gun, Hunt, the men, still up, still working. The gun fired again, and Worth yelled, "Go! Send the infantry! Order the charge!"

The men on the roof were quickly gone, and Lee lowered the glasses, Worth moving by him, toward the stairway. Worth looked at him, said, "We'll have our victory now, Captain! The whole world will know what we did here!"

Then Worth was gone, and Lee moved to the edge of the roof, raised the glasses. He could see the storm still blowing out from the fight at the gate, but now the troops were moving up, the thick wave of blue building behind the low walls, and he watched, waited, saw the officers moving down the lines. The wave began to burst, spilling over their own cover, the troops rushing forward, straight through the shattered defense of the enemy.

THE TROOPS HAD SPREAD OUT INSIDE THE GATE, HAD MOVED into the houses and buildings that once held the enemy muskets. The Mexicans were still there, a heavy force, infantry mostly, their big guns left behind, captured by the surge of American troops moving past the gate. There was no easy advance now, the dense buildings inside the gate offering protection for soldiers on both sides. Worth's men began to spread farther into the city, burrowing through basements, fighting their way in a slow push from house to house, musket fire above and below, from cellar and rooftop. If the daylight would be gone soon, there would be no retreat, no pulling back to regroup. At the Molino, these men had made the good fight for no good reason, had occupied a place that had little value, endured the shock of a fight that left many of them bitter at the commanders who had ordered them forward. But that was forgotten now, Worth's men focusing on the fight straight in front of them, pushing hard into the city, each man driven by the fire, by the raw heat, moving house to house, pushing the bayonet closer into the heart of the enemy.

THE SHARP SUNLIGHT HAD BEGUN TO SOFTEN, THE LONG AFTERnoon giving way to a cool dusk. Lee forced himself to sit upright, held himself high in the saddle, the horse perched alongside the intersection just west of San Cosme. Worth had ordered some of the units out of Chapultepec, men still fresh from the celebration of their victory, now on the march again, reinforcements for the thrust through the San Cosme gate. Lee had been sent back as a guide, and he accepted the duty numbly, did not have the strength to protest, to insist anymore that he was overdue for a report to General Scott. He sat now at the obvious intersection, watched as a small column of troops moved quickly past, pointed the way to officers who did not need him to tell them where the fight was still hot. The column was past now, and Lee tried to clear his eyes, his mind, thought, Where should you be? What . . . else is there?

He had not seen Scott for a few hours now, thought, I should find him . . . report to him. He will be angry if he is kept in the dark. I will explain that General Worth required my presence. He should know that General Worth would have expected me to stay. . . .

His vision began to blur, and he blinked hard, wiped at the fuzziness in his eyes with the back of his hand. This is not good. Get hold of yourself, no excuses, no apologies. Do the job. He will tell you what he wants done. Now, just find him. He spurred the horse, moved south on the wide road, could see riders moving toward him bearing a flag. He tried to focus his eyes, moved to the side of the road, waved them on impatiently, *Come on, move on.* He gave them the guidance silently, could not even speak the words, the directions any officer would see for himself. He felt himself sagging again, suddenly jerked himself upright, fought it, sat upright, another hard blink through bleary eyes. He began to wave now, automatic, motioning them past, said, "Follow the road . . . turn right at the intersection. General Worth is near the front. . . ."

The riders stopped, and Lee focused through a fog, saw now the broad chest, the grand uniform, and he blew the fog from his mind, a sudden stab of panic.

"General Scott! Sir! I wish to report—" He stopped, the words a tumble of confusion.

Scott moved close to him, leaned forward, said, "Good God, Mr. Lee, are you all right?"

Lee was feeling the fog again. "No wounds, sir." He fought his exhaustion, the words forming, said, "Sir, we have advanced into the city. General Worth's division has made a strong foothold inside the gate. The general is waiting for you, sir. He is quite pleased to be the first one into the city."

Scott shook his head. "Is he now? This has been a magnificent day for this army, Captain, and they're more concerned with who wins the damned race. Mr. Lee, you should know that General Quitman's people broke through the Belén gate three hours ago. I guess it's up to me to break that news to General Worth. Maybe the shame will cause him to resign."

Lee felt his head swirling, tried to focus on Scott's face. "That is . . . wonderful news, sir. General Worth will certainly be pleased."

Scott looked at him closely now, and Lee blinked hard, tried to focus on Scott's face. "When was the last time you slept, Mr. Lee?"

Lee tried to think, realized he had no idea what time of day it was. "I'm not sure, sir. It has been . . . a while."

"Stay with me, Captain. I don't think you're in any condition to be out here on your own. Your detached duty is concluded for now."

Lee nodded, felt a small alarm go off in his mind. "Sir, I can still perform my duty. There is much to be done. General Worth is still heavily engaged."

"Thank you, Mr. Lee. We're on our way there now. Let's ride, shall we?"

Lee turned the horse, felt himself sliding away. He pulled on the reins, felt the leather slip from his hands, tried to see Scott, wanted to speak, his brain shouting at him, fighting through a swirl of dizziness, I'm falling . . . help. . . .

"HE'S ALL RIGHT, SIR."
Lee tried to see the face above him, heard the familiar voice of the young major. Lee sat now, his hands pushing into soft dirt, felt a sharp stab in his back, and the young man said, "He's awake. You all right, Captain? Nasty fall."

Lee shook his head, saw Scott standing above him, huge, his face far away. Lee said, "I'm sorry, sir. I must have fallen. . . ."

The young Scott said, "You fainted, Captain."

There was faint disgust in the voice, and Lee felt embarrassment, pulled his legs under him, forced himself to his feet, fought past the pain in his back. "My apologies, sir. This is most . . . inappropriate. Please allow me to return to duty. I am fine now, sir."

Scott reached out, put a heavy hand on his shoulder, and Lee straightened, pushed against the old man's hard grip. Scott said, "I would like you to accompany me to see General Worth. Hell, I don't even know where he is. I suspect you do."

Lee tried to stiffen his legs, holding up the weight of Scott's hand. "Of course, sir. I can take you to him by the most direct route."

Scott seemed to be watching him, measuring. "Let's move, shall we? From the sound of it, he still has his hands full of a fight."

Scott moved to the horse, climbed up, and now Lee saw his own horse, the reins held by an aide. He took the leather straps in his hand, pulled the horse toward him, felt another unsteady moment, a small wave of dizziness. He reached up, gripped the saddle, held himself against the side of the horse, thought, Stop this, get control. This is not the time . . . there is much work still to be done.

He climbed up, held himself upright in the saddle for a moment, saw Scott, the others, all watching him. Scott shook his head, spurred the horse forward, still looked at Lee, said, "Mr. Lee, once you have taken me to General Worth, you will do a greater service to this army if you will just . . . get some sleep."

34. SANTA ANNA

E HAD LEFT THE BELÉN GATE, HAD NOT BELIEVED THE ENEMY could penetrate there, and when the guns from Worth's batteries began to pound San Cosme, he had led the reserves close to the fight. He had stayed out of the carriage, walked among the troops, led them in the chorus of song, patriotic hymns, the great rallying cries that kept the fire in their eyes. When he learned that the defenders at Belén had given way, he directed his fury toward the men at San Cosme, and for a while they had responded. He was not usually in the middle of the fight, and he had seen the troops' faces light up with the inspiration, the sight of their commander, so close to the danger from the guns of the *yanquis*.

He believed it was treachery that had allowed the enemy through the Belén gate, but now, at San Cosme, it was the steady persistence of the enemy, the artillery that pounded his defenses into rubble. His men could not endure, had pulled back completely from the gate now, and the *yanquis* had moved into the defenses, had turned his own guns around, the Mexican cannon now pouring a new horror onto the men who could no longer defend them.

He tried to slow the retreat, limped forward through the smoke, shouting into the faces of the men who still looked at him with that vacant stare. Even the most panicked began to slow, some stopping in front of him to just stare at him, hearing his words. His anger was complete and consuming, and at first he had shouted into their faces with the fire of God, blaming *them* for the unspeakable act, running from the enemy. But the anger was gone now, and he felt the exhaustion, drew it from the faces of his men, beaten back by the relentless wave, the hard assault by their enemy.

He began to direct them into cover, the officers standing aside as he moved past. But his troops were still there, paralyzed, the mad retreat away from the gate blocked now by their attention to him, the sight of him, the glorious uniform, the long golden sword held high in front of him. He watched them gather, the voice screaming in his mind, No, I do not want an audience. I want an *army*. Now the anger had returned, and he waved the sword in a wide arc, shouted, *"Move, go, fire back! Fight!"*

The faces began to turn away, some men moving to new cover, men appearing on rooftops, kneeling, crouching low, the muskets firing again. He watched the troops fall slowly into some kind of line, an officer slapping his men with the sword, and Santa Anna shouted at the man, "Yes! Turn them around! Give the Devil a taste of hell!"

He had seen the first wave of blue as it came through the gate, saw them again now, still moving forward, darting quickly into the gaps, small spaces, pieces of cover. He moved forward, up close to the men with the muskets, stared hard through the smoke, saw one man falling now, sprawling into the street, the blue uniform ripped apart, the man's life flowing out on the hard stones, and he cheered, raised his hand, shouted again, "Kill them . . . yes, kill them!"

He could see more blue, the *yanquis* still coming forward, more of them now, lining up behind low walls, filling the narrow ditches. The man beside him suddenly backed away, disappeared into the smoke, and Santa Anna shouted a noise, no words, a sharp scream of rage, thought, What are you doing? You are no man. . . .

He looked down, saw the man's musket, reached for it, the rage pounding in his chest, searched the smoke in front of the low wall, held the gun upright, thought, A target, any target. I will kill them myself! He tried to fire the gun, felt nothing, the gun empty, and he threw it down, looked out, saw the targets, many targets, moving closer to the thin lines of his defense.

The musket fire was a storm now, and he began to back away, some voice in his brain, calm reason, Leave this place, do not die here. He saw his guards, the men surrounding him now, pulling at him, and his own anger was answered by the desperation of the men who protected him, one man shouting close to his face, the voice rising above the roar from the growing fight, "Please, Excellency, we must find cover!"

He saw an opening in a fat stone building, moved that way, moved behind its thick hard walls, felt the ground jump under him, the impact of a shell close behind. The floor of the crude house was a pile of rubble, the ceiling already coming down, the walls crumbling from the impact of the *yanqui* guns. The guards followed in close behind him, and he fought through the smoke. Through a small window he watched the chaos following him in the street, his troops still flowing back away from the gate. Again his hot anger grew, the voice of reason pushed away, something uncontrollable filling him, animal rage, and he began to shout through the window, *"Turn around ... fight them! You will all burn in hell!"*

He felt a hand pull him back, heard the sharp whistle of the shell, the road in front of him bursting into flame and dust. He turned, focused his rage at the man who held him, thought, I will kill you ... and the man released him, glanced down, said, "Apologies, Excellency. You were in danger."

Santa Anna felt his hands shaking, wanted to reach out, grab the man by the throat, unleash all the frustration focused in his fingers, take the life away from this one impudent man. The other guards moved close now, and the man backed away, faded out of sight. Santa Anna looked at their faces, felt his control coming back, the hard pain in his chest giving way to the cold black reason.

"How has this happened? Who is in command here? What traitor has allowed the *yanquis* to enter this city? There will be punishment!"

There was no response, and he thought, No, there is never a response, no one will admit his treachery. But I will find him. I will know who has done this! And he will die by my hand! He moved to the doorway again. "Let us move back. I must find some order. We must organize the men, bring the commanders together. We are still strong. This fight is not over!"

He stepped into the street, the guards filing out quickly, and he felt them moving him along, past the gathering lines of his men, his troops now finding the will, the courage, to stop their own retreat. He could see muskets firing again, holding the blue flow back, holding the enemy tight in their cover, and he shouted again, "Yes! Fight them! *Kill them!*"

He looked for officers, saw a young captain, the man moving his troops forward, spreading them along a garden wall, giving the order now, directing the volley from their muskets. Santa Anna pulled free from the guards, moved close to the man, said, "What is your name?"

The young man appeared stunned, saluted him, said, "Lezar Menendez, Excellency!"

"Captain Menendez, you will command a division today! This is an army of traitors! I need good men, men who know how to fight!"

The young man nodded, his face still holding the shock of Santa Anna's words, and then there was a rush of hot wind, the ground bursting between them, the shell ripping into the wall, blowing rock into the air. Santa Anna covered his eyes, the sharp blast pushing him back. He felt arms holding him, pulling him again. He tried to see through the smoke, saw the bodies of men blown back from the shattered wall, one man twisted horribly. He wanted to shout again, but there were no words, no voice, just the hands, still pulling him to some safe place.

THE LAST OF THE DAYLIGHT ECHOED WITH THE SCATTERED shots from the muskets, the snipers firing still at the single glimpse, the blue uniforms of the *yanquis*.

He sat at a wide table, stared into a fire blazing in a great stone hearth, looked past the plate of food that had been set before him. The room was still filling, the commanders now finding him where the day had begun, the word spreading that he was here, again, at the headquarters, the great palace in the center of the city. He did not eat, did not even see the food, heard them moving slowly into the room, kept his gaze hard at the fire, the dance of hell, the laughter of the enemy now holding fast to a piece of the city. There were low voices, but no one spoke to him, and he waited, closed his eyes, leaned back in the big chair, said aloud, "Who among you has the courage to admit your treachery?"

There was silence, and he opened his eyes, looked across the room, saw the familiar faces of his senior commanders.

"No, of course not. Cowards will never admit they are cowards. Traitors will never reveal their treachery. But I know. I know very well what you are."

He stared at the faces, saw the eyes look away, and still no one spoke. He looked at the plate of food, felt his stomach turn, pushed it away.

"Only a traitor will have an appetite this night." He glanced at the fire again. "Only a devil will find warmth."

He pushed the chair back, pulled himself up, the stiffness of the wooden leg rocking him forward. He leaned on the table, let out a long breath.

"Because of your failures . . . because no one would keep the enemy out of our city, we are faced with grave choices. Belén and San Cosme are in the hands of the *yanquis*. Tomorrow they will certainly be reinforced, and they will continue their attacks. I had thought . . ." He paused, closed his eyes, saw it in his mind, the rows of troops, his great strength, the big guns staring out where no fight had come. "I had thought the enemy would come at us from the south. All of your reports told me that. We were prepared, we were ready for them! It would have been a glorious fight!" He moved around the edge of the table, close to the fire, stared at the flames again.

"How did the *devil Scott* know to come at Chapultepec? How did he know we would be weakest at the western gates?" He looked up, the faces again avoiding his eyes. He began to feel a small shake, his hands quivering, the heat growing in his chest, the rage filling him again. "Perhaps it was because my *trusted* commanders betrayed their country? Perhaps it was because someone in *this* room . . . is a traitor? How could the *devil Scott* know where *I* would be? How could he know I would not be out *there* with my glorious army, that I would be here, preparing the strategy, ensuring that my trusted generals would do their jobs. How did the *devil Scott* know that Chapultepec could be assaulted, that our great fortress was defended not by the power of my army . . . but by a mere thousand men? A thousand men and *boys*, the innocent children of the military academy?"

He paused, flexed his fingers, felt a sudden weakness, moved to the chair again and sat heavily.

"Today was to be the final stroke, the plan realized after so much blood. It was to be the one great fight that would finally drive the *yanquis* away. But Scott knew . . . he *knew!*" He shouted the word, could see the men squirming, the impact of the message. Yes! You know what will happen! It is what always happens to those who betray their country! He clasped his hands together, said, "The enemy is now inside the city . . . because he was informed that only the traitors guarded the western gates. Now, I have no choice. I must sit down here with those who have betrayed me. I must rely on the advice and the counsel of cowards."

He felt himself shaking again, closed his eyes, waited for someone to speak. No, he thought, there will only be silence. They are still cowards. There was a voice then, low in the back of the room. "We cannot destroy the city."

Santa Anna looked up, saw the heads turning, the glow of the firelight reflecting on the face of one old man. He saw the man slowly rising, saw the face of Manuel de la Pena y Pena. He saw more suits now, civilians lining the back of the room. Santa Anna addressed them. "This is a meeting for soldiers. I do not recall asking for civilians, for *bureaucrats*, to offer their opinions. Señor Pena y Pena, you are in charge of the Supreme Court. There is no court decision to be made here."

Pena y Pena stepped forward, made his way up past the men who were seated, all eyes on the dignified man with thinning gray hair. "General Santa Anna, the civilian government does not believe there is anything to be gained by bringing this war into our streets. The population is at great risk. The refugees have come here in great numbers because they believed there was safety here. Tonight there is already panic. Tomorrow, if you fire your guns at the enemy, there will be slaughter."

Santa Anna stared at the old man in the dark suit. He contemplated the man's words, said slowly, "Would you have this great and glorious army . . . withdraw? Retreat *away* from our capital? Is that what you bureaucrats have been sent here to tell me?"

"General, there is no glory in continuing a fight that holds no promise of victory. We placed our confidence in you. We believed you could lead your army successfully against this invasion of our country. For reasons none of us can understand . . . God has turned against us."

Santa Anna laughed and stared at the ceiling. "A bunch of traitorous old men has decided that God is no longer behind me."

Pena y Pena shook his head, his face calm, yet revealing a deep sadness. "We speak for the government ministers. It is the government that is no longer . . . behind you. It has been decided that we should ask General Scott for terms of surrender. If we do not, there is great danger that this city could become a battlefield. There would be no victory, no glory in such destruction."

Dulled by the man's calm, Santa Anna felt the last bit of his anger slipping away. He looked again at the fire, the flames low now, the fire collapsing into a pile of white ash. His eyes moved slowly with the dying flames, and he tried to fan his anger, to strike out at this old man. There was complete silence now, a long moment. He saw a small burst of sparks from the fire, the final collapse, the ashes only a faint glow. He looked again at the sadness in the old man. "I cannot give up this fight. I will not tell my glorious army they have been defeated. There is still a war in those men. There is still a war in this country!"

Pena y Pena moved close to the table, said quietly, "No, General, there is not. The army has already begun to leave the city. Look outside, you will see for yourself. Men are leaving in great numbers. They understand what has happened here."

"I am still in command."

"You cannot command without the will of the people. The people . . . are turning away. There must not be a war *here*, in this city. If you would destroy Mexico City just to keep fighting your war . . . you will not *have* an army . . . you will not have the people behind you."

Santa Anna studied the old man's face, saw the calm, the eyes watching him in soft sadness. He tried again, looked down in some dark place, wanted to feel the anger, to shout the old man away, clear the room of the treachery, the demons who had brought him to this moment. But the strength was gone, and he felt only the weakness, the hopelessness, saw it clearly in the old man's face.

"I cannot surrender to General Scott. I must find a way. I will make them pay for what they have done. I will punish the traitors. There are still loyal soldiers, men who will fight for me."

The old man nodded. "You are certainly right. But there must be an end to this. There must be a treaty. In the end, you *will* abide by it. There is no other way."

Santa Anna stood again, looked out at the faces watching him, the eyes not turning away. He raised a hand, clenched it into a fist. "My enemies would have me surrender. You would wish me defeated, shamed, disgraced in the eyes of my people. There is a price for treachery. You will all pay the price."

He looked at the old man again, leaned close, felt the anger coming back now, the glorious heat rising in his chest.

"I will leave the city. I will take my army away. You may do whatever you must do to appease the enemies of Mexico. But while I have the strength and the will, I have the power. The soldiers will follow me as long as I will lead them. There is no treaty . . . *yet!*"

35. SCOTT

SEPTEMBER FOURTEENTH, TWO A.M.

THERE HAD BEEN NO SLEEP NEAR THE BIG TENT, THE OFFICERS and staff moving in one continuous flow, the reports going in both directions. The only quiet spot was closest to the enemy, inside the two gates, where Worth and Quitman had held their men tightly in place. There would be no retreat, no giving of ground, and once the dark had settled across the city, the Mexicans had not made any attempt to drive them back. At both gates the men in blue had dug in hard to the houses, the basements and rooftops. Even the artillery had been rolled through the gates, up close, prepared to sweep the empty streets of anyone foolish enough to mount another assault. But when the muskets grew quiet, and the soldiers could absorb what they had done, where they would spend the night, the joy had given way quickly to exhaustion. They slept now, men holding muskets, some curled up between the spoked wheels of their own cannon. To those who could not find sleep, the muskets pointed out at darkness, at the strange calm, the city waiting, as they would wait, for the first hint of daylight.

Scott sat, leaned on his arms, the small camp table straining, settling into the dirt under him. He blinked hard, tried to focus, the lamplight behind him throwing one fat shadow against the wall of the tent. He picked up the paper again, read, had already seen the reports, casualties, the position of the troops. He pulled out his watch, thought, Too damned late . . . too damned early. Can't even get a good nap before the sun comes up.

There had been celebrations in the camps, cheering from the men who were still outside the city, and around the big tent the staffs and

gathering officers were filled with the glow of the party. He had tolerated the noise at first, knew it had been an extraordinary day, thought,
They will remember this one. September thirteen. Six thousand men,
if that many. And we marched straight into the power of a much
stronger enemy, straight into his home, his heart, and by God . . . we
won. But there should be no celebration, not yet. We are in the city . . .
but it is a big city. If we have to fight house-to-house, this could turn
into some kind of serious mess. We will have to threaten them, bring
up the big guns, threaten to take down the whole damned place, the
palace, the national buildings. But if the Mexicans are fool enough to
call our bluff . . . then we have a problem.

Polk will never go for that, pouring artillery fire into the city
itself, blowing the place to hell just because we can. Not the kind
of thing that looks good in the newspapers. The opponents of the
war will have a field day, and that *will* look good in the papers: we
made it to the enemy capital, and it just wasn't enough. We didn't
have enough of an army to finish the job. Polk would have to relieve
me of duty, make all kinds of excuses. But even that would take time,
and so here I sit with a hundred guns. If Santa Anna wants to fight this
out to the end, I will go down in history as a butcher. Very smart. This
might have been his plan from the beginning. Welcome to Mexico
City. Now what the hell are you going to do? He'll know it's a bluff,
the threat itself sounds ridiculous. Watch out or we just might have
to toss a few shells into your national cathedral. What the hell good
will come from that? It might even bring Mexico a bunch of new allies,
give Polk a new problem, maybe some damned war with, who knows,
maybe Spain.

His head was spinning now, and he closed his eyes, rubbed his fingers hard into his temples. He tried to see numbers, to add the strength
together, the men who could still make a fight today. He sat back,
blinked hard again, looked at the paper, saw it was Quitman's casualty
report. You damned fool, he thought. What cost this time? Damn him,
damn that slick old lawyer. Just like Worth, chase the damned glory.
They learned nothing from Worth's mindless tactics, the disastrous
planning at Molino. They're all still so eager to claim the prize, to try
luck instead of strategy. San Cosme should have been the target, the focus of the attack. But Quitman thought it would be simple, just a stroll
in the park, march right through the Belén gate. He had to have the
glory, had to rub that in Worth's face, the volunteers outfighting
the regulars. Hell, if that was true, we wouldn't need the regulars in the
first place. Quitman's not any different from Pillow, or any of the rest

of them. If Davy Twiggs had been there, he'd have probably done the same thing: full speed ahead and damn the consequences. The attack at Belén was reckless and it cost us twice as many casualties as it should have. But Quitman's probably got it all figured out. He knows I can't raise hell about it. He won his damned fight. He was the first one inside the city. That's all Polk will want to hear, all that the newspapers will print. Just what we need, another stiff old peacock who wants to go home a hero . . . or President. Scott put the paper down, looked at his shadow, the exhaustion complete, said aloud, "This is a young man's job."

*H*E WAS HOLDING HIS DAUGHTER'S HAND, THE LOVELY CORNELIA, *very small, tiny fingers. He watched her pull the white flower from the stalk, smiled as she held it up, the word coming from her through the beautiful smile, the small music of her voice, "A daisy, Papa . . ."*

"Sir!"

The image jarred aside, and she was gone now, and he saw the glow of the lamp, the uniform, and the voice again: "Sir!"

He sat up, his head swirling, saw the face of his son-in-law, the urgency, wanted to pull him down, grab him by the throat, said with a low growl, "You . . . *you* took her away, you know. She was mine."

The young man backed up a step, said, "Sir? Who, sir? I'm sorry, I don't know what you mean. . . ."

"My daughter, you . . . you . . ." The words faded, and he saw now there were other uniforms outside the tent, felt the fog lifting in his brain, looked again at the young man, said, "Nothing, Major. A dream. I was napping, it seems."

The young man stepped forward again, said, "Of course, sir. I try not to do that myself. Dreams are very distracting, sir. Serves no purpose."

Scott sat back, was awake now, annoyed with his son-in-law's smugness, thought, She *married* him, for God's sake. "What do you *want*, Major?"

"Oh, sir. The Mexicans are here. General Worth brought them to see you, sir. He did not feel authorized to speak to them. Should I summon Mr. Trist, sir?"

Scott looked outside, saw only shapes, dark forms in the shadows of the small fires. He stood. "I don't need Mr. Trist's permission to speak to the Mexicans, Major. Who are they?"

The young man moved to the opening in the tent, lowered his voice. "Civilians, sir."

Scott stepped outside, felt a cool dampness, took a long breath, saw officers moving toward him, Worth, who bowed and then spoke. "Sir, these gentlemen entered my lines a short time ago. I believe you should speak to them."

Worth stepped aside, and Scott focused on the shadows, saw three men coming forward, saw the hats come off, more bows, and one man said, "General Scott. The government of Mexico wishes to negotiate with you the terms for your occupation of Mexico City."

There was silence, and Scott worked through the man's thick accent. He could see other men, officers moving up behind the gathering, the word already spreading through the camp. Scott waited a long moment, thought, Ceremony, Trist said . . . ceremony. Take your time.

"I am honored that you would visit my headquarters," he said slowly. "I am surprised to be speaking with . . . civilians. Forgive me for asking, but is your visit here authorized by General Santa Anna?"

The man turned to another of the civilians, and there was a small whisper, a reply, and Scott waited, thought, Where the hell is Trist? Now the first man faced him again, said, "General, I am informing you that as of eight o'clock last night, General Antonio Lopez de Santa Anna evacuated the city with his army. There is no official military presence in Mexico City."

There were voices now, men back in the shadows, responding to the man's words. Scott felt something open up in his brain. He straightened, a warmth began to fill him. He held it tightly, nodded, a small show of formality. "We are pleased to hear that, sir."

"General Scott, we are here to begin negotiations for your occupation of the city."

He could hear sounds echoing out through the camp, men running as the word spread. He waited, thought, Careful, do this right. No insults. "I am pleased you have come here."

He was beginning to feel foolish, thought, Negotiations. They want to negotiate . . . what? Damn it, where's Trist?

The men watched him, respectfully patient as he stared into the dark. He thought of the troops, the men who would wait for the daylight, who were ready to carry the attack again. They do not yet know, there is no enemy in front of them. There is only . . . the city.

"Gentlemen, I have the honor of informing you that negotiations are not necessary. This is a simple matter, I'm sure you will agree. In a short time, the sun will rise. Your people will be able to see that we have lined up a considerable number of cannon, all pointing to the center of the city. Assuming you are correct, and there is no armed resistance, the army of the United States of America will march into the heart of Mexico City, and establish command there."

The men glanced at each other, and Scott waited, thought, That may have been a bit blunt. He thought of Trist again, Save face, give them something to save face. He looked down, ran the words through his mind.

"The Mexican citizens may be assured that no harm will come to them. We have the utmost respect for your institutions. No harm will come to your city."

The man bowed, expressed his relief. "General Scott, the people of Mexico City will welcome you."

The man backed away, and Scott returned his bow, heard a commotion, then a voice, saw another man rushing forward. The man stopped, seemed to gather himself, emerged from the shadows with slow dignity, and Scott said, "Ah, Mr. Trist! Welcome to our . . . negotiation. Sorry you weren't here sooner. I believe we have finished."

Trist bowed slightly, and the Mexican spoke to him in Spanish, his tone quiet, respectful. Trist nodded, the polite smile slipping from his face. He looked at Scott, said something in Spanish, made another bow toward the men. The Mexican's conversation seemed urgent, and Scott watched, thought, At least he seems to know them. Wonder how badly I offended them?

The men bowed toward Scott again, moved away, and Trist moved up beside him. "I don't know what you said to them, but they were . . . impressed."

Scott shrugged, moved to the tent. "I was pretty plain about it. Trying to get the hang of this diplomatic business, remembered what you told me, tried to give them something to take back to their people. Told them I wouldn't destroy their city."

He moved into the tent, Trist following, and Trist said, "That's it? That's all you said?"

Scott moved to the chair, sat, saw the shadow again, said, "Something wrong? We got a problem?"

Trist shook his head, tried to say something, turned, took a step, seemed nervous now.

Scott said, "What, dammit?"

Trist stopped moving, looked at him now, said, "I'm not sure if this is a problem or not, sir. It seems . . . you have been offered an opportunity, sir. I'm not sure how to phrase this. It appears there is a position they feel needs to be filled, and they believe you are the man for the job."

Scott was confused now.

"Job? What the hell are you talking about?"

"General Scott, they have requested . . . they are wondering if you might accept the position of . . . dictator of Mexico."

36. SCOTT

SEPTEMBER FOURTEENTH, DAWN

THE DAYLIGHT CAME QUIETLY, AND HE STOOD OUTSIDE, WATCHED the glow spreading up behind the big mountains in the east. He had not slept, did not take time for the small naps, had spent the last hour of darkness putting the uniform together. He was assisted by the young Sergeant Dunnigan, the nervous little man picking through the wardrobe, holding each piece of clothing for Scott's inspection. When the ensemble was complete, Scott sent him away, began to dress himself with a slow, quiet intensity, creating the uniform one careful step at a time. He watched the process in the mirror, pulled and fastened and straightened each layer, smiling his approval at the thoroughness of his young sergeant, each piece of cloth cleaned and pressed perfectly, the gold braid freshly stitched, the medals shined. He had to kneel to see the hat, the thick burst of white feathers at the top, as he pulled and adjusted the slight tilt over his brow. When it was all in place, he had enjoyed a long moment with the mirror, simply admired, something he had not done in a long time.

He knew it was vanity, had long accepted what others said behind his back, knew that whether it was said in kindness or with mean spirit, "Fuss and Feathers" was an accurate description. On all the special occasions, he spent long minutes before the mirror, admiring the spectacle of himself, his uniform, his posture, all those things that created the *presence*. In Washington he had often gone through this same routine, had thought then, They may not care for me, but they cannot ignore me. But today would be very different. Today he would go before his army, and they would know by his appearance that this was his finest day as a soldier.

Now, in the light of the new morning, he stood outside the tent, a last inspection by the young sergeant, earning his smile, the approving nod. Now he was ready for his army.

He could hear the sounds growing around the headquarters, Harney's cavalry gathering, his own formal escort falling into formation. He looked toward the sun, was suddenly nervous, thought, One more moment. I had thought I would be ready for this. But, no. Give it time.

He felt his breathing, hard and sharp, felt the pounding in his chest, was embarrassed now. Stop this, you are the damned commander. You are not supposed to be this damned nervous. Commanders don't get excited.

He turned, saw Harney himself at the head of the column, tall in the saddle, his grim face calm, unchanged, and Scott thought, He doesn't show a damned thing, just another day to him, another ride. Well, dammit, he's wrong. This is a special day indeed. We're going to ride straight into the heart of that city. We're going to take charge.

He moved to the horse, admired the big white bay, standing perfectly still, and ran his hand along the horse's neck, ruffled the mane. Yes, you're ready for this day too. Very good, you've taken me this far. You should damned well take me the rest of the way. Quite a portrait, this uniform, this fine big horse.

He climbed up, the horse moving slightly, adjusting to the weight. Scott looked at Harney, read the impatience in his expression. Scott smiled. "Colonel, we have time today. No need to hurry."

Harney sniffed. "Certainly, sir. The men have had time to prepare, I imagine. Should be a nice reception."

Scott had assumed the troops would not wait for him, would move quickly at both gates once the daylight came to occupy the main buildings in the center of the city. Yes, he thought, there is still a damned race. By now Worth and Quitman are probably fighting a duel in the grand plaza to see who gets the prize.

He looked at Harney. "Actually, Colonel, perhaps we should ride. No time like the present."

THEY MOVED IN A QUIET, DELIBERATE PROCESSION, HARNEY holding his men in tight formation, the men out front carefully watching the rooftops. They moved toward the San Cosme gate, through the wide plaza, surveying the destruction. The fight had ripped through the homes, the small shops, a shattered church, its stained glass a spray of color on the gray rubble. He looked into the church itself, could see the uneven rows of pews, could see the people now, civilians, gathering, emerging from the darkness of the awful ruin. The people began to gather outside, lining the street, all faces watching him, staring at the grand uniform, this big man on the great horse. He passed through the gate itself now, saw more rubble, jagged masonry walls, pieces of a broken cannon. The streets narrowed, and he saw the crowds growing. Despite the mass of civilians, it was eerily quiet, the only sounds the click of the horses' hooves, the marching steps of the troops. The people seemed to be flowing up from some unseen place, like water from a spring. They came out into the light, shading their eyes, all staring at him, watching him move slowly past. He saw motion from above, saw blue, a soldier on the rooftop, a guard, saw more now, Worth's men moving to the edge, watching him as well. They held their muskets upright in quiet salute, and he let out a breath, thought, Of course, there is security. I hope . . . we don't need it.

The procession moved past a wide intersection, and he could see out in both directions, more civilians gathering, moving close to the column of horsemen, and now there were voices, men calling out, women responding, the sounds of children. He saw them coming out of the houses still, a great mass of people, the citizens of this grand old city, the people whose lives had been trampled by the turmoil and politics and the violence of war. They surged forward, held back only by Harney's horsemen, and the voices grew louder, the word passing from old to young, fathers to sons. He could see it in their faces, recognition, the crowd understanding what this was, why these men marched slowly past on horseback, what was so important about this small parade. Hands began reaching out toward him now, some pointing, some beginning to wave. Then he heard his name, carried forward like a wave, saw one woman step close to the horses, the cavalry officer holding her away, but the woman would not stop, pushed past the horse. Harney said something, a quick shout, but the woman slipped behind Harney's horse, moving close to Scott. She raised a cloth bag, and he watched her hands, reaching inside, felt a cold stab, heard Harney again, thought, A weapon . . . a pistol, and then the woman drew out something else from the bag, a glorious red rose. She reached out to him, held it up, and the guard stopped behind her, his sword raised, ready to strike her down, but Scott said, "No! It's all right."

The woman ignored the men moving close behind her, stared at him still, held the rose up toward him, and he reached out, took it from her hand. "Thank you. *Gracias, señorita.*"

She said something he could not understand, but he saw her expression, the emotion it revealed, her eyes holding on to a deep sadness. He saw her age now, older, the time etched hard in a face that had seen much, that knew something of war and death and loss. She did not smile, looked at the rose now in his hand, backed away, moved past the guards, out through the throng of people, disappeared in the crowd.

Harney gave an order, and the column began to move again. Scott spurred the horse out of instinct, moved as well. He searched the crowd still, thought, That face, the sadness. But there is no anger. She wants this whole business to be over. He looked at the rose in his hand, shook his head, thought, A pistol. There's a lesson. Don't underestimate these people. Don't assume the politicians control the hearts of their people. Not all of them are our enemies.

The voices came again, the street filled with sounds now, and he heard his name again, the hands waving, the faces alive with celebration. He saw a ragged uniform, a Mexican soldier, and the man was waving as well, another part of the joy of the growing crowd. He nodded to the man, a small salute, and the man smiled, a broad, beaming grin, and Scott could feel the man's joy, said to Harney, "It appears, Colonel, they're happy to see us."

Harney did not look at him, was watching the guards on the rooftops, said, "I would accept that as a positive sign, sir."

Scott heard the flatness in Harney's voice, smiled. "Yes, Colonel. I believe this means . . . we won."

THE SOUNDS WERE STILL GROWING, BUT NOW THE WORDS WERE in English, the crowds wearing blue uniforms. The streets were lined with soldiers, ragged, filthy troops, many with bandages, torn uniforms, other signs of the fight. There were muskets, all raised high, hats in the air, and he could not help but smile, had seen this before, always drew excitement from the troops. But now there was something new, something missing. The grim reality of the next duty, the next fight, of *tomorrow*, was not in these men. The cheers were for him, would always be for him, but he could feel the difference, something beyond the usual rally around the flag, the victory celebration. Even when the victory had been clear and glorious, the grand sweep at Cerro Gordo, the great triumph of Chapultepec, the men cheered him with relieved exhaustion, finding some piece of themselves to feel good about. But the reserve was always there, the losses fresh in their minds, the friends who were gone, or those who might be gone the next time.

But today the celebration was complete, the reserve gone. They cheered each other as they cheered for him, the emotion pouring out, uncontrollable, tears and laughter.

Ahead the road opened up into a wide plaza. He rode to the end of the street, but the soldiers were held back by officers, the great open plaza nearly empty. He stopped the horse, heard Harney order the halt. He stared across to the National Palace, and close by he could see the spires of the grand cathedral. On the roof of the palace a line of soldiers snapping to attention, above them the American flag snapping in the breeze. He smiled, thought, Of course. They couldn't wait after all. He rode forward, alone, sat up tall in the saddle, heard the roar behind him, the soldiers all watching him. He felt his throat tighten, thought, No, not now, don't let go . . . just a moment. He blinked hard through the tears he could not stop, saw the wave of color, the Stars and Stripes moving with a small breeze. He took a long breath, but the emotion would not pass, and he lifted his hand slowly, stared at the flag, raised a salute, held it for a long moment.

Behind him the voices of the troops exploded into a salute of their own, and he turned, looked back to the mass filling the street. The voices were echoing down other streets as well, Quitman's troops, and he thought, Good discipline, good order. They held back, waited for me to arrive. Generous, indeed. But this is for them, this place is *theirs*. He raised his hat again, held it high, answered the voices of the men, the narrow streets now rivers of sound and motion extending away from the plaza. He could not stop the tears, did not try, thought, I should say something, tell them something. But the words were choked away, and he thought, No, let it go. There are no words to describe this moment. They will remember. There will never be another day like this.

T HE STAFF FILED BEHIND HIM, AND HE HELD THEM IN A TIGHT formation across from the entrance to the palace. He could see the Mexican officials waiting for him, other faces at the windows. The staff was beside him now, and he held the horse still, thought, Ceremony, show them respect. He saw horses now, officers moving toward him from across the plaza, waited, began to smile, thought, Well, how about this. It's both of them, together. And no duel.

Worth and Quitman were side by side, rode up close. Both men stopped, saluted him, and Scott said, "Good morning, gentlemen. Everything in order?"

Worth replied, "General Scott, as you can see, we have occupied the government buildings. The government ministers are awaiting your presence, sir."

Scott looked again at the palace, the small crowd of men in black suits, thought, My God, it's as simple as this. We will just walk in. He could not help thinking of the word, had begun to think of Cortez, the awful comparison. We walk into that building . . . as *conquerors*. He glanced up at the flag again, thought, What does this mean for us, beyond Polk, beyond this war? Our flag flies over the capital of a foreign nation. Surely, it was never supposed to be like this.

He shook his head. No, this is not for you to decide, to pass judgment. The duty is right there, in that building. You're just an old soldier who is supposed to be having his day. This is your finest moment. Enjoy it, dammit.

He looked along the line, saw the staff watching him, waiting for the order. He glanced at Quitman, still stiffly formal, solemnly dignified. That's what this is about. This is what soldiers do, what inspires armies to fight, this moment. It's time for us to . . . claim the prize.

September fifteenth

Worth stood in front of him, the frown creasing his face. Scott waited for it, thought, All right, let him have his say. Get it over with. He expected anger, more of Worth's strange bitterness. Worth seemed to search for the words before finally speaking.

"Sir, was your decision based on something I did? Could I have done something differently?"

It was not what Scott expected, and he said, "General, you seem to be taking this decision . . . personally. I don't have any reason to keep you in some corner. He's simply more qualified. Besides, as I'm sure you are aware, there was some considerable noise made about a . . . race."

Worth seemed wounded by the word, said, "Certainly not, sir."

The voice was flat, a lame denial, and Scott said, "Let's make this brief, General. John Quitman is a lawyer, and from what I hear, back in Mississippi he was pretty good at it. It seemed entirely appropriate to appoint him Military Governor of Mexico City. He earned it. If anyone should be wrinkled up about this, it's Gideon Pillow. Funny I haven't heard much from him. He's too preoccupied with that thorn in his foot . . . oh, forgive me, his *wound*. I suspect he's got his eye focused on going home, probably doesn't want to stay down here any longer than he has to. Glory awaits, I'm sure." Careful, he thought, stay with the issue at hand. "Quitman's volunteers fought as well as anyone in the army. And, after all, General, it was Quitman's division who broke into the city first. Even if I didn't pay much attention to all that race business, you cannot deny that . . . you did."

Worth nodded slowly, smiled now. "Suppose I did, sir."

"Face it, General, it's not exactly a pleasant job. He has to sort out all the civilian matters, all the complaints. It's a grand sounding title. But it's not a job I'd want myself."

Worth thought a moment, seemed resigned now. "No, sir. I suppose not."

"Good. Anything else?"

Worth seemed to energize, said, "Yes, sir. The sniping is getting worse, sir. We know now that Santa Anna opened up the jails on his way out. We're being fired at by criminals, all over the city. It seemed to be little more than a nuisance at first. But there are also reports of Mexican troops infiltrating the city, out of uniform. There's no safe place to walk, and no man dares to go out alone. As you know, sir, Colonel Garland was seriously wounded by a sniper. He will recover, but it could have been much worse."

Scott nodded. "I know about Colonel Garland, I know about the reports. The war is not over, General. We simply have to keep up the pressure. Work the streets, house-to-house if you have to. Don't hesitate to use power. Take some artillery, make a presence. If you have to level a few buildings to make a point, do it. Spread the word, 'You shoot at us, we'll take down your house.' But keep it orderly, keep your men in control. No looting, no reprisals. We will not become a mob here, General."

Worth seemed to glow at Scott's words. "My thoughts exactly, sir!"

"Good. We through?"

Worth thought a moment, said, "Sir, I was hoping . . . there would be time for you to speak to the reporters. There are a number of men here from the foreign papers, apparently have been here from the beginning. I'm hearing requests for your time, sir."

Scott grunted, thought, Bad enough to be misquoted in American papers. Now the whole world hopes I'll say something idiotic. To hell with them.

"General, I don't have time for the luxury of interviews."

Worth seemed frustrated, strangely nervous, said, "Sir, you *must* . . . you have to speak to them, open the dialogue. If you don't, none of us can either."

Scott sniffed, thought, So, of course, that's it. They know the rules, no discussion of military affairs that don't begin in this office. And they're all itching to talk, to tell grand tales of their exploits. That's reason enough for me *not* to.

"I'm glad you understand protocol, General. There will be plenty of time for official reports, plenty of opportunity for everyone to get his name in the paper. Anything else?"

Worth took a breath, and Scott saw the man's frown, the disappointment etched on his face. "No, sir. Thank you for the time, sir."

Worth moved out of the office, and Scott waited for the door to close before he pushed the chair back from the desk. They'll all push me now, he thought. They all want to talk about it, make damned sure their names are mentioned. It's time for the politics again, the great clash of ambition. And out there in the field, their men are still getting shot at. His anger rose, unexpectedly; he had not wanted to feel this way. He picked up a pen from the desk, rolled it hard between his hands, his heart pounding. This is a time for celebration, and still they find a way to infect everything with their pettiness. How dare they feather their own nests, how dare they look to the newspapers, while their soldiers are still under fire. He slapped the pen down on the desk, stood now, moved to the tall window, looked out toward the grand cathedral. He tried to relax, put the anger out of his mind, thought, Such a beautiful place, a grand old city, a country with so much of the charm of old Europe. And such chaos in running it.

They unify in war, fall into line behind one strong leader, but Santa Anna goes away, and the problems return. He thought of the Congress, the ministers. No one has come forward yet. Santa Anna is still out there somewhere, that damned charisma of his, and he still has followers. No one here wants to risk offending him. They know we'll leave eventually, and when we do, anyone who dealt kindly with us could find himself branded a traitor. Hell, Santa Anna or someone just like him could march right back in here and take over. Who would stop him? The best they can do, the best idea anyone came up with around here . . . *me*. Let me do it. And not as president, not even some kind of occupying administrator. No, let's just jump right to dictator, another strong man to run the show.

He heard noise outside the office, voices, and there was a knock on the door. He turned, said, "What is it?"

The door opened, and he saw his son-in-law, and the young man said, "General, it's all arranged, sir. They're waiting for you in that big staff room down the hall."

"What the hell are you talking about, Major?"

"The reporters, sir. General Worth had said there was a great need. I assumed you'd enjoy the attention, sir. They're quite eager, and I understand the Mexican government is providing transportation to the coast, so they can get their reports out quickly. They're ready whenever you are, sir."

He felt the heat rising, said, "Reporters? Now? Who the hell authorized you to bring in . . . *reporters?*"

The young man's face drained of color, and he said, "I thought it was a good idea, sir. General Worth and I discussed it earlier. He agreed, was very supportive. I assumed you'd want to get it over with as soon as possible. They've been waiting all day."

"Damn!" Scott turned to the window again, thought, Damn you, William Worth. I have no choice now. They think they've been invited by *me*, and if I send them away, they'll write God-knows-what. And sure as hell, something will get back to Washington. He took a breath, said, "What are they expecting me to say? How much time do I have to give them?"

"I don't know, sir. A few words, I guess. Take questions."

Scott moved toward the door, reached for his hat, saw the young man pressing back into the wall, waiting for him to move past. He stopped, put a finger in the young man's face.

"Major, if you or General Worth ever make another *arrangement* without consulting me, I'm sending you *both* out on sniper patrol."

He moved into the hallway, could hear the hum of voices, the open doorway at the end of the wide corridor. He straightened his coat, saw a uniform rounding a corner, a tall thin man, the familiar face.

"Ah, General Twiggs! Excellent, good timing. I need some support, reinforcing. Follow me, please."

Twiggs seemed confused, said, "Why? Where are we going?"

"Reporters, General. Foreigners, Europeans, hell I don't know. I've been ambushed into talking to them. You can help."

Twiggs stopped, said in a whisper, "Reporters? But I came to see you about . . . God, no, I can't talk to reporters. I have nothing to say. I can't, sir."

Scott saw how wide-eyed he was, thought, My God, I've never seen him look this way. He's . . . afraid. Looks like he's going to cry.

"All right, General. I'll go it alone. Wait for me in my office. If my son-in-law gives you any trouble, shoot him."

He turned, moved toward the open doorway as Twiggs moved quickly away. He waited a moment, stepped into the room. Faces turned, men in suits, and the room was abruptly quiet. He moved through the center of the room, saw a small podium, moved behind it, said, "Hello, gentlemen. I have nothing prepared. You have questions, I'll try to answer them."

There were small sounds of shuffling paper, then one man cleared his throat, raised a hand. He was small, bony, and wore round glasses on a long hooked nose. Scott pointed to him, nodded.

"General, is the war over?"

Scott heard the accent, thought, French maybe. "We have won the Mexican capital. We have whipped Santa Anna's army completely. But, sir, I am just a soldier. It was my job to make the war. It is up to the politicians, to the men who write treaties, to make the peace."

He stopped, thought, Good, I like that. This might not be so bad after all.

Another man motioned, short, heavy, thickly bearded. "It is widely accepted, *señor*, that the United States has waged a bully's war. I believe that is the English word for it. Mexico was a weak adversary, helpless, much inferior for your army. Do you have a response?"

Scott let the man's words hang in the air. Of course, they would all ask this. He looked down, thought, Remember this, you'll be asked again. He looked squarely at the man. "*Señor*, there are a good many American soldiers buried in the soil of this land who were killed by the soldiers of that army you call inferior. General Santa Anna brought an army to the field that outnumbered us by three to one. But to say that we prevailed because the Mexican fighting man was inferior to us is a grave injustice to soldiers of both sides. I cannot tell you why the United States won this war. History will make that judgment. If there is a difference between our people, it might have something to do with leadership. Sir, the people of Mexico did not elect Mr. Santa Anna to lead them. He commanded his army, his generals, by the strength of his hand, by intimidation. It's not a system that works very well, anywhere. In our system, our President, Mr. Polk, appoints me to command—"

He stopped, felt the words choking him, swirling around him in nonsense. His face began to flush, the heat filling his head. The journalists watched him, seemed to lean forward, waiting for his next words. He tried to breathe, held the podium with his hands, thought, This was not such a good idea after all. They want a damned speech.

"Enough of this, gentlemen. I can't explain war to you. I can't explain it to myself. You all go write up whatever you like, send it on back to wherever you're from. Print whatever you like, you're going to do that anyway. But I would ask you . . . no, I challenge you, any one of you, to write about what really happened here. I am surrounded by generals who can already taste their glory, are already imagining the great big parade that waits for them back home. I've heard that General Taylor is being asked to run for President. Well, that's all fine with me. But I challenge you to tell your people what these soldiers did. Men on both sides were ordered to march into the guns of the enemy, and they obeyed, they stood tall, and most of the time they did not run. The Mexican soldier who stood up to us at San Cosme gate is as much a hero as the man who finally pushed him back. A great many men bled and died on the ground around this city. They marched into the fight because their commanders told them to. That is what being a soldier is about, gentlemen."

He paused, felt the heat slipping away, felt a rhythm now, the words building inside him.

"I have read how newspapers describe war. I have seen accounts of great battles, always quick to single out which general did God-knows-what wonderful thing, but I have never read, anywhere, what it *felt* like. I have never read about the soldier who takes his bayonet and charges the man who fires the cannon, or the cavalryman who spurs his horse straight into the face of a thousand muskets. I have never read of the man who is *first* up the ladder, climbing over a wall into certain death. Generals aren't heroes. The heroes are still out there, patrolling the streets, walking their post, or . . . buried in that ground. That's my challenge to you. Write about *that*. And leave the politics and the damned generals out of it."

He stopped, and there were no more words. He saw nods, men writing on pads of paper. He stepped away from the podium, moved through the silent room, into the corridor. He stopped, was surprised to see a group of officers, an audience gathered outside the room. He saw Twiggs, and his son-in-law, more familiar faces. They spoke in low voices, *sir*, and he moved past them, felt his uniform cold with sweat, his heart beating heavily. He stopped again, looked at his son-in-law, said, "Don't tell General Worth, Major, but I rather enjoyed that. . . ."

37. LEE

SEPTEMBER TWENTIETH

THE STREETS HAD BEEN CLEARED, THE SNIPERS NOW GONE, AND
the worst behavior of the American soldiers had been brought
to a halt. Despite Scott's published orders, despite efforts from
the senior commanders to avoid problems with the civilians, there
had been looting, mindless destruction, the soldiers letting go of the
months of anger, all the emotions boiling over, the horror of death and
fear replaced by a need for revenge. Scott's orders had been strict and
clear, respect for the city, for the citizens, but in the end the emotion
had won out, reinforced by liquor and temptation. The spoils of war
were easy to find in a place where the people could no longer protect
themselves.

Order had finally come with the silence from the rooftops, when
the threat from the hidden muskets of the snipers ended. With the
enemy finally gone, the attention turned inward, and the officers could
finally take control. The sources of liquor began to dry up, the guards
could patrol the streets without risk of attack, and finally the army
took to their own care. The camps were spread throughout the city,
every open plaza, every square, the officers finding quarters in the
larger haciendas. The wounded were tended to, the uniforms cleaned
and repaired. The nights were growing cooler now, and there were parties, a spirit of playfulness the men had not felt since the war began.

There were still details to work out, and so, technically, the war
was still in place. They all knew there was some kind of treaty, men
working long hours behind closed doors, the strange and sickly Nicholas Trist, the Mexican officials who still insisted on some fragment of
honor. Whatever final document emerged from behind the doors of

378

the palace would not matter to most of the men. What they waited for was that final command, each day bringing them closer to the words they dreamed about, the order that would take them to the coast again, where the big ships waited, the ships that would take them home.

L EE RODE SLOWLY, TURNED HIS HORSE INTO A NARROW STREET, passed through a cloud of wonderful smells. There were no shops now, the street lined tightly with small houses, and he stopped the horse, thought, No, wrong again.

He had been advised to take an escort, but the men were busy with their own duties, or they were out, like he was, exploring the city for the first time. He had thought, Just stay out in the open, stay with people, it should be all right. But now, as the horse moved back along the same street he had come, he felt a nervous stab in his gut, thought, Admit it, you're lost.

He had gone beyond the big plaza, searching the small shops, where the boisterous commerce of the city, the joyful enthusiasm of the street vendors, was returning to full speed. He had bought toys for the children, bright feathers on straw animals, the gifts that would eventually find their way to Virginia. But there had been a treat for him as well, for the eye of the engineer. He had marveled at the architecture, the beauty of the stone and tile, even the most modest shop adorned with great care. Everywhere there was color, from the walls of the buildings to the dresses of the women. As he rode farther away from the camps of the army, he had felt more out of place, thought, There is no enemy here, no evidence of war at all. I'm just . . . a visitor.

He knew the sun would set soon, moved the horse at a faster pace, saw a wider street ahead, felt a wave of relief, assumed it must lead to the plaza. He stopped the horse, was bathed in more smells, something sweet, suddenly felt the rumble of hunger. He looked around, saw a narrow alley, dark, a small glow of light from a window, a small sign in Spanish, *Pan*. Perfect, bread, eat something. He climbed down from the horse, saw motion in the window, shadows, said aloud, "Hello? *El pan, por favor?*"

A face appeared in the window, an old woman, and she looked at him strangely, said something he could not understand. He felt frustrated, thought, You should know how to speak to these people. This is their country. He put a hand up to his mouth, motioned as though eating, said, *"El pan?"*

The old woman shook her head, spoke a long sentence of words that meant nothing to Lee, and she pointed down the alleyway, seemed anxious now. He looked that way, saw only dark walls, and he thought, All right, no bread. He bowed, said, *"Gracias, señora."*

He moved back to the horse, sensed something, stopped, saw a man moving toward him from behind the horse. Lee felt an icy chill, watched the man's hands, saw a large coil of rope cradled in them. The man said something, and Lee saw his smile, dull yellow teeth, saw him touch the side of the horse. The man now took a step closer to him, his free hand slowly loosening the coils, the smile gone now. Lee put a hand on his pistol, thought, It's loaded . . . I think it's loaded. He drew the pistol, let it hang low, pointing at the ground, and the man looked at it, smiled again, more words, and now stepped back. The rope was still now, and the man nodded to Lee, said, *"Buenos noches, señor."*

Lee looked at the horse. "Yes, *noches.* Getting late. Excuse me, sir. I'll be leaving now."

Lee moved slowly to the horse, the man still watching the pistol. Lee climbed the horse, the pistol still in his hand, and he turned the horse back to the open street, spurred hard, and the animal jumped forward. He did not look back, saw the light ahead from the wider avenue, moved the horse quickly around the corner. He felt his heart pounding, gripped the reins with icy fingers, put the pistol in its holster. He rode hard, the hoofbeats rattling across the stone pavement, and he saw more people now, heads turning, watching him move past. He saw a familiar storefront, a cluster of black-haired children, pointing and laughing at him as he rode by, and he slowed the horse, thought, Enough, you're all right now. He stopped, looked behind him, the street busy with people, some looking at him, many more ignoring him, doing their own business. He laughed. No need to report this. General Scott would not appreciate that his staff officer had been sent in a mad retreat by one man armed with a rope.

He looked around the familiar street, turned the horse toward another avenue, knew it would take him to the great plaza. The sun was nearly gone, the street coming alive with flickers of lamplight from the windows. He rode through more of the smells, felt the rumble again, thought of the old woman. She was either out of bread, he thought, or she knew I wouldn't live long enough to pay her. He laughed again. Next time, Captain Lee, take an escort.

October fifth

He climbed the short white steps, moved into the grand hacienda that was now his quarters. He passed a group of officers engaged in intense conversation, moved into the hallway, toward the door to his room. He heard voices coming from an open doorway down the hall, smiled at the sound of one familiar voice. He moved that way, stopped at the door, peered around, saw Johnston sitting on the bed, two other men standing, the discussion a flurry of arms and hands.

Johnston saw him, said, "All right, enough talk. I have to make preparations."

The two men glanced at Lee, gave smiles, short nods, then moved past, disappeared down the hall.

Lee stepped into the room, said, "Sorry. Didn't mean to intrude."

Johnston shook his head, laughed briefly. "You're too polite, Robert. Politics . . . that's all they want to talk about. Who's getting promoted, who's getting the recognition, who's been slighted. They argue about who's the greater hero, which general should become President."

Johnston began to pull on a boot, and Lee saw he was wearing his dress uniform, the pants a crisp white. Johnston grunted, his face a twist of pain. Lee stepped forward. "Here, let me help." He pulled the boot up, and Johnston let out a breath.

"Still feel it. Hurts when I try to do anything at all." He looked at Lee, lowered his voice. "I didn't say that. Don't tell anyone. They tried to keep me out of action as it was. The wound at Cerro Gordo was bad enough. Seems I can't keep myself out of trouble."

Lee stepped back, looked at the rumpled bandage that lay on the bed. "How bad?"

Johnston pushed the bandage off the bed. "Nothing serious. More aggravation than anything else. But, three times . . . three holes in my uniform at Chapultepec. I'm lucky, Robert. I'm blessed. Any one of them could have killed me. I should have been dead at Cerro Gordo."

Lee moved to a small chair and sat. "God has something else in mind for you, some road you haven't traveled yet."

Johnston reached for the second boot, slipped it over his foot. "I had thought it was the infantry, the Almighty deciding I needed to pull my head out of engineering manuals and lead foot soldiers into battle."

Lee wasn't sure if Johnston was serious, saw the man's face twist in pain again as the boot slid on. Johnston leaned back on his elbows, took a deep breath. "I insist you try it some time, Robert. I swear, going up that road, leading those men into Chapultepec, it was horrible, it was magnificent. I'm counting on God to agree with me on this. It's what I was born to do. It's what I *want* to do."

Lee shrugged his shoulders. "I don't know what God expects from us. But if you are happy charging into musket fire . . . and God has anointed you with a talent for avoiding mortal wounds . . . then, by all means, it sounds like you've found your calling. I just hope God doesn't change his mind without telling you."

Johnston looked at him, surprised. "Humor? From Captain Lee? God works in mysterious ways. Well, I should have my chance to find out. There's still quite a bit of guerrilla activity. Rumor has it that Santa Anna himself is still leading troops, is making a move toward Puebla again, hopes to cut us off from the coast."

Lee nodded. "Heard that, yes. There's a column of troops coming from Vera Cruz, reinforcements. From what I hear, General Twiggs is preparing to go east, take command. If there's a fight, if things get hot again, this war could be a long way from over. It puts a lot of pressure on those people doing the negotiating. Makes it so important to get the treaty signed."

A quiet moment passed before Johnston said, "So how about you? You still going to stay with the engineers?"

"Certainly. It's what I'm comfortable with. I've already been assigned to do some mapmaking, prepare some detailed sketches of the valley. I might be here for a while yet."

"Comfortable? I'm not convinced, Robert. There's more to a man's career than settling for something that makes him comfortable. What about challenge? What about the unknown?"

Lee did not answer, thought now of Henry Hunt, the lone cannon in front of San Cosme, one man's assault that opened the hole. Hunt survived, was considered a hero, and Lee had wondered about that, how Hunt felt now, what had changed.

"I'm ready for whatever task God assigns me. If it is in His plan for me to lead troops, or charge some enemy somewhere, then I will obey the calling. You can't decide in advance what you are meant to do. It may be that I'm meant to be an engineer. Mapmaking can be interesting."

Johnston stared at him for a moment. "If you say so, Robert. How long you figure to be here? Word is, the infantry will occupy all the outposts between here and the coast, secure the route, get rid of as much guerrilla activity as we can. Shouldn't take more than a couple of months. Once we have a treaty, most of us . . . maybe all of us can go home."

"I hope to finish my work by then, but I don't know. General Scott was most insistent on detailed topography of the valley. It might take three or four months to complete."

"You don't sound too sad about that. You may be the only man in the army who isn't chewing nails to leave here. Peace means boredom. Especially for us men of action."

Lee smiled, but there was something serious in Johnston's eyes, something beyond Johnston's good mood. Lee waited a moment before asking, "What about Preston? Have you made the arrangements yet?"

Johnston's smile faded. "Working on it. As soon as I get orders to move to the coast, I'll have his body shipped with the supply wagons. He should be buried in Virginia." He stopped, looked toward the window.

Lee said, "I'm sorry. It's not my place. I shouldn't have said anything."

Johnston continued to stare away for a moment, then looked at him, pushed the sadness away, sat up. "You seen my hat? Had to get a new feather, somebody sat on the old one."

Lee focused on the uniform again. "Why are you so formally dressed? Is there a reception?"

Johnston looked at him, puzzled. "As a matter of fact, Robert, there is. If anyone should know that, it should be you. General Scott is toasting the officers tonight, the grand ballroom of the palace."

Lee jumped to his feet. "That's tonight? Now?"

A broad smile split Johnston's face. "I was wondering where you were all day. Everybody around here's been preening and feathering and blowing themselves up like balloons, all hoping to catch the general's eye. Not that it should matter to you. You've already made your impression. But you should attend."

Lee felt a small panic. "Yes, of course. I had intended to. I lost track of time. The work . . ."

Johnston walked over to the window, limping slightly. "You better get moving. There's already a crowd gathering in the plaza."

The sounds of voices, calls of greeting, laughter, came in through the window.

"Yes, won't take me long. I'll see you there."

Johnston was staring out the window, waved now to someone below, and Lee backed away, moved into the hall. He opened the door to his room, moved into musty darkness, then pulled open the window and looked out. He saw clusters of blue, small groups of officers talking, gesturing. Men were moving quickly, joining their friends, and Lee watched the faces, so many familiar now, saw many of the younger men, the junior officers, thought, No, they're not so young anymore. He saw one man approach a group of his friends, and the hands went up, and he heard the men all saying the same thing: *"Major!"*

The word was exaggerated, and Lee smiled. Promotions. There are a great many promotions now. He backed away from the window, thought, They deserve it, certainly, all of them. Maybe even you. He put that out of his mind, thought, No, this is not a time to flatter yourself. Do not concern yourself with personal achievement. He could hear the voices again, the celebration, felt a small shadow of guilt. You have no right to fantasize, to daydream about your own glory. Your place is already chosen. Your only responsibility is to do the job you are given. He thought of Johnston, the satisfaction at his new command, leading men into battle, thought of Magruder, Hunt, the artillerymen so possessive of their guns. God has opened up their future, shown them a path to follow. Not all of us are destined to have such adventure. Some of us must . . . draw maps.

He felt a small wave of depression, pushed it away, looked for some distraction, put his hand on the letter to Mary he had begun the night before. I should finish this tonight, he thought. Maybe in the next few days, we will finally be able to send the mail. So many letters, so many experiences waiting to be told.

He put the letter in a small drawer, closed it, looked again in the mirror, saw his rough beard, the accumulated dirt of the many days in the countryside. The voices outside were fading, the men beginning to move away, the spirit of the party flowing toward the grand palace.

H E HAD DONE THE BEST HE COULD WITH THE UNIFORM, COULD not scrub away all the stains, a stubborn smear of dirt on the white pants, the dust of the campaign finding its way inside his trunk. He had put the hat on carefully, the final step, posed for the mirror, appraising, frowning, could not help feeling sloppy. He had even considered staying away, spending the evening by himself, finishing the letter to Mary. But the image of General Scott would not leave him, and he knew, sloppy or not, he would be expected.

He stood now in the entranceway to the great ballroom, the noise of the men rolling over him, loud talk, friendship, relief, joyous congratulations, all the emotions letting loose from men who share the bond, share the experience of the great fight. He waited, watched them, could see the stains on the dress uniforms, many worse than his, and there was no mention, no one seemed to care. He glanced down, shook his head, thought, What does it matter? What matters is the men who are here, who brought this army to this place. That's the point of this whole evening, for General Scott to acknowledge them, to shake their hands, all of them.

He stepped into the room, saw men holding glasses of wine, cigar smoke rising in great clouds, the voices loud all around him. He moved past one circle of men, saw Magruder, surrounded by men with the red in their uniforms, the artillerymen. Magruder noticed him, nodded, gave him a friendly smile, and Lee nodded as well. He saw then the young lieutenant, the strange man from the mountains, Jackson, who did not look at him, seemed awkward, uncomfortable. Lee could hear the comments, all directed at Jackson, and one man said, "This poor chap could not find one quiet place to hide in this entire war! He couldn't help but be promoted. The Mexicans wouldn't leave him alone!"

There was laughter, a hand slapping Jackson's back, and the young man continued to frown, red-faced, staring at the floor. Magruder said, "He gets any more brevets, he'll outrank me! Hell, he stays here long enough, he'll outrank General Scott!"

Lee moved away from the new burst of laughter, could see to the front of the room, a wide platform, chairs arranged in a neat row. He moved that way, thought, The chairs might be for the general staff. I suppose they expect me . . . up there. He searched the crowd, looked for Johnston, saw more familiar faces. Moving close to the platform, he saw the young Scott stepping up on the far end, moving unsteadily to a chair. Lee climbed up as well, moved across the platform, close to the young man, said, "Good evening, Major. Do you wish me to sit up here?"

The young man looked at him, his face flushed, and waved an arm absently. "Sit wherever you like, Captain. No one will chase you away."

Lee backed away, thought, He is . . . intoxicated. He looked away, did not want to see this, not tonight. He saw other members of the general staff moving up, climbing the short steps, Colonel Hitchcock, Scott's Inspector General, followed by two more men. Lee moved to a chair, sat, looked out over the great crowd of officers, the room a haze of cigar smoke. He saw movement in the crowd, men parting, making a path, saw General Twiggs now, moving to the platform.

Twiggs climbed up, said, "I suppose generals are allowed up here."

Lee moved to the end of the row of chairs, watched Pillow and

Worth, the two men smiling, exchanging brief greetings with the officers. Pillow stepped up on the platform, looked at Twiggs, gave him a polite nod that Twiggs seemed to ignore. Pillow looked down the row, moved toward the staff, held out his hand to greet each of them.

He stopped in front of Lee, and Lee took the offered hand, but Pillow did not look at him. "Wonderful event, Captain Lee, wonderful."

Pillow was past him then, using the same words as he moved down the line until he took his seat as well. Lee looked down to the end of the platform where Worth, sitting now, was saying something to Twiggs, who tried to ignore him as well. Lee watched their faces, the two men falling silent, stoic, staring out at their officers, waiting patiently for the duty, the formality, of the evening to begin.

Lee let his eyes drift over the crowd, searched for Johnston again. He focused on the entranceway, saw guards stepping crisply into the room, standing at attention on each side of the door. The room began to quiet, heads turning, and Lee thought, Time to stand up. The men on both sides of him stood as well, and now he saw Scott, filling the entrance, the feather from the tall hat brushing the top of the doorway. One of the guards shouted out, "*Atten . . . hut!*"

The room was silent, and Scott began to move through the path opening in the crowd. Lee watched him come, saw the uniform, perfect, the medals on Scott's chest arranged in marvelous display, the long sword hanging stiffly by his side. Lee could see the quiet pride on the old man's face, the glow of respect from the men around him, the reverent silence as he passed by. Lee's throat tightened and he thought, My God, he looks . . . magnificent. How could any of us believe this night would be ours? This is for *him*. We will remember him long after he has forgotten us.

Scott reached the platform, moved slowly, heavily, up the steps. He stood and faced his staff, the commanders, the men standing stiffly in a neat row before him. Scott nodded, smiled, looked into the face of each man, and Lee waited for it, saw Scott now looking at him, saw a smile, then Scott was past him, moving toward the end of the row. The greetings complete, Scott turned, faced the room, said aloud, "At ease, gentlemen! This is a party, not an inspection!"

The sounds began to flow through the room again, men gathering at one end of the room, wine being poured, great trays of food. Lee was suddenly very hungry, thought, Should have gone there first. But not now. You'll have to wait. He saw a waiter, a young soldier in a neat white uniform, and the man held a tray of wineglasses as he stepped up to the platform. The officers reached out, each man removing a glass, and the waiter passed by Lee, who shook his head, no. Scott took a glass, looked at Lee. "Temperance is a virtue, Mr. Lee. However, quenching thirst is a necessity."

Scott drank from the glass, emptied it, handed it to the young man, turned to the room again, stood quietly, waited for the return of their attention. Lee watched the crowd, saw the men closest to the platform turning to face Scott, the talk growing quiet again. Scott held up his hands, the talk fading, and he waited for a moment, until the room was silent.

"Gentlemen, there will be no speeches, no politics, no long-winded blather. I would like each of you to move up here in line, a reception line. I will shake your hands, every one of you. Many of you . . . I do not know your names. Please forgive me. I expect to hear you introduce yourself. No one in this room should leave here without my hearing his name."

Scott stepped back, close to Lee, and the staff all stood now, lined up on either side of Scott. Lee moved forward, was next to Scott, thought, No, this is not right. I should be down the line. This does not look good.

He glanced to the side, saw the young Scott looking at him, standing unsteadily, moving behind the line of men, and Lee stepped back, whispered, "Major, here. Stand here."

The young man looked at him, said, "He would prefer . . . you. . . ."

Lee stared to the front, thought, This is not the time, and moved to the side, made a space between him and Scott.

He felt the young man move in beside him, and the young man whispered, "You're a kind man, Captain."

Scott now motioned toward the room, waved them forward, and the officers began to fall in line. The first man stepped up, moved slowly, awkwardly, down the line, took the hands of each of the command staff. He stopped in front of Scott, snapped a salute, said, "Lieutenant Landers Grey, sir. Sixth Infantry."

Scott repeated the man's name, and the line began to flow past now, developing a slow rhythm, the good order of men who understand order. Lee shook their hands, felt their hard grip, soon felt his own hand beginning to ache, thought, This is for politicians. I still have to hold a pencil.

The line moved past, some men making the brief nod, the men Scott recognized, others waiting to see if he would remember them from a chance meeting, some event, some command he'd issued. When the silent moment told them Scott did not recall them, the men would give their names, salute him, their pride slightly bruised. Others did not wait for recognition, would not chance embarrassing the commander. They gave their names when everyone knew the names were familiar, and Lee enjoyed hearing some of the senior officers make their own introductions, Bennett Riley, Persifor Smith, men whose confidence did not require a boost from Scott.

As the line passed and the men left the platform, the crowd at the wine bottles grew and the sounds from beyond the platform became more festive. Lee still shook the hands, felt a dull tingling in his right hand, could still hear Scott speaking to each man, making some comment, something the man would take home. Lee saw Magruder, the group of artillerymen following behind him, and Magruder said to Lee, "You may check my aim any time, Captain!"

Lee smiled, and Magruder moved to Scott, exchanging more comments. Lee saw the young Jackson now, the man stiff and formal, the eyes staring straight ahead. Lee took the hand, and just as quickly the hand was gone, Jackson's eyes staring through him, moving past him now. Jackson reached Scott, said, "Brevet Major Thomas J. Jackson, sir. Magruder's battery."

A silent moment passed. Scott suddenly dropped his hand, left Jackson's hand in the air, said, "I don't know if I will shake hands with Mr. Jackson!"

There was a quiet hush, and Lee leaned forward slightly, saw Jackson's face, a look of embarrassed horror. Scott held the silence, waited, the dramatic pause, then said, "If you can forgive yourself for the way you slaughtered those poor Mexicans with your guns, I'm not sure that I can!"

Jackson glanced to the side, and Lee saw a look of quiet panic, but then Scott reached out, took Jackson's hand, gave it a firm shake. There was laughter now, and the men close to the platform began to applaud. Lee watched Jackson's face, saw his relief, the horror fading, the stare returning, Jackson's eyes holding the calm blue light again.

The line moved again, and Lee was smiling now, could feel Scott's good humor infecting them all. He heard more laughter, the familiar sounds of the artillerymen, more teasing of Jackson. Lee couldn't see them, his vision blocked by the line of men in front of him, thought, There is still something in the man's eyes, something unsettling, something that says he *needs* a war.

He took another hand, heard more greetings, names he did not know, some he did, finally saw Johnston limping toward him. "Captain Lee, you seem at home up here." Johnston leaned close now, whispered, "Tell you what. We ever do this again, I'll lead the infantry, you can wait back here to shake their hands!"

Johnston moved away, and Lee was not smiling now, took another hand, another face he did not know, Johnston's words still punched in his brain, hard and cold, and he tried to see Johnston's face again, but the line had moved on, and he thought, Of course, he was teasing. . . .

38. LEE

H E HAD BEEN IN THE SADDLE MOST OF THE DAY, HAD RIDDEN UP to the north, close to the hills that led to the vast wilderness, the great open space that eventually became Texas. The maps were still a work in progress, and he carried the fat leather pouch with him as he climbed the long stairway to Scott's office.

He stopped at the last step, felt the stiffness in his back, brushed again at the dust on his uniform. He saw officers emerging through the wide doorway, followed by Trist, the pale, thin man weighed down by a heavy black coat. Lee stood aside, and they nodded to him as he passed. Trist's own leather case was fat with papers, and Lee thought, *The treaty,* glanced down at the case under his arm. Certainly more interesting than what I have here.

He moved through the office door. Sergeant Dunnigan was sitting behind a small desk, and rose to greet him. "Sir! Welcome. Wish I could tell you different, but sorry to say the general is not in a very good mood."

Lee smiled. "Sorry to hear that. I don't have much to report that will change that."

Dunnigan leaned forward, lowered his voice. "There was quite a bit of fireworks earlier. Mr. Trist seems to bring that with him. Not sure how things are going with the Mexicans." The door to the inner office opened and the young Scott appeared, looked at Lee, scanned his dirty uniform, frowned his disapproval. He looked at Dunnigan. "If Captain Lee wishes to see the commanding general, there should be a few minutes now."

Lee wanted to say something, thought, I am *here*, it would be all right to speak directly to me. He was still not comfortable around Major Scott, the strange barrier between them even now. He never believed he had done anything to offend the young man, had tried to find small ways to be sociable, even friendly. But Major Scott still kept his distance, exercised cold formality.

Lee accepted it now, would play the game, said to Dunnigan, "I would very much like to speak to General Scott. If he is available . . ."

The young Scott moved behind him, left the office, and Dunnigan watched him go. "It's not you, Captain. He's just . . . different. Doesn't seem to like anybody that General Scott approves of."

Lee said, "We all have our peculiarities, Sergeant. It is God's pleasure to give each of us something unique."

"Excuse me for saying so, Captain, but God's gotta get plenty of entertainment if He's watching this place. I never seen so many odd characters—"

Dunnigan stopped abruptly, stifled a moan. Scott stood in the doorway to the office, said, "Tell me, Sergeant, does your insight into God provide you with some explanation as to why I am so thoroughly tormented?"

Dunnigan cleared his throat. "No, sir. My apologies, sir."

Scott grunted, said to Lee, "You're not here to see *him*, dammit. Come in."

Lee moved past Scott into the big, empty office, saw the chairs scattered around. Scott moved to the big chair, sat.

"Take a seat, Mr. Lee. You look as if you could use a rest." Lee moved to a chair, set the leather case on the floor beside him. "I won't take up your time, sir. I just wanted to let you know that I had completed the survey of the hills to the north. . . ."

"Tell me about it later. I'd rather have you just sit there for a minute, if you don't mind. All day long I've had people in here complaining, saying things to each other they're afraid to say to me. Sometimes they just send notes, so they don't have to look at me when I place a well-chosen profanity in front of their names. And my sergeant talks to God . . ."

Lee said, "No, please sir. That was my fault. He didn't say anything out of line—"

Scott held up his hand. "It's all right, Mr. Lee. I give him hell all the time. He's used to it. You can say things to sergeants you can't say to officers. Officers are infected with pride. They're like big fat tomatoes. They bruise easily. They still threaten to fight duels, for God's sake. I've had men, right here in this office, make hints that if this was back home, or some other circumstance, they'd challenge *me* to a duel! Been through that before, you know. Did you know that Andrew Jackson, our beloved President, our great national hero ... did you know he challenged me to a duel?"

Lee was surprised, said, "No, sir. President Jackson?"

"He wasn't President then. Not long after the war with England, maybe thirty years ago now. We never got along, not from my earliest days as an officer. Good thing we fought the British from posts so far apart. Worked out best for the country, I was in New York, he was in New Orleans. Well, after the war, somehow somebody's words got twisted, somebody else stirring the pot, anonymous letters, accusations. All a big storm over nothing. Only time in my life I ever really felt backed into a corner. Wasn't scared of the duel, about whether he'd kill me or not. I knew I'd win. Dodged a bullet plenty of times in the war. Didn't give that much thought. But, imagine if I'd killed *him*? Old Hickory? I'd have become a national disgrace, lost everything I ever worked for. Learned a lot about diplomacy then. Had to come up with something to cool him off, without costing me my job. Tricky situation. He outranked me, but I was the commanding field general of the army. Two big frogs in a damned small pond."

Scott sat back, stared far away.

Lee smiled. "You should write a book, sir."

Scott focused again, looked at him. "One day. No time now. Besides, enough people despise me as it is. I start telling the truth, putting their names in a book, and they'll be lining up with their dueling pistols. For all I know, they're lining up already in Washington."

Lee had heard about new controversies, feuds, had stayed away from the talk. He was beginning to feel uneasy, thought, Maybe this isn't the time.

"Sir, I can make my report later if you'd prefer."

Scott laughed. "Makes you nervous, eh, Mr. Lee? Intrigue in high places. I can't seem to get away from it. We finally open up the communication lines again, and the first thing I hear is reports being sent home from two of my esteemed commanders, each claiming they're responsible for our great victory. I knew it would come from Pillow, that's the only reason he came down here in the first place. Now, it's coming from Worth too, some ridiculous claim that this was all his idea, the assault on Mexico City, the whole plan. Before it's over with, maybe even before we leave here, if it gets nasty enough, I may have to do something about it. Hell of a note, putting me in that position. The great victorious army, returning home to parades and celebrations, and oh yes, by the way, two of your generals are under arrest."

Lee shifted in the chair. "Surely it will not come to that, sir. Reason will prevail. It must be . . . frustration, the eagerness to go home. Once this army returns, it is the victory that will matter."

Scott tilted his head, looked at him and frowned. "You actually believe that, don't you?"

"I would hope so, sir. We have accomplished a great feat here. We have prevailed. The country should be proud of her soldiers."

"Mr. Lee, I finally received copies of the newspapers in Washington, New York. Did you know there have been public protests? There has been an organized movement calling for an end to this war. Even congressmen have made speeches, great public outrage, end the war, stop it, pull out. Polk has been under fire from the start. I knew the Europeans would howl, they howl at anything we do. But it's not foreigners, it's Americans who say that we have no business being here in the first place."

Lee felt a dull shock. "Why, sir?"

"What's going to be the final result of the war? What do you think Mr. Trist is working so hard for? Our treaty will eventually include our annexation of lower Texas, which was always a foregone conclusion. But it will also include the United States of America assuming control of California, and most of the land in between. What is being negotiated right now is not whether all that land becomes ours, but how much we will pay for it. We're actually going to pay the Mexicans millions of dollars. And since we won the war, we have the upper hand, we can decide how much we *ought* to pay. Our leverage . . . our strength, Mr. Lee, is that if they do not agree to our terms, we will threaten to annex, say, half of Mexico as well, put a dividing line, maybe the new border of Texas, right through here. I heard some of that talk before I came down here . . . this is nothing more than a land grab. I never listened to all that nonsense. I came here knowing something about duty, about fighting for your country. Now, I see the treaty, what Mr. Trist was really sent down here to do. It is indeed a land grab."

Lee was numb. "Sir, if this was not a just cause . . . if God did not approve—"

"Hell, Mr. Lee, I don't know what God approves or doesn't approve. There's quite a few people in Washington who seem to know for certain that He approves quite nicely. Have to admit, in the beginning I did too. It's Manifest Destiny, Mr. Lee, it's our birthright. It's plain English, right there in the Monroe Doctrine. This land is ours, because we say it is. President Polk made this war, not Santa Anna. Hell, in the beginning Santa Anna wasn't even here." He paused, thought for a moment. Lee leaned forward, waiting for the words.

"Mr. Lee, it took me a while to realize that even though I command this army, I'm not in command of this war. This war belongs to the politicians, not the soldiers. You and I, we did our duty, we are trained to believe we are fighting for right, for what is just. We won, for God's sake. We have a right to expect to go home to a hero's welcome. But, be prepared, Mr. Lee. It may not be like that. There may be no parades, no glorious triumphant march. Once the treaty is signed, the politicians take over. This army will have no place, no part of the prize. Men like Pillow understand that. Men like Worth are grabbing for their own place in history, latching on to some piece of fame. Frankly . . . it's sad, Mr. Lee."

Lee could feel Scott's depression now, said, "Sir, it cannot be that way, not completely. There are still the families of these men, the people in the towns who will see their soldiers returning home . . . triumphant, victorious. There is inspiration in that, surely. These men didn't fight for Washington, or for a piece of land. They saw the Mexicans as the enemy."

"They were well-trained, Mr. Lee. I agree, they did not fight for Polk, or whether they could start a farm in California. I have to admit that I am sometimes amazed by that, by the spirit." He stopped, and Lee saw the general's sadness. Scott rubbed his hands slowly on the desk then looked at Lee through red-rimmed eyes. "I'm not one of the soldiers anymore, Mr. Lee. I miss that more than anything. I watched them charge up Chapultepec, and I forgot all about Polk and land and newspapers. There is purity in those moments, and every man holds that in his heart, every man knows what he is fighting for. He fights for the man beside him, for the man up ahead holding the flag, for the sergeant who screams at him from behind. That's when a man knows God is with him, with all of them. It's why they climb the ladders, it's what sends them over the wall."

Lee could feel the weight in the room, the air growing heavy, the sadness etched in Scott's face. There was a silent moment before Scott said, "What about you, Mr. Lee? You have some yearning for politics? Or are you still a soldier?" Scott laughed, then continued, "No, I know the answer to that already. Just, don't change, Mr. Lee. Your place is here. There will be other wars. Not for me. This is all for me. Too many years, too many enemies. The future is in your hands, commanding all those young officers, all those West Pointers. Your place will be . . . right here, some room just like this one, some other godforsaken place. I hope you're comfortable with *your* Cause."

Lee searched for words, thought, He cannot be right, not completely. He is tired, exhausted. He is entitled to that, after all. "Sir, perhaps when the army returns home, you should take some time, some reflection. Things may not appear so . . . pessimistic."

Scott laughed, leaned back again in the chair, said, "Maybe you're right. Thought about taking up the challenge myself, fight them at their own game. I've learned enough about politics from these peacocks around here, might try my hand at it."

Lee smiled, thought, He's not serious. "Really, sir. Would you be President?"

Scott nodded slowly. "That would work. Hard to be a subordinate, should go straight for the top job." He leaned forward again. "Not this time, though, too soon, and besides, Zachary Taylor's already campaigning, got his foot in the door now. Can't have two military men run against each other. Lacks . . . decorum. Have to wait four more years."

Lee saw that Scott was serious. "Do you . . . mean it, sir? You'd run for President?"

"Why not? Can't do any worse than these characters now. If Old Hickory can do it, no reason I can't. Might even cause him to rise up from the grave, just so he can vote against me."

Scott shook his head, seemed to drift away now, and Lee waited for a long moment, before saying, "Sir, I do need to go over these maps with you. If you prefer, it can wait."

Scott looked at him, and Lee felt the stare, the full strength of the man, felt like the small son before the great power of the father. Scott leaned close, said quietly, "Mr. Lee, I meant what I said. You have a future in this army." Scott paused, seemed to think a moment, said now, "Mr. Lee, I have been making notes, working on the reports, all the damned paperwork that will go to Washington. Sometimes, things get lost, buried somewhere in a report almost no one will read, no one who matters anyway. I'd prefer that didn't happen this time."

Lee replied, "I'm sorry, sir. I don't understand."

"No, of course you don't. Mr. Lee, I was a soldier before most of these soldiers were born. I have fought warriors, savages, gentlemen, and politicians. I have been attacked by nearly every disease that the soldier's life provides him." He paused, seemed to search for words, and Lee waited, could feel the silence, the hard energy of Scott's mind.

"I have seen every kind of soldier there is, Mr. Lee. I have seen the quiet ones who become heroes by accident. When the battle is hottest, I have seen the loud talkers turn into cowards, and I have seen foot soldiers rise up to lead regiments. There is education in that, Mr. Lee." Scott stopped again, leaned back in the chair, and Lee waited patiently, thought, He needs this, to say these things. Do not forget this moment. . . .

"Mr. Lee, despite what they teach you at West Point, not every soldier has value, not every officer is a leader. In the great battles, there is no equality. A commander has to know that, has to understand that there are those he can depend on and those he cannot. But always . . . *always*, I have seen the good men, the best men, step forward."

Lee nodded slowly. "Yes, sir. I understand."

"Like hell you do. You have no idea what I'm getting at, do you?"

Lee felt a slow burn now, the embarrassment beginning to rise up inside him. "No, sir."

"Captain Lee, these reports will go to Washington with one very prominent mention of one very good officer. That officer is you. I had thought this might wait, but hell, everybody else around here is strutting his promotions like some damned princess at a ball. Never mind that it's all just brevets. Half those promotions will never become official. Once things calm down and the War Department shuffles the papers, we'll find out we need more sergeants and fewer majors. But it puts everybody in a good mood. However . . ."

Scott pushed aside a paper on his desk, read for a moment. "Ah, yes, here. Mr. Lee, as I said, it won't be official until some damned clerk files the paperwork, but as far as I'm concerned, it's official right now. It is my privilege, Captain, that for your service above and beyond . . . um . . . most everybody else around here, you are hereby breveted the rank of colonel."

Lee stared at him in shock, saw a broad smile, felt a strange uneasiness. "Sir, that's . . . three ranks. Shouldn't it be just . . . major?"

Scott put the paper aside, laughed. "Got to hand it to you, Mr. Lee. Never had an officer argue with me about his promotion. Consider this to be three promotions. If I have to justify it to you, well, that's easy. One for Cerro Gordo, another for what you did in that damned lava field. And there's your fine work in scouting and placing the guns at Chapultepec. Give me some time, Mr. Lee, I'll probably remember a few more things you did. But for now, does that sit all right with you? Put your mind at ease?"

Lee was numb, saw Scott's beaming smile, tried to say something, but his mind was a blank. Scott seemed to wait for him, and Lee shook his head slowly. "This was not necessary, sir. I did nothing anyone else would not have done."

The smile vanished and Scott said, "Spare me all of that, Mr. Lee. There are times when a man must accept his . . . medicine. I expect you to say one thing, and one thing only."

Lee fought his embarrassment. "Thank you, sir."

"You're welcome, Mr. Lee." Scott smiled again. "See? It's not that damned hard."

Lee smiled, felt the tightness loosening in his mind, felt that small hidden place opening up, a dark place he kept wrapped inside a hard fist. He began to feel good now, could feel the affection from Scott, the warmth behind the words. "Thank you, sir."

Scott stood, moved to the tall window, and Lee felt himself smiling still, took hold of it now, thought, All right, enough. There is more work to do. He glanced down to the thick bag on the floor, then looked up at Scott. No, it should come from him. He knows why I'm here. He sat back again, watched Scott.

"I don't know what your plans are, Mr. Lee. Certainly, Colonel Totten will expect you to resume some kind of engineering work. That's not a bad thing, I suppose." Scott turned, looked directly at him, the huge man framed by the light of the window.

"Yes, sir. It's a good assignment. There is a great deal of work to do."

Scott grunted. "Building forts. You want to grow old building forts, Mr. Lee?"

"I will do my duty, sir."

"I've seen the kind of duty you can do, Mr. Lee. I can tell you right now, it will happen to many of them, and they don't know it yet. And it will happen to you. You will go home to peace. And you won't like it. No matter where they send you, you will remember what it felt like at Cerro Gordo. You'll try to hide from it, the way I hid from it for thirty years. But it will find you, it will come back to you in the middle of the night and jar you awake. All the sounds and smells, all the horror, will be fresh in your mind. You'll think you've tucked it all away, memories you can tell your children about, trimmed and edited, packaged carefully so the horror doesn't show. But it won't work. Because the horror is real. And now it's a part of you. That's what war does to soldiers, Mr. Lee. You will always be a soldier. A damned fine soldier. And you won't forget that."

Lee sat quietly, felt a powerful mix of emotions rising inside him, knew it was a moment he would remember, a wonderful compliment. After a long moment he said in a low voice, "Thank you, sir."

Scott sat back now, stared away for a moment. Lee waited, saw Scott focus again. "All right, Mr. Lee, let's have a look at those maps. . . ."

39. LEE

JUNE EIGHTH, 1848

THE SHIP HAD PULLED AWAY FROM THE WHARF, MOVED PAST THE walls of the great old fort of Uloa. He stood far in front, near the point of the bow, could hear the sails above his head rolling into full bloom, pushed hard by the wind. He was alone now, had heard the call to dinner, knew most of the men were below deck, had thought, Just a while, stay up here, watch the shoreline.

He focused on the old fort, could still see the guns that had never fired on the invaders. The memories were already fading, the details of the great siege, *his* siege, the sight of the walls of Vera Cruz coming apart under the heavy shelling of the guns he had positioned. He tried to hear the sounds, remember the deafening roar, the great clouds of smoke that rolled over him, choking him in sulfur. But he stared instead at calm water, the slow, quiet movement of the big ship, stared at a city that showed little of the damage now, a city that might never have seen a war at all.

He moved to the other side of the bow, looked out to sea where the sky was growing darker, the sun falling away behind him. The scene before him was calm and empty, no fleet, none of the great men-o'-war that had controlled these waters for two years. Most of the fleet was already moving north, as he was, the sailors returning to duty close to their own ports.

He had seen Scott leave the city, watched with enormous sadness as he climbed the great horse, moved slowly through the gathered troops. There were cheers, as there had always been, but this was no celebration. They were astounded that Scott had been recalled, his position taken away by a President who insisted this man was the enemy.

With the coming of the peace, all the focus had been on the politics, the disease of ambition. Lee had testified at the Court of Inquiry, a circus of charges and countercharges between Scott and Pillow and Worth. The court had convened in January, while the delicate negotiations of the treaty were still fragile and uncertain. Lee had tried to stay far away from the ridiculous name calling, Scott's arrest of the two commanders, their countercharges against him, inspired by Polk's own need to pull Scott down, to remove the commanding general from any of the bright lights swirling around victorious Washington. There was even an attempt to implicate Lee in some kind of vague conspiracy, as though by his loyalty to Scott he too was dangerous to the administration. In the end there had been no finding of guilt for anyone involved, the court merely an exercise in rhetoric and excuses. But the damage had been done to Scott's reputation.

Now, Scott was already gone, and Lee thought, He's already in Washington. He must already be enduring more of the same political horror that caught up with him even this far away. It was never right. It never should have come to this, to take him away from his troops. The treaty was so close, and after all, it was *his*. The treaty belonged to *him*, not just the glory of the battlefield, but the completion, the final acceptance. He had earned that, to see it through, to march out of Mexico City leading his men to the ships, not leaving them behind.

He did not know William Butler, the most senior commander after Scott, who had been sent to Mexico City to replace Scott, but Lee thought he was at least a decent man. General Butler seemed uneasy, moving into that position. But he understood, knew better than to stir things up, or even make changes. That was smart. The treaty was so close, and he could only have done harm.

The Treaty of Guadalupe Hidalgo had been signed in late February, and though not yet ratified, the terms were clear and final, and no one believed the government would allow patent stupidity to stand in its way. Lee had hoped to hear of ratification before he left, had thought it was important to all of them, leaving Mexico feeling as though the job were done. He felt the familiar anger now, the frustration, stared at the growing darkness, the night sky wiping the horizon away, thought, Must General Scott continue to endure this? Must this army go home now to such pettiness, such ridiculous arguing over issues that will be so quickly forgotten? The troops know better, they do not care about Courts of Inquiry and the vanity of politicians. No matter what happens to General Scott now, history will tell his story. These soldiers will make sure of that.

Lee thought of the letter to his brother Smith, long sent now, his anger spilling out, something he rarely allowed to reach the written page. He had written to Smith of some of the ridiculous arguments, the petty claims of the generals, the grab for headlines, for some piece of glory. Beyond that, Lee had felt offended at the outrageous lack of respect to the campaign itself, to the accomplishment of Winfield Scott. He wondered now, Should I have written that? Smith will be discreet, after all. He is my brother. But still, the letter was unwise, I should have tempered the words *"with all their knowledge, I will defy them to have done better."* It is not my place to defy anyone. I'm just . . . an engineer.

He had received word from Colonel Totten that he was to report to Washington for a new assignment with the Engineering Corps. There was no surprise there, and Lee thought, General Scott does not need such a large staff anymore. I had no reason to believe I would stay close to him. He has his son-in-law, and Colonel Hitchcock, some of the others will certainly stay in Washington with him. I can be of more value somewhere else, certainly.

He remembered Scott's words, *always a soldier,* but it didn't seem so important now. He had spent so much time thinking of home, of Mary, the children, thought, For a while at least, the soldier will become the husband, the father. The memories of this place will have to sit quietly for a while. There must be time given to children, to all of them. It can never be like this again, being gone for so long. Just because I have been a soldier . . . what kind of father does that make me? No, there will be time now, no matter what duty Colonel Totten assigns me. I will find a way, stay close to them, watch them grow.

He moved to the point of the bow, leaned out, tried to see down to the water, the ship cutting through. He caught a glimpse of silver, a small reflection, a flying fish, leaping away from the great ship. He watched it curiously, saw it skip along the top of the water, then just as suddenly dive away, disappearing. He stared down again, hoping to see another, but the water was growing darker. He waited, his eyes adjusting, but there was nothing to see. He could feel the ship rising slowly, then dropping in a slow rocking rhythm, stared into darkness and suddenly thought of his name. *Colonel Lee.* He smiled, felt self-conscious, turned and looked behind him, but the deck was still empty. He looked back along the ship. Far astern the sailors stood coiling the ropes, men moving with quick efficiency. A good commander, he thought, good officers. *Colonel Lee.* He was still smiling. I do like the sound of that. Maybe someday it will become official, and there will be some duty, some place far away from the horrors, where death is not so much a part of the plan. *Colonel Lee, Commanding.* He could see his name on an office door, gold lettering, *Colonel Lee, Engineer,* in Washington, perhaps, some fine office overlooking the Potomac, a view of Mary's home, Arlington. Perhaps one day it could be . . . *General* Lee. . . .

He shook his head. There is no time for this. You have no right to daydream, to fantasize about your own glory. And none of it is official, and might never be. Brevets are handed out to anyone who catches a commander's eye. The official promotions come from Washington, from hidden rooms where papers are shuffled, not from anyone's headquarters in the middle of a battle. Even General Scott can't change that.

He looked up, could see stars now, looked ahead to the darkness. How brave . . . how much courage it took men to do this when they didn't know what was out there. How long ago was it, when there were no instruments, only the stars? Now, there is no uncertainty at all. We sail to New Orleans, and none of us is even concerned about that. Amazing changes. He thought of the young soldiers, some below deck enjoying the evening meal. What changes will you see? It was not so long ago . . . war with axes, clubs, spears. Now it is war with cannon, muskets. Every man came down here, even the volunteers, each man with his own idea of how this war would be. How many of them are changed now? Some were changed right away, like the San Patricios, or others, men who simply quit, disappeared. But so many more stood up and faced it, could never have known what they would see and hear and smell, some with no idea what a violent death was like. I didn't know . . . could never have known what to expect. And General Scott believes I'm a soldier. I've seen the worst of what war is, the worst things we do to each other. And I don't feel changed. But . . . he is probably right. The memories may not sit quietly after all.

He felt the rumble of hunger, thought, All right, enough of this. God is trying to tell me something. Less thought, more food. He stood away from the railing, felt the motion of the ship, glanced up at the stars again, thought, No, not just yet. This is so rare . . . to feel so . . . alone. He moved again to the rail, stared out. Will we do this again? Perhaps here, or maybe somewhere else? If the politicians have their way, it will certainly happen again, some other dispute, some other opportunity. And the army will go out again, young men just like these, maybe the same men, sooner than we could ever predict, marching in line again to face the guns of *more* men like these. And surely God will judge us for that. Whether wars start from politicians or generals, from broken treaties or disputed boundaries, whether the weapons change or death becomes more horrible, no man can be made to do this unless he believes it is the right thing to do. If I am to be a soldier again, that path, that destiny, is already laid out. But for now . . . I'd just like to go home.

AFTERWORD

Major-General Winfield Scott

Scott's departure from Mexico City on April 22 is heralded by another of the glorious tributes he receives both from his men and the citizens of the city, who acknowledge the extraordinary fairness of his policies and his generous behavior toward the Mexican civilians. He sails from Vera Cruz on May 4, but cannot escape a final insult from the hot climate of the Mexican coast. He endures the three-week journey home suffering from a case of the *el vomito*.

He reaches New York on May 20, joins his wife and three daughters in his home in Elizabeth, New Jersey, soon settles in New York City. He avoids Washington, remains quietly in the background as Zachary Taylor is elected President in November 1848.

Scott is disappointed with the country's lack of appreciation for the amazing success of his army in Mexico, but he is not ignored by the men he commanded. He is celebrated in a number of rallies and parades, and even Washington cannot ignore his prominence as a national hero. Congress awards him a special gold medal for his achievement on the field of battle.

Though still active as General-in-Chief of the army, he stays away from Washington, but his supporters pull him out of his quiet office, convince him that generals make good candidates, and better Presidents. He is chosen the Whig nominee in 1852, but his inability to turn the soft phrase plagues him yet again. He loses the election to Franklin Pierce, who had served in a mediocre capacity as a brigadier general under Scott's command.

In 1855, Scott is promoted to Lieutenant General, the only man to hold that rank since George Washington. He remains in New York, more a symbol than an active participant in the army's day-to-day affairs, but in 1859 he is given the opportunity to travel to the Pacific Northwest, to intervene personally in the controversy with the British over possession of San Juan Island in Puget Sound. In one of the nation's final displays of the heavy-handed application of Manifest Destiny, General William Harney, Scott's disagreeable old cavalry commander, has seized the island, despite British objections. Harney is supported by his subordinate, Captain George Pickett. Scott soothes the ruffles of the British, negotiates a compromise, and returns home with the satisfaction of victory, which few will notice.

As General-in-Chief of an army with no war to fight, he watches his own time passing, is held inactive by an administration helpless to confront the issues tearing at the country. As the angry talk in the South inevitably gives way to secession, Scott urges the War Department and President Buchanan to strengthen the army's forts around southern seaports, as well as outposts in all parts of what will soon become the Confederacy. The request is ignored.

He observes the election of Abraham Lincoln with curiosity, knows nothing about the man from Illinois, and though he never becomes close to Lincoln, he immediately understands the vital importance of protecting Lincoln's authority over the Union. Despite the strong pull of his native state of Virginia, and the resignation of most of the army's southern officers, Scott never hesitates in supporting the Union cause. As the new President struggles to confront the explosive events of April 1861, Scott formulates his own plan for the quick defeat of the rebellion. Called "Anaconda," the strategy calls for strong occupation of the Mississippi River, and the blockade of southern ports. The strategy eventually becomes reality, though Scott receives little credit for devising it.

He is considered a thorn in the side of the new powers in Washington, Stanton and Halleck, who believe him far beyond usefulness and an obstacle to their own ambition. Thus, in July 1861 when the North is shocked by their army's first momentous failure, the first great bloodbath at Bull Run, Scott considers the outcome with a stoic detachment. He is not surprised that of the South's fifteen general officers on the field, eleven had combat experience under Winfield Scott.

His official command of the army is terminated on October 31, 1861, and his administrative duties in Washington are given to Henry Halleck, with overall command in the field passing to George McClellan.

Aging and increasingly weak, Scott spends the remaining war years in New York City, suffers the death of his wife Maria in 1862. He passes his final years eagerly offering the grand stories of his life to frequent visitors, and maintains a passionate grip on the details of the progress of the Civil War. He is often heard to remark on the accomplishments and rise to prominence of his favorite subordinate, Robert E. Lee. But his sentiment does not diminish his admiration for the new Union commander, the man he remembers vaguely from the great fight at the San Cosme gate, Ulysses S. Grant.

He visits West Point frequently, unannounced, walks the grand halls, surprising instructors and cadets alike, enjoys the captive audience the Point provides him. He travels to the Point in May 1866 to observe the graduation ceremonies, but falls ill, and dies on May 28. He is eighty years old.

It is a little known tribute to his lasting influence on the military culture of the nation that the uniforms of the cadet corps of West Point are fashioned after the same gray pattern that Scott's troops wore in 1812.

T HE DUKE OF WELLINGTON, BRITAIN'S MOST FAMOUS SOLDIER of the nineteenth century, the man who defeated Napoleon at Waterloo, upon hearing that Scott had cut himself off from his base at Vera Cruz, remarked:

"Scott is lost! He has been carried away by successes . . . He won't leave Mexico without the permission of the Mexicans!"

Upon learning of the capture of Mexico City, the duke had a change of heart:

"His campaign was unsurpassed in military annals. He is the greatest living soldier."

CAPTAIN ROBERT E. LEE

"Robert E. Lee is the very best soldier that I ever saw in the field."
—Winfield Scott, 1858

Lee reaches New Orleans, travels up the Mississippi, and finally reaches Washington in late June. Along the way he begins to see the newspapers, and experiences firsthand the controversy of the war and the terms of the treaty. Though he remains fiercely loyal to Winfield Scott, he grows uncomfortable with the political results of the war, believes that Mexico was indeed bullied into submission.

Still officially part of the Corps of Engineers, Lee is assigned by his friend Joseph Totten to Baltimore, to supervise construction of what will later become Fort Carroll.

In 1849, Lee is approached by representatives of the Cuban government-in-exile, offered the command of an insurrectionary force to overthrow the Spanish authority in the island country. Lee considers the post briefly, understands ultimately that his duty lies with his own country, and rejects the offer.

As Fort Carroll nears completion, Lee travels to Florida, surveys sites for additional forts along the lower East coast, is entirely absorbed with his duties as an engineer. He is thus surprised in the spring of 1852 to receive orders for a post he had not sought, that of Superintendent of West Point. He lobbies for the appointment to be passed on to someone else but is unsuccessful and finally accepts graciously, then moves his family from Virginia to New York. His tenure at the Point is mostly free of turmoil. He brings an efficient sense of discipline and dignity to the academy, which many believe had become diminished. He serves in the post for three years, graduates men with names that later become far more than merely familiar: John Bell Hood, Philip Sheridan, and the young man who will become his favorite cadet and close friend, James Ewell Brown ("Jeb") Stuart.

Despite his good work and the labor of administrative life, the peacetime inactivity of the army is difficult, and Lee feels himself growing older in a military system that fills the higher ranks with men who have no incentive to retire. Thus, he accepts a unique opportunity, becomes second-in-command of a new regiment of cavalry, under the command of Albert Sidney Johnston. The duty is in the wilderness of central Texas, and for the second time he will leave his family in Virginia with no expectation of seeing them for many months. But he accepts the duty with an enthusiasm his friends and family do not understand, and in April 1855 he arrives in Louisville and assumes command of troops in the field for the first time.

The duty is harsh and difficult, involves the protection of new settlers who are pushing the American influence westward, often resulting in hostile confrontation with the Indians.

In late 1857 his father-in-law, the patriarch of the Arlington estate, dies. Lee is granted an extended leave from the army, returns to Virginia to manage the plantation, must endure a difficult legal and financial storm. He spends all of 1858 and much of 1859 at Arlington, but still performs duties for the army that arise because of his proximity to

Washington. In October 1859 one of these duties involves quelling the insurrection of radical abolitionist John Brown at Harper's Ferry. He performs this duty with efficiency, and Brown is ultimately hanged. In February 1860, Lee naively returns to Texas, having no idea about the explosive effect Brown's execution will have on the growing hostility over the issue of slavery.

Lee now commands the Second Cavalry Regiment, under the overall command of General Davy Twiggs. Twiggs has grown more bitter since his days in Mexico, and regards Lee with disdain, as merely a puppet of Winfield Scott. If the duty in the Texas wilderness is disagreeable at best, under Twiggs, Lee suffers miserably.

As the angry forces begin to drive the country toward civil war, Lee seems unaware of the depth of the passions, maintains an idealistic view that God will not allow such foolishness to engulf the country, and he writes frequently that reason will certainly prevail. In a letter to his son Custis, Lee says, *"The southern states seem to be in a convulsion. . . . It is difficult to see what will be the result, but I hope all will end well."*

In February 1861, when Texas votes to secede, Twiggs suddenly surrenders the army's property in Texas, and Lee is recalled to Washington. Lee writes his son again, *"I can anticipate no greater calamity for the country than a dissolution of the Union . . . If the Union is dissolved . . . I shall return to my native State, and share the miseries of the people, and save in defense will draw my sword on none."*

With the shelling of Fort Sumter and the start of the war, Lee receives an extraordinary offer from Francis Blair, an old friend. Speaking for Lincoln, Blair extends a Major General's commission and command of the Union army which Lincoln is organizing to put down the rebellion. The offer is endorsed strongly by Winfield Scott. To the dismay of official Washington, Lee turns it down, resigns from the army and returns to his home, believing his service to his country is at an end. Winfield Scott tells Lee, *"You have made the greatest mistake of your life."*

In Lee's letter of resignation, he states again, *"Save in defense of my native State, I never again desire to draw my sword."*

Invited by the governor of Virginia to assume command of the state's defensive forces, Lee finds himself caught up in the growing passions of the war, cannot escape from the memories of and the attraction to combat he experienced in Mexico. Thus his devotion to the defense of Virginia brings him closer to an increasing involvement in the South's military cause. After serving in the relatively unimportant and unfulfilling role as military advisor to Confederate President Jefferson Davis, Lee is offered command of the Confederate Army of Northern Virginia. He accepts.

ANTONIO LOPEZ DE SANTA ANNA

In late 1847, Santa Anna continues to command what forces will remain loyal, still refers to himself as the "Napoleon of the West." He orders the assault against American garrisons in Puebla, but American reinforcements from the coast arrive in time to prevent any significant Mexican advantage. Frustrated by the slow collapse of the army under him, he tries but cannot muster enough men to wage any kind of campaign with any hope of doing damage to the American occupation forces.

With the signing of the Treaty of Guadalupe Hidalgo, the government, under the interim leadership of Supreme Court Justice Pena y Pena, demands that Santa Anna relinquish all control of the army. In late February 1848, General William Butler, replacing Winfield Scott, provides Santa Anna with a passport, and permits him free passage to the coast, to leave the country. Santa Anna narrowly misses capture and a possibly violent end by a renegade group of Texas volunteers under Colonel John Hays.

Santa Anna accepts exile in Jamaica, and in 1850 moves to the island of Granada. He never considers himself retired, stays close to events in his home country, always searching for opportunity. When a new crisis overcomes the Mexican government, his leadership is sought again, and he returns in April 1853 to assume, once more, the control of Mexico, and is named "Perpetual Dictator." His rule is brief again, however, and he falls victim to a new revolution, led by Benito Juarez. Exiled again, he lives first in Cuba, then moves to the Bahamas. In 1864 he enters into negotiations with the United States to place him back in power against the French puppet Maximilian, and at the same time attempts to win over the friendship of Maximilian himself. The negotiations with Washington are short-lived.

After the removal of Maximilian, he returns to Mexico in 1867, believes his time has come again, expects a hero's welcome, but is arrested and put on trial for treason by officials loyal to Juarez. Avoiding a political and public relations disaster, Juarez allows Santa Anna to escape the obligatory death sentence. But Santa Anna is exiled again, spends six more years in Cuba, the Virgin Islands, and the Bahamas, where he writes his memoirs. The book is a stream of attacks on enemies real and imagined, and seeks to justify every act of his life as a response to the traitors and enemies that constantly threatened him and his country. Described as the ultimate patriot by some, and a brutal and abusive despot by others, when questioned as to why he does not believe liberty is appropriate for the Mexican people, he responds: *"A hundred years to come my people will not be fit for liberty. They do not know what it is, unenlightened as they are, and under the influence of the Catholic clergy. A despotism is the proper government for them, but there is no reason why it should not be a wise and virtuous one."*

He completes the memoirs in 1874, at age eighty. Crippled and nearly blind, he nevertheless outlives his bitter enemy Juarez, and is allowed to return to Mexico. He is welcomed only by a small party of old friends and is ignored by the government. He dies in 1876, a bitter man, still believing it is his enemies that prevent him from again rising to power, serving a nation that only he understands. In its obituary, one newspaper says: *"The last hours of his life inspire the saddest reflections: the man who controlled millions, who acquired fortune and honors, who exercised an unrestricted dictatorship has died in the midst of his greatest want, abandoned by all except a few of his friends . . . A relic of another epoch, our generation remembered him for the misfortunes he brought upon the republic, forgetting the really eminent services he rendered to the nation."*

Another says, *"His career formed a brilliant and important portion of the history of Mexico, and future historians will differ in their judgment of his merits. General Santa Anna outlived his usefulness and ambition, and died at the ripe age of eighty-four [sic]. Peace to his ashes."*

It is a strange footnote to his long and controversial life that despite spending nearly as much time in exile as he spent in Mexico, he served as leader of that country on *eleven* separate occasions.

NICHOLAS P. TRIST

He pursues the treaty with the Mexican authorities with dogged determination, often at the expense of his own health. His distance from Washington causes him to assume somewhat more authority than the administration had thought appropriate, and despite the unqualified support of Winfield Scott, or perhaps because of it, in November 1847, Trist is sent a recall letter by Polk. It is an order popular to no one in Mexico, least of all the Mexicans themselves, and so, encouraged by Scott, his British friends, and his Mexican adversaries, Trist ignores the recall and completes the negotiations. The resulting Treaty of Guadalupe Hidalgo provides for the Mexican government to relinquish all control of the territory of Texas above the Rio Grande, the territory of New Mexico, and all of what is today California. As compensation, the United States pays the Mexican government fifteen million dollars. The treaty is all that Polk and his allies in Washington had hoped for, and thus they are caught in the difficult situation of pushing for ratification of the treaty by Congress while at the same time condemning Trist, the man who engineered it. The treaty is finally ratified on May 30, 1848.

Trist returns to Washington, but can no longer find employment with a government he has embarrassed. Polk is so outraged at Trist's show of independence, he will not recognize Trist's legitimacy as a government agent, and thus Trist is not reimbursed for his considerable expenses until 1871, twenty-three years after his return.

He practices law, is never particularly successful, and fades into obscurity, made notable only by his appointment to the job of Postmaster of Alexandria, Virginia, by President Grant in 1870. He fills the post until his death in 1874.

PRESIDENT JAMES K. POLK

Elected at forty-nine years old, the youngest President up to his time, and the man who defeated the enormously popular (and favored) Henry Clay, Polk does not seem like a man who will build a healthy gallery of enemies. He enthusiastically embraces the policy of Manifest Destiny, has no difficulty dismissing the moral questions that much of the nation wrestles with over the war with Mexico.

Polk states early in his presidency that he is a one-term officeholder, promises to retire without running again in 1848. Upon his retirement, he says, *"I feel exceedingly relieved that I am now free from all public cares."* The retirement is brief. After leaving office he travels extensively, contracts cholera in New Orleans, and dies on June 15, 1849.

"[Polk] is a bewildered, confounded and miserably perplexed man."

—Abraham Lincoln, 1848

"James K. Polk is a great president. Said what he intended to do, and did it."

—Harry S. Truman, 1960

CAPTAIN JOSEPH E. JOHNSTON

Recognized by his superior officers for conspicuous command of his volunteer infantry, Johnston receives two brevets for exceptional service under fire. He serves in garrison duty as the war concludes, returns home to immediately begin duty in the newly acquired territory of Texas and New Mexico. With little need for infantry commanders, the army recalls Johnston's skills as an engineer, places him in charge of an effort to construct a lengthy railroad line linking Texas to California. But the scramble for financial opportunity in the new territory creates chaos in Congress, pulled by lobbying interests on all sides of the question, and the railroad, and thus the duty, is never completed.

In 1852, Johnston seeks and is granted extended leave from the army, and returns to command various engineering projects along the Mississippi, Ohio, and Arkansas rivers. He suffers similar frustrations that plague his friend Lee, looks to command infantry again as a means of advancement. He is thus surprised and somewhat disappointed when, in 1855, he receives assignment as second-in-command of the First Cavalry Regiment in Fort Leavenworth, Kansas, and soon finds himself in the middle of the growing hostilities of Bloody Kansas.

In 1859 he is appointed Inspector General of New Mexico, but serves only a short time, has his eye more strongly than ever on promotion. When Quartermaster General Jesup dies in 1860, Johnston recognizes the opportunity offered by the vacancy and vigorously lobbies for the post, which carries the automatic rank of Brigadier General. Winfield Scott nominates four men for the position, including Robert E. Lee, but Johnston's efforts at self-promotion are rewarded. He receives the appointment and thus becomes the first graduate of West Point to rank as a general officer in the regular army. But Johnston finds the difficult position unfulfilling, and the complicated administrative duties are not easily dealt with by a man who prizes most his own talents for leading troops in the field.

As the issues dividing the nation grow hot, Johnston agonizes over the issue of secession, decides to place his loyalties with his home state of Virginia. Despite personal pleas from Winfield Scott, Johnston resigns from the army the same day as Robert E. Lee. However, unlike Lee, Johnston seeks service beyond the defense of Virginia, is soon appointed Brigadier General of the Confederate Army, the highest ranking regular army officer to join the Confederacy. He is immediately placed in command at the first major engagement with Union forces at Manassas (Bull Run).

As the war progresses, Johnston has great difficulty adapting to the ways of Jefferson Davis, and begins a feud that boils the rest of his life. The result for the Confederacy is destructive, and when Johnston is wounded in 1862, Davis uses the opportunity to place Lee in Johnston's place. The relationship between Lee and Johnston deteriorates, to the great dismay of Lee, who cannot understand Johnston's increasing hostility to everyone around him, and his suspicions of anyone in power. Their friendship suffers, and the closeness, so important to both men in Mexico, will never rekindle. When Lee dies in 1870, Johnston expresses deep regret that their relationship was not closer. He dies of pneumonia in 1891.

Major General William Worth

Cleared of wrongdoing at the Court of Inquiry in spring 1848, Worth's career nonetheless suffers. He will never receive the glory he feels he deserves, and after the war, he settles reluctantly for command of the Department of Texas. But his own fears about his health prove to be accurate, and he contracts cholera, dies in San Antonio in May 1849, at age fifty-five.

Major General Zachary Taylor

"Old Rough and Ready," the crude and plainspoken Indian fighter, achieves an unexpected reputation for heroism in northern Mexico, surprising even himself. He begins to accept what those around him are saying, warms to the idea of running for President, and in June 1848 receives the nomination of the Whig party despite similar ambitions from Henry Clay and Daniel Webster. He defeats Lewis Cass, and is inaugurated in March 1849. He proves to have no tolerance for the enormous wave of details that confronts the office, and suffers from a complete inability to understand the necessary concept of compromise. He does not complete one term, suffers heatstroke at a Fourth of July celebration, and dies July 9, 1850. He is succeeded by his vice-president, Millard Fillmore.

Major General Gideon Pillow

President Polk's law partner brings on much of the controversy that results in the Court of Inquiry, insists that he was responsible for the American victory at Padierna, goes so far as to write an anonymous report of the battle in which he is named principal hero. The article is published in New Orleans in September 1847.

His political strength is too solid to be affected by the controversy, and he returns to law practice in Washington and continues to be active in the politics of the day. He actively supports his former subordinate, Franklin Pierce, who defeats Winfield Scott for President in 1852. It is a source of lasting satisfaction for Pillow. However, he is denied his own political goal, is not considered electable as a vice-presidential candidate, seeks the nomination again in 1856, and is again rebuffed.

As a native Tennessean, he is nonetheless outspoken against secession. However, Pillow cannot reject another opportunity for personal glory, and he accepts a commission as Brigadier General in the Confederate Army in July 1861.

His service to the Confederacy consists of a brief term as subordinate to Leonidas Polk at the battle of Belmont, Missouri, and later he is given command at Fort Donelson, which he almost immediately passes off to Simon Buckner, who ultimately surrenders to Ulysses Grant. It is not a distinguished act, and Pillow is suspended from service by Jefferson Davis.

Pillow's investments in Confederate bonds ruin him financially, but he resumes his law practice after the war in Memphis, Tennessee, and survives until 1878.

BRIGADIER GENERAL DAVID TWIGGS

In December 1847, Twiggs leads a column of troops that assists in clearing the army's main route to Vera Cruz of the threat of guerrillas. Appointed Military Governor of Vera Cruz, he serves that post only briefly; he returns home in March 1848. Taking no part in the controversy surrounding the clash of personalities, he thus keeps himself immune to political backlash. He is appointed to command of the Army of the West, and then command of the Department of Texas, where among his subordinates is Robert E. Lee.

A Georgian, his sympathies lie with the southern cause, and with secession he does not hesitate turning over the army's property to the rebellious Texas authorities. Branded a traitor in Washington, he is dismissed from the army, and returns briefly to his home state. In May 1861 he accepts appointment from Jefferson Davis as Major General in the Confederate Army, in charge of the District of Louisiana, but the command is insignificant and he sees little action. His age betrays him, and he dies in July 1862 at age seventy-two.

COMMODORE DAVID CONNER

One of the most efficient and accomplished naval officers of his time, Conner returns home in spring 1847 to no fanfare, spends two years in relative obscurity, but is remembered by the veterans who rise to prominence in the new administration of Zachary Taylor. He is thus appointed to a token position as Commandant of the Philadelphia Naval Yard in 1849, but it is a short-lived duty and his poor health keeps him from further service. He dies in 1856, at age sixty-four.

MAJOR GENERAL JOHN QUITMAN

Quitman returns to Mississippi with the full attention due an honored native son, despite the fact that he was actually born in Rhinebeck, New York. He receives much fanfare for his exploits under both Taylor and Scott, and is elected Governor of Mississippi in 1849. He involves himself in the Cuban insurrection of 1850, the controversy Robert E. Lee had avoided, but it is a violation of Federal neutrality laws, and Quitman is forced to resign in 1851. He is elected to Congress in 1854 for two terms, dies in Natchez, Mississippi, in 1858, at age sixty.

COLONEL BENNETT RILEY

Arguably the army's most competent brigade commander, Riley receives two brevets for his efficiency and gallantry at Cerro Gordo and Padierna, and leaves Mexico as a brevet Major General. After the war he is appointed commander of the Department of the Pacific, and subsequently becomes Military Governor of California. He provides full support to the creation of a civilian government in that territory, oversees a constitutional convention, and turns over control of the territory to elected officials in December 1849. Considered by his superiors as a shining star of the army, he is appointed commander of the First Infantry in January 1850, but is struck by illness, retires from the service, and dies in Buffalo, New York, in 1853, at age sixty-six.

He is honored by having his name assigned to a new fort under construction in Kansas, soon known as Fort Riley.

CAPTAIN JOHN BANKHEAD MAGRUDER

Magruder leaves Mexico a brevet Lieutenant Colonel for his outstanding command of his artillery battery, but returns home only to fade into an inconspicuous career. Stationed in Newport, Rhode Island, he builds even more on the reputation that had given him the nickname "Prince John." He is always the center of his post's social scene. A Virginian, he resigns from the army in March 1861 and joins the Confederacy. Magruder is instrumental in the defense of the Virginia Peninsula from McClellan's invasion in 1862, and performs with competence during the Seven Days Battles. But ultimately he is judged by his commanders to be slow to react and inefficient as a manager of troops in the field. He eventually supervises Confederate efforts in the Southwest, captures Galveston, Texas, and serves with some distinction in assisting the command of Richard Taylor in Texas.

After the war ends, he refuses to accept northern control of his home, returns to Mexico, serves briefly as a Major General under the command of Emperor Maximilian. As Reconstruction wanes, he returns to the United States and settles in Texas, where he dies in 1871 at age sixty-one.

BRIGADIER GENERAL JAMES SHIELDS

The Irish-born brigade commander leaves Mexico with a brevet for Major General for his conspicuous actions at both Cerro Gordo and Churubusco, but he does not see a future in the army, resigns July 1848. Shields is soon appointed Governor of the Oregon Territory, resigns from that post to run for Senate from his adopted home state of Illinois. His election is voided by the U.S. Senate, which does not fully recognize his U.S. citizenship. The matter is resolved, and Shields is elected again and serves from late 1849 through 1855. He is active in the organization and settlement of the Minnesota Territory, and is elected again to the Senate, this time from Minnesota, in 1858. He serves an abbreviated term and does not win reelection in 1859. He moves to San Francisco, pursues the mining business, establishes some connections with Mexican businessmen, but the Civil War finds the army in search of experienced brigadiers, and he accepts appointment as Brigadier General of volunteers in August 1861. He serves under Nathaniel Banks in the Fifth Corps, is remembered most for his exploits in the Shenandoah Valley. He is victorious at Kernstown, then suffers total defeat at Port Republic, both actions becoming part of the legendary Shenandoah campaign of a former artillery lieutenant, Thomas "Stonewall" Jackson. In March 1863, Shields resigns again from the army, moves to Missouri, practices law, and is active in the state legislature and the state's railroad commission. In 1879 he is elected to the Senate for a third time, from his third state, but he dies in Ottumwa, Iowa, in 1879.

LIEUTENANT PIERRE G.T. BEAUREGARD

Beauregard is breveted twice in Mexico, receives a permanent promotion to Captain of Engineers in 1853. He serves throughout the 1850s in his home state of Louisiana, but in January 1861 receives the extraordinary appointment as Superintendent of West Point. He serves in that post less than one week, resigns to return to Louisiana, anticipating the defense of his home state. He joins the Confederate army as a Brigadier General, is most known for commanding the artillery that fired on Fort Sumter, in Charleston, South Carolina. He serves as second-in-command of the Confederate forces under Joseph Johnston, and serves competently throughout several theaters of the war, including an amazing defense of Petersburg, Virginia, against the overwhelming numbers of Ulysses Grant. But he is never content with his place in history, feels he has not been allowed to reach the heights of fame and glory he believes is his destiny.

After the war he is president of a railroad in Louisiana and fills various public positions in his home state. Always involved in some dispute over his place in history, he writes a memoir of questionable accuracy, feuds for the rest of his life with Jefferson Davis and Joe Johnston, and dies in 1893 at age seventy-five.

COLONEL WILLIAM S. HARNEY

Known primarily throughout his career as an Indian fighter, the disagreeable cavalry commander makes the mistake of opening a bitter dispute with Winfield Scott, refuses to relinquish command of the cavalry to a subordinate, Edwin V. Sumner. Scott thus has him court-martialed. Because of the odd politics of the day, Harney is not punished, while Scott himself receives a reprimand. After the war he is assigned again to Indian duty in the plains, earning a reputation as a relentless and efficient fighter, and contributes to the unfortunate reputation that many in the army earn for extraordinary brutality to the Indians.

Promoted to Brigadier General in 1858, he is given command of the Department of Oregon, and nearly starts a war with the British over the possession of San Juan Island. Recalled to Washington, he is given command of the Department of the West, is headquartered in St. Louis. As a Tennessean, he is actively courted by Confederates, including Robert E. Lee, but resists, yet his close ties to his native state arouse suspicion of Confederate sympathies in Washington. He is removed from command in mid-1861, resigns from the army in August 1863. In 1865, Union Commander Ulysses Grant looks beyond the suspicions, and though Harney is in retirement, Grant awards him a brevet for Major General, a recognition of a lifetime of service. He dies in Orlando, Florida, in 1889, at age eighty-nine.

COMMODORE MATTHEW C. PERRY

The successor to David Conner performs with the same efficiency and spirit of cooperation with Scott's command that had so distinguished his predecessor. As Scott's army moves inland, Perry continues the war from the sea, leads expeditions to still-active Mexican ports south of Vera Cruz with considerable success. After the war he returns to New York, serves four years in relative obscurity, but in 1853 receives assignment to visit the closed and mysterious island of Japan, where, after much difficulty, he finally succeeds in opening a diplomatic relationship between the two nations. He returns to the United States in 1854, co-authors a book detailing his Japanese adventures, and dies in New York City in 1858.

LIEUTENANT ULYSSES S. GRANT

Grant is awarded two brevets, for his gallantry at Molino del Rey and his ingenuity during the assault at San Cosme. He leaves Mexico in July 1848 with the bulk of Worth's division, returns home to St. Louis to marry his young love, Julia. He accepts assignment first to New York, then to Detroit, both of which allow his family to remain with him. However, in 1852 he is assigned to the Pacific coast, at Fort Vancouver and San Francisco, posts he must attend alone. Though promoted officially to Captain in August 1853, the difficulties of life and the temptations of gold-fever San Francisco become his downfall, and he resigns under disciplinary pressure from the army in July 1854.

He proves to have no talent for civilian life, fails as a farmer, then as a real estate agent, and finally accepts work with his own family in Galena, Illinois. With the outbreak of the Civil War, Grant receives a commission in July 1861 as colonel of an Illinois regiment, finds great comfort in his return to the army. He rises quickly to prominence by commanding the first significant northern victory of the war at Fort Donelson. His subsequent victories at Shiloh and Vicksburg propel him to overall command of the Union army in March 1864. His amazing skill and perseverance in the field of battle eventually wear down the forces of Robert E. Lee, and Grant accepts Lee's surrender at Appomattox, Virginia, in one of the most poignant and documented moments in American history. In 1868 he becomes the third veteran of the Mexican War, along with Taylor and Pierce, to be elected President. His own memoirs of his experiences in both wars is a monument, both for his clear-headed descriptions of events and personalities and his surprising talent as a writer. He survives until 1885.

LIEUTENANT JAMES LONGSTREET

Breveted twice, for gallantry at Churubusco, and Molino del Rey, Longstreet remains bedridden for much of the winter of 1847. Finally able to sail, he leaves Mexico in January 1848, returns to St. Louis and immediately marries Louise Garland. His recovery from the wound is difficult and lengthy, and is spent mostly with his mother at her home in Mississippi. His career in the 1850s is remarkable for its near total obscurity. He serves as paymaster for posts in El Paso, Texas, and Albuquerque, New Mexico, receives the official promotion to Major in 1858. He resigns from the army in 1861, volunteers for service in the Confederacy, expecting to receive the minimal attention that his paymaster duties have earned him.

In fact, his reputation as a leader of infantry is remembered by Joe Johnston, and Longstreet is astounded to receive the rank of Brigadier General. He is conspicuous in leading troops at the battle of First Manassas, and becomes conspicuous again for protesting vigorously when his brigade is ordered to stop their pursuit of the fleeing Federal forces. It is a trait that will accompany him through his entire career. Despite his stubborn adherence to his own point of view, there is arguably no more consistent and reliable commander in the Confederate army. But his stubbornness and lack of judgment cost him dearly after the war, and attempts at remaining close to his friend Ulysses Grant are seen by many in the South as betrayal. Despite working to ease the strain of Reconstruction, Longstreet is branded a scapegoat for the South's defeat at Gettysburg. He eventually writes his own memoirs, which contain many lapses in accuracy, and thus he again defeats his own efforts at redemption. In his later years he serves as Postmaster of New Orleans, U.S. Minister to Turkey, and U.S. Marshal for the state of Georgia. After Louise's death in 1889, he marries a woman forty-two years his junior, again inviting scandalous comment. He dies in 1904 in Gainesville, Georgia.

LIEUTENANT THOMAS J. JACKSON

Breveted three times for his astounding enthusiasm in every fight he is allowed to wage, he nonetheless seems to enjoy the peacetime as it evolves in Mexico. Jackson spends much of his time exploring the ancient and modern wonders of Mexico, though he puts a priority on the pursuit of religious enlightenment. Unlike most of the soldiers who consider Mexico a place to be left behind, and quickly, Jackson is attracted to a charm in both the country and the people.

In mid-April 1848 he is named quartermaster of his former unit, returns again to the command of Francis Taylor. He leaves Mexico on July 7 and is assigned to mundane duties in Fort Hamilton, New York, and Carlisle, Pennsylvania. In New York he vigorously explores his increasing need for religion, and in April 1849 he is baptized at St. John's Episcopal Parish, though he continues to examine and find fault with Church doctrine. In mid-1850 the boredom of peacetime life is replaced by the misery of a new assignment to Fort Meade, Florida, under the command of Colonel William French, a man Jackson quickly grows to dislike. The duty is stifling beyond Jackson's tolerance, and he finally resigns from the army, seeks to fill a vacancy as instructor at the Virginia Military Institute, in Lexington, Virginia, a teaching position for which he has neither experience nor talent. But his experience in Mexico and his West Point credentials land him the job.

His years in Lexington are a contrast of quiet devotion to his duty, his new passion for the Presbyterian faith, and stunning personal tragedy. In 1855 his first wife dies in childbirth, and four years later his second wife gives birth to a daughter who lives only a month. The pain of these events carries Jackson more closely than ever to his absolute obedience to his perception of God's mission. Thus, when war breaks out, he does not hesitate to volunteer for service, and commands the VMI cadets as drill instructors for the new Confederate regiments. He commands the First Virginia Brigade in action at Manassas in July 1861, where both he and the brigade receive the nickname "Stonewall."

He rises to become the symbol if not the actual leader of southern passion for duty, and along with "Pete" Longstreet is responsible for much of the Confederacy's successes under Joe Johnston and Robert E. Lee. Jackson's greatest victory is also his final accomplishment. During the Battle of Chancellorsville he is accidentally wounded by his own men, and dies of pneumonia eight days later, on May 10, 1863. During four years of war, no other incident has such a devastating emotional impact on the South, until Lee's surrender.

There is one quote often recalled, attributed to several sources, which was given following Jackson's extraordinary performance on September 13, 1847. It is a comment that could have applied to so many, to an extraordinary generation of American soldiers:

"He will be heard from again."

ABOUT THE AUTHOR

Jeff Shaara was born in 1952 in New Brunswick, New Jersey. He grew up in Tallahassee, Florida, and graduated from Florida State University in 1974. For many years he was a dealer in rare coins but sold his Tampa, Florida, business in 1988 upon the death of his father, Michael Shaara.

As manager of his father's estate, Jeff developed a friendship with film director Ron Maxwell, whose film *Gettysburg* was based on *The Killer Angels*. It was Maxwell who suggested that Jeff continue the story Michael Shaara had begun, the inspiration that produced Jeff's first two novels, *Gods and Generals* and *The Last Full Measure*.

Visit the author online at www.JeffShaara.com